Boys in Bedrooms:
The Prison of the Mind

A Call to Action

For sufferers of male social withdrawal
and their enabling systems

 A catalogue record for this book is available from the National Library of Australia

Publisher:
Inspiring Publishers
P.O. Box 159, Calwell, ACT Australia 2905
Email: publishaspg@gmail.com
http://www.inspiringpublishers.com

National Library of Australia Cataloguing-in-Publication entry

Author: Jay Freeman

Title: **Boys in Bedrooms: The Prison of the Mind**

ISBN (Print): 978-1-922792-81-5
ISBN (eBook): 978-1-922792-82-2

This book is dedicated to:

Mal, the most inspiring man I've worked with in many years. Thank you for your never-ending encouragement, and your belief in my writing.

Though an adult and a businessman, you were determined not to be a product of your thinking; to marry your emotional age with your biological age, and robustly walk down the aisle of life. You turned the heat up on your pain and drove down the messy backstreets of your childhood, freeing yourself from your chains and walking into your destiny.

PREAMBLE

IMPORTANT THINGS TO KNOW

This book is written as a Call to Action — we urgently need our young men to step up and protect our way of life. Sadly, thousands are living in mind prisons, wounded on home ground, with no defence and repair armour, voicing their concern for their lack of adulthood, with no psychological immunity in sight.

Lest we forget, as we live in the land of milk and honey, smothered in the luxury of freedom, that ... young men were once prepared to protect our way of life. They valued our culture and our land and they were prepared to die for what they believed. Our ancestors left us with an important legacy to pass down to the next generation — is their legacy now compromised within our peace time slumber? Parents, wake up: Australia needs our warriors!

- The Title: *Boys in Bedrooms: The Prison of the Mind* describes a middle-class social development disaster in terms of the large and increasing number of (mainly) males who are being supported to remain dependent (emotionally and financially) upon others for their long-term survival.
- Risk Assessment: The intent of this writing is not to vilify the social withdrawer. It is important to remember that change for those caught in long-term cycles of social withdrawal and addiction can be a frightening experience. Alarming rates of self-harm and suicide are prevalent across all age groups. This book does not adequately cover

chronic trauma and post-traumatic stress disorder, nor does it replace the need to work collaboratively with medical and mental health professionals. Also, please remember — when it comes to mental health, child protection and family domestic violence it is *everybody's* responsibility.

- Stages of Social Withdrawal — Early Withdrawal: 1-3 months — early intervention and prevention measures recommended. Chronic Withdrawal: 3+ months — Urgent need of intervention — risk of developing secondary conditions. 6-12+ months: highly urgent disordered state — an illness requiring complex intervention with the whole system urged to participate in a recovery plan.

- Severe Long-term Withdrawal (6-12+ months): This book is NOT to be used as a form of threat, manipulation or eviction. This book has been written as a Whole Family System Change Model: Regression and social withdrawal do not exist on its own — *the whole system is unwell.*

- Theme: Discomfort to Grow — Moving Forward with practical strategies. This book is less about reading and ALL about doing. For those serious about breaking patterns of social withdrawal and enablement, please provide a copy of this book to each member of the system. Highlighting relevant sections is considered a form of communication.

- This book does not cover male or female sexuality or gender complexities. The term 'transition' refers to the bridge between childhood to adulthood.

- The main focus of this book is targeted to those who identify as male, respecting fluid gender identity and the changes in terminology that may (at the time of printing) not be correctly reflected in this edition.

- Unintentional readers and those who would like to assess the level of possible dependency within your household — please refer to Chapter 6 — The Financial Formula.
- The Family Meeting Process is considered a vital part of breaking cycles of retreat. Each family member is encouraged to read their own copy of this book and highlight relevant personal sections. Highlighting is a form of communication and is often a first step forward.
- Due to the distinct lack of literature or research on social withdrawal in Australia, Japanese research has been referred to (Hikikomori), respecting the valuable work of Dr Saito Tamaki.
- I welcome a wide range of individuals and professionals to read my book to ensure the information is responsible. The first edition of this book (and e-book) is limited. Feedback for alterations, deletions, additions and relevant stories are welcome for the second publishing of this book. Strategies are also provided as a separate e-book.
- Ad Lib — Controversial Notions — it was recommended that I place this section at the back of the book as some of the content is highlighting unchartered topics such as brain chipping through brain-computer interfacing and trans-humanism. The intent for this section is to highlight the urgency for us all to be aware of government policy and human trials as we continue to protect the geographical landscape of our brain!
- This book is not intended as a guilt trip — it is written as an Action Verb — A Call to Action. Please free our men!

TABLE OF CONTENTS

Disclaimer: The content of this book is intended to provoke a discussion on male social withdrawal and to challenge family systems. This writing is not intended as medical or psychiatric advice. Neither the author nor the publisher or illustrator can be held responsible or liable for any loss or claim arising from the use or misuse of the content of this book.

Every effort has been made to contact the holders of copyrighted material. The publishers will be glad to rectify, in future editions, any inadvertent omissions that have been brought to their attention.

Strategies:
1.1   Identifying the Primary Trigger Event
1.2   The TED Strategy – Topic/Emotion/Decision
1.3   Anchoring
1.4   Replace Problem with 'Dilemma'
1.5   It's JUST A Trigger
1.6   Divorcing Possessive Pronouns

INTRODUCTION

The Boys in Bedrooms: Prison of the Mind epidemic became apparent to me around 15 years ago, both in my professional life and within my friendship circles, hearing somewhat unusual stories from dozens and dozens of emotionally and physically drained Australian parents who were labouring over their adult sons' bizarre **social withdrawal behaviour** and/or lack of emotional adulthood. Parents appeared to be stuck in a somewhat frozen-in-time, psychologically perplexed state, unable to transition or re-transition their boy-man (and occasionally daughter) to adulthood. They seemed powerless in their confusion as to how this mind prison and lack of adjustment had now become a never-ending adolescence, as evidenced by persistent and chronic dependence within the family system, with no psychological immunity in sight.

Parents often discussed Primary Trigger Events (such as sudden changes, failure, betrayal or rejection) from many years earlier, though expected their son to have 'gotten over it' by now. Years later parents were confused as to why their sons were *still* not taking any practical steps to transition to adulthood, or to change their circumstances, nor appearing to even *want* to transition or adjust from his worldly **brain bruising events**. Instead of a bounce-back approach, he had chosen a **bounce-inwards**

lifestyle, turning to the farmland of his bedroom and rejecting wider familial and community systems, such as peers, extended family, coaches, counsellors, career advisors and employers.

At times, there were sporadic attempts to work, orchestrated by parents negotiating a deal with **nepotism**, such as pleas to their wider family professionals or business-owner mates to employ their son, even *just* part-time or temporarily as 'a favour'. As we are well aware, the **partiality of favouritism** requires less discomfort, such as (often) an elimination of job applications, interviews, nor many of the realities that those transitioning on their own to new employment must endure. Though, for the 'right time, right place' people, an opportune leg-up provides a sustainable concrete foundation, whilst others, even with 'a leg up' will still sabotage their opportunity to launch or re-launch into adulthood.

Overall, there was a noticeable decrease in the typical at-risk behaviours that we often view as 'common' to young people who are exercising their developmental right to endure consequences by **combining failure with success**, through the school of hard knocks. 'He *needs* to change, he *needs* help', parents pleaded, though they continually rejected practical change-advice, preferring to maintain their strange and never-ending rupture-repair cycles behind closed doors. Parents' minds were closed and so too were the bedroom doors of their young people who had become increasingly dissociative, enmeshed within the technological era, internalising stress hormones that were now acting as immune suppressants.

Parents were unaware of the ongoing inner turmoil of their bedroom dweller, as well as the subtle decrease of natural immunity to life stressors, alongside the emergence of his value-changing mindset, thwarting his ability to build psychological antibodies. With little pressure to change, nor reality-check his emerging bedroom mindset, parents were completely unaware that their son's **view of the role of his parents** had changed and over time he had also altered his relationship with values and ideals such as reciprocated love relationships, earning an income, establishing (or maintaining) a career and gaining even basic work-to-eat employment. At the same time, parents often lacked interest, nor took responsibility, in the vital role of *discomfort-to-grow* opportunities, as well as whole-of-family-system change models that require humility, assertive communication, consequences and exposure.

As time moved on, frantic parents tried desperately to fast-track an employment opportunity, often walking into businesses without advertised positions, unaware of the 'demand' in their voice that said 'you need to employ my son'. What they didn't realise was that their **over-focus on nurture and attachment after 18 years of age** for their man-child was the wrong currency for the leap into (or back into) the world of sustainable employment and responsibility. A world where adults, particularly bosses, aren't jumping to desperate parents' wishes, a world where employers don't expect to take over the role of nurturer, nor piss in a young person's pockets during an interview. If the young person does become the successful applicant, bosses aren't interested in forming a deep or even terribly meaningful collegiate relationship, nor wiping anyone's backsides — they 'just want the bloody job done'.

Where he once might have held promising relationship and career goals and valued sweat, money and lifestyle as drivers to his manhood, he had now defaulted to a new system of opt-out and mere basic survival under the roof of his enablers. The blood-brain barrier was broken, there was no firewall within his new self-imposed reign of psychological terrorism. At the same time, the subtle new family cultural theme, 'if you're emotionally or physically wounded or not quite on your feet, we will enable you to regress' had emerged. With little motivation for a solution-focused whole-of-family-system change, as well as stubborn determination to remain focused on an individual pathology, alongside the demonisation of addictive technology, parents simply turned back to the other parts of their lives that made more sense, and left their man-child to his own demise.

I was eager to ascertain whether young males, in general, regarded themselves as *protectors* of our way of life, and also how they imagined they would cope if they were called to arms? Many young people looked at me with blank faces, stating 'no bloody way — I can't even protect *myself* from the war in my own head'. They agreed that the introduction of the tech era had reduced their psychological immunity, though they were often experts as to how to protect their devices against viruses and hackers. Terms such as proxy server firewalls, next-generation firewall (NGFW), packet filters, circuit-level gateway and rogue wireless access points were easier to rattle off the tongue, than their knowledge or ability as to how to build their own personal firewall or re-configure their personal thinking systems. It had become nearly impossible to protect themselves from themselves by blocking insidious viral thoughts from breaking through their blood–brain barrier, nor were they creating vitally rich bounce-back chemicals absorbed through connections within their social systems and nutrient-rich environment. **Natural immunity** was nowhere in sight.

Asking males between 18 years and 55 years what age did they *feel* like an adult, their reply was often slow and awkward: 'I still don't *feel* like an adult', 'I'm a six-foot-four stunted adult', 'I know I don't *think* like an adult', 'adulthood hasn't arrived yet', 'do men *ever* reach adulthood?' Although awkward answers abounded, men still *wanted* to talk about the concept of manhood and rites of passage or the lack thereof. Men initiating counselling stated that their main goal for improving their mental health was linked to 'wanting to *feel* like I'm adulting', or to 'stop feeling like a kid when I'm meant to be a man'.

Discussions with professionals working with youth suggested that skipping classes, absenteeism and persistent school refusal (truancy) from around 15 years of age was considered to be a common risk factor for social withdrawal. Truancy increased the risk for non-completion of high school, youth unemployment, criminality and future dependence on the welfare system. The government's truancy laws were not only policies to make parents accountable, they were considered a form of protection and early intervention. Government funding resourced truancy officers, counsellors and family support workers with reports of forced practices around school attendance such as fining parents and reduced Centrelink payments. As well as numerous attempts (albeit considered ineffectual intervention measures by some) to address important issues such as bullying, learning difficulties, mental health, physical health, abuse and complex family issues.

Discussions with males from lower economic families and complex family backgrounds as to how they defined their transition to adulthood began to provide insight into the plausible links between wealth and manhood. Many answers were definite and age identifiable, citing on average 14-20 years, attributed to a forced collision with reality. It was an Opt-In or an intentional decision to step 'into' manhood. Common rhetoric: 'When I was 16 and my father died', 'I was around 14 when I realised I wasn't going to stay at home and put up with this shit anymore', 'when I stood up to my father for the first time', 'on the sporting field when I knew I could keep up with the men', 'I didn't like school and made everyone's life hell, so I decided to work', 'when I realised I liked money and grog', 'when I realised my parents valued my opinion', 'when I knew I had to work if I wanted to eat', 'when I knew that no one else was going to do me any favours', 'when I was ready to give life a go on my own/with my mates', 'got sick of the old girl still *wanting* me to be around her', 'when I had to'; 'I wanted to be independent'.

It soon became evident that on average, young people growing up with absent fathers or raised in single-parent households or lower socio-economic families were NOT growing dependent offspring nor delaying adulthood. In fact, individuals raised in less privilege were more likely to understand responsibility, due to reality markers at earlier ages. Put simply, they *wanted to* begin to adjust to adulthood, or often had no other choice. Absentee fathers (and other absent male role models) are not, for the purpose of this writing, considered to be a risk factor for social withdrawal. This fact surprises many middle-class, double-income families, who often elevate their own family social standing by deflecting the troubles in society to 'other' groups, such as single parents or lower socio-economic families.

My ongoing focus for stunted male emotional growth, causing men to be held up in their bedrooms and/or behind their screens, turned to **links between class and mismanaged privilege**. It eventually became clear that the demographic for stunted emotional growth was common to: males from largely educated and/or middle-upper class families; often the eldest sibling who was once high functioning, such as the sport captain or A-grade student, Mr Popular, once regarded as 'most likely to succeed'; elite sportspeople; males returning back to the family home past the age of 18 years for financial or housing issues; as well as young people who were previously 'reasonable' in their functionality, aside from maybe a few typical developmental quirks.

Where once the home environment acted as a pseudo 'real life' agent or a brief healer, it became evident that many bedrooms had become 'mind prisons'. Instead of the home environment acting as a short-term solution-focused growth centre to launch or re-launch, there was now a whole of family 'buy in' to regression — a form of kindness-blindness was now the new norm. Parents were loading the gun of retreat, rather than 'walking alongside' their young person, when relatively typical (as well as overwhelming) **primary trigger events** showed up. Eventually, the protective shield around their bedroom dweller became only one layer, with gaping holes. Outsiders were rejected, and eventually tapered off in their confusion and sadness for the plight of the home dweller, who appeared to be living in a strange new home-based social debit system, with no social credit in sight.

It soon became evident that **delayed healing timeframes** had escalated to the onset of serious and potentially irreversible secondary conditions, shifting the 'primary' focus to pathology. Sadly, the lack of bounce-back as seen in thousands of Australian families had created a new, behind-closed doors, middle-class, *barely* surviving **Failure to Thrive community.**

Often female siblings were living independently and achieving their goals by smashing through glass ceilings, initially drawing the attention away from their ever-retreating sibling. These (often) highly elevated young women were attending counselling in increasing numbers, unaware they had joined a new fraternity with their acquired, non-intentional matriarchal mindsets. Unlike her wisdom-retreating parents, she had become the face of reality for the family, enmeshed within repetitive cycles of dis-enablement as she watched her brother deteriorate under the rein of

familial kindness-blindness. Sisters were continually distraught at the way their parents had become strangely brainwashed, and they were saddened by the deterioration in their mother's physical and mental health.

Daughters' genuine pleas to parents to instigate a family system change was simply returned back void — the proverbial boomerang effect. After a number of years, she felt like a detached family participant, resembling a monkey in an odd zoo — a far cry from previous family dynamics that could once be described as reasonable, privileged or relatively unremarkable. **Boomerang Sisters** clearly loved their brothers, though they remained visibly distraught when discussing their powerlessness in terms of their brother's lack of adulthood, citing 'my brother is still a kid but he's living in a man's body', 'he only seems like he's 13 but he's actually 25', 'he's turning 30 and nothing is changing'.

These generous-hearted, often high-achieving Boomerang Sisters had unknowingly taken on the role of co-dependent Matriarch for their whole family. Whilst they empathised with their brother's initial trigger point setbacks and their parents' broken hearts, they had been forced to sit by as voyeurs, caught in cycles of rupture and repair, listening to emotionally and eventually financially drained parents who continued to make empty promises of change, as their brother's situation only worsened, not improved, as the years just kept rolling by. They knew only too well that the definition of madness is doing the same thing over and over again and expecting different results, and yet it was these remarkable young women who were the ones questioning *their* 'madness'.

Some Boomerang Sisters were adamant that their brother hadn't experienced any initial major setbacks, nor had they been terribly rebellious as a younger lad, arguing that although he's a 'nice sort', he's been taking cruel advantage of their parents' kindness, with no intention to adult, sucking off family goodness like a parasite — and now will likely never leave the family home or his addictive technology without some sort of professional help. There were very few reports of these parasitical brothers *instigating* work around the home in respect of his free existence, with a plenitude of examples citing external and internal home-based deterioration attributed to 'utter laziness'. Why now, they reasoned, would their brother *ever* want to change his status quo?

Most Boomerang Sisters agreed that their parents had naïvely entered into some type of strange three-way 'brainwashing' relationship, like enmeshed addicts within a defunct parent-son rehabilitation centre — living on their own detached island — The Isle of Denial. Boomerang Sisters' genuine words of concern were simply hitting the sides of the walls and then being chucked back, like sticky hot tar, scarring her face and her overall belief in her family system as an agent of growth. It was common for parents to defend their ever-retreating son by telling her 'you're just being a bully', 'you're just jealous of your brother, after ALL we've done for *you* in the past', 'leave him alone, he's just taking more time than you', 'you know boys are slower than girls'.

It was common for Boomerang Sisters to deflatingly quote a high number of their female friends who were *also* battling the same dilemma with *their* parents, and enquire as to whether these friends were welcome to refer for counselling. A new subgroup of frustrated female siblings had begun to emerge in high numbers within the therapy space. One young woman suggested that she's struggling to name one young man in her community who's working full time, or who lives outside the family home, or who can juggle education alongside other responsibilities, without the excessive assistance of his enablers. Addiction to his dependency, his devices, his pain or his substances had become the main focus of his life.

Then, an even more disturbed Boomerang Sisterhood enters the door of the counselling room. She's articulate, well-dressed, planned in her conversation, often professionally driven, though more elevated than the rest. The body sells us out and so too does hers. Trauma abounds as she describes the highly addictive lifestyle of her brother, alongside parents who have enabled his crime and addiction life for years: The Proverbial Bail-Out King of the decade. High-risk lifestyles — guns, knives and guerrilla warfare, the family has endured it all, and lost much. The family moral compass is defunct, there is now no radar in sight.

Although Boomerang Sister may not be the main enabler, she's endured barbaric consequences to her own life, simply due to her bloodline connections within her now over-compromised, family-imposed matriarchal role that she didn't even sign up for in the first place. She's been used and abused for many years, and now *she* needs support. The reward for her excessive sibling over-kindness means that she now meets criteria for an anxiety disorder — such as post-traumatic stress disorder, or a major depressive disorder. Where once her mental health was robust, she is informed that she may now require long-term professional support and/or medication — sadly, a ticking time bomb.

In many ways, my writing has become a tribute to the role of our societal sisters. My hope is that that they will stand up and not repeat the mistakes of the past, particularly when it's their turn to raise our next generation. I acknowledge their pain, rung out like prematurely aged dishrags and yet they remain independent and societally vital. How were you meant to know the dangers of parental inaction after three months, or even more so by six months? Is it time to stop your overfocus on your familial line, and shift the focus to your own psychological and physical survival?

Boomerang Sisters keep dissecting the vitally important topic of co-dependency (Melody Beattie: 1992) and assess how unwell you may have become as a result of what was imposed upon you through your bloodline connections. You must heal. You must maintain self-care strategies. You must focus on the other parts of your life that make more sense. Flip the script, sistas! We must remember that although dependent people and/or addicts desperately need help, unless they are actively seeking assistance and maintaining connection, THEY HAVE NO INTENTION OF CHANGING. There is no point pretending otherwise — reality is opening our eyes wide open.

In their heyday of destruction, addicts commonly report that they feel no remorse or empathy towards their enablers, due to their addiction/s morphing the role of their conscience and moral compass. Sending clear messages throughout their cognitive landscape that they are invincible, with God-like powers, socially exempt from responsibility. In fact, their enablers are nothing more than puppets on a string with a wallet, ripe to be manipulated on a regular basis. If an addict is medicating their pain, they will increase their risk-taking appetite and maintain their narcissistic 'scoring' — the pain of others is simply not on their agenda.

At the same time, addicts report waiting and waiting for their circus ride to end. They wait for their enablers to stop making excuses — 'when will *someone* stand up and stop me?' Technology addicts expect that eventually *someone* will turn off their access to technology. For those caught in criminal offending cycles, they are always waiting for the police to arrive, expecting that they will *eventually* be caught, because 'if you do the crime, you'll do the time.'

For **chronic addiction**, addicts know the only way they have any chance of becoming the adult they were always meant to be, will be when they are fully committed to some form of rehabilitation. When talking with addicts in prison or working with new clients in rehabilitation or detoxification, their first response is 'relief' that the circus ride has ended. Addicts admit that **'I cannot change on my own'.** They are shocked at how easy it is/was for 'my lies and bullshit' to be believed for so long. Often disgusted that their enablers truly believed that they would simply grow a conscience and 'wake up' one day and be ready (on their own) to change. Deep down they plead to their enablers to 'wake the fuck up and stop making excuses for me!'.

Who even knew that it only takes around six months of bounce-back inaction, before symptoms of social withdrawal can morph into an even more complicated reality — introducing the highly avoidable label of **Adjustment Disorder?** Who was even taking any notice from around three months after the trigger event at the young man's blank face and white knuckles obsessively massaging the key to the front door, increasingly reluctant to open the door to his freedom?

And ... 10 years later, the picture was still the same, only a lot worse. Parents were now concerned about the emergence of a whole bunch of **secondary issues**, and were referring their man-child to medical and psychiatry professionals for assessment, diagnosis and medication — 'He *needs* to change, but now he *can't* change, he's at a stand-still, it's like he's gone backwards'. Not only had these young men regressed socially, so too had their emotional age in comparison with their biological age. It was common for a man of 30 years to mirror the emotional life and reactivity of a young person of around 15–16 years of age.

No action at his first major trigger event, as well as extended periods of recklessness and care bombing, meant the emergence of a stark and very unusual new reality — a significant mismatch, **a divorce between his emotional age and his biological age.** Sadly, parents subconsciously began to connect more with his emotional age than his biological age, often referring to their hairy six-foot son as 'my boy' or 'he still needs his Mumma' and even 'my wee baby' or childish nicknames. A strange brainwashing or extreme family-denial state had now occurred, as the whole family system turned further and further in on itself as each new year rolled over, with many men now in their thirties or closer to forty.

It was like a disturbing time-warped, embryonic state of reality denial had become the new family culture — or maybe a psychologically dangerous regressionary hostage had 'grabbed' parents and adult children who were *all* now held up and enmeshed within the prison walls of their own homes? Eventually, parents appeared to take solace in their deflection game, *blaming their son* for his regressionary behaviour and denying any responsibility for the part they were playing, despite their own cultural and developmental norms, as well as typical societal expectations, suggesting otherwise. They also appeared oblivious to their family member's broken heart and broken relationships, as well as his inability to cope with general societal activities, which, unknown to many parents, was eventually based on their young person's chronic fears and shame and had nothing to do with laziness and boredom.

As their young person continued to decline community involvement and avoid familial and other relationships, parents began adopting a more justifiable **generational pathology** by finding comfort within their social groups or occasional sporadic counselling sessions as the normalisation of social withdrawal increased and the motivation or the belief in the family system as a transition or a change agent, decreased.

Glass-ceiling-smashing daughters continued to attend counselling sessions, some for many years, suffering avoidable anxiety and anger-related disturbances attributed to the way their parents were still 'smothering' their brother, who was *still at home being 'babied'*. During initial sessions, these women were surprised how I easily summarised their concerns, suggesting I was like a voyeur or a mind reader with cameras inside their family homes! When they understood my heart and passion in terms of male social withdrawal (MSW) after many years listening to the stories of males themselves who were honest about their lack of 'adulting', the parents of these daughters began calling to discuss their adult son.

Parents appeared relieved they were not alone in their struggles. However, I soon learned that there is a huge difference between parents *discussing* their adult socially withdrawn son, and an *actual desire or plan* to begin to move forward. My plea: **Change is an Action**, not an emotion, often fell onto deaf ears. I would ask, 'Is your son a "Boy in a Bedroom"?' I wasn't sure how appropriate this terminology was, though most were unified in their agreement that indeed there was a serious problem with lack of adulthood and social withdrawal.

It was common, particularly for mothers, to reject the notion of 'parental responsibility', nor to fathom the idea that the 'whole family system is unwell'. Though they did agree that their language needed to immediately change from 'boy' to 'man'. With this in mind, they suggested that due to my passion in the area of MSW, they would prefer to refer their son to my private practice as they were sure I could help him to change rather than *every-one* getting involved. 'Besides', they surmised, 'it's great that these days we don't directly blame the parents anymore'.

In a true circus style of communication, women were quick to admit that they had indeed become overly accommodating and were treating their son as if he were much younger than what was typical 'back in my day'. At the same time, mothers admitted to being tougher and more expectant of their daughters, who were now confidently independent. Mothers recalled stories of typical parental–adolescent conflict and plenty of examples of their daughter bouncing back from major and minor trigger events. Initially, it was a huge eye-opener how often mothers blatantly admitted to **gender double-standards**, whilst still continuing to talk about their son as 'loving his mumma', or 'we all know the bonds between mother and son are entirely different than with our daughters', 'it's a special type of bond with my boy, you know, he's my baby'.

Love, seemingly skewered, with many mothers appearing to have replaced their relationship with their husband to one that resembled a strange and somewhat **disturbing husband–wife relationship with their son.** Women usually rejected the invitation for couple counselling, deflecting to their partner as still being 'in denial' as to the extent of the enduring babyhood of their offspring. It was rare for both partners to attend counselling. Women in denial with unmet needs was a bigger issue than the limitations of a one-hour counselling session and even more so in the absence of her partner — her genuine motivation for change nowhere in sight.

Mothers were, however, prepared to study relevant literature such as **codependency** (high-level codependency is treated as a caretaking addiction) before booking their next session. Many women identified *entirely* with codependency, though they still continued their dangerous **'Yes—But' justification**: 'Yes—but everyone knows that girls are more adaptable than boys'; 'Yes—But females mature quicker than males'; 'Yes—But he's just a bit slower than others'. At times, it appeared that the worker had more belief in her son's ability to move out of his emotionally damaging and chronically dependant corner, than what the mother had in her own son.

It became clear that many modern women, particularly high-level professional women were less likely to change their enabling behaviour, DESPITE (1) agreeing wholeheartedly with their parental double standards, (2) professional concern for *her* serious and declining emotional and physical health, as well as (3) agreeing that her adult son was regressing towards possible serious and irreparable **secondary condition/s.** Many women sought counselling for de-briefing only, which of course was their prerogative as a client of any service. They continued to reject or stonewall offers for referrals to specialists, or for family systems therapy or to address relationship disharmony or even to seek advice from her respected tribe. It appeared that the role of professionals and supporters was typical of the new Aussie style — 'one must listen without placing undue pressure'.

As most workers in the social services industry are well aware, Family Systems Theory suggests that it's typical for one family member, generally a young person, to carry the illnesses of the family, rather than the family system as a whole taking responsibility. Rather than focusing on early intervention or prevention, parents had automatically programmed themselves to focus on an individual blame-game. Parents commonly attributed much of his withdrawal behaviour to the evil and alluring nature of technology (or other) addictions, as to his newly acquired and declining physical and mental health.

Had the **demonisation of technology** allowed parents to justify the alienation of his previous socialised self? Our new alien-nation, now held up in their rooms, with their tech-driven-gagged voices now bound? Change-resistant parents appeared to be locked in a holding pattern, trying to 'just get through it' by ignoring reality — the stark reality of our new community of gamers living alongside parents as 'false-hopers' had emerged. Parents began increasing their dependency upon psychotropic medication, at the same level as their emotional blockers, such as alcohol and workaholism — barely coping within their systems of work, rest and play.

Parents discussed their overwhelming guilt for past parenting mistakes, such as divorce, transience, financial disarray and time-neglect during their son's younger years. They were strangely overly-eager to 'make it up to him', though agreeing that indeed their primary parenting years had now passed. It wasn't rocket science to surmise that regret, buttered with guilt, were the entirely wrong ingredients for males reaching and/or maintaining adulthood.

Literature and media reports regarding the alarming rise in suicide rates (particularly for young men) with an estimated one in three struggling with mental health issues at any one time, prompted parents to raise the topic of self-harm. Many admitted that the 'self-harm card' was the main reason they didn't want to place *any* pressure on him 'just in case'. Confusingly, in the absence of previous indicators or disclosures of risk, many didn't believe he would act on it, though they preferred to be cautionary and suggested that his anxiety-driven behaviour could be a cry for help, though not wishing to support him to access help, because 'he probably wouldn't accept help anyway'.

Many parents often admitted to feeling unsafe within the family home, due to aggressive behaviours, such as verbal abuse, threats, physical abuse, emotional abuse, financial abuse and psychological abuse. Even simple tasks such as instigating the cleaning of his disgusting room, picking up his towels or taking a break from his addictive technology often resulted in alarming hostility, such as destroying items around the home.

Parenting styles often revealed an increase in a 'reward positive behaviour' by ignoring anti-social behaviour, citing that they 'feel sorry for him when he loses control' as a reason for the elimination of consequences or as a justification for medicating anger. Therefore, risks assessments and safety planning often steered sessions in alternative directions for many weeks, as other professionals and/or government departments were prioritised. Understandably, very few parents were comfortable discussing possible police involvement, child protection or preparing for ambulant services when risky mental health and physical health issues emerge. However, hundreds of families *are* prepared to maintain their secret hell for year after year.

When asking women where the older men in their son's life fitted with their story, there was often further admission of regret, that they had indeed, in the earlier years, stifled the older men, such as their son's father or grandfather or uncle or pastor, from input with typical transition markers. And, for some strange reason, the older men in their son's life, had eventually given up with what would've been considered normal bloodline rites of passage practices 'back in the day'. Had these men turned soft in their ivory towers? Or were they intimidated by the strong women in their lives or were they just plain lazy?

These older men knew only too well, that 'back in my day' a mother would NEVER have been able to thwart or influence the bridge from childhood to adulthood. Though it appeared that these strong male influencers had also turned back to the parts of *their lives* that made more sense, and had left their bloodline man-child to his own demise. Had male influencers abdicating their transition roles in lieu of other competing interests become yet another societal epidemic? Or was it now endemic, as we study the decline of the traditional nuclear family and reflect upon what could be fast becoming a generational norm?

Many conversations with parents was like being part of a crazy circus ride. Arriving at their first session late and still on their mobile, answering their mobile again mid-session for 'highly pressing matters', elevated and lively, often instigating the topic of unmanaged trigger events and robust family finances as an inhibitor to manhood for their son, at the same time as dobbing in their 'other' parent (or step-parent) as someone who is in denial and far too busy to take part in any whole of family change process. Phew! Long sentences and **mixed double-standards**, heads buzzing with no real plan — leaving the worker to sit and listen with few gaps left for advice, therapy or action planning.

Most parents agreed wholeheartedly that they would all benefit from a family systems approach, at the same time as starting each sentence with 'Yes–But': 'Yes–but money isn't an issue, so would you able to just "fix" our problem because we're just too busy'; 'Yes–but it's not his fault he got addicted to painkillers after the accident'; 'Yes–but he's such a nice boy and no real trouble'; 'Yes–but he's just anxious and I think a bit depressed'; 'Yes–but he left home too early and even though he's been out of home for five years, we need to work on attachment because it wasn't his fault we moved around when he was young'; 'Yes—but I know he'll get there one day, he's just a bit slower than most'.

It became glaringly obvious that 'Yes—But' had become a major stumbling block for males reaching adulthood. Parents attending counselling with energy, a targeted focus on their deteriorating situation as well as high motivation, agreed that language eradication or reversal was vital. They agreed to totally eradicate all use of 'Yes—But'; to ban this language from future counselling sessions; to water-pistol all use of derogatory words, such as 'boy or baby' by replacing with the noun MAN; and to remove possessive pronouns such as 'his anxiety' or 'her depression' or 'my anger'.

A high percentage of parents admitted that their main barrier for change was attributed to 'hating confrontation'. They like a quiet, easy-going life, believing that kids eventually find their own way in life. Other parents freely admitted that they were unmotivated and 'I really just want *'it'* all sorted'. Others became visibly distraught at the thought of being unpopular with their son or daughter as they believed in **friendship parenting**. Some surprisingly admitted that they were lazy and had quite an uninvolved or non-confrontational style of parenting, whilst others suggested that they would pay me generously if I would just come to their family home and start my work with their son — 'please just try to force him out of his bedroom' ... Seriously? Gweh!

I adamantly declined such an offer in lieu of a democratic Family Systems Approach, reiterating that although I'm passionate about male social withdrawal, my private practice will not accept referrals from individuals, couples, families or any other systems if there is force, coerciveness, threats to evict, bullying, bribery or any other general unwillingness to be involved in the counselling or family intervention process. My suggestion that 'the situation will not change just because you *want* it to change, nor will money fix 'it', mostly fell on deaf ears, along with my concerns for potentially high level emotional reactivity by their son, as well as the potential for further regression, if cornered in an office or home-based counselling session that the social withdrawer had not given full permission for.

Furthermore, I explained, gone are my days in government positions such as child protection, youth justice, child adolescent mental health and addiction, where intervention and involvement in a government system for the client was often not an option. I was now working in private practice as an accredited mental health social worker with people who had referred *themselves* and who were *motivated* to change. Although I was deeply saddened by the extremely large numbers of MSW and highly motivated to support change by assisting with ways to improve re-connectivity with society, I did not believe it was my place to invade privacy, nor was I a leading expert in this vitally important area.

I knew deep down that parents are the experts on their own children, and under all their many layers of denial they were feeling helpless and just as frightened for him, as he was for himself... though justification still abounded.

Sometimes, though, my admin workers' gatekeeping failed. Or parents in their genuine attempt to seek help for their retreater believed he was ready for professional talk therapy, and I found myself sitting in a therapy session, opposite a Boy in a Bedroom unsuccessfully beginning his initial assessment... Clearly, motivation was not walking in the door...

The welcome handshake is slightly quivery, as a pasty, six-foot, solemn-faced man walks in the door with a slow gait. He is welcomed to the service and treated with respect; he declines water or coffee and any friendly initial banter... As he slowly sits down opposite me, he looks up with a seemingly disassociate type of disdain and disgust in his eye, that suggests there will be no winners today. Eventually, it becomes clear that far from a personal attack, his disdain is nothing short of a paralysing 'fear of others' partnered with chronic shame and awkwardness, though his behaviour and prosodic stress suggests otherwise. Alone and out of his bedroom comfort. A man, and yet a boy. Quietly sarcastic and dismissive, tidy and orderly, with a tone of class: on edge, waiting to pounce.

It's obvious the young man feels cornered, though at least he provides a brief glance of his past happiness when prying into the playing fields of his youth, coupled with the pain that had sabotaged his opportunity to adult and bounce-back. His brief trip down memory lane, coupled with fleeting bravery, alongside a caring ear, a small start, and yet, still to be applauded. Though, he soon sits backward in his chair, crossing his arms above his head, as the moat of his fragile world closes down once more. He, sadly, has no idea that although society is waiting with wide open arms, without the draw-bridge of his reality re-opening, his condition may never cure itself on its own.

Parents were genuinely unaware in those earlier years that they had abdicated their role as Transition Coach (the bridge from home to society) in lieu of their **new role as Regression Coach.** It also appeared that parents were unaware that their son's withdrawal behaviour was often a reflection of chronic shame that had eventually morphed into a paralysing fear of others, as well as ongoing fears of possible abandonment or eviction from the family home. The elasticity of his cognitive muscle memory system had become disrupted and opportunely medicated with withdrawal and less responsibility in an attempt to reduce his distress and improve his flat affect. Parents in their over-kindness and stupidity lacked the necessary parental-intelligence to understand that less responsibility and continued over-kindness is not a sustainable medication regime.

STUPIDITY
('Behaviour that shows a lack of good sense or judgement' — Oxford Dictionary)

In our fragile new world of sensitivity, discrimination and revised nouns and pronouns, it's now simply not Australian to be brutal with subjective descriptors of behaviour. Nevertheless, I began to throw caution to the wind by suggesting that parental abdication that supports an otherwise healthy individual to be left alone, inside their mind prison by buffering their discomfort, is not only stupid, it's also surely a form of extreme parental laziness or even abuse?

Had Wisdom (life skills) been replaced with Stupidity? Did parents need to be publicly urged to wake up and analyse their parenting styles? Family wealth was clearly not transferrable to mental wealth, particularly with parents' heads in the cloud, printing a licence called 'Failure to Drive'. Parents in their hundreds were driving 'our men' off the frontline, leaving our society wide open to invasion and forms of irreversible mind control. Doing the same thing for years on end and expecting different results was causing parents to feel like monkeys trapped in a bizarre zoo.

Previous straight-talking styles from a base of honesty, had been replaced with a softer and overly sensitive piece-meal style of communication, particularly noted in the middle class. Meeting in cafes rather than homes and sipping on fancy coffees of denial. The air refreshing, time with our people increasingly time-pressured, so why infiltrate our conversation with an ounce or two of healthy discomfort that may provoke parental reflection when the atmosphere of privileged café culture seems so perfect in this moment?

Though, back at home, with no pressure to transition, the young man fills his brain with dangerous self-talk, his head buzzes as the consequences of his choices and his family choices have become a regressionary risk. He knows only too well that there's something very wrong with his brain functionality. The rupturing of his highly productive fact-finding rational executive frontal lobe and the dangerous dance with his fear-based primal limbic system, continues to spew dangerous chemicals throughout his body — creating the perfect storm for an illegal frontal lobotomy procedure that is occurring unknowingly behind closed doors. More alarming side-effects, such as blunted emotions, volition and personality are soon walking around the home grassland in a dull state of confusion, unable to fathom how this strange new life has now become his new norm. No one had even signed the permission form for this dangerous and unsupervised lobotomising, nor were they even challenging its legitimacy.

As parents continued to climb further and further up the ladder of their career successes, enjoying their financial pockets growing heavy with capitalistic opportunity, they stopped *connecting* with the seriousness of the way their pale skin offspring had emotionally and developmentally regressed. Roaming around their homeland during the obscure night hours and sleeping away their daylight hours — the dangerous divorce from reality when we rupture the rhythms of our circadian clock routine. How was it even *possible* to ignore the absurdity of sleep/wake pattern reversals without the family sounding the alarm bells, or calling an urgent family meeting, or seeking advice from their tribe and professionals?

Avoidable secondary conditions had become the centre-stage norm requiring serious clinical attention. Eventually, the inability to bounce-back or 'adjust' from a single life stressor was classified as clinical depression or an anxiety-related obsessive–compulsive disorder, or personality disorder (such as avoidant personality disorder), or psychosocial disorder, or conduct disorder or any number of other highly avoidable secondary disorders. Fear of others had become the new best friend (anthropophobia). The diagnostic community was now treating and medicating secondary condition/s and addictions, as if they were part of the original psychopathy. **A Primary Trigger Event had now turned into a sinister and potentially irreversible Secondary Condition.**

Parents and social services workers within the child and youth sectors reminded me that millennial parenting is in a class of its own, incomparable with other generations, blaming the rapid onset of addictive technology and the pressure for young people and their families to continually 'buy in' to the pressures of modern gadgets and devices. Sharing books and library cards a thing of the past and general-knowledge intelligence at an all-time high with devices readily available to rapidly acquire facts, without even purchasing a book or learning how to spell. Pressured and anxiety-provoking educational deadlines achievable in bedrooms, at the same time as maintaining a secret social media or gaming life — all within easy reach of devices and socials.

In the earlier days, parents were unaware that letting their kids shut their bedroom doors was also selling their kids' souls to the global world, who had birthed the World Wide Web and had begun to study our tech patterns long before we even knew we were guinea pigs. We were unaware that our data was eventually to become the new gold. While the global elites were playing with our futures and digital data was doubling every three years, conspiracy notions were ignored as we focused on our trendy words: 'narcissism' and 'gaslighting'. Technology had also altered the stalking playgrounds of deviants, paedophiles, hackers, advertisers and cyber bullies, who were now free to attack us at home.

Is the 21st century, the de-stabilisation of our youth? Creating strange new sleep patterns and frantic deadlines. Submitting academic papers in the middle of the night, alongside strange new early-onset avoidable physical health conditions. We ignored unusual mood fluctuations as 'just typical teen behaviour' rather than considering the possibility of unmanaged situationally triggered realities or prodromal states. The era of subtle, hidden and emerging avoidable secondary conditions — simply referred to as 'the new norm'.

Parents began to blindside advice from professionals, such as optometrists who were warning us of the serious myopia epidemic (short-sightedness attributed to lack of exposure or involvement with the environment). Deteriorating eye sights and diagnosed spinal conditions in our young were emerging at the level of the very old. Life had become too frantic and increasingly complex, so we stopped noticing the environmentally rejected pale faces behind the pimples, and the emerging obsession of the bedroom, as the secrecy of bullying, stalking and other primary triggers were hidden behind the over-reliance on addictive technology. Whilst the safety net and retreat of the bedroom simply just grew and grew - Plan A lay hidden underneath the sheets.

Parents from lower socio-economic families reported feeling emotionally drained due to financial pressures keeping up with technology. The salt of the earth plodder parents were angry and confused — why are there now so many bloody gadgets? Little did they know that their socio-economic lifestyle may have been a preventative for social withdrawal and secondary conditions.

Keeping their kids grounded as well as focused on transition to adulthood markers, due to not being in a financial position to 'buy in' to the allure of technology (particularly the over-reliance on hobby tech) as they insisted their young people maintain their connection with their outside environment.

Over the past two decades, financially stressed parents reiterated how difficult it was to manage technology pressures within their households. Stories abounded of whole sibling groups forced to share rooms, share devices, negotiate equal access time on one computer or laptop and often co-located in the lounge for access equity. They were forced to cope with escalating internet costs by time-locking devices, not extending night-time use, forcing their offspring to *complete* educational deadlines within reasonable timeframes. This was in direct contrast to their wealthier counterparts who were often unsupervised for extended time to game, then *demanded* more time to complete rushed educational deadlines.

Financially pressured families reported preparing their offspring for early independence by teaching their children the principle of reciprocation as well as budgeting skills such as gaining after-school jobs, purchasing mobile credit and age-appropriate device restrictions. Older siblings helped with younger siblings due to parental workload and childcare costs. Devices and food were banned in bedrooms: the bedroom was for sleep only, with no sleep/wake disturbances in sight. Parents could not afford to buy their teenager their first car, therefore commitment to work (while still at school) was important. The outside environment was once the main supply chain for vitamins, with REM sleep and morning energy common.

When reaching 18 years of age many young people raised in healthy tough-love families, stated that they were more than ready to move out of their family homes. Eager to flick the olds and earn their own full-time income, soon after completing their education (or low-paid apprenticeships). They were ready to adult due to the dearth of discomfort to grow opportunities experienced throughout their young life — the simple fact was that these young people knew that they had outgrown their child-hood. They knew 'if it's going to be, it's up to me'. They were pre-pared to lose the confidence of their youth and to embrace the unknown challenges of adulthood.

The Direct Voice of our Young People — parents be aware!

'I think my parents have guts to ban technology, like mobiles from my bedroom, even though I yell at them every night and give them shit about it.'

'I'm never as tired as my friends, they can't even concentrate.'

'My parents think I hate doing my jobs because they've gotta nag at me at least three times before I do them. I feel useful when I do them - like I'm needed.'

'My parents are idiots because I know how many times they're going to nag before they're gonna crack it, they've got a system and so do I.'

'I hate being treated like a kid, even though I don't act like a man.'

'I don't mind going to the library - plenty of computers, it's easy to concentrate and the old workers are helpful.'

'The consequences of NOT doing what my parents ask me is too high, so that's the only reason I do it.'

'I'm tired all the time; I hardly get any sleep and my parents have no idea I'm up late most nights, they never check.'

'My parents don't really care about me because they never check-up on me. They've got no idea how much freedom they've given me and now I'm in over my head.'

'It's easy to get away with things coz my parents are too nice.'

'Why do my parents think I need a friend? I've got enough friends.'

'It's so easy to get money out of my olds. I'm not going to hand over money to my kids. Don't tell them, though, I've got a system.'

'When I'm a parent I'm going to give my kids heaps more boundaries than what I've been given.'

'I like the way my parents have the guts to stand up to me. I feel sorry for them, though, coz they think I don't like them, they put up with a lot from me.'

'I don't have to do anything extra around the house because I'm at Uni, it's easy.'

'Mum feels guilty for not working, so she does everything at home. That's her job, anyway, isn't it?'

'I'm the kid, so they should provide for me.'

'My mother does all my thinking for me, probably because Dad isn't interested.'

'The real world is tough. Wish my parents had been tougher on me. I got away with everything.'

'We know we've become the "grunt, huh?" generation — that's because it's hard to have a convo with an adult when we're used to our devices being our world.'

'ISO messed things up a lot. It's much easier to get away with gaming instead of school work and only do the subjects I want to.'

'I didn't even know my parents were treating me like a kid until I got my first job.'

35-year-old – 'When I'm a father I'll never let my kids loose in their bedrooms. It's a bit like handing a kid a loaded gun and a bottle of gin every day, as well as the keys to the local brothel, and then expecting him not to become a grog addict, a porn addict and a masturbation addict. It's taken me years to learn how to relate to women after all that porn, and I'm still single.'

The Toughest Act on the Planet — Parenting

Gone are the simple days of the sixties and seventies where hard work, simplicity, predictability and boundaries were the norm. It was a given that we worked hard between fifteen and sixty. Discussions today, with frantic modern parents suggest that there's no comparison between 'back in the day' and the current era. So why then does the older generation still want to talk about 'their day'? Their frantic life, feeling choked within labour-intensive cycles, forced double incomes to afford current lifestyles, high childcare costs, unreasonable housing prices in comparison with pay packets, fears of bankruptcies, interest rate hikes, completing career-driven studies, caring for ageing parents, keeping up with advances in technology, at the same time as desperately trying to adequately afford a privileged 'lifestyle' for children who now demand or expect to be constantly fed with their fancy toys... all on top of our new global madness.

Parents face merciless emotional and physical exhaustion nearing breaking point, alongside stress hormones and rapid heartbeats, only to be told by medical professionals that 'it's not a heart-attack, you're *just* suffering anxiety'. When a same-age peer recently dies from a heart-attack, they become fearful, wondering whether it was attributed to a genetic predisposition or purely from unmanaged stress? Over the past few decades, the numbers of **high-achieving women** with impressive careers and qualifications have risen. Acting like Wonder Woman without a protective bullet-proof shield, working full-time and yet, according to research, still coordinating and completing most of the home environment responsibilities.

Often, the main income earner pleads to their partner to help generate more income to cover the ever-increasing costs of living or to at least engage in household equality, 'what about even part time wages?' The never-ending cycle of enticing partners to re-enter the workforce is now a challenge within many relationships: The Underground Secret Retirement Club. One partner may have experienced a major trigger event, such as a retrenchment or a health condition or maybe a psychological injury though, when the time seems right to launch back into work, there is an entirely different internal agenda.

The anticipation or belief in change, without evidence of *motivation* is the over-givers' greatest demise. While one partner is left holding the financial fort, often feeling lonely, detached and highly resentful, society refers to her/his boisterous exhaustion as being too controlling — or 'you're such a Karen'. As the love tank runs dry, the punishment for sacrificial over-giving is evidenced in the subtle emergence of avoidable and sometimes chronic mental health issues or the triggering of potentially irreversible and/or predisposed physical health conditions. The long-term homebound partner has had plenty of opportunity to muddy their own mind with failure to re-launch chatter as well as negatively impact the bounce-back role modelling to the younger members of the household. Their spines and eyes become weary, evidenced by their relationship with their screens and their ignorance of the washing basket, the grubby floor and weeds in the garden, justifying their lack of reciprocation as a self-imposed work-exclusion clause. So, all one needs to do is simply *pretend to want to work*, to be thought of as *still* a worker? Once upon a time, a wounded Tarzan of the jungle who had fallen from great heights could be found humbly cleaning toilets or cold canvassing — whatever it took to put food on the table. Has peace-time slumber and unduly leaning on others taken us off the frontline of responsibility and decency, turning us into our own worst enemy as our relationships crumble around us?

Denial is a very powerful and stubborn force. Working partners pretend that they're loved, whilst being 'trained' to believe that their partner *could soon* 'feel' work-ready ... despite the months and years that pass by, still naively waiting for the launch of the ever-promised new project (or qualification) to launch the promised million-dollar jackpot. The tribe keeps reiterating that unless the unemployed is updating their resume, constantly talking to recruiters, attending job interviews or volunteering, then THEY ARE NOT INTERESTED IN GENERATING AN INCOME.

How does all this shemozzle compare to our grandparents' day? Older adults suggest that 'back in the day' adulthood was expected to arrive quickly upon leaving school, due to an 'earn or learn' culture that reflected a 'no earn, no eat' philosophy. Parents recall their own transition journey into adulthood, often feeling reasonably adult at around 15 years (particularly if tertiary education was not on the cards) through hard work, initially generating a low income as the 'shit kicker' trainee or office junior, succeeding and failing at relationships, tons of consequential learnings with plenty of hard knock-downs and back-up experiences, especially if alcohol, sex, money recklessness and other risks were involved.

Talking with older men, they suggested 'back in the day' there wasn't always easy choice employment options. It was expected that young men would work in the family business until it was handed down to them. Other families were labelled as 'the butchers', 'the builders', 'the mechanics', 'the tradies', 'the health workers' or the blue-and white-collar workers. There was often the opportunity to join the family and also take advantage of bloodline skills as well as the experiences of fathers, grandfathers and uncles.

Older men indicated that 'back in the day', there was more pressure to avoid revealing the 'real' you. Differences in sexual orientation, mental health or preferred career paths were often hidden under more typically gendered roles. Women were once expected to cease all formal employment when married. Conscription for the armed forces was considered to be one of the most important paths to adulthood (and still is in countries such as Israel). Many older men believe that without a 'duty to country' mindset the younger generation will not learn to stand on any front line. Many older men categorically 'told' me to not bother writing this book — 'give up on the younger ones, they're too far gone, they'll never change'. Brutal!

Migrant families recalled their stories of significant hardship and trauma from their country of origin, grateful to immigrate to the land of golden opportunity, with strong mindsets of 'in kind' reciprocation, proving that reward through hard work can be achieved against all odds. They proudly taught their own children, who were often born in Australia, the values of hard work. Now they're feeling helpless as they watch their grandchildren being parented from a decreased responsibility/increased luxury-device 'sit in' culture. I challenged many older people as to whether they were making excuses by 'sitting back' or had they too formally abdicated their Transition Coach roles?

CALL TO ACTION

After many years discussing the Boys in Bedrooms epidemic, it was evident that the professional community was also confused as to why and how the condition of social withdrawal had become so prolific. Discussions with numerous doctors and psychiatrists, social workers, psychologists, counsellors and education staff revealed an eagerness to support the reversal of social withdrawal, particularly in our young people. Medical professionals reported confusion as to why able-bodied men weren't initiating their own medical appointments nor exercising their right for privacy.

Doctors were disturbed at the way these child-men were sitting strangely close to their mother during *their* consult — 'pawing her arm like a cub in a cave' while she eagerly talked on behalf of her son, suggesting that 'it isn't anyone's fault he's anxious or behaves obsessively, or avoids people and likes his bedroom or needs to sleep so much', because 'maybe he was just born this way?' The man-child sits in his consult with a dazed face, muttering barely a few words to the doctor, at the same time as not disagreeing with his mother's defeatist chatter. The enmeshed unhappiness between mother and son, now clearly a liability, as she seeks medical and/or psychological answers to the product of neglect.

Doctors began discussing how mothers had become 'frenzied doctor-shoppers', blaming professionals for not building rapport with her son, as she frantically searches for a diagnosis. Doc desperately explains that this style of doctor-shopping and self-diagnosis is irresponsible. The concerning words of the medical (or other) professionals fall onto deaf ears. The swift-talking parent has often self-diagnosed a convenient (secondary) condition, such as obsessive-compulsive disorder, social anxiety or depression, eager for a formal label (rather than an opinion) as well as medication to ease the family's conscience.

Once a professional does come out of their diagnostic closet with their prescription pad, there's a strange relief seen in the eyes of the parent, though the pit of their gut tells a different story. The parent knows only too well that 'back in the day' their son was a happy kid, that there's nil family genetic link to his new diagnosed state and that his story began with ... a mismanaged bump on the road.

Working in various states of Australia between 2011 and 2019, within different contexts such as headspace and government mental health, I found the issue of male social withdrawal within the middle class was a concern in *most* communities. Doctors and psychiatrists listened to my rhetoric, though we all knew I was punching above my qualifications as a mental health social worker in terms of suggesting that the diagnostic world was labelling *secondary* issues rather than focusing on their patients' primary issue. One psychiatrist respectfully challenged me, 'If you act like someone, for example, with significant and ongoing compulsive behavioural patterns that cause disruption to most areas of your life as well as a disturbed sleep/wake pattern, we will diagnose you with depression and/or an anxiety-related condition such as obsessive–compulsive disorder, so what's it *now* got to do with the primary issue, anyway?'

One doctor agreed with my concerns and optimistically told me to stop talking about the issue and spend more time writing my book as a Call to Action. He agreed that although I was still in the early stages of understanding this condition, and intervention was not yet documented nor unified in Australia, it was still important to start my writing as an initial provocation, as well as a plea for professional comradery to confront this issue and to plan a way forward. Furthermore, he stated, 'If you write your book, I'll have a pile permanently on my desk to hand out to my patients and their families — the numbers of male social withdrawers (and now female social withdrawers) are high, yet the reversal rates are very low, so just get on with it'. Thanks for your encouragement, Dr Matt!

As a novice writer, I appreciated the encouragement from my incredibly patient writing coach, Lyn Jackson and the medical and psychiatry sectors who all agreed that my writing is primarily a Call to Action. I wondered if there would be a 'shoot the messenger' type of initial reaction, given the references to our middle classes, as well as the humility that would be needed by parents to acknowledge and participate in a disaster recovery model that must involve the whole family if longstanding change is to occur. I respectfully know that when/if psychiatry supports my notion, or agrees that there is an overfocus on secondary diagnosis, it will indeed become an even stronger call to action. Is it assumptive to suggest that due to the fact that many doctors are also in the upper echelons of society and are maybe raising their own socially withdrawn adults, they are not quite brave enough (yet) to publicly agree, that there may indeed be a link between class and mental health, leading to the alarming level of stunted male growth that I now refer to as a generational norm that has triggered a national social development disaster.

What is a Disaster?

'A disaster, whether actual or threatened,
relates to a society or a self-sufficient group in society,
when it undergoes severe danger,
resulting in a disruption to its social structure and
the inability or the prevention
of fulfilling the essential functions of that society.'
(Drabek: 1996)

I set off on a journey to begin researching and writing and listening to families in an attempt to better understand the barriers associated with transition to adulthood. I discovered a relatively empty basket within Australian literature, with little media nor public concern for the growing issue of Boys in Bedrooms. Was there a middle-class gag order in place?

Social Withdrawal — Japanese Contribution Hikikomori

> **Hikikomori:** *A Japanese word that describes individuals who slowly withdraw from society and eventually spend extreme amounts of time on their own.*

It was a relief to discover the pioneering work of Japanese psychiatrist, Dr Saito Tamaki, specialist in youth psychology and family intervention, who had coined the noun 'Hikikomori' in the 1970s to expose the chronic issue of social withdrawal in his country. Saito published his research findings and family intervention strategies in 1998, which was then translated to English in 2013 by Jeffrey Angles, *Hikikomori: Adolescence without End.* Saito coined the noun, 'Hikikomori' 'staying indoors (social) withdrawal' as a way of identifying the distinct behavioural pattern of social withdrawing or avoidance of society, as a 'condition' which has now been added to the *English Oxford Dictionary* (Third Edition, 2020) and is now widely adopted by sufferers of this condition.

Saito was alarmed by the large proportion of young mainly male adults who had become recluses in their parents' home, unable to work or go to school for months or years. They also withdrew from their usual social activities and jobs and became isolated, often not *ever* leaving their homes, instead spending most of their time sleeping, watching television, playing video games and surfing the Internet. At the time of his first publication, Saito boldly suggested that there was possibly an estimated one million Hikikomori (Japan's Missing Million) which was initially met with an outcry of shock and disbelief as to the extent of this abnormal adolescence that rejects all forms of socialisation with the outside world.

Similar to my own discovery, the main demographic were mainly young men, from middle class or above families, the eldest sibling, an average age onset for first major trigger around 15.5 years whose initial behaviours were skipping school and there were no other prior underlying diseases such as bipolar or schizophrenia. The concept of Hikikomori was thought to only be linked to collective cultures, such as those who were pressured to remain connected long term (or lifetime) to the family for survival, as well as those with extreme educational and professional pressures, initially referred to as 'just a Japanese issue'. These days, most Western countries now agree that within many households there are individuals who are regressing at an unusual pace for their developmental age and decreasing their opportunity to (ever) adult.

Western psychology is more likely to explain or diagnose the abnormal avoiders of social contact as more of a secondary issue (rather than focus on the initial lack of adjustment trigger point). For example, diagnosis begins *with* social withdrawal and *then* focus is placed on the *proceeding* anxiety-related triggers such as 'social anxiety' or 'agoraphobia' or a 'fear of open places'. Unlike Australia, the Japanese government over the years has spent millions of dollars to address the severity of social withdrawal, with high public awareness, institutions and effective psychiatric intervention. Although professional assistance is often vital, it has been discovered in Japan, that the most enduring source of healing comes from ex-hikikomori themselves who support others to recovery by providing opportunity to gain work experiences, responsibility and daily social interactions.

I am presenting the issue of social withdrawal from the ground level with permission from many voices (families, sufferers, professionals and supporters) while continuing to work in private practice in Queensland, Australia as a mental health social worker. I am not going to throw too many 'isms' at you such as feminism, cultural relativism, or sexism. However, I will refer to *spiritualism* (disconnect from identity and purpose) as well as *capitalism* (over-focus on family wealth) and controversial notions of *globalism* and *transhumanism* (located at back of book) attributed to evolving systemic mind control measures that I believe is accelerating MSW in Australia.

Rather than adopting the Japanese noun 'Hikikomori', I interchangeably use a variety of phrases and words, such as home dweller, social withdrawer, man-child, early retiree, home-grasser, dependent, mowing the home grass, bedroom long-grasser, recluse, excessive bedroom dweller, permanently housebound, young person at home, retreater, night stalker, on the bosom, home stayer, home wonderer, living as a permanent resident and prisoner of the mind. Due to the high prevalence of males, I'm more likely to use nouns and pronouns such as he, his, boy and man more often than female pronouns.

Although male social withdrawal and addiction is the main focus of my writing, I would like to reiterate the concerns from many professionals and families, in terms of the escalating numbers of young women, the LGBTI+ community, those with chronic eating disorders and addicts who have become increasingly home-bound, particularly with the introduction of enduring social isolation practices since April 2020.

This book does not adequately address the growing reality of **parasite singles** — described by Japanese writers as otherwise functioning, non-contributing individuals with no stated major or previous primary triggers, choosing to remain or re-emerge back into the family home, long after graduating, by relying on their parents for their basis existence. If this applies to members of your household, please refer to Chapters 6, 7 and 8. If you are unable to instigate the concepts in the above chapters you are encouraged to seek professional assistance and/or consider the relationship between enablement and regression.

Risk Assessment

Please note that any boisterous comments, recommendations and strategies that sway more to a 'tough love' style of intervention are definitely NOT recommended for any long-term sufferer of social withdrawal, such as eviction from the family home nor verbally forceful styles of change management. The way forward can be slow and arduous and extremely painful. Therefore, kindness and empathy must be provided in order to provoke the initial stages of change. Sufferers inform me that change can be a frightening experience in terms of community re-integration — like being teleported into an unknown war-torn culture with no protection.

If you or your family members are engaged in any form of self-harm, experiencing suicidal ideation or there is a threat to others, it is VITAL that you seek assistance immediately. Please reach out and maintain connection as well as consider the urgency of risk at all times. I make no apology for reiterating risk throughout this book.

SUMMARY

Australia once boasted one of the best-known lifestyles on the planet. It's my hope that my writing will be received as a genuine, albeit robust contribution to the topic of social withdrawal, encouraging all Australians, despite global disarray, to continue to protect the type of lifestyle that so many of us are eternally grateful for.

I am appreciative of all the professional support received during the writing of this book. I am also hopeful that the readership will be able to sift through my brazen and somewhat nomadic style of conversational writing and join me in a Call to Action for sufferers of social withdrawal and their families, who are frozen with uncertainty and hesitant to interact within their nutrient-rich environment.

My message to all our young people, particularly our young men, is that society is eager for you all to transition to adulthood — we desperately need your tenacity, your strength, your ability to problem solve, your technology intelligence and particularly for you to help us protect our way of life. You are born into this time for a reason. We need you to become psychologically fit by building psychological immunity and to venture out of your mind prison and *stay* out. You deserve to stand up and be counted. You deserve to participate in the adulthood that was destined for you, before time even began.

BUILDING PSYCHOLOGICAL IMMUNITY

Assisting our system to recognise and defend against natural and biologic invasion

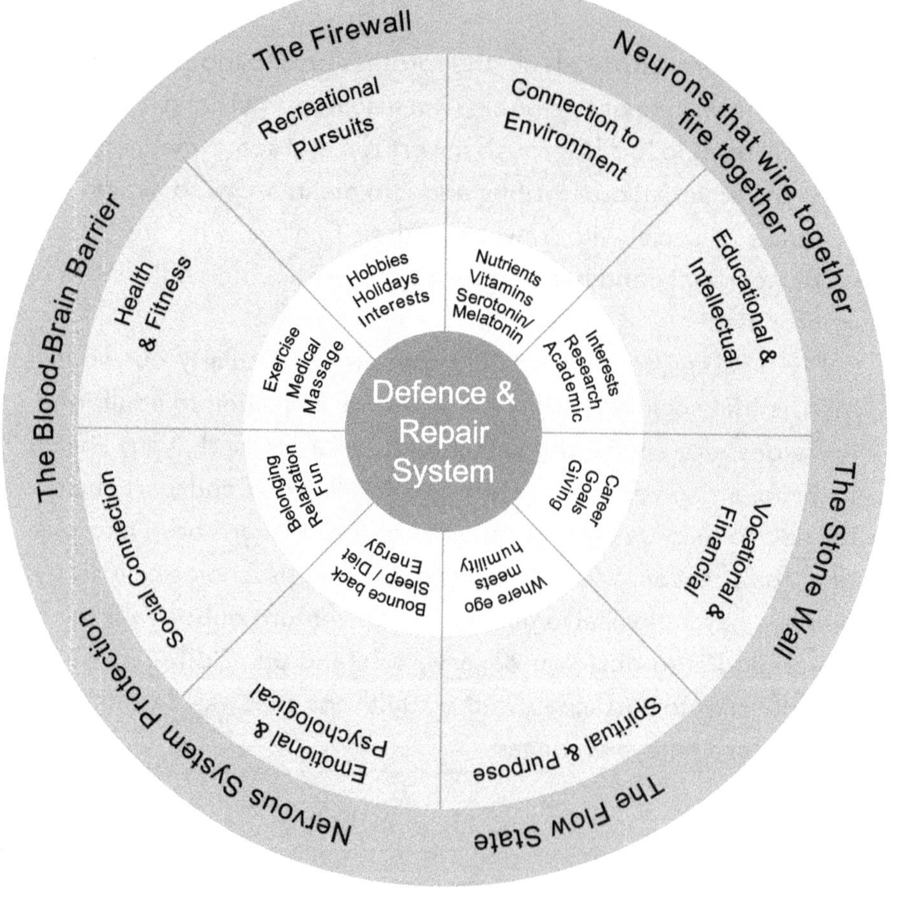

The Firewall

Neurons that wire together fire together

The Blood-Brain Barrier

The Stone Wall

Social Connection

Nervous System Protection

The Flow State

Recreational Pursuits

Connection to Environment

Health & Fitness

Educational & Intellectual

Vocational & Financial

Emotional & Psychological

Spiritual & Purpose

Hobbies
Holidays
Interests

Nutrients
Vitamins
Serotonin/
Melatonin

Exercise
Medical
Massage

Interests
Research
Academic

Defence & Repair System

Career
Goals
Giving

Belonging
Relaxation
Fun

Where ego
meets
humility

Bounce back
Sleep / Diet
Energy

www.get-a-grip.com.au

Chapter 1
Unmanaged Primary Triggers &
Emerging Secondary Behaviours

In this chapter, I discuss the proposition that the 'condition' of long-term social withdrawal is the behavioural response of unmanaged Primary Triggers that have occurred to an otherwise reasonably functioning individual. A 'condition' in this instance refers to the way that, when left untreated for six months, an unmanaged primary trigger event has the potential to become clinically significant, as evidenced by impairment in social, occupational and other important areas of functioning.

I have provided a collection of 12 strategies for prevention and early intervention, rather than over-focusing on the slippery slope of pathology that is enriching the trillion-dollar pharmaceutical industry. It is with sincere hope that early exposure, treatment and/or self-help will see our young people and their enablers continue to participate in the life that they are destined to live.

Theme: Links between affluence and parenting styles that are avoidant of discomfort-to-grow opportunities as a catalyst for emotional regression.

Primary Triggers: Events that can overwhelm individual capability; such as sudden or forced changes, failure, betrayal, or rejection.

Recognising Reasonable

For the purpose of this writing, you agree that prior to the trigger event (or the period of over-reliance) the individual was functioning at a 'reasonable' level within their developmental age. This would mean that:

1) The trigger event did not exacerbate a pre-existing disorder (nor was it considered normal bereavement).

2) There were no serious issues or major disruptions to general functioning as a result of physical health, disability or mental health, including neurocognitive and neurodevelopmental conditions.

3) The individual was engaged in education and/or full-time employment.

4) Movement between jobs was limited, and periods of unemployment (or part-time work) was minimal (freeters).

5) There were no major interruptions within interpersonal relationships or social activities. Participation within family life was reasonably healthy with only minor relationship challenges. When needed, the individual had access to a reasonably functional social support network.

This writing focuses on individuals and their enabling system, who, at the time of their withdrawal period, were not professionally diagnosed with any other major underlying condition/s. In other words, there were no genetic, biological or other conditions, as a result of disturbances in brain function present before the decision to socially withdraw, for example, physical disability, intellectual impairment or neurodevelopmental disorders (please refer to the list below).

A large proportion of adults diagnosed during childhood with attention deficit/hyperactivity disorders such as ADHD or ADD suggest that as adults, this diagnosis has not impacted or hindered their ability to bounce-back from major life stressors, nor to reach their developmental milestones. In other words, their ability to maintain meaningful employment, relationships and recreational pursuits has not been hindered. Based on their comments, I am suggesting that readers are cautious before including ADHD or ADD as an exclusion (refer to point 2).

Examples of genetic, biological or other conditions, including disturbances in brain function:

o Neurodevelopmental Disorders — intellectual disorders, communication disorders, autism, motor disorders
o Neurobehavioral Disorders — Attention Deficit Hyperactivity Disorder
o Neurocognitive Disorders — Alzheimer's, Parkinson's, epilepsy
o Schizophrenia Spectrum and other Psychotic Disorders (included drug-induced disorders)
o Bipolar and Related Disorders
o Depressive Disorders — disruptive mood dysregulation disorder, MDD
o Disruptive, Impulse Control and Conduct Disorder
o Substance Related and Addictive Disorders and Medication-induced Disorders
o Physical Disability or Abnormality
o Severe Trauma — diagnosed trauma and stressor-related disorders, for example, Resignation Syndrome such as child refugees who have become chronically unwell and unable to function at even the most basic of levels

  o Psychosocial Disability — a disability that may arise from a mental health issue. This may cause functional impact and barriers when interacting within a social environment.

I am highly respectful of complex and co-morbid mental health and physical health conditions that often require management through specialist intervention and/or psychotropic medication, including case management under the National Disability Insurance Scheme (NDIS) program.

It's humbling to meet inspiring individuals with diagnosed disorders such as bipolar, schizophrenia, chronic medical and physical conditions and mood dysregulation who are unstoppable in their determination and tenacity to reach their goals. Individuals identifying with condition/s as per the above list are welcome to join my frank discussion on social withdrawal, particularly, if you are motivated to re-connect with society or to remain connected to your environment and social relationships, and you have not been pressured to read the content of this writing. I sincerely hope that my strategies will make a difference to your life, as they have done in mine.

Please note: this chapter does not focus on parasite singles — a Japanese notion describing individuals who have not been diagnosed with a psychological illness, or an injury, nor have they suffered from the effects of a significant trigger event as a reason for non/minimal contribution within the home environment. This includes adult family members (18+) and those returning to their family home (often with partners and children). For entrenched parasitical behaviour, please refer to Chapter 6 (The Financial Formula), Chapter 7 (Moving Forward) and Chapter 8 (Family Meetings) to break patterns of regression and entitlement by focusing on the principle of reciprocation.

What is a Psychological Illness or Injury?

For the purpose of my writing, a psychological illness or injury is a mind problem attributed to the structure or constant re-structuring of perception. It's likened to a type of brain bruising or structurally fragmented, dangerously sparking, overloaded brain circuitry system that occurs to otherwise reasonably healthy individuals. People most at-risk of overloaded thinking styles are those who are constantly eliciting their primal response system as evidenced by perfectionism, procrastination, people pleasing, avoiders of conflict or confrontation, workaholics and people with a vendetta belief system.

Stages of Withdrawal

- Early Withdrawal: 1-3 months — early intervention and pre-vention measures recommended.
- Chronic Withdrawal: 3+ months — Urgent need of intervention — risk of developing secondary conditions.
- 6-12+ months: highly urgent disordered state — an illness requiring complex intervention with the whole system urged to participate in a recovery plan. Keeping in mind, for long-term social withdrawal to exist there has been a long-term partnership of dependence — *the whole system is unwell.*

Contribution from Neuroscience — Cultivating our Emotional Intelligence

The wisdom and flexibility we apply to the construction, monitoring or reconstruction of our thought pathways is described within the neuroscientific field as neuroplasticity. The plasticity (flexibility) or speed in which we are able to construct or reconstruct (cognitive restructuring) our thoughts, particularly at our trigger points, provides us with vital opportunities to continue to strengthen our bounce-back skills and resume our preferred emotional and behavioural state. Continuing to develop our speedy bounce-back system, as well as rigorously test our primally-charged irrational, repetitive thought-looping means we are progressing our emotional age, as well as controlling the chemicals in our body. No practice, no progress.

Our brain will always be in need of care and protection. Our mind is considered the last private part of the human. At this time in history, no one can read your mind or force you how to think. YOU have the capability of being the Chief Executive Officer of your own brain architectural system. You also have the capability to restructure or re-catalogue your messy stories: When you are ready to dig deep: The Deep Dive.

Is the greatest enemy of your State, you? When you are emotionally or behaviourally triggered, do you quickly recover and move forward, or do you snap and sway? How elastic is your brain functionality? Do you require others, or emotional blockers to think for you as a way of avoiding pain? Are you psychologically resilient? Do you have a plan for your hype and clutter? How strong is your psychological firewall?

Taking aim at rapid advances in neuro-technology that seeks to eventually control or "Wi-Fi" all human behaviour through brain computer interfaces (BCI's), it's with this 'hot potato' topic in mind that I invite the reader to prioritise the protection of the geographical landscape of your brain. One day we might hear parents threaten their kids — 'get rid of that chip on your shoulder and change your thinking, before we chip your brain and *tell you* how you're going to think'. Building and firewalling our own direct, conscious link between the different departments of our brain has never been more important, so too are regular updates to our 'virus software', particularly after a threat to the system.

FINDING RATIONAL REASONABLE

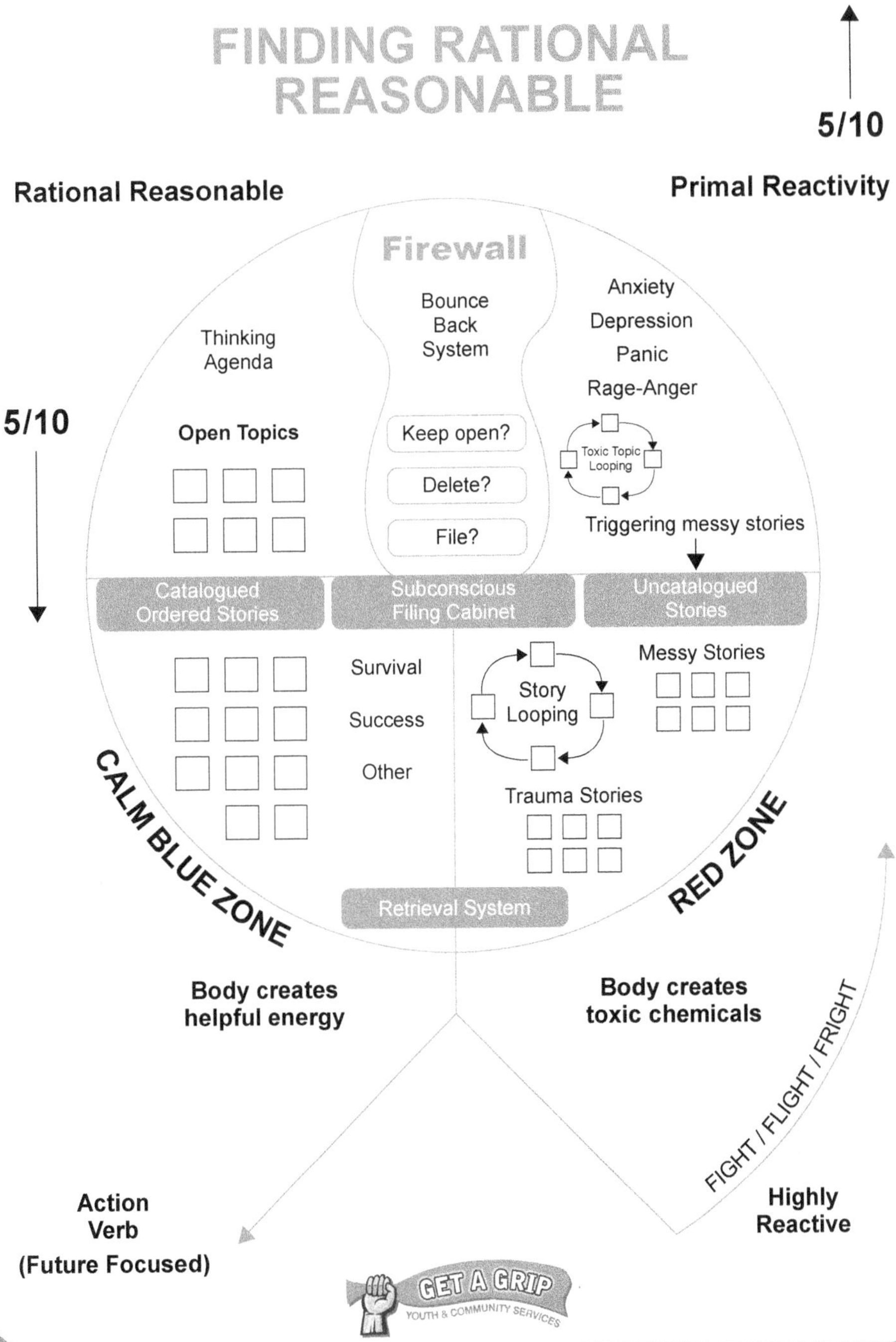

www.get-a-grip.com.au

The Primal Limbic System

Challenging and complex new events often force us to significantly narrow our world view and react to the circumstance: As an act of survival. Most of us can identify with a relatively typical, highly uncomfortable or provocative trigger event, followed by the induction of toxic primal fear-based (or anger-based) chemicals, as we attempt to manage the event, particularly when faced with an actual or perceived threat to life, such as a truck mistakenly moving into our lane on a busy motorway. We move from a semi-relaxed state to one with an 'emergency' mindset that requires swift decision-making.

Thankfully, our fear-based primal limbic system responds with lightning speed and our thoughts (instructions) have the potential to create sufficient protection chemicals to successfully manoeuvre a life-and-death situation. When our situation has been reality-checked and the crisis is over, we are required to return back to our 'rational reasonable state' in order to carry on with our day — *regardless of the chemical disturbance that still lingers in our body.* When we adequately manage these emotionally provocative trigger events a number of times, particularly within four seconds (bounce-back optimum), the brain eventually catalogues (files) this adaptive and highly effective instructional system in our retrieval system — The Library (Hippocampus). Then the next time a high-risk situation arises, we are offered the *same system.*

Faulty Instructions - the Greatest Risk to Our Life

Our instructions (thinking styles) about a range of Topics can be *highly functional, reasonable* or *frantic.* Some of our instructions may have been left in their unchallenged state or not reality-checked for a while, simply filed somewhere 'back there' in our sub-conscious. A barking dog runs out of his driveway towards you in the absence of his owners — what are your instructions? Run? Freeze? Assess body language? Prepare for aggression? Lower your voice? Look for the owner? Freak out?

Instructions form the base or the foundation of our emotional life. Not that it's anyone's business to *tell* you that your instructions (your rules and beliefs) are faulty, or that they are on shaky ground, are too wishy-washy or that they need to be deleted or modified. It's entirely up to the individual to decide the legitimacy of their *own* thinking styles by analysing whether the benefits outweigh the risks?

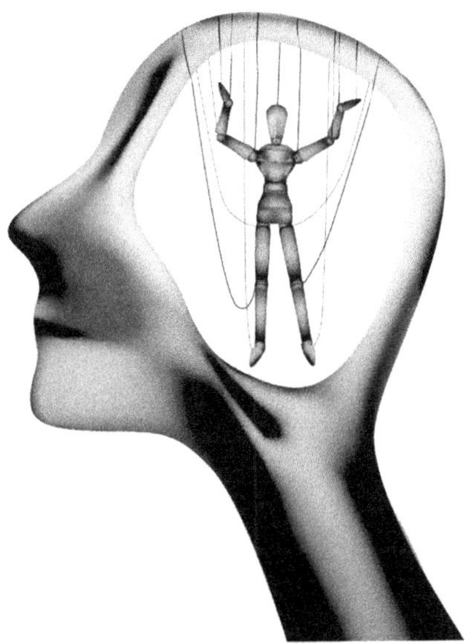

In many ways, we are a puppet on a string to the range of our filed instructions and our life is simply played out as a stage performance. Thankfully, we have the freedom to be the editor of our story or the author of a new story, and we are also more than capable (unless impaired) of laying aside our excuses and rewriting our script — or sacking some of the actors in our story. We can also press Total Reset and re-hire a fresh new cast.

Aside from dealing with a life-and-death situation (immediate threat) or engaging in an act of spontaneity (skinny dipping in the middle of the night!) most of our trigger events give us plenty of opportunity to practice building our executive bounce-back skills. Most days have a multitude of simple occasions to practice elasticising our muscle memory system, such as: completing/planning deadlines; dealing with the boss; coping with annoying colleagues or teachers; completing tedious household tasks; sorting out our Monday-morning attitude; our toxic Sunday afternoon dread-of-Monday vibe; practising assertive communication skills or communicating/negotiating within a power imbalance relationship (parent-child, boss-colleague, police-citizen).

Emotional management does not require perfectionism: The goal is to achieve at least a reasonable C and simply keep building executively from there. We aren't required to be brilliant communicators or gifted decision-makers, we just need an Opt-In Mindset. As for the hundreds of older people who suggest 'but you can't teach an old dog new tricks' — please read the research that suggests otherwise, and re-join the brain gym! The body may age, though the mind requires its human to stay young. We may score an A-plus in our business prowess, sporting or academic life, though more of an F-minus in our emotional management life.

The Tyranny of the Bedroom Walls

When a major event arrives, such as a complicated transition point or a trauma event, the brain is put to immediate work and tries to make sense of our situation. In the face of abuse or horror or a situation that our memory system has nil, weak or irrational instructions for, our mind can turn a big event into an even more complex event. Why does our brain do that? Our brain just does its best initially, in order to protect us, and when the initial danger is gone, it attempts to make sense of our current situation by giving it *some* type of meaning and order.

A long-term unmanaged primary event is similar to emotional pendulum swinging in a boxing ring with only yourself as your own head-bashing opponent. Stuck in the corner ring, slipping on your own sticky blood and barely able to breathe, then rushed to hospital in an ambulance. Waking up in hospital to your new unrecognisable deconstructed self ... you begin to wonder if the damage is irreparable. Your medicals and your people are frantic, as they work their magic, to stop you from enduring further torture. Though, sadly, your people are unaware that your physical pain is secondary to the horrific emotional torture of lost dreams, crippling your ability to heal and altering your moral compass.

Rather than the physio pushing you out of your hospital bed, you continue to worship your pain and you are led by the hype and clutter of your new story. Released back home, the physical *body* starts to heal, though the *mind* has succumbed to the dark, detrimental tunnel of Plan A Lost Dreams. Your medicals are hopeful that your body will heal over the next few years, though your concussed head has another two weeks for a full clearance. Strangely, rather than employing optimism as the main actor in your new story, you choose to exacerbate psychological inflammation by employing messy octopus thinking, that quickly grows arms and legs, internally screaming, enmeshed in a cesspool of anger, degradation and imposed shame.

Who knew that the hit to the ego was, by far, the greatest hit of them all? Why was no one warning you that the trade-off for continual volatile and toxic head chatter is nothing short of a secondary smash to the head, which everyone knows, is far more dangerous than the first. Soon, your medicals refer to your 'injury' as a 'condition' with the brain acquiring an even newer prognosis of its own.

When the meds and the walls of the bedroom become a solace, and there's less pressure to de-toxify the mind, it becomes impossible to cut off the roots of your dangerous octopus thinking, now split into juvenile pathways, aimlessly looping around and around with no end in sight. From the cells of your mind prison, the news reporter asks you, 'So, what's your game-plan now, mate?' You disdainfully reply, in true Mike Tyson style, 'Doesn't *everyone* have a plan, until they're punched in the face?'

Complex Trauma Events

Life in our modern world is not perfect; in fact, it has become quite bizarre! We are facing unprecedented times in our history, with most of us shaking our heads in confusion, as well as in anticipation of what new surprise could be lurking around the corner. Therefore, unlike any other time in our history, it has become imperative to tidy up the geographical landscape of our brain, as well as process our past messy stories in order to strengthen our stamina for the future.

The neuroscience field provides a dearth of information and resources to explain the different departments within our stored memory system that explain the interesting (albeit somewhat complicated!) interconnection between these brain regions. Such as explicit memories (episodic and semantic), implicit motor memories (basal ganglia and cerebellum) and our short-term working memories (prefrontal cortex).

Analysing the impact of unresolved or uncatalogued past stories begins with 'Mapping' (refer to the Grief and Loss Mapping template in Chapter 2). Respectfully revisiting and re-cataloguing our stories (stored memory system) can have a profound effect on our functionality, as well as improve our mental health and our physical health.

The brain expects us to know whether our past stories are either **success stories** or **survival stories**. Sometimes our 'sense' at the time of the event didn't make *actual* sense, or was hugely out of proportion to reality, because we didn't spend enough time gathering the correct facts, or we may not have *catalogued* our story correctly. Sometimes we didn't provide the story with rational instructions, or the right name, nor did we give it the attention it deserved at the time.

The brain is like a sophisticated librarian system that requires order. The goal for us all is to store our success stories as well as our messy or survival stories in the 'orderly' catalogued area of our memory system.

Unfortunately, there's often a bunch of unruly books chucked into the corner of the library that represent our messy, sassy and uncatalogued memories, such as our non-sensical stories and our trauma stories (refer to Finding Rational Reasonable template).

Until we transfer our messy uncatalogued stories into the sophisticated library system, by respectfully spending time correctly cataloguing (healing and planning) we can remain vulnerable to the same Event and its triggers, even 10 or 20 years later, experiencing emotional volatility AT THE SAME LEVEL — as if the event had *just* occurred.

Individuals with long-term unresolved messy stories, describe their long-term partnership with constant fear-based thinking like living on planet Earth as a visitor, enmeshed with their highly protective, on-guard armed soldier, sheltering together in the corner of an island on their own. During brief patches of rationality on the Isle of Smile, there's a sense of freedom and joy. Though, like any imposter they soon sabotage their freedom, due to their complex mistrust of mainstream culture. Their tidy exterior does little to elicit attention, though internally, they keep their finger near the panic button, where the predictability of chaos makes more sense than the strange normality of calm.

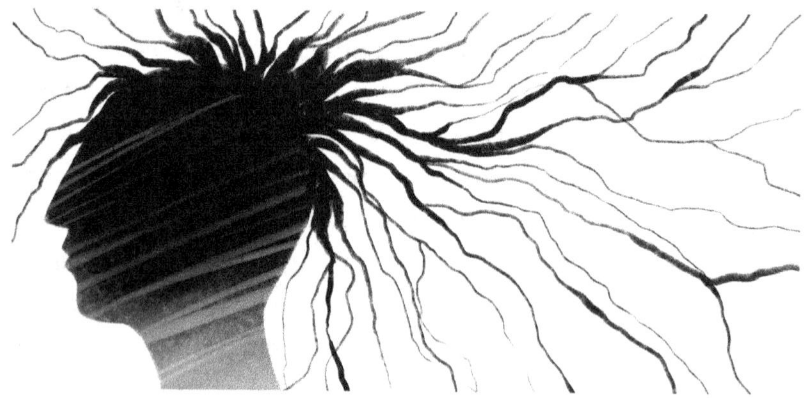

THE JOB OF FEAR

The Great Protector Enemy

Unmanaged *fear* is one of our greatest *enemies*. Fear is also one of our greatest *allies* when we are faced with a life and death situation, where swift thinking and action is imperative. The job of fear is to provide information, particularly accurate information from the brain to the body, in order to determine the level of protection chemicals we need at the time. Therefore, harnessing and controlling fear is one of the greatest, and also, one of the most challenging achievements of them all.

Our fear-based system can be appropriately reactive in terms of dissecting *real danger* in the moment, such as an aggressive animal within our close proximity. Speedy changes in our limbic circuitry (amygdala) can regulate the brain to produce neurochemicals, such as adrenaline and noradrenaline, which mobilize the body to manage an emergency situation (Golman, 1995: 205).

In the face of danger, the brain needs its human to produce a clear instructional rationale based on facts. Though, sometimes our brain struggles to understand our instructions, as well as the *real truth* or the reality of a situation in order to create (set in motion) the *right* type of chemical responses for each situation. Often our rational thinking is ignored or stonewalled in favour of a narrowing or over-prioritising of our primal fear-based thinking. This forces our body to try to protect us, by inducing toxicity, triggering a **fight, flight or fright** behavioural response system.

If our body believes we are in need of protection, it will be *compelled* to respond to this threat by producing what it believes are the 'right chemicals' to enact behavioural responses in order to successfully 'manage' our situation. Our instructions command our body to either:

(1) Freeze or become immobilized
(2) Run quickly from the perceived risky situation
(3) Fight to win what it believes is a battle — the ultimate survival of the fittest

The commander of an army has the authority to instruct the soldiers to load their guns and prepare for a battle in order to kill their enemy — when instructed, the soldiers will shoot. **Our highly reactive Primal System is likened to a pending missile launch attack. Primal mind bombs are nothing short of chemical explosions, so without a plan to manage this system our life will continue to be compromised.** In other words, unless we learn to become speedy Rational analysers and re-constructors of our fear-based self-talk (particularly self-talk that has split into messy roads, like an octopus on steroids) toxic emotions such as anxiety-panic, rage-anger and morbid depression will continue to infiltrate our life and minimise our opportunity to win even a simple battle — likened to living with an internal bomb, with no 'off' switch in sight.

To live life on the edge of an easily triggered state is considered to be maintaining our **Primal Child State**. It's easy to see this in motion when our adult Aussie baby rooster doesn't get his way on the international tennis circuit — screaming, yelling, abusing umpires and breaking tennis rackets in a brazen fashion likened to an ancient king who believes he owns the universe! Although we're not yet perfect (nor is perfectionism a requirement for a happy life), we *must* practice trigger point management at *every* opportunity, rather than bombing, suppressing or excusing our reactivity as a developmental weakness, or due to entitlement, special privilege or baby rooster giftedness in one area of our life.

During a counselling session with a young person in Broken Hill, NSW, he admitted he had acquired an internal primal bomb mindset, which was switched to 'permanently on-alert' (rage-anger), described as 'only seeing black'. He felt like a scared two-year old living in the body of an old war vet. He had been told that he would probably end up in prison by the time he was 10 years of age. He knew that he wasn't even fully grown into his adult body and yet he was assaulting children and adults like they were matchbox toys.

After learning about Mr Primal, my new young client looked at me right square in the eyes and said, 'Well, I'd better learn to switch that little primal fucker off then, huh!' He was only eight years of age and earlier in the year he'd only been allowed at school for two hours per day, with two youth workers at his side at all times, due to the chronic safety risk to other pupils. When his mind bombs were detonated, he had no conscious awareness of his violent actions at the time: with his memories left in raw form, he was accumulating innocent victims like a single armed enemy on a battlefield.

When I first met Master Eight, he described his head as 'full of dark black clouds, with only a few white fluffy ones'. He described deep shame and a sense of disbelief that his reign of terror had hurt so many of his peers and family. He clearly stated that his goals were to (1) 'have more white fluffy clouds' (2) 'to control Primal' and (3) 'to get back to school'. He wanted a Total Reset.

Master Eight eventually achieved his goal of winning his 'head-battle' and began negotiating his slow graduated return back to school with his principal, clearly apt at articulating his 'toolbelt' strategies. It was indeed, an incredibly proud day when his principal shook his hand and eventually welcomed him back to school as a full-time student. Master Eight was instrumental in passing his 'tools' to other students, and he also urged me to talk about his story. If a young person with a horrific trauma history can eventually defuse the battle in his mind when triggered, so too can all adults (more on Master Eight later).

Right Topic, Right Response

Our thoughts are processors of information: simply a bunch of ideas, propositions, perceptions, judgement, truths, mis-truths, as well creative ideas for solutions, whether for harm or good. Research and studies on memory and thought analysis is interesting, such as phenomenology (experiences and sensory), metaphysics (mind and matter), psychoanalysis (the unconscious), the law of thought (contradiction and identity), counterfactual thinking, critical thinking (reasonable, reflective), positive thinking (optimism) and so on.

Regardless of theories, models and general views around thought management, our trigger point moments can provoke a bunch of toxic *first-layer* (often quickly followed by second-layer) emotional reactions if we choose to rapidly over-analyse our circumstance. Our brain is not built for chaos, nor were we created for personality disordered behavioural patterns. We were created to master our Adult Rational Reasonable State and to guide our brief moments of emotional reactivity into safer waters.

Our brain requires its human to be strategic. Our brain also requires us to be able to *accurately* name each topic that we have placed on our thinking agenda. Although this is no easy feat, if we are at least working towards *developing* this strategic skill, we are heading in the right direction (refer to template Finding Rational Reasonable, pg. 59).

Topics Demand a Solution

When we place a topic on our thinking agenda, our brain expects us to connect with fact-based rationality, *as quickly as possible*. Our brain's favourite meal is rational decision making! The body listens for our clear instructions in order to produce the right type of energy to manage the situation. Our body abhors inducing toxicity and partying with chaos, though its hands are tied if our instructions are faulty and we hand ourselves over to Primal.

The Boss of our instructions is the brain — US! The Boss of the story sends direct instructions to the body, and our legs are sent in the direction of these instructions. No one 'makes us' or forces us to think the way we do. Regardless of our past, or the behaviour of others or our current circumstances, our thoughts are a choice. It is a huge risk to maintain a frantic topic. **The toxicity of highly volatile and ongoing stress hormones will eventually lead to the dismantling of our brain architectural system.** Over time, this can seriously impair learning, behaviour, physical health and mental health.

The hottest topic in psychology currently is linked to the alarming rates of anxiety within all age groups, including preschool children. Fear-based (or rage-anger) over-processing is often the reason young children living in volatile circumstances, who have been forced to employ their Primal basic survival system from a young age, are eventually diagnosed by psychiatry with *avoidable issues* such as chronic behavioural problems, attention deficit, significant learning difficulties, hyperactivity, and other complex mental health and physical health issues.

Many conditions are acquired — we are not born with unmanaged toxicity (respecting genetic conditions and neonatal abstinence syndrome). When we challenge or harness our fears by reconstructing our instructions, our feet automatically move in the direction they were designed to walk. Are black clouds confusing your thinking and red dust-storms stinging your eyes?

Toxic stress is a type of dangerous brain circuitry overload. Left unmanaged, it can damage our neural connectors, which are otherwise vital for our Higher Order Thinking Skills (HOT) such as our ongoing ability to effectively rationalise and solve dilemmas. In other words, the likelihood of our executive brain reaching adulthood is minimal or severely compromised, which is why, ever-increasingly, adults are describing themselves as 'young people living in an adult's body'. There are no winners when an individual disconnects or unplugs the executive connection to their rational brain. Pulling the plug, cutting the air supply, opening the moat to invasion, procrastination, stonewalling — call it what you want. We must remain lovers of our rationality, not reactors of our primally induced toxicity.

So, our view (perception) of our circumstances has a direct bearing on what type of productive or contaminating chemicals our brain is forced or instructed to smash into our body? Damn right! And unless interrupted, our legs will *only* move in the direction they have been INSTRUCTED to walk. Yep! Therefore, the rest of our life is simply a stage performance of these instructions. We are living a scripted life. Nothing more and nothing less. This means that (outside of genetic or hormonal imbalances) our emotional life does not exist: it is engineered as a result of our thinking patterns.

The Great Enemy of Change — Procrastination

Delayed rational decision-making is often attributed to the infliction of privileged procrastination. One luxury we cannot afford is procrastination! When we rapidly overthink or overanalyse a circumstance, we are teaching ourselves to remain on toxic alert. Why do we choose to party with Primal when we can run with Rational?

Toxic topics are often linked to our fear of failure, perfectionism or our lack of motivation to face our current reality head-on. When we open a Topic and place it on our Thinking Agenda, we open a neural pathway. Considering we already have trillions of these pathways in our brain, we must ask ourselves — what is the value-add of opening even more? If there is no rational decision (keep or delete or file) for a topic, we are left vulnerable to the content of our thinking. It's easy to turn a **Single Lane** neural pathway (new event) into a Road, left unchallenged it widens into a **Motorway** which then grows into a **Superhighway**, eventually morphing into a wide and dominating automatically programmed **Mega-Superhighway**.

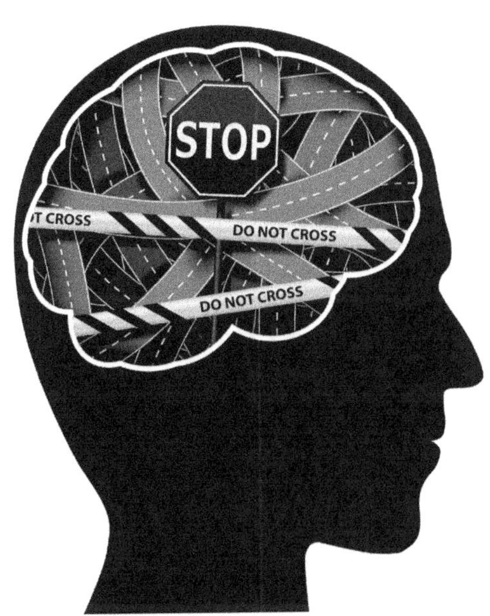

Over-using erratic thought pathways turns ordinary topics into hairy toxic beasts with long arms and legs, breaking through our blood-brain barrier, like a viral invader. This alters our view of the future, easily becoming brainwashed to our own notions of mis-belief, finding us spending serious and uninterrupted time selling ourselves lies and visualising strange abstract concepts.

Many of our topics and instructions are generally reasonable or functional, tucked away securely in our sub-conscious filing system — for example, *how* to ride a bike, drive a car, pay a bill online, send a txt, make a coffee and so on. Though, if our *instructions* about a particular topic are frantic, our head office (brain) will create a chaotic relationship with that topic. For example, road rage — I can drive a car (functional automatic pilot) — '*but I shouldn't have to deal with idiot drivers: they'll pay*' (toxic vendetta/payback).

If we string or link a number of our topics together with erratic instructions, and start cooking them into one big melting pot, we can expect our body to increase its confusion and provide us with a mixed pot of toxicity (the 'speed and weed' effect of unmanaged highs and lows). This system will eventually malfunction, particularly if we have other predisposing vulnerabilities, as well as messed up lifestyle routines. Therefore, to remain in control of our chemical responders, we MUST learn how to separate our topics and elicit a speedy solution at every opportunity.-

Decision Making One Two or Three — Keep / Delete / File

1. **Keep Topic Open** — working document. Leaving a topic open on our thinking agenda is a direct instruction to the body to produce helpful energy *or* toxicity, as per the content of our thinking.

2. **Delete Topic** — erase the 'content' of this topic.

3. **File** — save topic for retrieval at a later time.

Prioritising Primary Trigger Events

Changes and events are an inevitable part of life.
We must be Prepared, with a Plan, we will Move Forward.

Our Reality Point (Primary Trigger Event)

Our Reality Point is a trigger situation or a moment in time that forces us (often through no fault of our own) into a *new* reality, for example, a shock failure, a breakup, unemployment, relocation, job change or bullying. When this occurs, we will either pull out an intervention tool/s from our toolbox to cohesively manage the situation, *or* we will block our reality, abdicating our right to bounce-back. The chemicals in our body can be triggered in a way that overloads our capacity or stonewalls our rational brain from managing a situation. Prolonged toxicity or inaction can exacerbate physical and mental health issues, particularly when we binge on our pain-relievers, dependencies and addictions.

Primary trigger points are considered normal (as well as bizarre) events that occur throughout our lifetime. Our reaction to a primary trigger may only be temporary, *or* it may only cause temporary interruption to our general functionality, particularly **if** we are prepared to retrieve and implement our rational bounce-back. Unfortunately, when our brain has under-used bounce-back instructions or has no photographs (stored memories) of handling such an event, we often react in unusual ways.

It's fair to suggest that recovery is not always easy, particularly in the face of tragedy, tragic global events, feelings of inferiority, perceived abandonment, shame, rejection, isolation and dislocation. Though, at all times, we must ask ourselves what side of the road are we driving our thoughts along — prison-able Primal or lawful Executive? In Australia, we drive our cars on the left-hand side of the road. If we make a mistake as an act of accidental negligence, by accidentally driving on the wrong side of the road, or make a wrong turn into a one-way street, we usually quickly turn around to avert a potential traffic disaster and carry on.

If we remain driving on the wrong side of the street with full knowledge of the legal and moral ramifications, it is considered dangerous driving — a criminal offence that has the potential to cause grievous bodily harm or even land us in prison. Psychological progression occurs when we continually elasticise our bounce-back skills or we are prepared to make a U-Turn and head to our intended street. Decision-making under fire (bounce-back) is thought to create an ideal opportunity to practice or test our reactionary skills. James Kerr in his interesting read, 'Legacy: What All Blacks Can Teach Us About the Business of Life' (2020:112), suggests that bad decisions are not always made through a lack of skill or innate judgement; they are made because of an inability to handle pressure at the pivotal moment.

1.1 — Strategy: Identify the Primary Trigger Event/s

Name a significant Trigger Event (*excluding bereavement*) that you can relate to or (using only two-four words) circle from the following list: failed exam; discrimination; partner cheating; relationship issues; bullying; transition to high school; transition to university/TAFE; relocation; health prognosis; new job; workplace exclusion/bullying; sexuality; pregnancy; leaving home; mandates; vaccinations; other ....

Name the Event/s: _______________________   Year/Age _________

1.2 — Strategy: The TED Strategy
1. Topic   2. Emotion   3. Decision

Please note: Difficulty applying TED may be an indication of poor elasticity at your trigger points.

Bounce-back strategies (BBS) are rational instructions for our trigger-point events, increasing our cognitive flexibility. BBS are nutrients for our brain, forming foundational instructions to direct our feet and maintain our emotional intelligence. If our cognitive elasticity becomes weak or inflexible or loses its spring, we are left vulnerable to external forms of mind control and toxicity.

Join the brain gym and start exercising — build your cognitive biceps and triceps! The only criterion for membership is a flexible mindset and a commitment for discomfort-to-grow opportunities.

The use of TED does not mean the topic is fully resolved; it means that you have elicited your rational brain to take control of your action planning.

1. **Topic** - Name the Topic/Event (or refer to Event in 1.1). What is it about the situation that has triggered me?

2. **Emotion** — (Validation) - identify and rate the emotion — above or below 5/10 e.g. anger 8/10

3. **Decision** — What direction am I taking?
    Plan of Action = keep/ delete/ file (refer to decision making One Two Three)

TED example - My relationship broke up; I'm devastated; I'm moving forward

1) **Topic** — Relationship Break-up? What does this break-up mean to me? I'm single again? Therefore, is the topic 'being single'?

2) Emotion - Sad @ 8/10 — (Validation — I deserved better treatment'; they deserved better from me?)

3) Decision — It's time to move on — so I'm just going to ...... deal with sadness (grief & loss); contact friends ...

Topic: ____

Emotion/s: ____

Decision: ____

Topic: ____

Emotion/s: ____

Decision: ____

Topic: ____

Emotion/s: ____

Decision: ____

Topic: ____

Emotion/s: ____

Decision: ____

Anchoring to the Last Time Life Made Sense

An Anchor is a metaphor or a picture that captures a happier or a higher functioning stage, by focusing on what was happening in your life at the time.

1.3 — Strategy: Anchoring — your last 'happy'

Let's travel back to the last time that life in general made sense or was at least reasonable within the context of your lifestyle. Can you visually capture the last time your circumstances weren't dictating your mood — when life was moving forward, rather than at a standstill or moving backwards? If it's difficult to remember the last time life made sense (due to long-term social withdrawal or enabling) start by heading back to 5 years of age, 10 years of age, then 14 years of age, then reaching adulthood from 18+ years of age.

What metaphor and colours capture this time — for example, a beach sunset/sunrise, surfing wild waves on a windy day, a peaceful outback scene, climbing a steep mountain, the tree of life, the joker in a crowd?

Other examples — wild waves — symbolising passing challenging milestones or maybe a beach scene — symbolising time in life before your shock break-up. What else was happening in your life at the time such as working, studying, friendships, hobbies and goals?

Example: Year 10 (2016), 15 years — life was simple/sporty/school/healthy — Anchor — bush scene — calm, friendships, achieving goals. Colours — grey and blue.

If Anchoring is difficult for you, the below Anchoring Questionnaire may be helpful. Please complete your example on the next page.

Anchoring Questionnaire

Identify your last general functioning age or stage and rate the below in terms of your functionality at the time:

- Daily attendance in employment or education
  (achieving basic goals) /10
- Connection to your peers, love relationships
  and interests /10
- Ability to make reasonable decisions within
  your developmental age /10
- Connection to family/others within your
  home environment /10
- Connection to community and recreational pursuits /10
- Connection to wider family, such as grandparents,
  uncles, siblings, cousins (weekly/fortnightly/monthly) /10

TOTAL **/60**

Calculate your anchoring score, add this to your metaphor as well as capturing the facts in your life at the time. This may provide you with a solid, powerful base to begin your re-launch.

Example — Anchoring Age (20yrs), Anchor Score — 35/60 — connected to peers and other relationships, working, achieving basic goals. Colours — Life was mostly white with only brief moments of black.

PRIMARY & SECONDARY INTERVENTION STRATEGIES

Tackling our messy thinking, particularly after trigger point events, by employing **primary intervention strategies** (cognitive restructuring) is vital if we are to avoid habitually medicating, suppressing or distracting ourselves from our reality. The goal for us all is to develop the art of 'hearing' what we are 'saying' and then challenge the legitimacy of this thinking. As we are well aware, ignoring reality is a fool's way of travelling through life — ask any person currently at breakdown level or an addict currently in a detoxification unit or an offender living behind bars subject to a lengthy incarceration order.

Suppressing fear as well as our anger-based stories is similar to creating a direct link to a weapon — weaponising our thinking is a ticking time bomb. Explosions leave us on an island on our own or becoming a player in someone else' story, creating automatically programmed rupture-repair cycles — for year after year, after exhausting year.

<u>Benefits of primary intervention strategies</u> — clearer thinking, better prepared for trigger point management, increased focus on rational language, increased ability to validate as well as quickly identify primary emotions.

Secondary intervention strategies are often a brilliant way of inducing a relaxed state, as well as taking the brain on a holiday, such as deep breathing, mindfulness, yoga, relaxation activities, new hobbies and time on your own. They can also provide the head with a thinking break, particularly powerful when combining socialisation and environmental nutrients. Though, used in the wrong way, it's easy to be distracted from addressing our *actual* circumstances, such as challenging our fear or shame-based thinking and restructuring our anger stories in order to move forward from our current circumstances.

Suppression, internalisation, distraction and deep breathing have the potential to cause our body to internally toxify our stories, as well as exacerbate medical or mental health issues. *However!* - if you're a recidivist offender on the street with a knife in a vendetta rage, then by all means suppress, deep breathe, think about your next holiday, walk on the beach or in the bush, talk to the sky and distract or block your mind from vicious thoughts of payback — do whatever it takes to keep your community safe!!

As long as we remember that psychological forward movement, particularly fear-based/anger-based stories, requires activating primary intervention strategies with a plan for primary trigger point management. Keeping in mind that the combination of both primary and secondary intervention strategies optimises the balance between work, rest and play.

Our Brain Thrives on Order

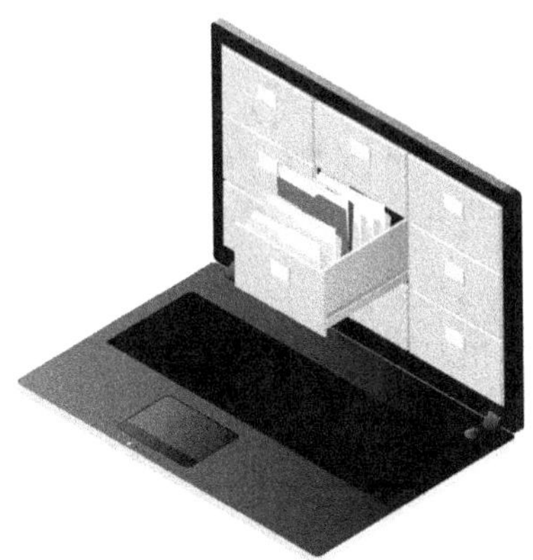

The IN/OUT Filing System

An ordered system is one in which we are able to clearly name each topic on our current (open) thinking agenda, *as well as* the names of our filed stories (such as our success, survival and messy stories).

Although life can be rather chaotic and messy at times, we must remind ourselves that our brain functions at its peak when we are in control of our current thinking agenda, and we are at least working towards an awareness of our filed stories (most of our stories are stored in our sub-conscious and felt in our body).

An ordered system seamlessly coordinates our Keep/Delete/File system by managing and prioritising the range of our topics. The intensity of our relationship with each of our current topics will determine the level of energy or toxicity the body creates, particularly at our trigger points. Once we can clearly:

(1) name our Topic/s

(2) validate (identify the intensity of the emotion/s and where they sit in our body ...... and then

(3) swiftly move to a solution
   We are considered to be compartmentalising.
   TED-it at all times!

Females on average report managing around 10 topics at any one time (some report up to 25!) with men reporting 2-4 topics. Psychological distress and physical pain can arise when we continue to link (rather than separate) all our topics and cook them together in a crockpot. Maintaining 10 topics means at least 10 primary emotions. If left unmanaged, there is the potential for a bunch of secondary emotions to join the story, which is why it feels like, at times, we're running around like a headless chook in a barnyard. Is it any wonder we armchair-diagnose ourselves with anxiety, depression or a personality disorder? OR (despite no genetic link) we diagnose ourselves with ADHD, bipolar, schizo-phrenia or any one of the wide range of personality disorders.

We must remain focused on executive decision making (ratio-nalisation) if we are to avoid undermining our own integrity. Our rational brain screams out for law and order and the body sells us out when there is a disconnect between our mind, body and legs. When we listen to our body, we may find a painful story-storage area that is competing for recognition, such as sore shoulders, stomach (nausea), lower back pain or ongoing head-aches.

Many agree that the alarming over-diagnosis of disorders is often attributed to an inability (or unwillingness) to control their body chemicals by *ordering* their thinking agenda into line. We must continuously remind ourselves that every topic on our think-ing agenda will generate an emotional and behavioural reaction

— whether good, very good, reasonable, bad or ugly. Therefore, it's entirely up to the individual to take responsibility for their own thinking agenda. For children under the age of 18, it's the role of parents to support and role model the TED system. Why focus on emotion when your body is waiting to assist you to safely enact your solution?

PARENTS AS ROLE MODELS

While children are in the care of their parents or guardians, they are constantly observing their role models' stress buffer styles as well as their parents' overall emotional and behavioural reactivity. They will trial or modify these skills with varying degrees of success, as well as test the consequences of their own emerging moral compass dilemmas, particularly when exposed to discomfort and pain. When parents decrease the opportunity to learn valuable life skills, the young person continues to live in Prince Town on the corner of Denial Avenue and Child-ers Crescent.

Adults must continue to provide a dearth of real-life opportunities for their young people to practice 'out of the corner of a boxing ring action-planning'. Society reminds us, when a young person has reached 18 years of age, they are 'a societal adult', with the freedom to make their own decisions, *without parental restriction*, though most are still dependent on the family system for their general livelihood. Leaving home at 18 years of age is the ultimate test of character for our young people, though nowadays, due to financial (and other) reasons, very few are ready to embark on such a life-changing event without considerable assistance, nor are parents providing a pseudo 'real life' opportunity while living at home (such as the Financial Formula). Many young people admit that they resemble an 18-year-old six-foot pre-schooler who is married to their parents.

Parents are increasingly admitting that the life of their off-spring is being played out through the vista of their own child-hood. These parents are hell-bent on providing the life for their children that they were not afforded themselves. Some parents are subconsciously overworking and under-expecting, by maintaining a superhuman standard that not even Superman or Wonder Woman could achieve themselves. Sadly, with such standards and privileges in play, and parents not owning or working on their unresolved childhood issues, their emerging young adult is unable to set their own standards. Young people report feeling inadequate in comparison to the standards expected of them, unskilled for life and over-babied – 'So, what's the point of even trying?'

Parents handing their adult children pocket money to 'play' with their mates are suggesting that their offspring are not capable of earning their own money. Young people are often desperate for their guardians to believe in their ability to adult. Each time he takes money from his parents he delays his childhood for a little longer. Underneath his disappointment, he still hopes that one day *his desire* to adult will match his *parents' belief* in his emerging adulthood, so he too can appreciate his independence while learning how to enjoy a sense of interdependence within his systems and culture.

Literally hundreds of young people who live at home report that they aren't expected to wash their own clothes, let alone the hanging, drying, folding or ironing process. Instead, they're morphing out of their rooms at midday, and their toast is being buttered on arrival, followed by fancy milkshakes as they sit at the table like expectant royalty. They are unlikely to ever be expected to pull any weeds out of the garden, or prepare meals on an ongoing basis for the household, nor would they have taken over the complete ownership of one major task in the household. It's very rare these days to see a young person pushing a shopping trolley at the supermarket on their own.

Parents, unaware they've adopted a 'friendship parenting' style rather than a 'modern realism' style, simply chatter together in their blindsided generational norming — at the gym, at the pub or over a café latte, grumbling in their martyrdom how ALL their offspring are so immature and selfish, 'so we may as well just give up and hope they'll eventually want to grow up'.

'It takes a village' is true — that is, of course, *only* if the village view of their young people is as capable emerging adults!

Premature Ageing

Research suggests that prevention strategies for cognitive decline includes activities and lifestyles (particularly new activities) that stretch our brain and activate our learning responses, particularly when we are in-tune or engaged with our environment. Many young people who have become indulged bedroom dwellers report feeling like old people, fully resonating with the notion of cognitive decline and premature physical ageing. This is a fact, folks! Many active, environmentally engaged, mature-aged people in their sixties and seventies do not resonate *at all* with the notion of cognitive decline, stating that their minds are still around 30 years of age, despite their external body suggesting otherwise!

Older adults often talk about the time in their history when computers didn't dominate life, when mobiles didn't exist and television was only black and white. Your word was your word — yes meant yes and no didn't change to yes as a result of children manipulating and bullying parents. Kids were fitter, healthier and leaner and 'random' activities such as staring at the sky or 'just hanging out' were common - *despite* the climatic extremes. There was no Netflix or big tech and kids didn't hang around homes in their bedrooms — they knew to 'be home before dark for dinner'. Today, young people are increasingly heard saying 'I wish I'd known a time such as yours'.

The 20th century had its own challenges such as the Spanish flu, vaccine disasters, population decline/culling, a number of wars, including WW1 (1914-1918) and WW2 (1939-1945), space exploration and advances in nuclear weaponry. By the end of the 20th century, new advances in communication technology had emerged, which were to become the key focus of consumerism leading into the 21st century. Today, regardless of horror, tragedy, terrorism, natural disasters or global health pandemics, our relationship with big tech has continued to dominate our lives and influence our pace beyond comprehension, leaving us as simply puppets on a chaotic technology string.

Technology Puppets on a String

New-born babies learn straight from the womb that they are sharing their parents' love with devices. Breast or bottle feeding, whilst lying underneath a mobile and laptop has become the new norm of parenting. It would be rare to find a toddler these days who hasn't had daily contact with a device from birth, or who hasn't been forced to listen to hundreds of hours of texting and mobile phone conversations or whose baby pics haven't been studied by strangers. Is it any wonder addiction begins from infancy? Is it surprising when devices are removed or used as forms of discipline, children immediately become distraught, often violent, at the same level as an alcoholic or a heroin addict?

Young people admit that they *can't cope* without constant stimulation and that they are literally chained to their devices, with no more than around five minutes' break before their mind addictively seeks device-consoling. It's not unusual for parents to seek counselling for a device-addicted four-year-old who displays frightening rage-level *violence at the mere thought of restriction* — their soul has been handed over to a greedy big tech industry that thrives on playing with our young people's mind and feeding addicts their 'hit'. When the four-year-old child becomes a hairy six-foot man-child with an insatiable addiction, their longstanding story of aggression becomes even more frightening.

There are thousands of parents domestically abused behind closed doors, as well as thousands of young people living under the reign of violent parents, who all lack the ability as to *how* to change their circumstances. Witnessing young children closed fist punching adults, scratching adults until they bleed, destroying property, kicking and biting in unconscious fits of rage-anger is horrific. Adults are maintaining their secret hell for years. It has now become a 'gen norm' for infants to be fully addicted to their devices before reaching primary school, with parents simply agreeing that this is now endemic within Australian culture. At the same time admitting to the avoidance of even *small changes* within their parenting styles — the new legacy of shame.

Chaotic expectations and advances in technology from the beginning of the 21st century have contributed to a frantically 'driven' rather than 'self-driving' society without a moment's rest to settle the farm! When we do have spare time, rather than ordering our thinking agenda and then relaxing, we let our brain 'free rein'. We're driving faster, eating faster, working longer hours, constantly multi-tasking and multi-device-ing, exercising faster and 'smelling the roses' less.

Rapid over-thinkers and deep analysers overtrain their brain to stay ON — even sleep is work, with their primal switch turned on 24 hours a day. Rather than moving through our REM sleep levels, strange distorted dreams confuse us, rather than alert us, to the way that we've simply left our thinking agenda (computer brain) still switched ON. Why would our body give us peaceful sleep (aside from initially crashing to sleep through sheer utter exhaustion) if the brain has been instructed to produce ener-getic chemicals to frantically drive up and down our thinking pathways?

Individuals with genetically wired hyperactivity report higher levels of emotional and physical exhaustion if they're not pre-pared to significantly modify (sometimes exclude) their use of devices before bedtime. They also report rapid over-analysis of multiple topics in comparison with the general population, and are more likely diagnosed with secondary anxiety-related labels such as obsessive-compulsive disorders. As employees, they're often used and abused for their hyperactivity and then tossed aside when they crash, or becomes too vocal within their exhaustion rhetoric. Toss-managers admit that it's like employing one person who can do the job for two or even three employees and then being able to predict when they will burn out.

The measure of success:
How we deal with disappointment.

Are we teaching our young people to avoid competition and failure? Are we agreeing to minimise success in lieu of par-ticipation rewards? If we need plenty of reality moments and disappointments in order to practice our executive bounce-back skills in preparation for adulthood, why is the education system fixated on 'rewards for all participants' rather than the old days where there was a clear acceptance of winners, losers, strengths and weaknesses?

Trigger moments assist us to develop the skill of cognitive elasticity, particularly for those potentially 'in the corner' moments. If we are capable of getting ourselves *into* a corner, we are capable of getting ourselves *out* of the same corner, even if that means asking for help or support. Whenever we focus on our *action* or our rational-response, we are increasing our bounce-back biceps and triceps and building our muscle memory system to cope with changes to our Plan A. When we *only* focus or specialise on targeted areas of our life such as career, hobbies, gaming and computer skills, and neglect other areas such as building our emotional management skills, we will grow UP in some areas, whilst growing DOWN in others: Progress or Regress.

Job interviews are an example of drawing on our muscle memory system. When preparing for a job interview, it's common to over-focus on our Primal Interview Relationship that prepares us for stress, anxiety and self-doubt — pre, during and post interview process. After the interview, it's common to bombard our system with active, worry-based talk of failure and 'stupidity'. If we operate within this system *every* time we approach interviews, our brain will file these instructions until the next time a job interview presents itself. That is, unless we challenge the legitimacy of this thinking and change our 'interview system' as well as continue to attend job interviews. Change requires opportunity and practice.

High functioning narcissists (and psychopaths) inform me that they usually secure jobs easily, due to nil focus on emotion.

They also find it easy to work (or stomp) their way up the ladder, leaving behind their 'emotional counterparts' — they eat risk for breakfast, enjoy their 'love' relationship with self and are happy with their preoccupation with their ego. Most of their interview rhetoric is highly believable, because recruiters want to believe that such a person exists. Sadly, people with 'helpful narcissism' (seen as an aid to self-assertion and success) constantly miss out on ideal career opportunities because of their preoccupation (or their 'relationship') with their negative (irrational) self. Rather than participating within a healthy 'entitlement' continuum, they *choose* intimidatory emotions (that easily cloud their true authentic self) by stonewalling rationality at the time they clearly need it the most.

If our instructions about interviews or our belief about our self remains the *same*, the *same* reaction is provided to us from our retrieval system. Why wouldn't the phrase 'fake it until you make it' make complete sense in terms of rewiring our brain — sending our feet in the right direction rather than our emotional direction, whilst the brain is catching up and storing (formalising) our new instructions.

The same process applies to the way we manage deadlines and tests. Do we automatically provoke worry-based thinking by inducing adrenaline and other above 5/10 stress hormones? Most deadline instructions have been well developed since our childhood days, and simply play out or flourish (negatively or positively) as we transfer to our working life or our tertiary education life.

Our brain must be instructed — told what it's going to think. Preparing for hurdles, before we find ourselves punched in the face without a Plan B, is OUR responsibility, rather than relying on others to 'adult' for us. Of course, there's no point denying that at times, our *actual* reality could be described as 'a total bitch'. Though, it's unlikely that *all* parts fit into the whole, and yet often, we risk the ALL for the messy part of the whole. It's like a mathematically unsound system. The ramification of constantly partying with toxicity will eventually make or break us.

Humans are designed for problem solving by facing 'dilemmas' head on. Unless we are significantly impaired, life was never meant for copious time on our hands to shit all over the inside of our brain or to let others clean up the diarrhoea in our diapers. Significant trigger moments are meant to allow us enough discomfort to provoke or induce our opportunity to create fair and reasonable decisions, or at the very least, to start trialling options. We were never designed to over-focus our energy towards our emotions, nor to medicate our discomfort, nor to grow toxic thinking pathways by wiping our priority for rationality.

The Slippery 7-Stage Slope

Are we becoming a version of a person we don't even know?

Most major events re-shape our belief in ourselves, others or the world in general and force us to think in different ways. Events are reality 'moments' that force us to either make rational decisions or induce toxicity. These days, it seems that we are increasingly choosing volatile fear/anger-based head chatter that disrupts (even paralyses) our neural pathways, resulting in a slippery downwards slope.

To ensure we maintain an effective recovery system that maintains our mental health and physical health, we must continually practice the art of bounce-back from our trigger points. By remaining closely connected with (1) our nutrient-rich environment and (2) our daily routines and (3) our 'people', we will maintain the marriage between our developmental age and our emotional age.

When a trigger event turns up, we must not allow ourselves or anyone else in our life to stagnate for more than

THREE MONTHS!!!

Regression can occur when the brain is bruised and we engage in a slippery seven-stage downwards slide ....

(1) a significant, avoidable or unavoidable life event occurs, that...

(2) collides with our over-use of/or creation of unchallenged primal language, coupled with...

(3) low executive bounce-back expectations and...

(4) extended healing timeframes, due to...

(5) lack of financial pressure (or other factors), that allows us to...

(6) withdraw from usual activities, increase social withdrawal and other medication or addictions, that soon become our...

(7) new best friend – as the need for others is rejected and the bedroom increasingly cossets our pain and shame, reducing our perceived need to bounce-back and join society.

LANGUAGE IS POWERFUL!

The word 'trigger' is NOT a dirty word

As discussed throughout this writing, changes in our body, mind and emotions are only meant to be fleeting warning signals to steer us towards our decision making. Our job is to return to our rational reasonable state as quickly as possible by eliciting the assistance of our Executive brain. Feeling pissed off with the boss is secondary to your rational brain trying to elicit your attention, asking you, 'So, what are you going to *do* about this situation?' What's your game plan? Constantly talking *about* the boss or any other non-action-ary overthinking that messes with our rhythms (such as sleep and diet) does little to address our actual *reality*. Therefore, neglecting the art of decision-making is a fool's way of travelling through life.

The body provides uncomfortable feelings or warning emotions for a very good reason. It's trying to elicit our attention! Our thinking sends an alert through our system (from brain to body) as a result of opening a particular topic. Fear-based thinking is likely to create a rapid-response (above 5/10) that requires immediate action. The trouble is, when we only focus on the emotion and not the topic or action planning, our response system learns that chaos is acceptable (and for some, highly addictive). Toxicity is highly confusing — why is my human narrowing their vision to only emotion? Why is my human not making a decision? What exactly does my human want me to do? Is it a war? Is it a freeze-down? Are we running in the opposite direction? What the *fuck* does my human want me to do?

Personality, past experiences and genetic predisposition often excuse us from taking responsibility for action-planning the topics that WE HAVE PLACED ON OUR OWN thinking agenda. When we avoid transparency and reality-checking by over-focusing on weakness, we're more likely to remain oblivious to the dangers of repetitively (and eventually automatically) travelling along the same thinking pathways.

Toxicity left unmanaged over time becomes a dangerous cesspool of chaos and brain bruising. It's like constantly punching ourselves in the head, in the same spot, over and over again and expecting different results, then becoming alarmed when we're diagnosed with a secondary concussion.

Are you medicating toxicity rather than challenging your thinking? Are you convinced your mental health or the mental health of others is at risk? Are you reluctant to engage in action-planning due to avoidance, exposure and discomfort? Do you believe that your situation will miraculously change on its own because you have faith? Are you constantly bathing in acid rather than reality-checking? Is denial, laziness or boredom easier than choosing to deal with discomfort? Are you living in a dilemma-adverse household? Are you a brain-bruiser? Do you want to increase your bounce-back? The choice is all yours.

Choice Dethrones Boredom

When we have choice: boredom ceases to exist

In the presence of choice, the notion of boredom does not exist. Boredom is a self-generated mindset that focuses on a state of induced excuse: a privileged statement of laziness.

The notion of boredom was once a dirty word. 'Back in the day' a child daren't utter the word 'bored' to their parents or it would've started a war with no survivors, reminding the young person of the 'less fortunate days of child slavery' followed by a ton of chores as a punishment for such meaningless, lazy sentiment.

Dilemma — the Best Friend of Discomfort

1.4 — Strategy: Replace 'problem' with DILEMMA

Eradicate the word 'problem' and embrace your 'dilemma/s' and life will open up a range of creative solutions. According to the *Oxford Dictionary*, a Dilemma is a situation in which a difficult choice can be/must be made between *two or more* alternatives, especially ones that are equally undesirable. Therefore, sacking our relationship with our negative 'problem' mindset reduces the opportunity to alert or induce our primal thinking. Are you a glass half-full person? Or do you automatically default to a glass half-empty?

1.5 — Strategy: It's JUST a Trigger

Emotional intelligence is not a complicated process. Do you rationally respond or primally react to your trigger point moments? The simple strategy — 'It's JUST a trigger' can place us securely back on our rational firewall, when forcefully applied at our trigger point moment (elevation of emotion). Remember — no Force No Results.

Triggers are a typical part of being human and they are expected to turn up on a regular, sometimes daily basis. We are not designed to be a species that teaches ourselves or our loved ones to avoid triggers. Nor are we designed to give ourselves permission to stop in our tracks, over-react, over-analyse or spotlight maladaptive emotions and behaviours. 'It's JUST a trigger' provides the brain with an ordered response system as well as validation that a circumstance is real, raw and requires a response (not reactivity). We need triggers to grow — hiding, running or overly reacting to triggers decreases our emotional age.

1.6 — Strategy: Divorcing Possessive Pronouns

Our words send clear messages to the body. Possessive pronouns refer to a strict ownership or possessive relationship with a notion. When we attach pronouns such as 'my', 'your' or 'their' to unwanted toxic emotional states such as anxiety, we have made a strict cognitive contract. For example, 'his anxiety', 'she wants to work on her depression' or 'his anger'. Pronouns can create complex patterns of reactivity, avoidance, suppression, medication and addiction.

If our goal is to eliminate toxicity from our body and lead a balanced lifestyle, we must be prepared to cut up the contract that binds us to dangerous mental states by focusing on healthy language. After all, does it make any sense to live a life of constant reactivity, and pay professionals to talk about 'my anxiety' if our goal is to develop strategies for managing *stressful events?* Being consciously aware of our language and keeping it simple creates clear action-thinking pathways that indicate possessive pronouns are now the declared enemy state of our mental health.

If we're not interested in developing a relationship with conditions that contaminate our mind and body, such as rage-anger, depression, anxiety-panic and constant worry-based thoughts or unsubstantiated doom-day predictions, then we must immediately stop attaching dangerous possessive pronoun language. Otherwise this has the potential to enhance our relationship with, what it is, we detest!

Anxiety is no respecter of age, gender or culture. We aren't born with anxiety — we TRAIN OURSELVES TO BE ANXIOUS people by fucking with shame, fear and rage-anger thinking. Constantly partying with toxicity, stonewalls us from rationally analysing and acting creatively.

Thankfully, we are not defined by the behaviour that others have imposed upon us, nor the words that have been spoken over us in the past, nor our own destructive words that we have spoken over our functionality. You know, all those words that have had a contaminating impact on our lives or have formed a habit loop. Individuals diagnosed with obsessive-compulsive behavioural disorder (OCD) linked to fears and complex thought-looping, report speedy return to their previous functioning when they begin to treat anxiety as a hostile or temporary visitor, by entirely eradicating all use of possessive nouns and pronouns from their vocab. Dismantling fear-based thinking begins with reality-checking the topics on our thinking agenda, then devising clear opposing themes that indicate a new decision has been contracted.

I made a decision many years ago to stop being triggered by 'my debt' and 'my anxiety' by focusing on financial freedom: divorce papers were sent to 'the' mortgage (rather than 'my mortgage'). I decided it was a total waste of my thinking time to continue to develop a relationship with what it was I was trying to get rid of (debt and anxiety). Therefore, my first step was to begin to force-fully or rigorously detach all possessive pronouns from my vocab — for example the notion of debt.

New notions (such as 'the mortgage') needed an action-verb statement in order to solidify forward progress. Moving Forward as an action positively challenged my current reality, perception, ability and past patterns. So, what would this look like? What is my goal — financial freedom? Improved financial management? By becoming a rebel of my defunct worry-based thinking (such as mortgage-anxiety) and replacing with clear action-'able' verbs: the hostile takeover began!

1.7 — Strategy: Theme Statement: Action-Verb

A theme statement is an Action Verb that directs a goal (no more than four to five words). This is a short, sharp, concise statement that formulates an action plan.

Example — 'financial freedom'; 'improved financial management'; 'one step at a time'

- **Visualise to Actualise** — what will my goal look like if it is achieved?
- **Opt-In** (non-negotiable) statement ('no gain without pain').

- **Neurogenesis** — create new thought pathways (instructions) that will create new habits loops.
- **Eradication** — unhelpful messy stories stored in the filing cabinet (Hippocampus), such as past failures. No trips down toxic memory lane!
- **Increasing Discomfort** — (practicality and humility) - talk to a professional or a broker? Tribal wisdom? Gain financial advice? Create a spreadsheet? Sack procrastination and perfectionism?
- **Personal Reflection** — strengths, weaknesses, barriers and past success stories. Eradicate Don't and start saying DO!

In relation to financial freedom, my daughter recommended the internationally acclaimed book, *Barefoot Investor* (Pape: 2017). Pape challenges the reader to eliminate *reactionary* spending by goal planning, inducing rational financial functionality and increasing spontaneous spending, whilst still maintaining a healthy financial system. Pape's financial coaching eliminates addictive, sloppy spending habits (that leads to bankruptcy) replaced with a type of dopamine reward system — a sexy, flexible, bouncy style of financial management.

PRUNING AND WEEDING

We are a species that are hard-wired for growth. We are also designed to dismantle areas of our false self and move towards positive somatic markers. Somatic markers are feelings in our body linked to emotions and are strongly influenced by our decision making.

The process of creating new topics and discarding old topics (neurogenesis and synaptic pruning) encourages us to cull unused or maladaptive neural pathways, and create space for new adaptive pathways. One example of pruning and weeding is the eradication of our maladaptive 'Yes-But' rhetoric. This switches off our bullshit voice and switches on our reality. Let's take a drive down Honesty Lane and put our butts on the line.

When we entirely eradicate 'Yes-But' from our vocab, we are eliminating toxic language and long-justification sentences, as well as switching off our 'blame-game'. No longer the 'butt' of our story, as we talk in shorter sentences and focus on one topic. When our ears become rationally engaged, it's easy to *hear the content of our chatter.*

1.8 — Strategy: Eradicate 'Yes-But'.......

Growth comes from discomfort. Be honest!
Truth builds psychological immunity.

Circle your theme-repetitive language. Risk discomfort by also asking your tribe for 'feedback' by circling from the below list.

Yes-But ....

'He's such a nice boy, he's never really been any trouble before this'; 'he just loves his mumma'; 'he was a promising academic back in the day'; 'he was a top sporty kid in his day, a bit of a hero'; 'he once had so much drive and ambition'; he's just a bit more sensitive than most'; 'if it wasn't for all that bullying, she'd be fine now'; 'it's just a stage'; 'it's not his fault about the accident'; 'he's just my baby though'; 'he got cheated on and hasn't been able to recover'; 'she's just got a bit depressed'; 'he's too anxious'; 'but I think he was abused as a kid'; 'he's lived out of home before so I know he can do it again'; 'she's had a lot of trouble with her mental health'; 'I'm sure he'll just grow out of it'; 'we're guilty for...'; 'I think Uni was a bit of a shock and he just wasn't quite ready'; 'it's our fault for pushing him'; he's just a bit different'; 'he used to work'; 'he's still trying to work out his sexuality'; 'he's probably going to be a millionaire programmer, so all his time in the bedroom is going to be worth it'; 'we believe in attachment'; 'he's shy and a bit awkward so it's hard for him to just rock up to a prospective employer'; 'doesn't know if they want to be a girl or boy'; 'we'll get around to charging board one day, we can afford it'; 'we hate confrontation'; 'we're a gentle family'; 'it's our fault we didn't push more'; 'he's working in his bedroom, though'; 'he just got caught in addictions'; 'it's just taking some time for him to grow up'; 'I'm sure it's just because he's got away with being a bit lazy'; 'we don't believe in invading her privacy', 'it's not his fault that we over-parented him'; 'he's just taking his time to grow up because he likes being around the family'; 'there's always someone in a family who hangs around for ages'.

ANALYSE YOUR EMOTIONAL BLOCKERS
Are you No-Gap Charlie?

Robust mental health is like a three-way survival system. When we are naturally (1) maintaining our commitments, at the same time as (2) working through the impact of our changed reality, as well as (3) maintaining our connection to our nutrient-rich environment, without the use of maladaptive coping strategies, we are sending very clear survival messages to our body: our feet are mobilised for action.

We must not weaken our commitment to our basic survival system, nor weaken the opportunity for our loved ones to develop this system. Is over-giving or over-caring undermining an individual's opportunity to develop their own survival system?

1.9 — Strategy: Name Your Emotional Blockers

List the areas in your life that reduce your focus on reality? Many suggest they spend approx. $400 per month on maladaptive coping strategies, or waste around 30+ hours a week on their devices. Example: alcohol, exercise, drugs, nicotine, porn, gaming, socials, Netflix.

____

____

____

Investing in your mental health means that you are taking over the role of CEO of your own company. You are making a declaration that you are not interested in forms of mind control that reduce your ability to adult. There has never been a more important time in our history to maintain the control of our own mind. This includes high-achieving, overly goal-orientated, A-type adrenaline junky perfectionists who admit they create so many toxic chemicals on a daily basis that they're often not even sure who they are anymore!

Is it time to cut up all the contracts we signed for employees who entered through the back door, such as maladaptive food and relationship patterns, weed, porn, nicotine, withdrawal, cocaine or gambling? No one is interested if you've been dependent or addicted for 10 or 20+ years.

Emotional blockers, dependencies and addictions are the antithesis to growth, causing stagnation and regression. Try putting your mobile on silent for a day or going out without it, or leaving it in another room for extended periods of time — how incestuous is your relationship with big tech? Remember that no one is holding a gun to your head to force you to sleep with your devices or to feed your addictions, nor are they forcing you to drive to the local BottleO.

Maladaptive Investment in our Mental Health

Research suggests that in the face of adversity, including economic depressions, there are two industries that are not under any threat. The multi-million-dollar global cosmetic industry runs to our beauty rescue with promises of memory bounce-back skin-recovery treatments attributed to the unavoidable visible effects of ageing and stress. Clever cosmetic marketing campaigns understand changes in consumers choice and motivation, as well as our *reaction and vulnerability* to global trends, on a background of past consumer choice and loyalty.

Intertwining human needs with so-called basic needs by calling the beauty industry 'health'. Words are powerful, though if we look good, we'll *feel* good. Right? 'No worries', though, if we're still feeling vulnerable, we can invest in the now considered 'essential service' liquor industry to dull or medicate our emotional life, just enough for us to remain alive and synergising within our systems. Our thinking gaps have been filled by our focus on our physical exterior, while our interior is medicated and pain free leaving us to behave in a 'nice' fashion that continues to deflect our reality. Are you a No-Gap Charlie?

1.10 — Strategy: Eradicate 'Nice'

The word 'nice' is not a personality type, it's simply a learned (and often calculated) behavioural pattern. We learn to modify our behaviour to suit our social setting, such as within our work-place or social interactions. Try eradicating the word 'nice' — initially you'll probably stutter and stumble! Hiding behind this notion is often a system of justification or a one-layered account of reality.

It's interesting how many clients state that their goal for coun-selling is to 'break addictive or compulsive layers of pathologi-cal lying'. Many admit how easy it is to fool people when you're labelled with 'nice'. No word of a lie! Many years 'getting away with lying' and then trying to remember complicated layers and patterns, eventually takes a toll on the moral compass. Many describe high levels of shame for their long-term patterns of com-pulsive, pathological lying, seeking medication for depression and becoming socially withdrawn in their struggles breaking these patterns. Though, of course, not all people who hide under the label of 'nice' are caught in cycles of pathological lying.

Describing someone as 'nice' is a way of explaining their *behaviour*, not their personality. We all have a unique personal-ity, enmeshed within our character, influenced by our upbring-ing and culture. We need to mould our character throughout our lives — as opposed to spending exhaustive (and sometimes fake) time developing our relationship with 'nice'.

Many caught in long-term social withdrawal cycles are described as 'nice' people, though are often terribly sad, anxious and awkward, desperate to break their chains, though unsure how to fit in with their fast-paced, seemingly chaotic society. Perceived social awkwardness is often behaviourally managed through non-invasive quietness in order to decrease attention. A 'nice' modus operandi could be linked to an overarching fear of eviction or exposure or not meeting the expectations of others or living in a state of potential abandonment and rejection.

Workers, particularly emerging professionals, often refer to themselves as struggling with an 'imposter syndrome' as they frantically avoid exposing their 'perceived' weaknesses. Working longer and harder, whilst maintaining a 'nice' persona, eventually leads to burnout.

So, if someone describes you as 'nice', regard this as an insult, and ask them to start the sentence again without this word! They will likely describe your endearing as well as (maybe) your less-than-perfect qualities — at least truth is in the room! There is no perfect person — nor is this a requirement of living on this planet. Are you overfocusing on 'nice' and constantly saying 'yes-but' to explain your behaviour, or the behaviour of others?

INVESTMENT IN OUR MENTAL HEALTH

Can I afford NOT to invest in my mental health?

It's brilliant the way modern men often attend counselling for the first time. They usually don't want airy-fairy counselling that resembles 'So how'd you *feeeeeeel* about that' type of questioning. Once an event and its trigger-link is established and validated, they're not usually interested in excessive dialogue around their background stories, nor breathing techniques and mindfulness, and definitely not sweet 'skipping through the tulips' Mary Poppins advice. They're often after bullshit-free action-planning. They want to know *how* to stop the emotional pain, rather than being given a script for medication to dull their pain, particularly with a past history of maladaptive coping strategies, complicated background stories, addictions and pain medication mismanagement.

Many new clients walk into their first session seeking psycho-education, as to *why* their head is literally spinning off its socket, with goals around maintaining their current life, at the same time as eager to begin their healing journey. When stating their reasons for attending, there is often a clear and concise rationale – 'Life is shit, I can't lose my job, my boss is on my case, my heart is all fucked up after being cheated on/messing up my relationship again, and I don't want to drink my way out of this mess like last time'.

Walking into counselling with humility, vulnerability and an action plan is one of the most productive starts for counselling and, in my opinion, men are leading the way with their goal planning rationale. Links to uncatalogued stories and a desire to steer away from addictive patterns, are on their agenda before even walking in the door of their first counselling session (or via telephone or video sessions). Whether the professional service on offer is bulk billed, or charges apply, or we need to wait for the right worker to be available, investment into our mental health can be a highly cost-effective way of moving forward.

Viewing therapy as an investment in mental wealth creates the perfect storm for the establishment of an effective client-worker relationship, with less likelihood for retreat and dependency. On average, individuals with less robust financial health will access counselling within speedier timeframes of a trigger event. When we do not have the financial luxury of extended healing timeframes, we force ourselves to exercise humility, and seek a solution-focused way to bounce-back. Although the costs of intervention can be challenging, early intervention is seen by many as cost effective, particularly if delayed healing timeframes could place livelihood or the wellbeing of others at risk.

Families with more robust financial health are, on average, less likely to expose their truth, often significantly delaying access for themselves and their loved ones for many years. They agree, that their *family wealth is not creating mental wealth*, though, their lack of humility and action planning (in lieu of denial) is often tragic. Have you given yourself or others longer healing timeframes due to economic circumstances or double-standards? Is your cleaner or handyman a pseudo-parent as your loved one remains imprisoned in their comfort, unable or unwilling to initiate even basic household tasks?

For those readers inflicted with the privilege of robust financial health and primary trigger point inaction, my plea to you is to consider the fact that unmanaged primary triggers, coupled with delayed healing timeframes, will eventually cost thousands of dollars in the long run. It's a bankrupt system. Eventually the welfare system is likely to pick up the bill, particularly when the enabling system is not available. Would you exclude your loved one from seeking medical care if they broke their leg or needed a heart operation?

The Australia government takes mental health seriously, funding a range of programs accessible through government and non-government services, attributed to escalating rates of self-harm, suicide, domestic violence, systemic abuse and global disarray. Millions of government dollars are provided each year for medical and therapeutic professionals to subsidise support for motivated Australians who recognise their current limitations and seek change as a result of life events and complicated background issues. When ordinary people like you and I want support to bounce-back and engage professionals (or others) to 'walk alongside' us, while reality-checking our story, then Australia is (for now!) the country to live in.

Professionals are expected to maintain costly and time-consuming qualifications as well as continuously develop their skills in line with their professional association's yearly requirements for registration. Professionals work extremely hard to maintain relevant best practice industry knowledge to deliver appropriate and modern services that meet their patient's/client's goals. Although, some professionals have long wait lists (post-2020) and are charging exorbitant fees, most are fair — taking into consideration that the social services industry is *not* creating millionaires! It's an industry of professionals who are ready to support and who are focused on positive outcomes and ready to walk 'alongside' motivated individuals who believe in their right for a better life.

Alongside government and non-government agencies, accessing subsidised assistance for clinically significant mental health can be discussed with your local doctor. General practitioners (GP's) complete mental health care plans for psychological intervention with referral options to professionals, such as accredited mental health social workers and psychologists (x10 sessions in a calendar year).

Sacking an Early Retirement Mindset

The prognosis of long-term social withdrawal is very bleak indeed. Undue trust in the dead reckoning has produced more disastrous seaworthy shipwrecks than all other causes put together. The further we drift from our 'true authentic self', the harder it is to find our way 'back', and the easier it is to employ an early retirement mindset. We don't *get* old, we *grow* old! Prematurely aged behavioural patterns reflect prematurely aged retirement mindsets, often resulting in avoidable psychological illness that morph into serious secondary condition/s.

As reiterated throughout my writing, the *type* of thinking we choose or employ to manage a situation is considered to be, by far, one of the most dangerous aspects of being human. A divided mind is a liability. It's daunting to consider that the body is FORCED to provide a **mirror image** (chemical response) as directed, dictated or instructed by our thinking.

Our behaviour, our choices, our view of self and others, even our clothing style is a result of our thinking style. For example, if I tell myself I'm hopeless at public speaking and I'm fearful of embarrassing myself, my body will prepare for an ultimate showdown of humiliation by increasing fear-based chemicals — and, I'll likely dress like I'm heading into battle! Becoming a rebel of our defunct story means we are re-authoring our role in a new story. Abdication of reality-checking for longer than three months is dangerous, hardening our arteries and starving ourselves of air.

Share Your Story

The greatest act of humility is to *begin* to share your story.

There is no fence: we are either moving forward or moving backwards. Standstill is not an option — with honesty and exposure we will move forward. Sharing your story with your people (or professionals) means you will begin to slowly chip away at the barriers that have been holding you back.

Across the entire generational age-span, since 2020, our conversations, beliefs, norms, debates, and hopes have taken new and interesting U-turns — the word 'socialisation' has a new face. Therefore, there's never been a more important time for those caught in cycles of social withdrawal and addiction to join or re-join the new socialisation era. We are all, in our own way, bravely and simply *trying* to move forward.

Can you name three people or organisations you would consider as your current or possible accountability system or tribe?

1.11 — Strategy: Accountability Coaches (names/contact numbers/address/hours available)

1. ____
2. ____
3. ____
4. ____

1.12 — Strategy: Tribal Truth Questionnaire

Choose three people in your Tribe who you regard as fair and honest — ask them the following three open-ended questions. They may include family from home or away, friends, colleagues, peers, partner, siblings, children and so on.

Question 1 — What is your opinion of the socially reclusive behaviour within my household?

____

____

Question 2 — What are three (3) of my main excuse statements in relation to social withdrawal or my parenting style (provide the 'Yes-Buts' list)

____

____

Question 3 — What advice have you given me in the past? Have I followed through with any advice you have provided?

____

____

Please note: reluctance to complete the above strategy may reveal long-term regression and patterns of secrecy.

In summary, the home has been identified as an initial source of healing as a result of primary trigger pain and discomfort, though inaction after three months is considered a catalyst for developmental regression. It's a bit like owning a lively and highly hyperactive cattle dog and forcing him to live a minimalist life-style, after recovering from an initial injury, alone in a dull one room apartment, without a backyard, and expecting him not to become depressed and continually bark and rebelliously shit all over the home in despair. The RSPCA would likely remove the dog from its owners, the law would prosecute and the neighbours would ensure the owners are media-shamed for such neglectful behaviour.

Though we're prepared to leave our human boy-men locked away in their bedrooms, with endless support to crap all over the inside of their brains, or ignore their parasitical behaviour by dulling their voices — without enablers ever being held to account. A delayed time to heal is a luxury. Over-caring, toxic language, procrastination and ignoring early warning signs have the potential for psychological regression, damaging long-term functionality, and altering the moral compass of all members of a system. It's important for us all to be given the opportunity to develop executive bounce-back skills and to prepare for the predictability of the highs and lows along the pathway of life.

Action within the first **three months**
of a primary trigger event is vital!!

Chapter 2
Strategies to Avoid Secondary Conditions

The focus of *Boys in Bedrooms* is to break open a frank discussion about a hidden condition in our society — social withdrawal. Thousands of families are suffering in silence as they struggle to manage this chronic social condition that has infiltrated their home. The individual and family are unaware that as each month passes, they are supporting the slow psychological decline of their family member as a hostage of their own mind, battling with psychological injuries that eventually mirror chronic trauma. Fraught with fears and shame, the protective allure of the bedroom provides initial comfort, though quickly becomes an entangled web of addiction and regression, exacerbated by enablers who abdicate their roles by minimising pressure to heal.

Chapter 2 (a mini book in itself!) focuses on prevention and early intervention strategies in order to continue building our psychological firewall and avoid the emergence of secondary conditions. Avoidable secondary conditions are psychological and medical disorders occurring to otherwise previously reasonably functioning individuals, attributed to mismanaged trigger events and long-term enabling behaviour. I have provided a further collection of 14 bounce-back strategies (BBS) throughout this chapter, keeping in mind there's not one size that fits all.

Toxic thinking is a viral invasion. These unwanted visitors respond to prolonged inaction, like viral invaders with no antibodies in sight. Particularly dangerous when the hostage has imprisoned themselves within the layers of comfort and wealth, creating an overall impoverished 'whole of family' mindset.

The reader is encouraged to interrupt toxic cycles by becoming a wedding planner, where the marriage between our emotional age and our biological age begins to walk robustly down the aisle of life — at least most days! After all, why would we knowingly let our body succumb to a bucket-load of potentially serious (and for some, irreparable) secondary medical and psychological labels such as Adjustment Disorder, Personality Disorder, Psychosocial Disorder, Anxiety Disorders or Depressive Disorders, when we can interrupt its progression in mid-flight?

Are modern families afraid of placing loving pressure on their offspring, when pressure is a requirement of growth? Are we robbing our young people of an equal opportunity to participate in our society — to enjoy relationships, career choices and the fruit of their labour such as wages and healthy spending choices? If so, is this nothing short of a form of wage theft, without the taxman banging on the door? Why didn't someone yell from the rooftops that serious regression and reduced functionality in all areas of our life, attracting potentially irreversible psychological and medical labels, can insidiously creep in after only six months of in-action?

Za Brain Za Brain

The organ of thought

What's all the fuss about our brain? How does the brain relate to achieving our goals, as well as maintaining our mental health? The role of the brain is to send clear messages to the body and create the right type of chemicals and energy to manage a situation — the good the bad and the ugly moments of life. It's incredible that something so small has such a large impact on our life. Reportedly, our brain only weighs around 1.5kg and is only about two percent of our total body weight (the heaviest brain ever recorded weighed 2.3kg). By around two years of age, our brain is around 80% of an adult size and the growth in the number of neurons added every minute is an estimated 250,000!

The brain and the spinal cord make up our central nervous system (CNS). The brain is a complex organ, controlling thought, emotion, memory, touch, motor skills, vision, breathing, digestion, temperature, hunger and every other process that regulates our body. When the brain is in charge of 'flexibly' managing our thinking, learning and emotions and our body is connected to its 'internal switch', we increase our ability to prevent disease and induce peace and happiness.

Delayed Adjustment to Primary Trigger/s — Adjustment Disorder

Adjusting to typical and complex life stressors is considered a 'normal' part of life ... up to a certain point. When our lifestyle patterns and choices are deconstructing our reality and our back-pocket of opportunity is empty due to running our car on the smell of an oily rag for too long, and we've been declining society's invitation to bounce-back, we turn to pathology for answers.

Psychiatrists refer to the *Diagnostic and Statistical Manual of Mental Disorders: Fifth Edition* (DSM:2013) when assessing and diagnosing clients who present in disarray or prolonged distress as a result of a trigger event, particularly when major areas of functioning are impaired. The DSM-5 refers to an Adjustment Disorder as a stress-related disorder that occurs in response to an identifiable stressor(s) within three months of the onset of the stressor(s).

A medical or mental health professional may diagnose an individual with an adjustment disorder when the intensity, quality or persistence of reactions exceeds what normally might be expected when cultural, religious or age-appropriate norms are taken into account. Adjustment disorder is characterised by a range of changes in mood and behaviour, though generally excludes normal bereavement, or an exacerbation of a pre-existing mental disorder.

<u>Fluctuations in mood</u> may include the emergence of: anxiety, depression, boredom, feelings of helplessness, constant fearful or rapid thoughts, increased anger, irritability, erratic mood swings, stress and suicidal ideation.

<u>Fluctuations in behaviour</u> may include: seeking or increasing intake of prescription and non-prescription medication, withdrawing from normal activities, seeking repeated medical certificates, reduced accountability, noticeably altered bounce-back compared to previous months/years, over-reliance on family/others, less motivation to generate an income, reduced contact with peers, reduced focus on goals such as education or employment/career, obsessive behaviours, hiding injuries/self-harm, compulsive food patterns (alcohol, weight gain or loss), excessive focus on cleanliness, change of sleep/wake patterns, glazed stare, excessive sleep, rejecting friends and family, impulsivity or intermittent explosiveness.

It's exhausting living on the poverty line of reasoning, where the bruising and wounding of the mind sucks the laugh dry, contaminating the body with dangerous chemicals. It soon becomes easy to dissociate ourselves from our elusive external world, hiding within the walls of our self-protective sabotage mindset. Until we decide to become the genesis of a new story, by slowly taking back the years that the locusts have eaten, only then can we move forward.

Messed Up Sleep/Eat/Wake Patterns

If you are hesitant to instigate discussions or instigate strategies around the serious issue of sleep/wake pattern reversal due to threats or violence, please discuss this with relevant professionals and/or your support system.

The sun and our environment are rich sources of chemical gold. Our internal body clock (circadian rhythm) thrives on routine and environmental nutrients. Significant changes in our mood, energy, appetite, weight and sleep patterns often reflect erratic routines, as well as a divorce from our natural nutrients. Unless we are paid nightshift workers, nursing babies, caring for the sick or the elderly, it will NEVER be considered normal to support our loved ones to alter their vital routines by turning a blind eye to circadian clock disruption.

Though the home grazier may be clean and orderly, their sleep and diet hygiene may in fact stink, remaining quietly nestled behind the walls of secrecy, shame, entitlement and addictions. Reversing our sleep/wake patterns IS NOT TYPICAL, nor was it ever a 'generational norm' to sleep all day and roam around at night, and then simply pretend that this situation will change on its own. Nor was unproductive night-time roaming *ever* a trendy parenting style throughout history.

Sun-starved individuals often describe a type of Seasonal Affective Disorder (SAD) syndrome — a mood disorder characterised by depression, fatigue, hopelessness and ongoing social withdrawal when they spend excessive periods of time estranged from their otherwise 'typical' outside nutrients. Seasonal Affective

Disorder is linked to the adjustment we can all suffer from time to time as a result of seasonal changes, given the fact that there's less sunlight at particular times of the year, and persistent grey sky can sometimes reflect our mood.

Those *choosing* to withdraw from the great outdoors are increasingly (and avoidably) diagnosed with a disturbance in serotonin, with treatment recommended, such as cognitive behavioural therapy and/or antidepressant medication (selective serotonin reuptake inhibitors (SSRIs). Circadian clock disruption can also attract labels such as Cyclothymic Disorder, with sufferers experiencing extreme emotional highs and lows. Although less extreme than Bipolar, these patterns can have a significant impact on generational functionality.

Recidivist offenders, sexual deviants and creepy weirdos were once well aware that they owned the night-time prowl within a community. Has the new technological era, with Big Tech owning our private space, and neglectful parenting styles that call breakfast 2pm, made it easy to target home grassers? Are parents increasing the likelihood of their offspring seamlessly transitioning into the messed-up world of deviants, whilst other household members are tucked away fast asleep at night? Sleeping during the day and then prowling or computerising our brain into the small hours of the night can turn reality into obscurity and can hide pain from pleasure, in a world where adulthood is nowhere in sight. Why would *anyone* want to take that chance or support their love ones to develop these insidious patterns?

Why would we want our brains or the brain of our loved ones to be forced to believe it's on a stay-cation? Where night becomes day and the increasingly sad, pale-faced, old-young person becomes accustomed to aimlessly roaming their homeland corridors. Many caught in these patterns, underneath their many layers of frustration, are secretly desperate to find a way out of their strange seemingly never-ending cycles.

When pressure to change *finally* emerges, many sufferers admit to feeling 'nervously relieved' that someone had the guts to intervene in their dismal situation, as it had become nearly impossible to reverse their mixed-up sleep/wake pattern on their own. Initially daunting, feeling like one is in a boxing ring with the lights on dim, wearing a pair of flippers and barking like a dog with a sore throat .... until eventually the day, once again, becomes the norm.

Sleep/Wake Pattern Reversal

Maintaining our mental health means that we respect and appreciate the *vital* relationship between our environment and our regular daily routines. Enablers who are unwilling to support their loved ones to reverse their long-term messy sleep patterns must understand that they are complicit in the deterioration of their mental health and physical health, particularly when living under the roof of the family home. Numerous individuals have confirmed that sleep/wake reversal can be achieved within one week. Surely, one week of discomfort is worth the long-term return of our natural life rhythms?

2.1 — Strategy: I'm Adult (IMA)

1. **Inform** — Respectfully and calmly inform the sufferer that their night-time wake hours will not be tolerated anymore (or discuss during the Family Meeting process — Chapter 8).

2. **Maintain** — Normal household routines during the day, reducing the opportunity to sleep. Maintain typical noise from household activity throughout the day. Keep the door open.

3. **Adult** — Treat and speak to all adult members of the household as adults. An adult is more than capable of reciprocation and attending to their *own* meal needs, as well as washing, cooking and instigating household chores. Stop treating an adult as a child-man and avoid thinking on behalf of others. Focus on enjoyable moments. Introduce the Financial Formula (refer to Chapters 6–8).

Please note: severe, long-term patterns of sleep/wake reversal may require medical review, medication and alternative intervention. Light Therapy is growing in popularity. Happy lamps are designed to reset our internal clock by correcting disturbances to the circadian rhythm by imitating natural sunlight. During the morning hours, these lamps teach the body that it's daytime. For countries such as Australia, with natural sunlight and easy access to the outdoors, standing or walking outside for even 15-20 minutes *every morning* will have a profound impact on circadian clock restoration.

Growing Our Social Risk Appetite

Has the introduction of the 'social' media era, where we appear to have dozens of 'friends' as listed on our page, reduced our appetite for social risk? Do you use the excuse of 'not liking people'? Are your face-to-face interactions decreasing? Are online connections reducing verbal skills? Is your over-giving or under-giving causing others to decrease their opportunity to practice social risk taking? Are you socially rich in one system (such as your workgroup or peers) though neglectful in other areas of your systems, such as wider family, friends or recreation? Do you invest in your social capital?

Social Support Network (SSN)

Social capital is a term that refers to the 'capital' (social gold) that resides within our social relationships. The investment of time developing relationships is thought to produce happier and healthier individuals, increase our 'golden' opportunities, as well as maintain societal cohesion. The genuine building of social capital is a type of pro-social nutrient or glue that links us securely to our people as well as our systems.

Building (or re-building) our social capital is a decision to reject social stagnation. Maintaining social connection increases our social risk intelligence. A serious disruption or deficiency in the building of social capital is considered to be a form of anti-social behaviour. The combination of chronic stress, complex background stories and a decline in environmental exposure divides brain cells and messes with our body balance, ultimately altering our DNA. Serious stuff!

It's suggested that a government system that forces its citizens to disconnect from their nutrient-rich environment, as well as their dopamine-enhancing social connections for prolonged periods of time is potentially altering the DNA of a culture. Practices that cause societal division through leper-ising, fear mongering and increased isolation practices have the potential to mess with the DNA of an entire generation.

During social isolation periods throughout 2020–2022, thousands of citizens naturally rebelled to forms of social control, seen taking up 'new hobbies' after finding themselves surprisingly seeking connection in other ways — 'I've never been interested in gardening or buying plants in the past, and now I'm hooked'; 'I've bought a kayak and yet I've never been a water person'; 'I'm enjoying the simple things around me'; 'why didn't I bike more often?'; 'I can cope without cafes and restaurants'; 'giving things away feels good'; 'longer chats with people I haven't prioritised for a while'.

Are you a social investor or is your system in deficit? It's usually not until a disruptive event or a new circumstance arises that we become aware of our social surplus or our vulnerability. Do we join others in the great resignation? Are we pro-social by testing the robustness of our social support network? When we discover a social deficit do we press the Great Reset?

Males often admit that in terms of building social capital, they've abdicated or handed over the role of social connection to the female/s in their life, suggesting that their schoolboy mates were, by far, their deepest connections, with most subsequent friendships shallow in comparison to their school yard days. Whilst female social practices, on average, are more likely to *consciously* spend time investing into social capital by throwing themselves into numerous 'friendships' over the years, even if some relationships are for a *reason*, or only a *season*, rather than a *lifetime*.

When a major change or life event occurs, our social support network, as well as our stress buffer style is put to the test. Sadly, many find themselves at a loss as to *how* to reach out to their people, or they expect that others will naturally steer them back in the right direction, as they struggle to deal with whatever it is that has unexpectedly arisen. Some assume that their bloodline will simply know *when* and *how* to provide support. It often becomes glaringly obvious that the distinct lack of investment in *their* social capital and/or the social capital of *others*, has resulted in a socially bankrupt social currency, particularly when swapping 'people power' with 'tech power'.

Stress Buffer Styles

Research suggests that there is often a sizeable discrepancy between our stress-buffer style and the amount of support people *perceive* is available (Sarason, B. R., Pierce, G. R., Shearin, E. N., Sarason, I. G., Waltz, J. A., & Poppe, L: 1991 - *Journal of Personality and Social Psychology, 60, 273–283*).

Tested Fact or Assumption?

(1) I have inadequate support: my trigger events will be 'terrible' or even disastrous (Plan to Fail mindset), or

(2) I have a robust social support system (principle of reciprocation): support will naturally and readily be available (Secure and Planned) or

(3) People *should* know when to support me: I don't need a plan (People are Mind Readers).

Individual stress-buffer styles vary markedly between *low tolerance, high tolerance* or *catastrophe thinkers*. Low-tolerance stress junkies deteriorate rapidly with the onset of a challenging stressor. Others enjoy a higher-stress buffer style, viewing layers of stressful events as opportunities for growth and change, whilst others perceive even minor stress events as a major catastrophe.

2.2 — Strategy: Social Support Network Exercise (SSN)

All adults are responsible for building and analysing their own social capital. I invite you to apply the Social Support Network rationale and complete the SSN strategy (Template). The goal is to identify gaps — not to be defined by these gaps. Placing the same person in all the boxes may be an indication of dependence or lack of reciprocation. Blank boxes are seen as an opportunity to begin to grow — analyse and then Reset!

1. **Emotional Support** — (My Top Five): non-judgemental, emotionally supportive, induce feelings of connection, high empathy, positive listeners, readily available.

2. **Physical Support** — practical support, such as driving you to the doctor, financial advice, lending money, brief accommodation, help with a deadline, easily accessible.

3. **Emergency Support** — can contact 24 hours a day. Who would you contact to drive you to the hospital at 3:00 am?

4. **Esteem Support** — people who boost your confidence, allowed to be appropriately brutal if needed. May include professionals, educators, career advisors, friends, pastors, family, colleagues.

5. **Negative Interactions** — people in your life who trigger anger or frustration, such as family, peers, teachers, colleagues. Often these people are unavoidable such as the boss or a teacher, or maybe a family member who is part of your local community.

6. **Network Support** — belonging to a group: sports, workgroup, recreational, church, gym, parents' group, AA, lifestyle complex.

7. **Informational Support** — professionals who work within office hours: doctors, specialists, dentists, counsellors, lawyers, mechanics, physio, accountants, pastors.

SOCIAL SUPPORT NETWORK EXERCISE

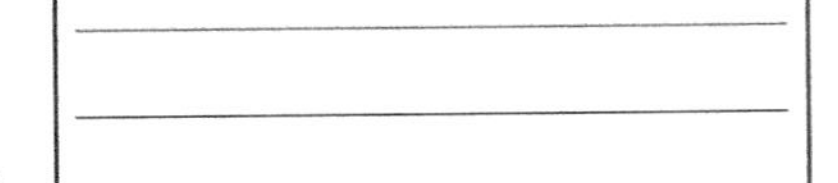

www.get-a-grip.com.au

Designed by Get-a-grip

2.3 — Strategy: Eradicate 'Don't Panic'

Words can make or break us. What we say about ourselves or what we say about others or the world in general impacts our health. If our brain is hot-wired to every word that we hang around with, we best take out the trash! A lazy mind seeks problems and re-acts according to the problem rather than the solution. Change your language and become a future-focused glass 'over-full' person — despite the crazy world or the body we are living in!

The government and other sensationalists are known to use toxic language as part of fear campaigns to gain maximum attention (particularly since 2020), such as phrases that start with 'Don't'. For example, provoking citizens to jump in bed with the big pharmaceutical, multi trillion-dollar industry by marrying psychologically damaging words such as 'don't panic' and then wondering why there is an alarmingly high level of people diagnosed for the first time with anxiety, who then seek government-subsidised treatment programs. Citizens are more than capable of understanding brutal truth — as long as it's accompanied by a rational future-focused action-plan (cognitive dissonance) that promotes 'choice' rather than coercion.

The mind is apt at sending clear messages to the body, as well as coordinating our filing/retrieval system in order to maintain our immune-efficient defence and repair system. For example — 'Diseases can kill. It's important to take our health seriously. Safe practices and wise choices will optimise our survival' (reality/rationality/action).

The Bounce-back GOLD!

Let's head back to tools that increase our trigger point management and continue build our emotional resilience.

2.4 — Strategy: Prefer/However/JUST

Use the word PREFER ... followed by the word HOWEVER ... finishing with the word JUST all in one sentence — in that **exact** order.

Rationale:

The rigorous use of the word 'PREFER' means we are validating our true authentic self — saying it how it really is, without holding back. No holds barred. Of course, this does not mean it is *ever* okay to induce abuse!

The grounding word 'HOWEVER' pole-vaults us onto our solid firewall (our rational-reasonable) by stonewalling irrationality (placing a full-stop on primal).

The rational word 'JUST' induces our objectivity, creating solution-focused options. This is our Action-Verb moment.

1. **'I would PREFER** .... **Primal self**
2. **HOWEVER** .... **Firewall of rational reasonable**
3. **So, I JUST** .... **Action Plan**

If we choose to remain engaged within the emotional context of a story for too long, we risk our body creating and maintaining toxicity. Who deserves *that?* Communicating at an emotional level does not require perfectionism, complex rhetoric or robotic over-analysis. If our aim is to *swiftly* move into an Action Plan mindset, particularly at our trigger points, we need to train our brain to utilise simple, straight-to-the-point brain-sweep strategies. The anti-inflammatory effect of a cold-water immersion by regularly elasticising our thinking is powerful!

Example

I would *PREFER* my son not to game all night; *HOWEVER*, it's been this way for years, so I *JUST* need to decide if I'm going to (1) talk to him or others about my concerns or (2) call a family meeting or (3) begin to instigate the financial formula.

Example

I would *PREFER* not to be so nervous (7/10) when I think about talking to my parents; *HOWEVER*, I admit that I'm not good at sharing my personal life, so I *JUST* need to (1) develop better communication skills or (2) write down what I'd like to say, (3) talk to someone outside the family or 4) maybe try emailing first.

Example

I'd *PREFER* to be able to hand my assignment in on time and not feel so upset with myself; *HOWEVER* it's not the end of the world if I lose a few marks, so I *JUST* need to (1) finish it (2) or apply for an extension or (3) learn better ways of time-management, so the next one will be handed in on time.

Validation – Deserve to Heal

I'm a huge fan of validation! When our past is still part of our present, or we feel stuck in the present with our past, we must validate our current reality! Validation is a swift brain-sweep of realism, rather than maintaining cycles of suppression or regression. Recognising, validating and devising a plan to heal our heavy and messy life experiences is the complete opposite to remaining owned and constantly triggered by the content of our stories.

Let's face it, life at times can be a huge confrontation. Humans feel pain at deep levels. This pain is often stored in our body or deep recesses of our brains filing cabinet. Depth of *pain* does not mean depth of *time* we need to swim in the messy mud of our past – unless, of course, we *choose* to do so. Choosing the word 'deserve' in relation to our complex stories can assist us to recognise the impact they have had on our life or on the life of others. Many of our complex stories may still need healing, tidying or a deep dive (please refer to my extensive elaboration of Grief & Loss processing, as well as Grief & Loss Mapping later in this Chapter).

2.5 — Strategy: I Deserve/They Deserve

(The notion of validation can be difficult for those identifying with co-dependency, people with low levels of empathy, high narcissism and younger children).

Example: 'I *deserved* to be treated fairly when ......'; 'I *deserve* to treat myself with more respect when I make mistakes/fail'; 'My partner/parents/others *deserve* better treatment *from me* when I ....'

Name Event:

I/They/He/She ________________ deserved to be treated/treat ________________ with respect when ________________

____

____

____

2.6 — Strategy: The Four-Second Rule (4-SR)

Can you apply *the Prefer/However/JUST* strategy within four seconds?

The Four-Second Rule (4-SR) is an extension of the Prefer/However/JUST strategy: a quick brain sweep that naturally induces our *action-ise*. The goal is to interrupt our automatic primal pilot by returning to the natural rhythm of our sexy executive neural networks. Remaining no longer than four seconds in our 'Prefer' state reduces the likelihood of creating toxicity.

We must remind ourselves that printing a licence to constantly bomb our mind and induce toxic chemicals that blasts nanoparticles throughout our body, is a morally dangerous drive along a one-way street to hell!

The time-delay between rapid-response thinking and the body producing toxic bombs appears to only be around four seconds. The role of our brain is to send messages (including protective instructions) to the body to create the type of energy it perceives as necessary to manage a situation. Most of the time, we don't need to reach deep inside our brain by smashing the glass and flicking on our Emergency Switch. The goal is to keep our toxic warfare switch turned OFF, unless faced with a perceived or real life-and-death situation.

I think we've all seen a two-year-old tantrum (after flicking their primal switch to ON) in a supermarket, after a parent is standing their 'no' chocolate ground, to know what triggered toxicity looks like! The child behaves like their life depends upon chocolate, enacting a vile vendetta! Adults with poor impulse control who visit their two-year-old self wonder why the people around them are intimidated, staring at them like they are a monkey in a zoo!

Master Eight informed me that the four-second rule totally changed his life and he was glad people weren't scared of him anymore. He eventually realised his family situation had been much harder than other kids his age (validation and extensive grief and loss work), which didn't give him permission to hurt others. He stated that the people around him deserved to be safe. He started listening to his trigger instructions and learnt to quickly reconstruct or genesis his thinking, rather than living his life inside a bomb. He was a true inspiration, given the arduous road associated with cognitive rewiring — once believed to only be an adult skill.

'HOWEVER', Master Eight informed me during one session: 'I'm not like other people, I reckon I only get around two seconds to hang out with *PREFER* — *not* four seconds, 'coz, my brain moves super-quick; I trained it from when I was a scared little kid'. Master Eight asked me if I could change the name of this strategy to The Two-Second-Rule! Those identifying with ADHD and long histories of anxiety, panic, rage-anger, perfectionism and avoiders of failure, also concur with the 'two-second rule'.

Example - 'I'd *prefer* my boss not to be so sarcastic; *however*, it's up to me to do something about my situation; and, at the end of the day, it's *JUST* a job' = sarcastic boss, just a job. My decision therefore, is to ....

Complete Prefer/However/JUST three times before moving on.

Captain Stand Down!

Our **dictator words** instruct our body to prepare for a (possible) battle, due to the enforcement of a rule or a belief. These little dictators are likened to the notion of a totalitarian or autocratic government, where one person holds all the power — such as the elusive North Korean dictator. A dictatorship rejects the notion of compromise, modification and democracy, referring to these as 'dirty words', due to a set of powerfully enforceable laws with no checks on power. The dictator's way is the right way, AND, the only way. Unless you conform to the establishment, you are likely sent on a one-way ticket to hell or at worst a bullet in your head — followed by your family being sent an invoice for the cost of the bullet!

Most of us party with at least a few little dictators, otherwise known as Rules and Beliefs. We file these in our subconscious for retrieval when we are automatically triggered, which instructs our body to react to a 'perceived' threatening trigger-point moment (such as during political debates, or the topic of vaccine mandates!). Our dictators are linked to our foundational stories, our values, our messy stories, our preferences and our goals. When they are triggered (positively or negatively) we *will* respond.

When we discover a maladaptive dictator, we have three choices: Keep, Delete or Modify.

1. **To Keep** means we have made a decision to maintain our strong relationship with a particular rule or belief.
2. **To Delete** means we are working towards eradicating that rule/belief (pruning and weeding).
3. **To Modify** means we are working toward reconstructing the notion behind a rule/belief in order to modify the risk to self or others.

2.7 — Strategy: Sack the Dictator

Let's start by getting to know our favourite (habitual) dictators and then begin eradicating!

Write the following words horizontally across a line and then rule vertical columns underneath:

SHOULD   **HAVE TO**   **ALWAYS**   **ALL**
EVERYONE   **NO ONE**   **MUST**   **NEVER**

Goal: Spend one week listening for sentences with the above words, placing a tick each time you or others use one or more of these words in a sentence. Remember that dictators highlight the imposition or entrenchment of a rule or belief, signalling a particular standard or expectation around our 'self, others or the world in general'.

Many rules and beliefs are linked to our 'fair enough' value system. For example, if you illegally break in to my home, you *should* face the law! Though, there are some little dictators that our brain has been over-trained to *immediately over-react to* — therefore, we've become an automatically programmed puppet on a string (often with little conscious awareness). When the dictator shows up, so does an emotional reaction and its twin toxic behavioural response.

Some say the definition of madness is doing the same thing over and over expecting different results. If we maintain our dictatorship thinking, we do so at our own risk (more on that later). Making excuses for our never-ending, over-active primal life that resembles more of a First World slum gets pretty boring (and dangerous) to the people in our lives after a while — 'yes-but my fuse has *always* been short'; 'but it's not my fault I come from a tough background'; '*everyone* knows I hate socialising'; 'they *shouldn't* push my buttons; 'they *should* realise that I was born this way'. Are we blah blah blah-ing to ourselves or others through the tulips? Not all our reactions are a result of dictators, though when we name, shame or cease blaming by eradicating the unwanted ones, we take a huge step forward in maintaining our adulthood.

Sometimes our reactivity is due to the lack of prioritisation within other areas of our life, such as processing (or validating) our background stories (Grief & Loss), OR we lack the awareness as to the real impact of a change (U Curve of Adjustment) as we move through the arduous stages of our life. Or, ALL of our stories are joined together with a long piece of string, running rampant and altering the overall geographical landscape of our brain.

Tribute to Albert Ellis

Passionate, albeit brutally frank psychoanalyst, Albert Ellis (1962-2007) is considered to be the leading contributor to the field of psychology, ahead of Freud himself. Not only is Ellis's work still relevant today, it is also easily understood and easily accessible online. Ellis was no fan of wishy-washy-bullshit therapeutic approaches. He also didn't pull any punches about the enormous risk to our mental health when we self-induce avoidable states such as anxiety, rather than viewing trigger points as typical stress moments that need immediate attention through cognitive restructuring (bounce-back strategies).

If we are serious about shifting our emotional state, Ellis believed that we don't need sweet skipping through the tulips rhetoric. A little like arriving at hospital via ambulance after a venomous snake bite — who needs wishy washy medicos when we're desperately trying to survive the snake bite? We need to be rushed into hospital for quick vitals only, then quick administer of the antidote before the venom reaches our vital organs. Imagine the same patient, upon arrival to hospital via ambulance, being wheeled into a room to engage in relaxing mindfulness, deep breathing, massage, distraction techniques or handed a bottle of gin!

Beginning his people-helping career in the early 1940's, Albert Ellis founded Rational Emotive Behavioural Therapy (REBT) due to his dissatisfaction with the inefficiencies and ineffectiveness of his own psychoanalysis work at the time. Ellis decided to shut down his own psychology shop and travel around the world, spending extensive time within numerous cultures and countries, including Greek and Roman stoic philosophers. He was fiercely determined to discover *universal principles* that disturb our mental health. Eventually, Ellis, together with his cognitive revolutionary philosophy, boldly declared to the psychology world ... that (outside of genetics) disturbance in mental health is not complicated at all, in fact, it's really quite simple.

Our mental health is directly linked to our perception or our VIEW of a situation, NOT the *actual* situation itself. Ellis linked temporary visitors, such as anxiety and situationally triggered depression, to maladaptive thinking patterns that had become chained or locked into a set of unsophisticated rules or beliefs. So, in order to 'get better and stay better', we must find these rules and beliefs and (in my interpretation) apply the antidote: Keep, Delete or Modify.

Ellis discovered the 'top 12 universal beliefs', eventually naming these rules as 'The Dirty Dozen' — a mix of self-crucifying, blaming or defeatism notions that can become automatically fused to our reactionary system (subconscious). It's easy to find these Rules and Beliefs in action whenever we elicit those demanding Little Dictators — 'You *should always* listen to me when I talk to you' (*should* I? do I *always*?). 'I *have to* pass my exams' (so, it's not okay to fail sometimes?); 'I *shouldn't have to* be pressurised, I *can't* stand it'; 'he *should* want to get out of his bedroom'.

Ellis suggested that a third of the population identify with at least one of the 'Top 3' Rules and Beliefs. These days, most enter counselling as their own personal assessor, stating that their disturbance is linked to either Perfectionism (fear of mistakes or failure), People-Pleasing (avoidance of disapproval), or behavioural issues associated with Payback/Vendetta (intermittent explosiveness). Ellis spent his entire cognitive revolutionary practice days labouring the dangers to our mental health and physical health, when we continually enforce a strong value on ourselves (or others) without analysing its role in our life, nor letting others rigorously challenge its legitimacy. To enjoy our life, Ellis believed, it's all about taming, or if needed, totally destroying those 'dictators' and being prepared to adjust to the constant changes that life is continually throwing at us.

The U Curve of Adjustment

Canadian anthropologist Kalverno Oberg (1954) first drew our attention to the impact of change (whether forced or invited) by coining the term 'culture shock', highlighting the struggles individuals often face when they are adjusting to new circumstances and environments, particularly cross-cultural challenges. The U Curve of Adjustment is a visual reminder of the highs and lows we may experience as we adjust to a new change. Particularly, the low-dip or three-to-six-month stage after a major change, that often finds even the most robust of people experiencing physical, emotional and psychological changes to their mood, behaviour and routines.

A few of many, Transition Markers include:
- Transition from primary school to high school — major!
- Transition from high school to employment or tertiary education — major!
- Transition from home to independence — major!
- Transition from singlehood to first love relationship — huge!
- Transition from first major break up — super major!
- Transition from failed Plan A to Plan B (e.g., divorce, accident, elite sports) — MAJOR!
- Transition to new career or management — full on!
- Relocation to a new suburb, city, state, country or overseas culture — culture shock!
- Transition from working to looking for new work.
- Transition from lifelong working to retirement.
- Transition from one identity to a new identity (gender, faith, role (eg. first time parent), socio economic, medical).
- Adjustment from health pandemic interrupters to new models of income generation.

When we embark on a change, we embark on a 'journey'. It's suggested that the journey to reach our 'new normal' is a minimum of 12 months (unless we become stuck in a stage). It's therefore, extremely important to consider our support system (particularly prior to the change) or to humbly reach out for support when needed. Reaching out for support is not a weakness: it is considered as an act of strategic change-management intelligence.

Any change in our life is considered important, whether the change is intentional or unintentional; or whether the change steers us into new crossroads, positive opportunities or unique dilemmas. Our emotional bounce-back intelligence, our support system, and our ability to problem-solve all form part of our evolving change-management style. Allowing us minimal scarring as we develop the flexibility to pole-vault through each of the stages (or hurdles) of our adjustment.

I've lost count of the number of adults who suggest that the biggest mistake of their lives was accepting a bail-out during a major transition event. While they don't blame generosity entirely, 'but what could my people do when I pulled out the poverty card or the self-harm card or the gambling bankruptcy card?', though they assumed that 'normal' pressure (such as financial payment plans) would be placed back on them to adjust/re-adjust *as soon as possible.*

Those returning home or not gaining employment were totally dumbfounded that they were treated like children, rather than an adult. *The Bank of Mum and Dad and/or the kindness of oth-ers had no reciprocation clause.* Furthermore, they were shocked that their lies, idle promises and pleas for change were believed, EVEN WHEN laziness, addictions or comorbid conditions were more than obvious to everyone else *but* their enablers. Many overheard their enablers tribal truth people pleading to 'treat him like an adult'; 'she won't respect you for bailing her out in the future'; 'you'll probably be in the same position in 10 years' time'; 'you've become brainwashed'; 'why are you asking my opin-ion when you don't *ever* listen to advice?'.

Others were shocked how easy it was to form a father-and-son 'Boys in Bedroom' duo, funded by other full-time workers such as their partner, mother, flatmate or the welfare system, with few pressures to 'action'-ise their declining reality. Technology-duo-retreaters suggest that if *they* were running the country, they would insist that Centrelink workers 'should' investigate each home of a welfare recipient. Stating that tens of thousands of retreating Australians are now comfortably 'milking the system', and would *not* be able to show-cause the reasons behind their lack of willingness to adjust and move back into their work-to-eat society. Is it time to flip the lid?

2.8 — Strategy: U Curve of Adjustment (Template)

The U Curve of Adjustment is a helpful way of analysing the Stages of Change, particularly when you name and analyse each current change process you are adjusting to (refer to Adjustment Mapping). Keeping in mind that most significant change events trigger a bunch of other change events that co-occur alongside each other.

The U Curve (adapted from Oberg's research) focuses on the *emotional* and *behavioural* changes. It is not an assessment of practical skills. In fact, many report higher levels of workflow or even accelerating their skills during adjustment cycles.

Please Note: Templates have not been designed for those living or working within abusive environments, such as workplace bullying or domestic violence – please seek professional guidance.

THE U CURVE OF ADJUSTMENT
The Stages of Change

Pre-Stage of Change
(one foot in / one foot out)

Return to Home/previous Functioning
(clear new goals)

Event: _______________________________

1 - 3 months
(The Honeymoon Stage)

relief
trepidation
nervous
excitement
embarrassment
euphoria
elation
exploration
enthusiasm

First non-adjustment
risk timeframe

12 months
(Adjusted/ Bi-cultural)

Balanced Lifestyle
Social Support Networks
Managing Grief &
Loss events
Psychological immunity
Bounce Back Strategies

9 - 12 months
(The Final Adjustment Stage)
managing workload pressures

3 - 6 months
(Low Dip Stage)

out of character reactivity
changes in mood
changes in sleep/appetite/energy

Low Dip
Culture Shock
Stage

6 - 9 months
(The Adjusting (resolution) Stage)
improved energy, open minded, humour returns, realistic,
minor adjustment issues, gradual acceptance

Shock

Acceptance

Forgiveness

Grief +
Loss

Eagle Eye

Denial

Resentment

Anger

(Adverse Reaction)
URGENT INTERVENTION

Adjustment Disorder

Based on Oberg's stages of culture shock

1-3 MONTHS — THE HONEYMOON STAGE

<u>Emotions & Behaviours</u>: excitement, nervousness, euphoria, shyness, trepidation, embarrassment, fascination, elation, enthusiasm, desire for exploration.

After all our action-planning and preparation (or lack thereof) in our Pre-Stage (one foot in/one foot out), we walk (or are forced) into the first one-to-three-month stage of our adjustment period. Considered a novel honeymoon season with feelings such as trepidation or euphoria, or maybe a sense of relief or dread as we stifle our humour with a half-smile and hope that 'things' will soon feel familiar.

3-6 MONTHS — CULTURE SHOCK/LOW DIP

<u>Emotions & Behaviours</u>: self-doubt, sense of conflict, hostility, bewilderment, anxiety, panic, overly critical, rejection, confusion, language barriers, frustration-anger, depression, embarrassment, timidity, insecurity, strengths turning to weaknesses, loneliness, hyperactivity, decreased energy.

The three-to-six-month stage (for some) is considered the most arduous road as we simply try to do our best to travel around the U Curve. It's common to feel depleted and to act out-of-character at times, eager (sometimes desperate) to improve our mood and reactivity and balance sleep/energy and appetite. It's common to 'miss the mark' and take offence due to mismanaged perception. We can be overly harsh on our ourselves and highly critical of our mistakes as well as fearful of upsetting others. Some debate or take action on matters that previously they would consider as relatively minor.

Humour can fly off to its own desolate planet, as our laugh becomes stifled or fake, and our new chemical responders begin clogging the engine. Physical aches and pains are common, as well as obsessing about what others are thinking — all competing with the *actual change* itself. It can appear that we're driving off-road onto unsealed pitted roads with only wild camels and dingoes for company, as we reminisce about the comforts of bitumen and long to return home.

Some reach the bottom of the U Curve by six months and they are ready to pay their tolls over the gateway bridge. They gather their humour, irony or the *right* to move forward as they begin to visit the vitally important Six-to-Nine Months Adjustment (resolution) Stage. The first six months resembles a 'preparation' stage: like trading in a foreign currency. Sadly, some hand back their keys and are driven back to the starting point, while others seek solace in their systems that allow inaction and comfort by pulling up on the side of the road, completely lost, unaware they've been reading the wrong map.

Lack of movement forward at six months is very serious. It's easy for time to slip by when there are few pressures to heal. If there is no bounce-back (return to normal functioning) after six months of the stressor (or its consequences), we are potentially AT RISK! Diagnosis and prognosis then turns to the *level* of disruption in social activity, relationships, employment and other important areas of previous functioning.

Lack of adjustment by six months is a serious and potential health hazard! A psychologically dangerous fine line begins to emerge. This has the potential to re-wire our brain circuitry and creating toxic chemicals, altering our future ability for rational decision-making. Land sliding our hopes and our dreams causes us to lower our watermark in lieu of nursing our avoidable, emerging, and somewhat painful 'conditions'.

6-9 MONTHS — ADJUSTING TO CHANGE (resolution)

Emotions and Behaviours: developing new relationships, coping with previously impossible situations, minor struggles in some areas (increased awareness), openminded, realistic and improved emotional competency.

It's pretty obvious when we've reached the six-to-nine-month stage of our change — our sense of humour begins to re-emerge within the irony (or not!) of our new situation. Our weaknesses turn to strengths, or we are, at least, aware of our weaknesses within the reality of our adjustment. We know in our gut that we are adapting, though it may be difficult to verbalise the 'how'. We are well aware of our compromises, as well as our *bottom lines*. Our ethics guide our decision making and we gradually move towards the final stage of our initial 12 months of adaptation.

9-12 MONTHS — Final Adjustment (bi-cultural)

Emotions and Behaviours: functioning effectively 'in flow' with only minor differences and disturbances, acceptance of reality, adjusting world view, values of the other culture accepted.

The final stage of our adjustment period is characterised by the acceptance of our new reality as well as enjoying the natural 'flow' of our routines. We are balanced within our systems of work, rest and play. We are eager to participate in reciprocated relationships, as well as focus on our goals and purpose (refer to Social Support Network and Balanced Lifestyle to assess gaps).

2.9 — Strategy: Adjustment Mapping

ADJUSTMENT MAPPING

Building emotional resilience through transition markers

GET A GRIP
YOUTH & COMMUNITY SERVICES

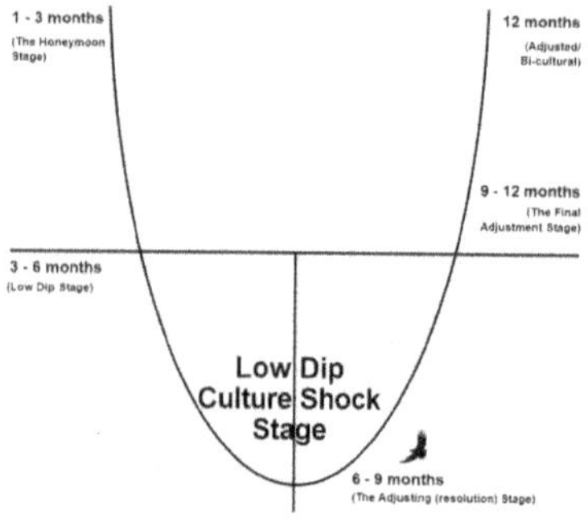

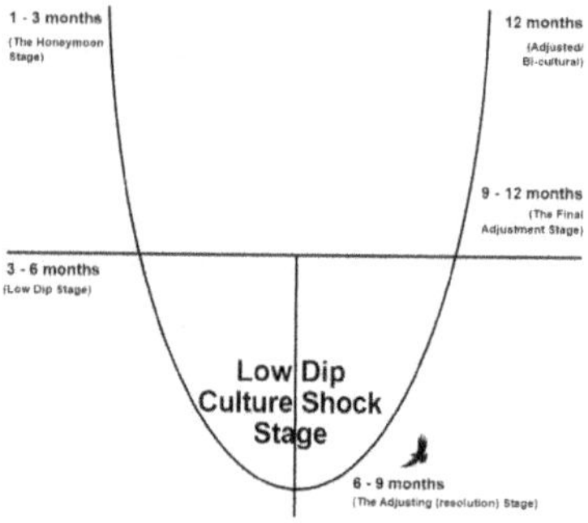

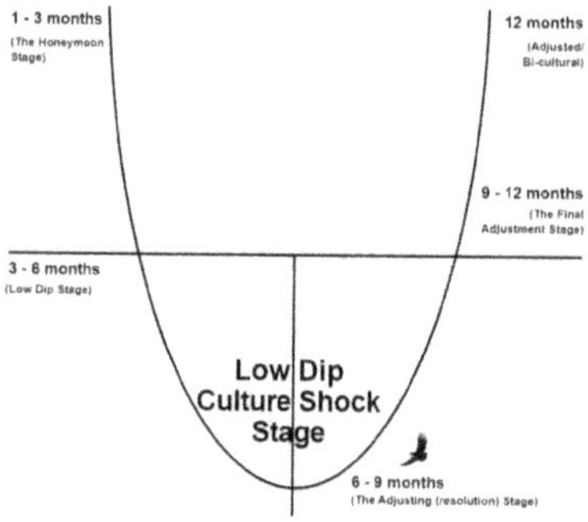

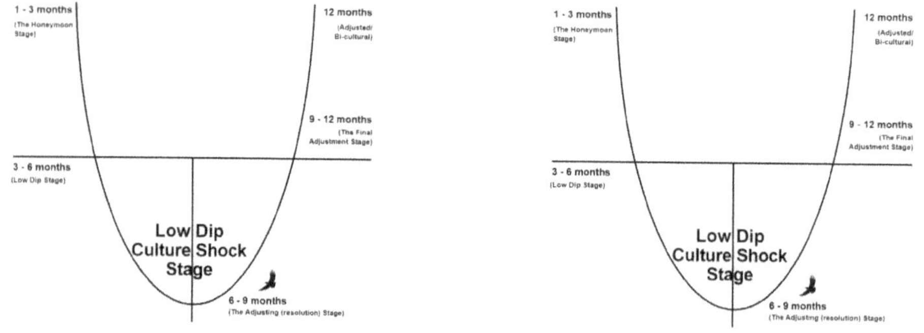

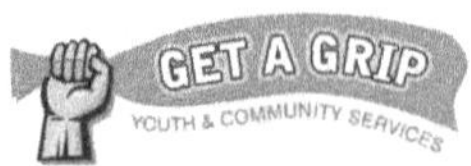

Based on Oberg's stages of culture shock

www.get-a-grip.com.au

Designed by Get-a-grip

The Balanced Lifestyle

Give Me 5!

'Balance' means different things to different people. There is a plethora of writing and recommendations within the medical and psychology fields regarding what it means to be living a 'balanced' lifestyle. Personality, working styles, goals, social preferences and a range of other factors often determine our individual view of 'balance'.

2.10 — Strategy: The Balanced Lifestyle (complete Template below)

The template I have re-adapted for use as a working document (original created as an addiction relapse-prevention tool — source unknown) provides an easy visual to begin to assess or plan our own balanced lifestyle, by focusing on five important areas. What is your self-rated score out of 100%?

Time for Food and Sleep (broken into 10% x2). When we analyse our sleep and diet patterns, we determine our mental state. Most of us are well aware of the link between mood, food and sleep, including our relationship with sugar, energy drinks, relaxants, blockers and coping strategies. Are you doing 'more of' or 'less of' than what would otherwise be considered as your 'reasonable'?

Time For Recreation — (20%) — FUN and PASSION. Recreation is considered the happy chemical moments of our life, where we initiate regular access to our environment or our preferred hobbies. Includes plans, dreams or past areas of enjoyment, such as holidays, projects, pleasure and physical activity.

Time For Work — (20%) — Workaholics often score 50/20 in this area! Work includes formal employment, housework, groceries, all parenting activities, financial management, transit to and from activities, favours, study, unavoidable interactions due to 'other' circumstances such as extended family and so on.

Time For Others — Fun, safe people only! These are the happy chemical people in our life, they are not our hard work interactions, or our obligatory relationships.

RESET is the declared enemy state of social withdrawal, addiction and co-dependency. Social gaps are opportunities to risk growth, such as initiating contact or re-engaging with friends, family and acquaintances. Respecting the fact that we aren't all natural 'people-people', with many preferring their own company. Though, increasingly social retreaters are cognisant of the way they've subtly reduced their people-interaction (particularly since 2020) as well as altered their perception of socialisation as a 'need'.

Time For Self — The relaxing date with yourself. This is not about sitting at home on your own watching Netflix. This is about getting out and about in your environment — such as sitting in an outside café reading the newspaper, having a massage, or maybe reading a book at the beach/bush. Some combine recreation with Time for Self, though it is important to separate the two in your intent for balance.

Complete the Balanced Lifestyle strategy on the next page or develop a new plan for your future. Are you over/under in your ratings? For example — no Recreational pursuits (0/20); over-working (50/20); infrequent Time With Others (2/20); excessive Time For Self (40/20); erratic Food and Diet (4/20).

> ### RESET your Balance — let's Move Forward!!

THE BALANCED LIFESTYLE

The High Five

Balancing our work/lifestyle is like being on a downwards moving escalator

- If we stand still we move backwards
- As long as we are moving upwards we are working towards balance
- One can never just stand still

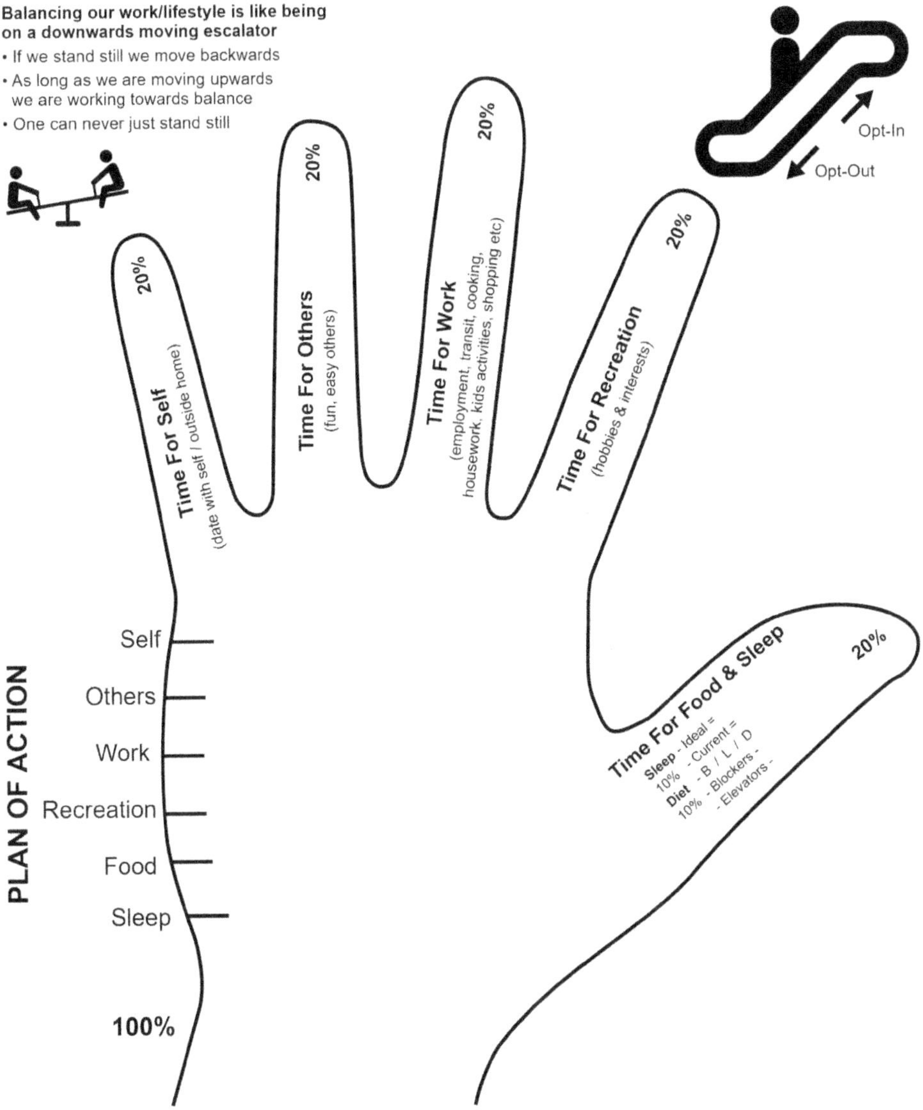

Opt-In
Opt-Out

Time For Self
(date with self / outside home)
20%

Time For Others
(fun, easy others)
20%

Time For Work
(employment, transit, cooking, housework. kids activities, shopping etc)
20%

Time For Recreation
(hobbies & interests)
20%

Time For Food & Sleep
Sleep - Ideal =
10% - Current =
Diet - B / L / D
10% - Blockers -
- Elevators -
20%

PLAN OF ACTION

Self
Others
Work
Recreation
Food
Sleep

100%

original source unknown: revamped by GAG 2022

www.get-a-grip.com.au

Grief and Loss

The measure of success: how we deal with pain and disappointment

> *Our Grief and Loss Intelligence — which requires a tolerance for discomfort, a recognition of pain and a plan/ desire to move forward, can determine the future of our mental health, our physical health, our spiritual health and our appetite for future risk.*

The DSM-5, states the condition of Persistent Complex Bereavement Disorder (PCBD) is codable as a 'severe and persistent grief and mourning reaction' under 'Other Specified Trauma and Stressor-Related Disorders'.

Most of us can relate to experiencing the rocky and tumultuous waves of grief and loss at some stage in our journey. The waves of recovery can be a lonely and emotionally draining experience, as we *slowly* begin to come to terms with our loss, at the same time as beginning to make sense of our 'new reality'. The normality of fluctuating emotional grief waves connects us to our pain in a somewhat haphazard tidal system, as we travel through the arduous stages of adjustment, particularly within the fragility of those initial 12 months.

Grief waves can feel like you're being dumped on the bottom of the ocean, then barely reaching the surface for air, before the next wave smashes you to the bottom again, desperately waiting for a break in the tide. The longer we live on this planet, the higher the likelihood of meeting that faceless white sea horse, and being forced to grab our aqua lung and flippers or other fancy underwater apparatus to help us breathe, as we try to pace ourselves through the rollercoaster ride of an unwanted journey. To be human is to survive deep-water tidal systems, tsunamis and giant sea swells. To heal is a rich part of the human experience: to stagnate our pain is to remain emotionally poor.

General Bereavement is considered distinct in its diagnostic classification to other life events or situational crisis trigger points. This is why the psychiatry diagnostic manual, The *DSM-5* (2013) treats normal bereavement separately from Adjustment Disorder (though this is under review). This is due to the assumption that *grieving individuals*, although distressed, will *generally* want to process their pain, *at the same time* as 'reasonably' manage normal commitments such as occupational/educational responsibilities and parenting responsibilities, whilst still maintaining routines of sleep, eat, rest and play.

Many of us can probably relate to an emotional stand-still, feeling 'emotionally stuck' in a particular grief stage, seemingly handing over our internal locus of control to an external black dog as we head into a vortex that sucks up our motivation like the grim reaper. 'Time' is an interesting beast. The subtle and delicate fine line between healthy healing and dangerous time-delay can stagnate our overall emotional growth. Our worldview slowly darkens, particularly when our pain is cosseted within the walls of retreat, subtly morphing into strange secondary states — it's like our aged self begins arriving thirty years too early.

Delayed grief and loss can attract labels such as an Adverse Grief Reaction, closely followed by Persistent Complex Bereavement Disorder, attributed to prolonged grief symptoms and impaired functionality occurring for at least 12 months. It's not unusual for people to describe their heart as if it's literally been broken in two. Medical professionals refer to Broken Heart Syndrome as a temporary heart condition, triggered by extreme stress and volatile emotions. Medicos may also call extreme grief as stress cardiomyopathy, takotsubo cardiomyopathy, or apical ballooning syndrome or a bunch of other hard-to-spell names.

The prognosis for radically delaying our healing is daunting, alongside the risk of clinical labels that may also show up for the ride. Internalising grief is like weeping on the inside, whilst our body is screaming out for ways to naturally externalise this pain. Although we don't get away with grief and loss 'work', we can minimise the risk as we learn to adjust.

Before we begin 'mapping' our deep-dive stories, it's important to Anchor back to positive events and achievements as a reminder of our flexible muscle memory system.

Grief and Loss Analysis

2.11 — Strategy: Positive Events — Adjustment Memories

Name 5 positive (major or minor) memories or achievements. For example — achieving an education or recreational goal.

1. ____
2. ____
3. ____
4. ____
5. ____

2.12 — Strategy: Worst Memories (analysis only)

Name your worst or most difficult memories or periods of time. For example — bullying between 10 and 15 years of age; relationship with parent between 5 and 10 years of age; car accident; loss of loved one; leaving school, failing education.

1. ____
2. ____
3. ____
4. ____
5. ____

Gone are the days where grief 'work' is a female-driven activity, while men are left to 'suck it up' and dull their pain with distractors such as drinking, relationship rebounding, working and maintaining typically gendered support roles. Healing can be a messy, haphazard process, with no 'one size fits all'. Men are increasingly aware that delaying the processing of complex grief is like putting a lid on a ticking time-bomb.

Referrals focusing on aggression, out-of-character violence within workplaces, volatility within relationships as well as the emergence of anxiety and depression, can often be linked to non-adjustment of a significant life event. Stuck-in-a-grief-stage is likened to feeling desperately alone without a life jacket and continually gasping for breath. It's heart-wrenching listening to stories of men who were placed in the role of first-responder or family 'strong man' (for example - after a shock death/suicide) and then entirely neglecting 'self' as they focus entirely on supporting other members of the system, rather than the whole family system healing at the same time.

When it's their turn to bravely face the pain of their loss, their loved ones have already moved forward many months earlier, and often treat their man with disdain for leaving *his* journey so late. His loved ones are unaware that he didn't even leave the starting block, so their negativity is doing little for him to even *want* to begin his healing journey. Men commonly state they are attending therapy to learn *how to grieve* without the use of their previous pain blockers and addictions (or relationship over-reliance) so they can still continue to juggle their 'general' life business.

Though incredibly broken inside, they still want to move forward functionally, *as well as* develop appropriate ways of recognising and validating their pain. If the brain has little or no recollection of dealing with extreme emotional pain, without the use of mal-adaptive blockers, therapy can provide an effective *grief and loss coaching support system* at the same time as addressing addictive behavioural patterns. Although no one on this planet can grieve for you, facing the pain of raw, unmasked grief is truly a brave person's journey. So, I invite you to put on your boots and put up the 'men at work' sign and value the arduous stages and waves of your journey.

Grief and loss often defies logic. Many find comfort drawing upon the healing environment of their land or local environment. Walking, talking, crying, kicking the sand, journaling, taking a bush walk, returning to areas that connect them with loved ones, group work or talk therapy — whatever *connects us to our pain and moves us forward*. Although grief waves can catch us off guard at any time of the day or night, people soon discover that the way to move forward lies within the prioritisation of their grief work, particularly in the early months.

Our bedroom is for sleep. Our bedroom was NEVER intended to be a long-term sustainable grief and loss processor, nor as a catalyst for an emerging psychosocial disorder. Mapping our grief and loss stories *as well as* our adjustment stories (U Curve Model) can be a useful way of analysing and separating the Memories stored in our subconscious (retrieval system).

GRIEF AND LOSS MAPPING

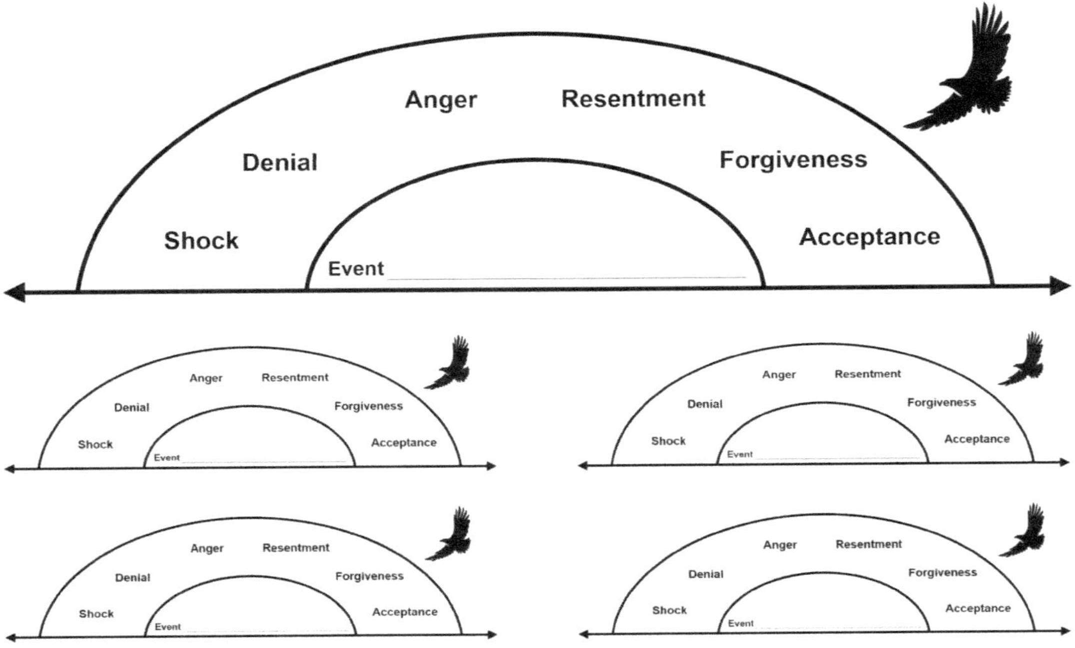

- Relationship breakdown
- Loss of loved ones
- Trauma
- Accidents
- Medical conditions
- Loss animals
- Global events

GET A GRIP
YOUTH & COMMUNITY SERVICES

www.get-a-grip.com.au

Designed by Get-a-grip

2.13 — Strategy: Grief & Loss Mapping (Template)

Transfer your 5 Worst Memories to the Grief & Loss Template and circle what stage you believe you have reached. This exercise is *analysis only*. It can be helpful to discuss with others or as pre-work before first-session work with professionals.

Shock and Denial Stage — This is the first stage of our journey, as we absorb the enormity of our trigger event or our loss. Shock can feel like we've been hit with a sledgehammer, trying to pick ourselves up, just in time to try to dodge the next blow! Emotions range from feeling numb, sad, a sense of disbelief, frightened, lost, distraught, lonely, despondent and confused. Some are frantic to deny reality and seek pain blockers, forcing themselves to bounce between shock and denial. Until we allow ourselves enough time to feel the volatile force of the next stage of our reality — raw ANGER!

The Anger Stage — is often the most misunderstood 'raw' stage of the grief and loss cycle. It's important to validate strong emotions, as well as the intense or complex relationship with your loss. The Anger Stage does not always elicit volatile emotions, with many feeling extreme sadness, disappointment and bewilderment. Many experience changes in their sleep, appetite and energy patterns as well as low mood, hyperactivity, super vigilance — feeling like they are constantly 'on guard'.

Internalising the Anger Stage can be extremely problematic for our physical health and our mental health: internally weaponising our pain as we become easily reactive or socially reclusive. Some prefer to remain calm and stoic rather than processing their pain: this is a direct stagnation of progress. Rather than processing pain, it's common for grieving individuals to try to 'jump over' the Anger Stage by avoiding and suppressing or trying to drive straight to the Acceptance Stage — bottling the other stages inside their denial crockpot, simmering on slow … Until an accumulation of life stressors ALL trigger to the boil.

The genuine end of the Anger Stage is characterised by feeling appropriately energy-depleted and battle-worn — finishing the raw race of survival, after a few months of exhausting rhetoric and erratic behaviour. Individuals who respectfully focus on grief-anger report relief when the toxicity of anger-based processing has been externalised. Those who've managed this stage without suppressants and other maladaptive coping strategies are grateful and proud of their journey thus far.

No one gets away without processing their pain: stories are simply stagnated and stored in our body. If we *maintain* a long-term system of avoidance and denial, our body will continue to sell us out. Our body sends us warnings to elicit our attention, such as an exacerbation of a previous health issue. We begin to notice new patterns, such as increases in headaches or aches and pains — stomach, back, neck or even heart palpitations. If we then talk to busy professionals such as the local GP, about our physical or emotional *symptoms*, they may diagnose and medicate a secondary condition such as depression or anxiety, rather than considering the impact of unresolved grief and loss, or our overall lack of adjustment.

The Resentment Stage — is less harrowing and reactive. Often turning to a somewhat 'it's not fair' rhetoric — 'why me', 'look at what I've lost', 'others have more'. Feelings of sadness and disappointment, associated with the reality of lost dreams, as we slowly come to grips with the *enormity* of our loss. Genuine resentment is normal, as well as confusion, loneliness and a sense of powerlessness, struggling 'on my own island'.

Some describe feeling 'like a stroppy kid' in this stage, with a somewhat increased or quieter sense of control, as they peer through the vista of their perceived unfair situation. Others report needing a well-deserved break before processing the next stage, preferring to focus on other areas of their life such as their relationships, recreational pursuits and work/education commitments. The journey between Shock-Denial and Anger-Resentment is definitely no easy feat.

The Eagle Eye Stage or Forgiveness Stage — we arrive at this stage when our executive brain shows up! We are ready to analyse the broad spectrum of truth, opinion, historical realism, genetics and choice from another perspective — an eagle eye. We are ready to change our focus from 'feeling my pain' to analysing and reconciling with the reality of our loss.

Col Stringer's portrayal of eagles in his book, *On Eagles' Wings: He Can Because He Believes He Can* (1983) suggests that with their steely, precision eagle eye view of the ground below, eagles can view reality and make decisions from a broader perspective, untouchable by any of their prey.

Most cultures, including indigenous Australians, hold the eagle in high regard, displayed on national emblems, reflecting a respectful awe for the uniqueness of their bold and tenacious feathered friends. These winged warriors are undaunted by the sheer ferocity of climatic extremes, remaining fearless in the face of adversity, easily harnessing the power of any ferocious storm by soaring above the turmoil to incredible heights in order to alter their worldview.

The race to trace requires rationality, brutal truth or being open to discovering the meaning behind our loss, rather than turning back to the comfort of denial or the primal processing of anger. This stage is *not* about excusing the abusive or bad behaviour of others (or self!) or exercising reckless trust. Nor is it about minimising or letting others walk over our boundaries, *despite* the 'word' forgiveness. Eliciting facts often triggers new realities.

This stage is almost impossible to effectively execute when our body is still suppressed or fuelled with unresolved issues that are best processed in the earlier stages. The fiery pain of loss and rejection, or the cruel demon of jealousy can torment our spirit and isolate our true potential from reaching freedom and purpose. Emotionally astute individuals often report frustration that they've arrived at this stage too early and head back, before moving on. Whilst others initially seek deeper explanations of what 'forgiveness' *actually means*, within their values, faith and culture.

Others realise that they've split or linked one topic or grief story into a bunch of other stories, complicating their grief and loss journey — such as the loss of a parent (one story), the abusive behaviour of the same parent (second story) and their choices of partners as a result of their upbringing (third story). This is why professionals will sometimes describe an individual as 'dealing with complex grief' or 'suffering an adverse grief and loss reaction' (refer to Grief & Loss Mapping template) particularly when movement forward is stagnated. It is of course, the business of the individual as to their own progress, though therapists and medical professionals remind us about the emotional and physical dangers of harbouring unforgiveness for self or others.

The emotional and physical benefits of releasing unforgiveness cannot be understated. Internalising unforgiveness is one of the most dangerous decisions on earth, and yet it is a decision only you can make or begin to break. Releasing the chains linked to those who have let us down, by handing our pain over to a higher power is true bravery in action — a recognition of emotional and spiritual intelligence.

The Acceptance Stage — is a healthy non-toxic place where we have reconciled with the enormity of our loss. We are fully aware of how the loss has impacted our personal life. This is not the time to excuse what is not right, nor neglect boundaries, particularly if these boundaries are linked to the safety of children, self or others.

The Acceptance Stage means that you are not internally 'owned' or permanently defined by the loss. Pain will still turn up from time to time. You are back on your feet and routinely engaged within all your systems of work, rest and play.

TERRSOP

(Trigger — Emotion — Response — Rule — STOP — Options - Plan)

Mental wealth could be summarised as 'control of our perception'. Afterall, it's the mismanagement of perception that often toxifies our body, particularly at our trigger point moments or when attempting to process our pain. TERRSOP is an analytical bounce-back strategy for those wishing to spend time deep-diving a tricky dilemma. Other readers may wish to move to Chapter 3 at this point.

Examples of misperceptions:

An A-grade student finding out they've *failed an exam* or receiving a *lower grade* than expected can experience a shock event likened to a head-on motor vehicle accident.

A person being *dumped* or *cheated on* (no matter what age) can experience a shock event likened to (and sometimes worse) than a sudden death.

A person being *yelled at* by a boss/colleague/teacher in front of peers can experience a numbing or petrifying shock event that mirrors heart attack symptomology.

Many students believe that a B or a C is a TOTAL failure and have left an entire university program after one or two failed papers or subjects. Their reaction to a minor failure has infiltrated every aspect of their view of self.

Many managers and CEOs are gracious to their employees, though they impose a 'zero failure' system upon themselves. Then, a mistake or a failure (finally) arrives and the impact is worse than a head-on car accident, often experiencing extreme anxiety-panic (sometimes blackouts). Many end up in hospital mirroring heart-attack symptomology or feeling like they've been teleported to a frontline war in Afghanistan!

2.14 — Strategy: TERRSOP - Template (below)

An EVENT opens a 'topic' in our thinking agenda. We must quickly (briefly) recognise (validate) the first raw emotional response (body sensation) and then move swiftly to a rational action plan.

Trial the following TERRSOP strategy to help shift a past event or to manage a current event.

Keys to success:
Be Real and Be Prepared to FLIP THE SCRIPT!!

TERRSOP - Template

1. **Trigger Event/s** — Name the Primary Trigger Event and Timeframe? 1-3 months / 3-6m / 6-12+ months

   ____

   ____

   ____

2. **Emotion and Behaviours** (Primary) — Name and Rate Primary Emotion/s and Behaviours?

   ____

   ____

   ____

3. **Response and Reactions** (Secondary) — Emotional and behavioural response as a result of inaction 1-2. For example, Social (reduced contact with others); Occupational (education, employment, household); Recreational (environmental); Medical

   ____

   ____

   ____

4. **Rules and Beliefs** (perception) — keep/delete/modify (find the absolutist words - should, have to, always, must, everyone, no one)

____

____

____

5. **STOP and Rewrite the New Script** — prefer/however/just; Validation; TED (topic/emotion/decision)
New rational theme:

____

____

____

6. **Options** — planning and consulting (U Curve mapping; G&L Mapping; SSN/Tribe; brain gym; words to eradicate...)

7. **PLAN OF ACTION** — new decisions - what is my next step?
   1. New Rational Theme _______________________________
   2. Tribe _______________________________________
   3. Professional _________________________________
   4. ____
   5. ____
   6. ____

Example of applying TERRSOP:
   1. **Trigger Event/s** — Relationship ending at the same time as failing an exam.
   2. **Emotions/Feelings** (primary) — sad, depressed, angry, confused, furious, shocked, relieved, petrified, abandoned, lonely, rejected, useless, humiliation, fear of retaliation.

Behavioural Responses (primary) — yelling, crying, with-drawal, fighting, embarrassment.

3. **Responses** (secondary) - emotional and behavioural (as a result of inaction) — eg. social withdrawal.

4. **Rules and Beliefs** (perception)

   Fact — my relationship is over; I failed my exam.

<u>**Maladaptive Perception**</u> — The fact my relationship ended and I failed my exam proves that I'm useless, so *no one* will want me. It's not okay to fail if I want to achieve. I'll probably be alone forever and I'll not *ever* pass my qualification. I *should* be able to depend upon someone; I *shouldn't* have to face the world; I'll *never* achieve my goals; I should've known better; it's not fair, why me, blame and punishment; need for control; need for love and approval.

<u>**Key dictator words**</u> - should, must, have to, no one, everyone, all, nothing, never.

FLIP THE SCRIPT!

5. STOP and Re-write the New Script (develop new rational theme)

Prefer/However/Just Strategy (four seconds) -

'I'd *prefer* to have passed, *however* failing or making mistakes happens, so I *just* need to get back on track with my goals' (erad-ication of all dictator/absolutist words).

Challenging the Rule (Fear of Failure) — 'What makes me so spe-cial that I can't fail?' It's normal to feel disappointed and sad when events occur. It's okay to take some time to re-evaluate what went wrong as well as grieve my loss.

A. New Rational Statement (neurogenesis — creating new superhighway) — My best is good enough so I *just* need to move forward.

6-7. OPTIONS AND PLAN OF ACTION

D. Social Support Network — Who are my people? Brutal Tribal Truth people? Reducing isolation by seeking connection with the environment or others; grief and loss counselling to address relationship cessation and seek opinion from academic advisors.

Common TERRSOP example of an individual who left their job and began to socially withdraw as a result of a workplace incident.

1. **Trigger Event** — Boss yelled at me in front of colleagues for making a mistake at work. Duration — 6 months ago.
2. **Emotions and Behaviours** (Primary) - belittled 8/10, embarrassed 9/10 (fright/flight)
   Hypervigilant at work, withdrew from colleagues. As a result of inaction above:
3. **Responses and Reactivity** (secondary) disturbances in social, behavioural, emotional, occupational and medical? Analysing options at the time.

Secondary Responses (as a result of no action at 1-3) — low mood, anxiety at the thought of going back to work; increased anger because the boss should pay for what they did/vendetta brought some relief initially; anxious at the thought of making other mistakes in the next job; grief realising I liked my job. Thought about taking legal action against boss, avoiding others, suppression with alcohol and technology, remaining unemployed, avoiding talking to others, considering applying for WorkCover for a psychological injury.

ANALYSING OUR SCRIPT

4. **Rules and Beliefs** — 'I'm a failure'; 'I'll *never* be of any use'; 'I *have to* get it right all the time'; 'I *should've* known better'; 'he *shouldn't* be such an arsehole'; 'I deserved better'; 'I'm going to pay him back' — Perfectionism and Payback.

5. **STOP and Rewrite the New Script**
   'I would PREFER to have handled my workplace situation in a different way. HOWEVER, I made the decision to leave instead of talking to my boss, so I JUST need to move forward.'

6. **Options** (hindsight) — planning and consulting
   Arrange a meeting to talk to the boss — did I have assertive confrontation skills at the time? Ask boss for support to gain new skills or where I went wrong. Ask boss for apology regarding the way I was spoken to. Separate perfectionism and fear of failure from the actual workplace incident. Accept that I will make mistakes and it's okay for my boss to point them out. Challenge my perception that my boss was targeting me. Gain opinion from others as to my boss's actions. Talk to GP about anxiety/blood pressure and any health-related issues and medication.

7. **Plan of Action** (Action-Verbing) — Reality and Fact Checking
   Organise a meeting with the boss;
   Talk to workplace human resources (HR);
   Book counselling session;
   Confidential employee assistance program (EAP);

GP — health check to rule out medical issues that may have caused issues with concentration in workplace — iron levels, cholesterol, etc.

Professional Assistance v Self-help v Prescription Medication

The body obeys our thinking and then mobilises our legs. If we toxify our brain with sad rhetoric and stop visualising future possibilities or cease to Anchor on past successes, the body has been instructed to stop the production of happy and productive bounce-back chemicals. This means our firewall is weak and our thoughts have broken through our blood-brain barrier. It's not the body's fault it has been instructed by the 'head office' to produce toxic chemicals.

If the body does not receive clear instructions to create functional energy such as oxytocin, and other bounce-back chemicals are on long service leave due to continual rejection of our vitally important environmental nutrients, our system has been instructed to turn in on itself.

Assessing whether the body is producing enough sexy daytime serotonin or sleep-inducing melatonin to maintain mental wealth can be challenging. Chemical imbalances, physical conditions, genetics, early life disruptions, unresolved grief and loss/ adjustment as well as self-imposed conditions of the mind, pose challenges for the diagnostic community. This is the reason the diagnostic community often suggest they are working in a 'grey zone' during their initial assessment process.

The decision to begin psychotropic medication for struggles with mental health is a personal choice in consultation with medical practitioners. This can be an important step towards moving forward, particularly low dose regimes that allow enough discomfort to practice bounce-back strategies and still build future momentum. At the same time, doctors often refer their patient for counselling as a form of co-care — with the therapeutic worker placed in the role of therapy and 'opinion only' in relation to medication, diagnosis and prognosis.

Respecting 'opinion only' and grey zone dilemmas, it is often disappointing working within a system that reduces, rather enhances, an individual's opportunity to thrive. For example, the increasing number of sulky clients who admit that they are unwilling to change their current circumstances, grieve or challenge their messy perception (hype & clutter thinking). Many admit that they are only attending counselling 'to shut my doctor up' after agreeing to at least one session before their doctor is prepared to prescribe medication.

A large number of individuals freely admit that they have no prior history of disturbance nor family history — 'it's just that I'm emotionally lazy' citing low discomfort intolerance and wanting 'a pill that will block all my frustrations'. The 'alternative agenda community' are obviously not impressed to be sitting opposite a brain-gym therapeutic worker who is perceived to be standing in their way of 'getting on meds'. It soon becomes obvious that;- despite relevant psychoeducation in relation to their presenting issues; the invitation to apply emotional management strategies through coaching; or to begin vitally important grief and loss work; or to engage in 'debrief only' sessions with a motivated worker who is easily accessible and is prepared to cartwheel and provide pavlova and strawberries on arrival — the forced new client still remains firmly convinced that 'meds are the only way'.

Increasingly, doctors report genuine concern that patients are rejecting 'matters of the mind work' in lieu of medicating their thinking with psychotropic medication that (1) dulls discomfort, (2) maintains 'nice', (3) reduces their future ability to manage situational stresses and (4) internalises rather than heals messy and trauma stories. People are the best experts on themselves? Or are we spoilt through choice due to low motivation and increasing admissions of emotional laziness?

Thankfully, many doctors and patients combine a 6-12-month therapeutic (and/or other) brain-gym approach AND an initial low-dose medication regime to allow enough discomfort to begin to support their presenting issues. This system allows enough of a buffer (medication) to lance, heal and reconstruct complex and deep-dive stories, at the same time as challenging unhelpful rules or beliefs.

Snarly, action-minded clients storming into their first counselling sessions with a grumpy disposition and a frown that engulfs the office provide the perfect storm for growth. Beginning their first sentence with profanity, under the guise of disbelief — 'Fuckin' doc sez I need medication, and I told 'em *not* to write me a script. I've never needed meds before and I've got no intention of putting that stuff into my body'. At the end of the first assessment session, the new client is assured that 'your doctor is clearly concerned about your mental health, for valid reason, and believes it has reached the stage that medication needs to be a serious option. *However!* The fact that your doctor has referred you to a therapist indicates that they have a belief in *you* personally as well as a belief in *your* ability to take back or resume the control of *your* mind'.

A perfect storm often creates a successful, albeit, whirlwind of a mind-gym therapeutic alliance in which, within a short space of hard-working time, natural chemical balance is restored and the smiley, cartwheeling worker is appropriately sacked!

> **Avoid the onset of secondary conditions
> by taking ACTION!!**

Chapter 3
(Avoidable) Secondary Conditions

The topic of Chapter 3 deeply saddens me. To be writing about avoidable, situationally induced, psychological and medical conditions that were once non-existent in an individual's life, and yet now, have become of clinical significance, due to the **mismanagement of primary triggers**, is nothing short of a tragedy. Let's scrap the Baby Bill and de-legitimise the act of storm-buffeting our younger generation's hurdles by fully eradicating the act of **care-bombing typical generational norms**, and walk 'with' rather than *for*.

If our response to events and circumstances causes us to spin anti-clockwise in a whirling mass of toxic, fluid air, exacerbated by the state of our globally chaotic world, it may be time to improve our psychological fitness by signing up for the brain gym — that is, if we are to survive the next stage of our ever-changing world. There are now hundreds of individuals of all ages who are deteriorating mentally and physically. They are developing a hostile relationship with their external environment — there is no skipper at the helm.

At the time of completing my writing, my paternal family in New Zealand was in shatters. The news of our young family members' suicide alongside his partner, rendered us all in disbelief. Two families battling with unanswered questions and broken hearts. It is indeed with a heavy heart that I remind readers, once again, of the fragility facing us *all*, in these unprecedented times of change and uncertainty.

The battlefield of the mind is real, and so is the war we wage upon ourselves, in a new era of controversy and confusion. Navigating our way back from deep states of despair after mismanaged situationally induced trigger events and rebuilding our social risk appetite, can be a slow and arduous journey. Turning theory into urgency and acting with purpose, we know that in order to find our way back to the dock, we must find our known starting point, as well as our estimated drift, and declare our RESET.

The Danger of Inaction by Six Months

When recovery from a primary trigger event has been extended for longer than six months, the risk to our mental health and physical health significantly increases. If our brain architecture has been foundationally laid on quicksand and we are not prepared to action a life stressor or mitigate the risks of inaction, we cannot expect the universe to be a mind reader and force us to heal. Nor can the universe heal for us. We must sound the alarm and recognise our right to heal as well as our right to be heard.

Many of us have watched heart-wrenching (yet inspiring) documentaries, or we have supported our post-accident loved ones, with what appears to be brutal medical and physio regimes, where the seemingly impossible collides with tenacity and determination. Patients' post-surgery are forced to mobilise their body quickly despite their pain (or other obstacles) in order to 'get out of that bed and get moving'. This contrasts with the 'old days' where recovery was synonymous with bed sores and healing timeframes were extensive due to the perceived role of the bed as the patient's main healer.

Modern stories of shocking prognoses with labels such as 'disability' smashed apart after an individual defies their physical barriers, attributed to the sheer mental force of maintaining torturous healing regimes. The brain and the body are synchronised, leading the healing journey. These tragedies would suck most of us into a dark vortex and yet these psychological heroes walk out of their inaccessible wilderness wearing their modern boots, after fighting their demons and forging a new life — one that defies all odds. These wounded heroes remind us that we will never win any battle if we fight the devil in our bare feet.

Empathy enables: sympathy disenables. We place extraordinarily high expectations on most groups in society, with minimal timeframes to get back on their feet. Mature aged people are expected to work until they drop, children are expected to cope with new teachers and classes every year of their school life, mothers are home within hours of giving birth, the disabled are pressured to work and the injured are graduated back to work.

So, WHY the *fuck* is it now fashionable to prolong emotional healing for our young people? Or, in the elimination of primary trigger events, to accommodate parasitical behaviour and then turn a blind eye to festering bed-sores, when *others* in society are expected to (or are forced) to speed up *their* healing and move forward? Does money buy extended time to heal? Are the upper class creating the new bedroom class? When did it become fashionable to hand our young people a hall-pass on discomfort, retreat, reckless spending habits and non-contributory lifestyles? What role have you played in the delayed healing or de-adulting or extended childhood of others, that has progressed into a psychological injury?

Are we bedroom-abandoning our loved ones by assisting them to ignore their primary trigger events? Is your household denying the obvious signs of decreasing immunity, rather than 'walking along-side' to maintain an immune-efficient firewall? Is your loved one's brain circuitry spitting and sparking, growing wiry arms and legs with grasping muscular tentacles that are gripping onto emerging secondary conditions? Are these new conditions acting like cognitive fatigue-lead-weights, on a system that's already under the pump?

When the brain weeps, like a type of sub-concussion with no obvious external signs, it will always place excessive pressure on the body. Though the body remains ever-hopeful its owner will develop genuine intent and become transparent by reorganising, reprioritising and then relaunching. If 'stress' is *not* a dirty word — why are we not teaching our younger generation that living on planet Earth means that stress will show up? Is it time to stop excusing addictive technology and global disarray? Are we willing to externally weed and prune our backyards to improve our façade, though reluctant to weed and prune our own grey psychological interior?

Are we teaching our young people that the measure of success is how they deal with disappointment? Are we living in a world where young people can easily name a *wide range* of guns with incredible accuracy, though they struggle to fire the pistol of liberation that can catapult them out of their own prison walls when triggered by tough events? Glued to their own self-imposed inmate called Sabotage, are they unaware of their contradictory by-laws or the density cap on erratic thoughts, as well as the need to delve into their own hidden recesses in order to heal? Are they wandering around in their fractured wilderness, ever-dependent on others, with excessive time to wage a war against the rulers of their own mind?

Maintaining the marriage between our emotional age and our developmental age is the lifetime goal for us *all*. Why, then, are adults turning a blind eye to signs of premature physical aging and cognitive decline? Our diggers fought for our protection under insurmountable conditions — are we dishonouring their legacy by rummaging around in our capitalistic mindsets, with our bulging tech-rich devices, unaware of our privileged peace time slumber? Has it become a fact that our socially withdrawn community are sporting psychological and physical wounds at the same level as our diggers walking in from the battlegrounds? Has it become the norm to be enmeshed with avoidable conditions then labelled as 'dis-abled'— meeting criteria for disability services such as NDIS?

Please note: This chapter is a 'discussion only' and does not negate the importance of maintaining current intervention, medication and professional consultation. The topic of post-traumatic stress disorder (as a result of a significant primary trigger event or a series of events or abuse) is not covered adequately. The writer assumes no expertise in psychiatry and medicine, nor recommends arm chair diagnosis or prognosis. Professional guidance at all times is recommended.

Avoidable Secondary Conditions

Adjustment Disorder

The *Diagnostic and Statistical Manual of Mental Disorders* (DSM-5 fifth edition) from the American Psychiatric Association, diagnoses **Adjustment Disorder (2013:286) as a stress-related disorder that creates significant emotional or behavioural symptoms within three months of a stressor(s).** The diagnosis of Adjustment Disorder refers to an overall lack of emotional and physical bounce-back, particularly after six months, as evidenced by significant impairment in functionality within important areas of general life, such as decreased performance at work or school, as well as changes in relationships. Of clinical significance are the number and/or severity of reported changes that are persistent, exceeding what is considered typical when cultural, religious or age-appropriate norms are taken into account.

Accompanying Adjustment Disorder is often a combination of depressed mood (feelings of hopelessness), anxiety (escalating to social panic) and conduct issues (such as threats of harm to self or others), causing loved ones to feel apprehensive or cautionary when challenging social norms, often the reason pressure is reduced, decreasing the opportunity to "adult".

Stress can sometimes overwhelm our capability to bounce-back, finding ourselves stuck in a corner, trying to ignore the bed bugs that are rapidly multiplying and beginning to leave infectious tracks on our arse. Although stress is uncomfortable ... we still *need* triggers to flex our trust in our own emotional management system so we can continue (even if we fumble) to travel along our developmental continuum. Abandoning or abdicating this responsibility narrows our worldview and continues to decrease our social intelligence (with respect of trauma events that can temporarily overwhelm our system).

Generalised mismanaged stressful event/s combined with a delayed plan of action and lack of cognitive bounce-back skills can give birth to avoidable Secondary Conditions such as Anxiety. For example, General Anxiety Disorder, Obsessive Compulsive Disorder, Separation Anxiety, Social Phobia, Panic Disorder (Agoraphobia) or Social Anxiety Disorder. Feeling anxious from time to time doesn't mean we're developing an avoidable condition as per above. It means that our over focus on our fear-based or anger-based thinking is dangerous, with the potential to malfunction our circuitry system, requiring urgent reconstruction or modification — preferably in four seconds (4-SR it! — strategy 2.6).

We are not born with anxiety; we grow anxiety. The combination of mismanaged (significant) events and delayed timeframes has the potential to turn a manageable primary event into the birth of a range of secondary physical and psychological conditions. Stress without an action plan easily turns into toxic fear-based anxiety — like a spaghetti brain on crack! It's not long before we become anxious at even the *mere thought* of being anxious (just *in case* anxiety turns up), placing our over-protection system into constant overdrive. The body *eventually* becomes *accustomed* to toxic invasion — like becoming best friends with a junkie in a clown's suit. In other words, our body becomes more comfortable with the normality of toxicity than normality itself.

Toxicity causes havoc to pre-existing physical (or other) conditions, particularly when we attempt to suppress, distract or force our denial brain into convenient notions of misbelief by befriending maladaptive survival and protection chemicals such as Panic and Rage. This system is an instruction to 'demobilise' or 'hyper-vigilise' or maybe 'hyper-civilise' by placing ON GUARD all our soldiers who often become instructionally confused — unsure whether to stand in position, load their rifles or stand down as they desperately attempt to decipher the instructions from their commander in chief.

It's not long until we need a break from our *head* and a break from our *toxicity* by desperately leaning towards maladaptive *coping strategies* as we begin to behave in compensatory ways, attracting new labels such as: Sleep-Wake Disorder, Insomnia Disorder, Major Depressive Disorder, Substance Related Disorder/other addictions disorder. It doesn't take long until our *personality* is then under attack, particularly when we continue to act in opposition to our typical cultural norms — enter General

Personality Disorder, Avoidant Personality Disorder, Dependent Personality Disorder, Intermittent Explosive Disorder, Conduct Disorder, Narcissistic Personality Disorder, or even the grand finale antithesis to cohesive societal norms: Mr or Mrs Anti-Social Personality Disorder (psychopath).

Avoidant Personality Disorder

Our social intelligence is a reflection of our emotional intelligence. Whilst some find social interaction easy, others prefer their own company. For most, social interaction is a learned skill, with a period of awkwardness as we progress our social appetite. Regardless of choices and personality, if we are not regularly exercising our social skills we will eventually regress and lose momentum.

The *DSM*-5 describes **Avoidant Personality Disorder as a pervasive pattern of social inhibition, linked to feelings of inadequacy, with hypersensitivity to negative evaluation in at least four contexts.** Overall, there is a chronic avoidant behavioural pattern within social, occupational, environmental or peer/intimate relationships, due to chronic fears around the possibility of being rejected, exposed, criticised, shamed or ridiculed. The avoidant *perceives* they are socially inept, unappealing or inferior to others, adopting an overall reluctance to take risks or engage in new activities.

Sufferers of chronic avoidance behavioural patterns are locked and chained into a very serious condition. Therefore, it's important that the system around them does NOT engage in forms of threat, such as eviction from the family home, as a way of instigating communication and change. Forcing change upon the sufferer against their will is considered abusive, particularly if the sufferer has been held hostage within a range of fear-based beliefs for a lengthy period of time (this includes individuals who are functioning in one system such as employment, though socially regress or refuse participation in other systems). If confidence and rationality are on long service leave, filed somewhere in the deep recesses of the subconscious, there is no point pretending or hoping otherwise. The pace of change is slow. Even small steps are considered a giant leap forward.

Rewiring social skills *begins in our home environment*, evidenced in our routines, for example our sleep/wake patterns, meal planning and increased reciprocation such as housework responsibilities. Any activities that also increases home-based verbal interactions are considered to be a positive move forward, particularly democratic negotiations and participation in family meetings: discomfort to grow opportunities.

Dependent Personality Disorder

The *DSM-5* describes a **Dependent Personality Disorder as a pervasive and excessive need to be taken care of that leads to submissive and clinging behaviour with fears of separation, evidenced in at least five contexts by early adulthood.** Keep in mind that chronic dependence requires a chronic enabler. Enablers need to be needed. Do you hover like a helicopter? Do you struggle to trust in another person's ability to grow?

Dependent young people describe themselves as 'home-grown', though do not *set out* to take advantage of others, nor do they want to develop enduring patterns of dependency. They want to live a life without chronic fears of abandonment, rather than hide in their cave sanctuaries. Much of the time they are not bored or lazy, as their volatile head chatter chews up hours and hours of erratic thinking space with the mysterious world of male responsibility nowhere in sight. Who would *ever* wish this disorder upon a loved one?

In the early days, many enablers focus solely on their Dependent. Then eventually the enabler becomes highly critical and embarrassed, as evidenced in their cruel gen norming rhetoric. Enablers rarely analyse their own behaviour, or the part they have played in creating a dependency system. Preferring to engage in cycles of *blame-the-retreater* and *reject-advice-junkies* as they sport the Aussie pattern of 'hoping for the best' because 'she'll be right'. At the same time, as ignoring their gut instinct that screams out — there is now absolutely *no* resemblance of 'right'.

Enablers victimise and criticise, at the same time as agree that their 'boundaries' are distorted. Often becoming *automatically programmed to martyr* their soul by continuing to cook, clean, wash and reduce expectations around board and chores. Most enablers eventually describe themselves as shells of their previous self, at the same time as stating 'though I'd probably be bored if there wasn't *someone* around to care for'. Enablers rhetoric becomes messy, with double standards galore that make no real sense to the outsider as they simply continue to reject the voice of wisdom.

Many enablers suffer from an overarching fear of abandonment, particularly pending empty-nesters, who perpetuate cycles of enmeshed dependence. Rather than facing their fears head-on or preparing for the transition from child-to-adult relationships with their offspring (within developmental norms), they hover like helicopters and reduce (rather than increase) expectations. In general, there is an overall distorted view of "relationships" with enablers suffering chronic fear of abandonment, often diagnosed with labels such as General Personality

Disorder, Major Depression, Co-dependency Addiction, Social Anxiety Disorder or Generalised Anxiety Disorder — take your pick, there are plenty to choose from. Are you choosing to extend your caretaking addiction into a full-time career called Chief Enabler?

Anxiety Disorders/Addiction Disorders

Fears that are out of proportion to the actual threat posed by the social situation, lasting persistently for six months or longer are often diagnosed within a vast range of anxiety disorders, particularly if this threat is unrealistic within an individual's sociocultural context, such as the perception that others will scrutinise, humiliate, embarrass or reject. If these unmanaged fears persist (anxiety-based thinking) they can attract clinically significant impairment and distress in important areas of functioning. It makes sense that, in the face of ongoing perceived threats, the individual will narrow their vision to a life with instructions that are focused on only *protection* or *survival*.

Addictively medicating high-level discomfort, as well as engaging in extended avoidance patterns, often morphs into Addiction Disorders. The Hidden @ Home Community often minimise the true chaos of their *inner* world by blocking their outer world. Though the mind is impoverished, they learn to behave as 'nice', after sending out instructions to 'stay low' and protect the cave from attack or invasion. With their basic needs for shelter and sustenance met, they can peer through the safe vista of their bedroom, as their co-dependent 'others' sip on their champagne of La' Denial and contemplate the family plight .... with all members of the system continuing to display little evidence of *any* change in sight.

Enablers as Codependent Addicts

Blind to Boundaries

Codependency is a system of **over-responsibility for others: taking responsibility for the thinking, feeling and behaving of someone else.** Melody Beattie (1992: *Codependent No More*) is considered a leading expert on the topic of co-dependency with her brilliant books read worldwide. Many workers in the social service industry dissect this vital topic, often suggesting that they, too, meet the criteria for co-dependency, or at some stage in their lives were functioning at a high level of co-dependency as 'wounded healers', until they re-established their boundaries and analysed their need to over-care by developing the skill of 'walking alongside'.

Beattie is not referring to 'the good stuff of life' such as our acts of love, kindness and compassion that are a natural part of our relational and familial commitment within functional relationships. Codependency relates to the way that people 'think, do, excuse and maintain secrecy' on a continuous basis for others, thus disenabling their person from learning how to take care of their own life, such as reaching out for assistance, risking discomfort and gaining professional advice. Partners (and parents) of addicts often identify with codependency, though not until many years later, realising their secret-keeping has become as addictive as the addicts' addictions. The damage this double-addiction lifestyle has on other members of the family, cannot *ever* be understated. It's like living in a system where Plan B is on permanent holiday and all members are declining in their functionality *at the same rate.*

Children raised in extremely complex families can unknowingly find themselves enmeshed into a type of early-years training station for codependency, particularly when young people are expected to (or chose to) grow up ahead of their biological age. When we are placed (or forced) into a care-giving role when we are young, such as continually coping with addicted parents; parents with mental health or physical health issues; chronic or chaotic families where career-driven lifestyles take precedence over developmental norms, our blueprint for participation within adult relationships can be altered. For example, the eldest child in an abusive, complex or low socio-economic household who was overly responsible for younger siblings. The 'man of the household' for a single parent can transfer this care-taking system to subsequent relationships, long after leaving home.

At its extreme level, co-dependency is treated therapeutically (or within a rehabilitation centre) as a Caretaking Addiction, with sufferers likely to die earlier than their dependents. This is due to sheer physical exhaustion and complex secondary health-related conditions, attributed to overextended, non-reciprocated patterns of caring. This is a form of self-harm under the guise of 'extreme kindness'. The body simply wears itself out! Caught in never-ending 'fix and solve' cycles or trying to make consequences simply go away, general health warnings fall on deaf ears for many years, until a major health event is diagnosed, often with astonishingly little change in the expectations of the receivers.

When discussing the notion of reciprocation as a two-way give-take street, many suggest that their compulsive over-giver just *can't* help themselves — 'so *why* would I want to stop Wonder Woman or Super Man from doing what they *can't* help doing?' At the same time as admitting that this system is 'unfair' and that Super Hero will probably just eventually crash head-on into an abyss'. The cruelty of Takers can abound for decades.

It's incredible how many adult children and/or partners who are living at home are not expected to 'work' inside or outside the family home. Why would they, when parents are cooking every meal and buttering every piece of toast for 'my baby'. Nor does the young person intend to *ever* operate within a system of reciprocation (if they can get away with it) while living under their pressure-free, privileged roof. It's easy to find this system in operation when you see weeds in the garden or basic painting jobs uncompleted as well as other typical household tasks untouched, in a home with otherwise capable, time-rich adults. Followed by a barrage of excuses such as 'yes-but I can't force them' or 'but we can afford to pay a gardener/cleaner', 'yes-but they just don't want to help', it's all too hard dealing with the sighing (or aggression)' or 'yes I know things need to change and I *should* expect more'.

This is in complete contrast to discussions with parents of 10+ year-olds, revealing that this age group are generally running rings around their older counterparts, particularly when the principle of reciprocation is a generalised expectation within the family home. This system is particularly powerful when reinforced by parenting styles that avoid 'hovering' and parents who provide plenty of positive family experiences with fair consequences, alongside an Opt-In theme with a range of 'discomfort-to-grow' opportunities.

Stockholm Syndrome and Lima Syndrome

The unusual bonds of survival

Stockholm Syndrome, though not found in the *DSM-5* (more likely diagnosed as post-traumatic stress disorder) is viewed as an unexpected emotional response some people have *towards their captor,* which can result in unnatural bond/s and long-term over-reliance. This differs from Lima Syndrome, which was first coined in Japan after the 1996 Japanese embassy hostage crisis in Lima, Peru where perpetrators or hostage-takers became *sympathetic to the wishes and needs of their victims.*

When our internal state has markedly altered over a lengthy (or intense) period of time and we have developed complex bonds with the people we are dependent upon for our basic survival, *someone* must sound the alarm bells! Psychology began studying the relationships between emotionally charged hostages and captors from the 1970s, attempting to understand situations in which the brain has been forced to send very clear survival messages in response to highly vulnerable and sometimes life-threatening situations.

When the brain attaches survival messages to a particular person/s or situation, it can trigger the formation of unusual bonds with captors, noted even years after a hostage situation. Research suggests that even in the face of enduring abuse, some hostages have fallen in love with their captors, some have refused to be witnesses or give testimony in criminal court, with others even paying for the legal fees of their captors. Could these notions provide a broader understanding of the serious long-term psychological enmeshment between enabling parents and their offspring? Are we now grappling to understand the complex relationship patterns between survival and protection, where boundaries are blurred and reality is altered? Or do we turn to Swiss psychologist Carl Jung's theories that focus on immature or absent fathering, blurred male/female archetypes (Anima/Animus), caretaker-imprinting and the collective unconscious?

It is suggested that there are also other settings for Stockholm Syndrome, noted within other imbalance of power relationships and institutions, such as when we are unable to achieve our **goals** without becoming highly dependent or reliant, followed by secrecy patterns. For example, coaches with elite sportspeople (particularly children) and sexual deviants luring innocent victims over a grooming process of many years. Are *you* living in a power imbalance situation where *you* hold all the survival cards for someone else? Or are you reliant on *others* for your *basic survival needs*?

Call to Action — The Implications of Doing Nothing

On the ground level of reality as outsiders, within our soft, relatively non-confrontational Aussie culture, must we continue to patiently sit by and say nothing when we witness bizarre familial behaviour? Do we have the confidence and conviction to expose bizarre behaviour and call it for what it is? Is writing such as mine persuasive enough to evoke a call to action, followed by families breaking their chains of denial? Or is it time to focus on our parents who are raising younger children (particularly 10+ year olds) to warn of the dangers of parental care misuse?

Are professionals (particularly doctors) ready to voice their concern for these bizarre bonds of survival? Particularly when important areas of functionality, such as full-time employment and social risk taking is nowhere in sight, replaced with unusual physical and mental health decline. Doctors are increasingly concerned and highly confused as to why adult males are unable to lead their own medical conversations. Why does Mumma sits glued to her son, 'taking over' the consult on behalf of her adult son — while he sits next to her, like he's a six-year-old child in a man's body, appearing to have become a feminised version of his mother?

Anecdotal evidence suggests that there *is* growing concern from insider-outsiders such as friends and extended family, who witness this bizarre behaviour over a long period of time. Such as an adult son sitting unnaturally close to his mother at the dinner table, pawing her arms like a cub in a cave, whilst looking deeply into her eyes like a lover — deeply disturbing! How is it possible to deny that sons are often mothers' emotional partner, when there's overt evidence to suggest that she's clearly his? Outsiders continually report confusion and awkwardness when they step inside the homes of friends or loved ones who are living in these enmeshed systems, when observing these somewhat odd behavioural bonds. Though, when they attempt to talk about their concerns, they are treated with passive hostility or contempt and leave feeling confused and rejected.

Where an imbalance of power exists, there will always be the potential for enduring patterns of vulnerability and in some cases, abuse. Living together within fear-based/basic-needs households creates disturbing anxious-attachment relationships. This refers to those who are reliant on others for their accommodation, food and other basic survival needs, particularly in the presence of ongoing fears around threats of eviction and decreased life skills.

Pain Disorders

Doctors report increased diagnoses for patients presenting with a psychogenic pain disorder — physical pain or movement that does not match symptoms, forcing the medical practitioner to turn to their patients' psychological state as a possible cause for the emergence of physical health issues. Left unmanaged, a patient could also be diagnosed with a psychosomatic disorder, which is a disease involving body and mind as a result of chronic stress, which has triggered hypertension, respiratory issues, migraines, pelvic pain or maybe dermatitis. Secondary to psycho-somatic disorder is the hideous widespread muscle pain condition of fibromyalgia which cannot be confirmed by x-ray, biopsies or blood tests (also linked to genetic issues, infections as well as general stress). At its absolute worst, a conversion disorder — a psychological condition whereby blindness, paralysis or other nervous system (neurologic) symptoms are unexplained under medical evaluation.

Back Pain and Curvature of the Spine

No spine, no life. Many young people are suffering conditions that once appeared in ONLY the very old. Research suggests that back pain is more common in people with mental health struggles, such as anxiety and depression, than those without — chronic physical pain triggers similar parts of our brain. Growing a backbone involves listening to our body and learning not to live our life in a spine-tingling suspense movie.

Supporting our young people to remain locked away in their rooms on devices without spinal health education and weight load management, is surely the same as handing a 10-year-old a bottle of vodka and a bottle of Bundy Rum every morning, then hoping he'll still have a backbone and achieve his goals on his road to full blown alcoholism. Our musculoskeletal system relies on our patterning and becomes stressed when forced to continually 'adjust' to prolonged periods of sitting, walking, standing, twisting and bending movements.

Chronic physical pain persistent over a period of time (particularly longer than six months) is often associated with undiagnosed mental health conditions. This has the potential to irreparably damage the body. Most of the time we associate back pain only with physical issues, such as sports injuries, strains, posture, falls, carrying heavy loads, pulled muscles, strained ligaments, bruising, accidents and infections. Even the basic links between stress and carrying loads (according to our genetics and our developmental stage) can be problematic, such as the link between stressful educational expectations and carrying heavy school bags?

Thousands of young people are displaying emerging spinal stress while their carers simply turn a blind eye. Scoliosis (kyphosis or lordosis) is where the spine twists and curves to the side, not uncommon, particularly in older adults, with diagnosis beginning around 10–15 years of age. Sometimes the spine is shaped abnormally, creating back pain from the pressure on the vertebrae. The emergence of physical pain may actually reflect emotional pain, as the nervous system employs intricate cells (neurons) to send a warning to *attempt* to gain our attention, before stepping up the pain to a level that *will, eventually,* stop us in our tracks.

The body sells us out, folks! Our body lets us know where our mental state is 'at' through the use of powerful (and sometimes painful) nerve cell prompters to force our thinking into action. These prompters are fulfilling the requirement of their role. They are warning us of serious trouble. Stress-related back pain that has arisen due to unmanaged primary psychological factors can turn our physical life and mental health life upside down and inside out, resembling a nightmare on steroids.

Neurons and electrically sparking nerve cells communicate with other cells (via synapses). If the spinal cord (column of nerves that connects our brain to our body to ensure we have movement) becomes hideously disrupted, a pain 'worse than child birth' can infiltrate our body's ability to function and immobilise our entire lives. Our spine or backbone is our body's central support structure and must remain healthy for our lives to remain viable! No spine, no ability to move our body or keep our organs functioning.

Adults, for whatever strange reason, expect young people to miraculously learn 'good posture' and 'good mental health' in order for their cells and neurons to party appropriately. Come on parents!! It will *always* be important to teach young people how to develop load management wisdom and to monitor the use of devices and socials, given the HUGE juggling act between educational expectations, peer group pressures and other developmental issues.

From Stress to Injury to Condition (SIC)

The Big Morph

How SIC would you feel to be informed that your loved one has a condition usually diagnosed in people 20 or 30 years older, though back in its *primary* days was highly preventable? Are we leaning too heavily upon our medical-aftermath *secondary* repair system (Big Pharma) as we wait with anticipation for prognosis and medication regimes to begin? Are we teaching our young people about The Big Morph — the fine timeline between typical stress management, the injury state and diagnosable secondary conditions of the body and mind?

The desert has its own rules. Desert people belong to their land and their customs. Many years ago, I began working in the Northern Territory of Australia after relocating from Queensland to begin a drive in/drive out community development role from Alice Springs (Mparntwe), to the very remote Aboriginal community of Nyirripi. Every second week I found myself driving to my workplace in my Toyota Troop Carrier (otherwise known as 'the troopy') off-road, over six hours along the bumpy, pitted Tanami Road (before bitumen) then heading west along the deep sandy slippery Nyirripi Road to work with the beautiful Warlpiri people of the Central Desert, who named me Nungarrayi.

In the early days of remote travel, my fear-based thinking was as juvenile as my initial lack of four-wheel driving skills. Wild camels, snakes, dingoes and wedge-tail eagles reminded me that Australia's outback is uniquely spectacular, particularly on the backdrop of picturesque cloudless blue skies and mass spinifex grasslands. Though, immature to life in the outback, it wasn't long before I realised, I'd let an unwanted visitor join me behind the wheel — toxic me! As a victim of myself, as well as a novice outback driver, the beginning weeks driving in the outback were like riding around the red dirt roads of hell.

Long-distance fear-based thinking was nothing short of an injury-condition waiting to happen. My brain and my troopy engaged in a fraught, toxic relationship, and when my lower back started talking, my ears weren't listening. I soon learned that if I blocked my ears and partied long enough with fear-based thinking, it feels like you're shitting on the inside of the brain, until it's not only a grotesque shade of brown, it's bruised you internally as well as externally. Repetitive, toxic thought-looping found me acting like someone who was blindfolded in a boxing ring with an eight-foot red kangaroo, trying to dodge his powerful foot claws from slicing open my abdomen, adopting the voice of a six-year-old, and hoping not to be labelled as 'that messed-up whitefella!'

Frantically clenching my teeth and frantically clenching the steering while frantically engaging in a toxic fear-based, death-in-the-outback thinking style for hours on end about a future event that had no place in the current moment was de-mobilising. Only to be repeated fortnightly. My fears about getting a flat tyre in 40+ degree heat and hoping that road trains wouldn't slam my butt as they spewed red dirt on my windscreen, caused my body to constantly mirror panic attack symptomology, like a never-ending heart attack on standby. It was a wild ride inside my head, at the same time as dodging wild camels and coping with deep slippery sand along the Nyirripi Road. Then arriving at my community on sunset, to the mis-managed routine of heavy-bag unloading, before my body collapsed at night under extreme physical pain and emotional exhaustion.

Anxiety, back pain, jaw pain and self-doubt had become my new norm. Until, eventually, others took me aside to inform me of their previous (much younger) colleagues who had developed irreparable conditions and were now deceased or permanently out of the workforce as early retirees! There were no formal workplace practices for new outback workers nor preventative measures to protect physical and psychological health, so I turned to research, shared my story with other outback workers and consulted with health professionals. I was determined to reverse my toxic relationship with the troopy as well as eradicate fear-based thoughts from my thinking agenda, in order to enjoy my work with the welcoming Warlpiri people.

I soon learned that when driving for longer than three hours, it is considered Long Distance Driving. I was warned that the effects of long-distance driving in the outback are hugely understated, attributed to thousands of outback workers burning out within only a few weeks. Stories of accidents, hospitalisations, a number of deaths after rolling vehicles, as well as the alarming revolving door of outback recruitment, costing taxpayers millions of dollars each year, as well as total devastation for families. And yet, OH&S documentation within organisational policies was sadly lacking.

Unmanaged physical and emotional stress can easily morph into a strain, *subtly*, morphing into an injury of the rotator cuff (the muscles and tendons that stabilise the shoulder) and other muscles, such as the neck or lower back. Prevention measures soon replaced fear, when I understood the important role of the muscles under our arms and around our lower rib cage, and how important it was to stop, stretch and raise my hands above my head, due to these small muscles easily becoming fatigued. I learned that if I didn't want to engage in the Big Morph, I needed to sound the alarm for support, listen to my body and to begin the *race to trace* of my maladaptive thinking and driving style. It took me a while, though I eventually averted a formal condition, through prevention and early intervention, particularly when I eradicated toxicity by looking at the bull *straight* in the eye.

Myopia – The 20/20 Rule

No level of myopia is safe. Turning a blind eye to the reality in front of us, may compromise our eye health or even lead to blindness. Myopia, described as the irreversible elongation and stretching of the eye, is a growing concern in all age groups, now considered endemic within our younger population (alongside the growing number of other comorbid conditions, such as diabetes). Optometrists are alarmed, working rigorously through publicity campaigns — urgently appealing to the public, particularly to parents, to change their habits before eye sight is permanently impaired.

Myopia is attributed to the excessive use of devices, as well as reduced time enjoying natural light and outdoor activity. The rapid early onset of this ocular disease leads to visual impairment, now considered to be a 21st century global public health issue projected to affect 50% of the world's population by 2050. High Myopia can raise our young people's risk of developing more complicated sight conditions later in life, for example, cataracts, glaucoma and detached retinas. Myopia complications can lead to blindness, therefore without regular eye examinations and early treatment, it can be overlooked. This 'common' vision condition, manages objects in closer proximity, though is often attributed to longer eye sight blurriness, due to the shape of the eye causing light rays to bend (refract) incorrectly by focusing on images *in front* of our retina instead of *on* our retina.

Our incestuous relationship with Big Tech and indoor screen scourge must change if we want to avoid irreversible and highly preventable eye conditions. The disconnection from healthy interaction and movement within our environment is causing our young people's eyes to become part of the prematurely aged society. This is nothing short of a tragedy, a total DISASTER! Although there can be a genetic predisposition, we *can* slow or halt excessive eye growth by re-evaluating our relationship between sunlight and our near-work, as well as the way we manage enduring social isolation and lockdown practices. It must become an active part of our conversations that decreased time in the outside environment is a *significant health hazard.*

Valuing our relationship with our outside environment will increase our opportunity for long-distance sight, particularly if we learn to reduce our near-work intensity. Neglect of eye health does not need to be a tragedy within your household, particularly with the Australian Medicare system providing free yearly check-ups with an optometrist of choice, alongside technological advances in myopia assessments. Why would *any* parent actively increase the risk of myopia, by turning a blind eye to closed bedroom doors?

Parents — we only get one opportunity to raise our children — so there's no point crying out years down the track — 'yes-but I didn't see that charter boat'. Is the 20/20 Rule an automatically programmed part of your life? Recommended lifestyle changes to manage risk include:

(1) spending 120 minutes outdoors
(2) reduction in near-work intensity
(3) adhering to the 20-20 Rule
   - 20 minutes screen time; 20 seconds long-distance viewing
   - 20 minutes of near viewing time (screens, reading, etc) followed by looking into the distance of at least 20 feet (6 metres) for 20 seconds.
   Mivision (December 2021: Issue 174: pg. 84) — 'Myopia Management: Why Eye Length Matters'.
   https://youreyesite.com' what-is-myopia-can-it-be-cured

Diabetes

Please note: This section does not include the genetic condition of Type 1 Diabetes (insulin-dependent diabetes) where the immune system attacks and destroys the insulin-producing cells in the pancreas.

Type 2 diabetes (once common from middle age) is linked to obesity and other enduring lifestyle conditions, yet another tragic epidemic within our younger population. Doctors suggest that it can take around 10 years before this disease is even diagnosed, by which time irreversible damage is often evident. Many doctors believe that current research findings are not reliable as they do not include thousands of those undiagnosed or misdiagnosed, as well as misreported statistics.

Type 2 diabetes is a chronic condition affecting the way the body processes glucose (blood sugar) due to not producing enough insulin. Diabetes can be managed with weight loss, medication and insulin. Risk factors include: obesity, erratic sleep, insomnia, reversal of sleep/wake patterns, increased sedentary lifestyles, insufficient physical activity, increases in sugar-sweetened and low-nutrient food as well as energy drinks.

Obese children often become obese adults, who have a higher risk of suffering breathing conditions, spine problems, chronic migraines, asthma, bone fractures, hypertension and early onset cardiovascular disease and even cancers. The abnormal build-up of glucose in our blood can be dangerous, such as kidney failure, loss of eye sight and limbs, disability, premature death or even ketoacidosis/DKA (excess of blood acid/ketones).

Our brain and our body send messengers to each other. When either or both are under attack and we are not listening, there are SERIOUS ramifications for our neglect. When our body stops producing happy chemicals due to faulty or contaminated instructions (internal flaming) and our maladaptive lifestyle backs up our thoughts, and our enablers reduce pressure to resume our reasonable routines — our body has been instructed to deteriorate. Unless we interrupt its progression in mid-flight, the Titanic will hit an iceberg and sink.

Erectile Dysfunction & Pornography

Therapists report increasing numbers of distraught male clients in their twenties and thirties presenting with general intimacy issues, complicating their love relationships, attributed to erectile dysfunction (a medical condition in which blood flow in the penis is limited or nerves are harmed). Tarzans of the jungle report feeling shocked, angry and confused when they are unable to connect emotionally with their partner, nor to enjoy normal sexual functioning, triggering major issues with anxiety, depression, body image, self-harm and social withdrawal.

General therapists are not sex therapists. Sex therapy is a self-regulated industry — untrained people can actually call themselves sex therapists. Qualified sexologists are professionally trained through university and belong to a regulatory body with guidelines for accreditation. They work in partnership with doctors, initially assessing whether erectile dysfunction or decreased sexual interest is secondary to early warning signs of more serious medical illnesses, for example, prostate, heart disease, high blood pressure or maybe high blood sugar from diabetes. Other factors are taken into consideration such as increased levels of sedentary lifestyle choices and maladaptive coping strategies, including excessive alcohol and drug use.

Men often refuse professional advice for many years, *choosing* instead to emotionally disconnect from their relationships or withdraw from general social interaction and increase their destructive or maladaptive coping strategies as a way of avoiding their demise. Their partners are left feeling anxious, rejected and angry, often questioning their own attractiveness, before becoming uncharitable and sometimes abusive in their confusion. Men, often a shell of their preferred state, are still desperate to seek meaningful connection, often experiencing deep regret when relationships end due to intimacy issues.

In the absence of medical (or other) issues of mind control, there are many males who are turning their focus to their formative years for answers, challenging notions of technology addiction, suggesting that their 'primary addiction' or dopamine drug of choice was not necessarily gaming or an overall addiction to technology. They blame their excessive and uninterrupted time in their bedrooms and their easy access to pornography, as well as 'addictive' masturbation as contributing factors to their 'real life' getting messed up by their 'fantasy life'. Admitting that their view or perception of 'love' relationships became highly distorted from a young age — their counselling goals are to 'reverse my messed up sexual brain architectural system' or 'to learn how to develop secure, respectful attachments, that will sustain future love interests'. (Therapeutic sessions do not continue if issues of criminality or sexual abuse are disclosed as per reporting mandates).

For those raised in privileged families, they are clearly grateful for their lifestyles of comfort. However, many are now analysing the 'style' of parenting they were raised under as a rationale for their current demise. Men who are now in their twenties, thirties or forties are appalled at the way they learned to objectify women from as young as 8–10 years, with many believing that easy access to pornography and addictive masturbation has now become 'impossible' to break. During such retrospective analysis, males are becoming increasingly angry with both parents (as well as other role models) attributed to early exposure to pornography provided to them as a rite of passage, alongside excessive, uninterrupted time in their bedrooms throughout their younger years.

The growing disgust of 'oh well, boys will be boys' is fast becoming a brutally-challenged notion by young people. Why would *any* mother normalise objectification? Why would *any* male role model view pornography as a 'typical' transition to manhood? Men refer to this as a 'damaging blueprint' or a 'lack of love or overall care': a form of parental neglect. Many are embarrassed to discover they are relationally behind by many years in comparison with their high-functioning male counterparts.

Some men begin counselling when they become fathers of daughters, with fears around their daughter choosing a relationship with 'someone like me', fearful of history repeating itself. At the same time, they are well aware of the dangers of maintaining their defence blame-game against their bloodline connections. They agree that eventually we reach an age where individual choice means taking personal responsibility for our *own* choices, as well as reversing our own blueprint.

Therapists report an overall decrease in younger-gen couples enjoying their sexual relationships (and an alarmingly high level of low fertility issues since 2021). Men report; performance anxiety, body image issues, sexual confusion, an overfocus on self with minimal ability to connect to their partner on an emotional level, as well as an increased use of sex toys. Others report not knowing *how* to sexually please their partner without toys, due to a shameful earlier life misbelief that the 'women's role is to please the man', such as roleplayed within his child-porn mindset.

As he begins to reconcile with the fact his brain was hijacked by the trillion-dollar pornography industry from a very young age, alongside uninterrupted time in his bedroom under a culture of privilege and 'porn-normalisation', he struggles to know *how* to transition from the world of youthful confidence (boy psychology) into the world of true intimacy within adult relationships (man psychology).

Introducing Anhedonia, the happy-chemical destroyer, the place of pleasure-less grey, where our usual activities are replaced with social withdrawal and lack of relationship. The ability to feel pleasure diminishes and not even the rewards of previous hobbies engender motivation. So, why would it *not* be a surprise when there's a loss of libido and an overall loss of intimacy?

Females suggest that during the 'love bubble stage' of their new relationship, she's eager to please, often becoming overly compromising and willing to overlook reality. Though, when erectile dysfunction or his lack of sexual intimacy emerges, she turns inwards to her own body image or wonders if her personality is to blame. 'Maybe he's threatened by me being an independent woman?'; or 'I'm probably too clingy and demanding'; 'I don't give him enough space'; 'is it because of his drinking or drugs'; 'maybe he needs more time for his hobbies?'

She chats with her peers, who also report similar frustrations, as they generationally norm their demise together. They all frantically self-analyse — 'maybe I'm just a sex addict', 'or too much of a Karen?', 'do I lack empathy', 'maybe he's intimidated by me?', norming the increased use of sex toys as well as 'giving in' to kinky preferences, though fully aware of the changes within their relationship contract.

Disappointment — the painful gap between our expectations and our reality, particularly by the people we trusted the most.

Her gut begins to churn when she thinks about how secretive he is — when passwords are unknown, when online chat rooms appear to be taking first place to her needs and his eye contact is increasingly flaky. Left rummaging around in her own thoughts, she begins to feel bored, bitter and confused rather than motivated to fit the pieces of the puzzle together. She begins her emancipation process, slowly pulling away and imagining her way out of the confusing, stunted, child-adult relationship she has found herself in.

Feeling emasculated, like a deprivation of his masculinity, a shadow of his former or future-projected self, he withdraws into the closeted walls of his inner world and disconnects from the outside world, not daring to share his demise, mourning the loss of the love of his life.

When the Table Turns — enablers becoming unwell

Turning back to enablers who have formed unusual bonds with their one-way street takers (partners or adult children), the sobering time eventually arrives when *they* are the ones in genuine need. Many enablers admit to experiencing 'shock likened to being in a head-on car accident' when it's *their* turn to experience kindness and yet they are treated with contempt. After a health diagnosis or other overwhelming circumstance, many are dismissed or minimised by their loved ones. The giver had always assumed that when (or if) they were placed in a vulnerable situation, their loved one/s would be super-eager to naturally pick up the slack or simply know *how* to support.

The sufferer, now in a new, fragile, position becomes reliant on the one-way kindness of others, as they begin to adjust to their frightening new reality. Sufferers are initially baffled when they are treated with remarkably low empathy from their loved ones, with some even experiencing hostility or victimisation from the people who are usually dependent upon *them* for their survival. These cruel dependents expect that *their* circumstances 'should not have to change', hoping that the sufferer's insurance or WorkCover *should still* cover the family's costs.

The devastation of realising that love has only been a one-way street becomes an increased health hazard for the physically unwell over-giver (such as those beginning cancer treatment programs). This massive reality or brain-bomb, sends toxic ripples through the body, like a scorched earth event, rendering some with shock reactions similar to being thrown overboard from a luxury liner with no life jacket and desperately trying to swim to shore in the middle of an arctic winter's night. The pendulum swings and the brain oscillates between hate and revenge, with words such as 'burnout' and 'breakdown' appearing on the public sphere for the first time, with 'nice' now, nowhere in sight.

The first counselling session reveals that the weary over-giver has been conversing with Dr Google, convinced that their loved ones' neural architecture must be the reason they are 'so abusively neglectful', as psychopathy is a disease of the emotional circuitry of the brain, particularly the part that deals with interpersonal emotions. 'Their brain is hard-wired differently so that's why there's reduced activity in the amygdala and they can't control or process their emotions'. Or, suggesting that their loved one is actually a 'true narcissist' and they have been 'gas lighting' me for years, or 'could even be a sociopath, *as well as* on the autism scale, which is why they have no social cues at all?'

Rather than viewing the role they have played in overkindness and disempowerment, these wounded heroes admit that their loved-one *once* displayed healthy patterns of empathy, engaged in healthy peer relationships, participated in the principle of reciprocation and met their developmental milestones with minimal reports of anti-social behavioural patterns. Sadly, as the psychiatry field reminds us — if any of us act in a particular way, for long enough, and then turn to pathology for the answers (with Dr Google in tow), it's pretty easy to meet criteria for at least a few labels, and medicated for a bunch of highly avoidable conditions!

Words from our Young People (earlier years of social withdrawal)

'I was too embarrassed to talk about my reality.'

'My parents shouldn't have rescued me back home.'

'I didn't need my parents to problem-solve for me.'

'My parents just chucked money at my problems.'

'I eventually didn't know how to get back to my old life.'

'My friends were around in the early days but then they just fell away, I don't blame them, I shut them out and then used them when it suited me.'

'It was like being in public with people but spaced out, like I was drunk but I hadn't even been drinking.'

'I started feeling like a freak, I lost my voice. Who wants to hang out with a freak?'

'I had everything I needed in my room. It was easy, until it wasn't easy to get back out.'

'I became petrified of the real world. It was weird, I was scared, maybe paranoid of others hurting me, even people I knew.'

'Big Daddy was always our family rescuer; it wasn't hard for him to bail me out.'

'Back in the early days, I didn't think I needed a career. My olds are rich, so I thought their money was mine anyway, or at least it would be my money and my house eventually.'

'My parents were embarrassed by me so they just turned a blind-eye and pretended that I wasn't hanging around home, it was like I didn't even exist.'

'When my parents had visitors, I hated it in case they joked about me, or their friends tried to convince my parents to get me to leave home or force me to get a job.'

'I don't know why my parents didn't expect me to do any jobs around the house, they just let me game for days on end, even though my back and neck always hurt and I had to get glasses.'

'My father gave up the fight, he started standing back and letting my step-mum just take over me.'

'Even though I ended up at home for years, it was like I was petrified of my parents abandoning me. How would I be able to provide for myself if I couldn't even get out of the house? I spent so many hours worried about the future.'

'There were plenty of times I thought about ending it all, there was no light at the end of the tunnel. I didn't do it because I kept thinking about the pain.'

'The day was my night. The night made more sense. I was left alone. I thought about topping myself all the time. It was part of my life. I had an escape.'

'I was forced to see counsellors. I was pretty rude to some of them, especially when they tried to talk about working. How was I going to work, the idiots.'

'When I left home, my parents bought my first car, set me up in their investment property, even bought me new furniture because they just wanted me to get through Uni. When things went pear-shaped, I was 'taken' back home.'

'My mates whose olds forced them to buy their own first car were jealous of me, telling me how easy my life was. Now they're nailing life and I still think the world owes me a favour.'

'My olds brought a counsellor into my house and he even came into my bedroom. It was one of the worst experiences of my life, even worse than the problem that caused me to retreat in the first place. It was like I had NO safe place on this planet, like an invasion, I lost my shit. After that, I punched holes in the walls and I tried to end it so they put me in hospital — after that everyone just left me alone and that's how it's been for 10 years.'

TOTAL RESET

Foundationally Re-wiring our Brain

Reject secondary conditions. Fight back by waging a civil war against the dark rulers of your mind. Take back the years that the locusts have eaten by rewiring and protecting the geographical landscape of your brain.

Let's turn to ad hoc notions of Reset by analysing your relationship with light, as well as the external and internal architectural design of your brain. If you *could* print out in glossy form your own architecturally designed home, what would your façade resemble? What style/s would you choose to internally decorate the inside rooms of your home? Would they reflect your personality, at the same time as adhering to your new blueprint and building codes as recommended by your structural engineer?

Would you create a new framework (blank canvass) by pressing the Total Reset Button and redefining your own external and internal foundational architectural system? Or would you re-vamp your current style by an upgrade, renovation or an extension to your current structure? Is your style architecturally intertwined within someone else's architectural system?

Rewiring our brain is more than 'doing' a bunch of sensible things and 'saying' a bunch of grateful statements for a few months and then 'trying' to skip through the tulips or bounce around on white fluffy clouds. Strategic visual planning and spontaneity, mixed with determination are vital ingredients for a Reset — that is, when we've made a decision to become our own architectural designer.

Roots, Reality and Dreams

The marriage between neuroscience and architecture is still in its honeymoon years. We are now learning that our connection to light and our relationship with our environment is often a direct indication of our overall physical and mental 'health'. Are you a shadow of your true authentic self, due to your reduction or dislocation from light?

What is your relationship with light? Stand in the middle of your bedroom and lounge — what do you see when you 360?

Is light restricted or dull? Is there clutter? Is everything minimalist? Is there a juvenile basic survival feel? Is light optimised in terms of the seamless integration between your inside rooms and the outside world?

Historically, architects have been influenced by science in terms of intuitively understanding the link between architectural structures and the influence on people's states of mind. Science is aware of the way that certain levels of light and noise in neonatal care units can interfere with critical sensory development in premature infants. For those impacted by Alzheimer's disease, there is now an understanding that group home designs incorporating space and connection between inside and outside maintains connection with the physical environment in order to improve functioning. It's also well understood how worship building designs can evoke immediate feelings of reverence or sacredness when people walk through arches, high ceilings or stained-glass rooms, such as cathedrals or places of worship.

It is now widely recognised that school children often struggle with energy and concentration, therefore modern learning environments are now being developed to optimise the relationship between natural light and air flow in classrooms. Such as pseudo-classrooms situated outside of the classroom for students to combine learning with environmental nutrients. Featured recently on television with students working in solar powered workstations — generous-sized undercover learning stations, powered with multi-plugs for devices and Wi-Fi, with easy access to their educators who were located in other parts of the school.

Workplaces are also increasingly recognising the growing number of absenteeism and poor work performance with staff reporting significant issues with depression, anxiety, lower back pain and so on. Work health and safety officers are mindful of the relationship between reduced environmental access and poor work performance as well as external building designs that do little to engender creativity. Sitting in dreary, windowless spaces for an average of eight hours per working day under artificial lights (as well as new work from home spaces) takes its toll on our mental health and our physical health.

Biophilia architecture is believed to improve worker wellbeing and increase productivity, due to the establishment of a visual relationship with light rather than shadows. The environment connects humans with nature, encouraging designers to scope characteristics of the natural world to fit into inside spaces, such as plants, stones, greenery and natural light, with elements like wood and stone. This is in contrast to ad hoc architectural styles that create dislocation, and distort reality by engulfing vision, such as de-constructive building design that appears to do little to engender creativity.

Our brain lives in a house. The structural design of our 'head office' is architecturally designed according to a blueprint or plan (within the professional expertise of the designer) taking into consideration the laws of the land and risk mitigation — such as an understanding of climatic extremes, building materials and tools (stone, sand, clay, wood, steel or copper), geographic location, environmental stressors and the cultural and spiritual norms of a region.

The foundation of our home bears the entire weight of the house, usually made of concrete, dug into the earth for additional stability. Once our base is secure, our building framework is erected with beams and walls, doors, as well as rooms with open spaces that often provide a visual link to the outside environment. The façade of our home is uniquely designed according to a particular architectural style/s, with roots often dating back many centuries and then modernised, climatised, culturalised and even politicised to match the current day. Our roof seals our shelter and provides protection and comfort from the outside elements, completing the overall framework for life inside our home.

Behind the walls of our home is an interesting life of internal circuitry (neuron pathways), working hard to ensure the continuity of our immediate heating and cooling (hormones, veins) and our connection to light to enhance our sleep, eat, play and work within our home environment. Neuroscientists are still discovering the way that neurons 'head-chatter' between the various rooms (departments) — like a system of genetically synchronised parts that seek order and pleasure, which takes into consideration our genetic makeup, strengths, weaknesses, personality and our predispositions. Are some of your rooms permanently hardwired? Is it possible for you to rewire your brain architectural system by challenging the legitimacy of your own building codes?

How well do you know yourself in terms of your brain architectural system? Does the geographical landscape of your brain reflect your Roots, your Reality and your Dreams? If not, is it time for a Reset?

3.1 — Strategy: Describe your Brain

How would you *currently* describe your brain functionality? What metaphors describe your brain? What percentage of your brain space is free for creativity?

Typical answers to the above — 'My brain is messy and sore, like a bunch of black clouds with around 20% functionality'; 'I desperately need to take my brain on a holiday: it sounds like a freight train with literally zero space to hear myself think'; 'My brain chatter doesn't stop, it's like I'm living in a constant whirlpool'; 'it's like I'm in a room full of people, and I'm only rational 40% of the time.'

TOTAL RESET

Gran's Story of Rubble to Ruby

As a young child, I remember my paternal grandmother's stories of survival in Hawkes Bay, New Zealand in the 1930s and 1940s. One such story was set in the middle of the worst economic downturn in history — The Great Depression, when a deadly earthquake, followed by destructive fires, dismantled the small seaside town of Napier, declaring a state of disaster. Gran recalled two and a half minutes of sheer torture as the earth shook and time stood still. Vivid stories of young mothers deaf-defying screams, trying unsuccessfully to save the lives of their babies as buildings collapsed around them and bricks and mortar became deadly missiles, landing in prams and targeting humans like demonic rays from hell.

My Gran could never forget the 3rd of February 1931 when an entire region was forced to endure the cruel 7.8-magnitude earthquake. There were over 250 lives lost and desperate attempts to pull bodies out of department stores and air-crushed vehicles resembling match box toys. The majority of buildings were damaged or in rubble, with remaining homes deemed unliveable. The land and sea floor were raised by as much as an incredible 2.7 metres, entirely changing the coastline and general landscape.

It was difficult to imagine Gran's account of the land ending up on 'a tilt' after the frightening, deadly earthquake had inflicted its worst. Unbelievably, the locals suffered around 520 aftershocks for the next two weeks, as well as the uncontrollable fires breaking out all over town (due to gas jets' close proximity to flammable liquids) that were unmanaged due to the earthquake cutting the water supplies. I imagined all those frightened little kids and adults living in their backyards and front yards, or on the side of the streets before they were moved to parks or other safer areas outside their local area. Life was indeed bleak. The future appeared dismal, without hope.

The government moved residents to makeshift tent towns in local parks and set up an emergency hospital in the racecourse, for what had become 'the city of the dead'. The residents in the heart of the rubble had no way of retaining their old life. Most buildings had collapsed or were deemed as an unsuitable risk for habitation. Hundreds were forced to seek other accommodation whilst mourning their reality and planning their future. Most residents, due to the economic depression, had no building insurance, which meant they were left to continue to pay mortgages on homes that didn't even exist.

Manipulating weakness to strengthen a region can change the overall DNA within an entire culture. While the world validated Napier's grief, their initial months were dark and daunting as the reality of their re-build began. Two culturally inherited predispositions found in most New Zealanders — stoicism and creative determination — turned up soon after the earthquake, forming a solid foundation for recovery. Failure to relaunch was not an option. Hardship will always provide humans with a launch-pad for instinctual survival, particularly when a 'whole of community' mindset unifies.

Reconstruction from a blank canvass takes only one creative recovery mindset to potentially influence the masses. Turning a disaster into a treasure is marked by a particular characteristic — *planting a seed of possibility.* Cultivating that seed and turning a disaster into an impressive infrastructural and economic system that sustains generations to come is truly a remarkable feat.

Prior to the 1931 earthquake, Stanley Nautisch, a local Hawkes Bay architect, had attended a building exhibition in France and was impressed with the new Art Deco building style that opposed the dark and dreary European architectural styles of the 19th Century. Art Deco (1920–1940) represented a modernised and optimistic change in building design and was considered a breath of fresh air known for its classical stripes, geometric shapes and colourful arches as well as economic viability (https://media.newzealand. com/ en/story-ideas/napier-new-zealands-art-deco-capital).

It's not hard to imagine this radicalised period of time when watching movies such as *The Great Gatsby* with its colourful glamour, opulence, charisma and energy. Art Deco first orig-inated as a European radicalisation with splashes of ancient cultural influences, such as Egyptian symbolism, alongside a tit-illating-for-the-time 'rule breaker' fashion for women, signifying new social freedoms — short skirts, short hair and jazz dancing. Mirroring the broader global reality at the time — power *and speed* — the new era of skyscrapers and developments in trans-port, technology and communication.

It was no doubt challenging upholding traditional Maori cul-ture by combining European modernism within a region with geographic, climatic and economic constraints, particularly the lack of availability of building materials. Laying aside ego and creative ownership, Nautisch pulled together a Building Tribe by combining four architectural practices, becoming a unified Head Office. They began working together around the clock, adhering to strict new building codes, to begin The Great New Experiment of Napier.

Art Deco was considered economical and safe, as well as eas-ily adhering to the new earthquake and fire building codes. The new colourful stucco concrete buildings were earthquake and fire resistance. Re-birth amongst insurmountable predisposed geo-graphical weaknesses such as ongoing earthquakes and volcanic activity was a sobering reality. Research suggests that there are around 20,000 earthquakes annually, with Mount Ruapehu, Taupo considered as one of the most active volcanoes in New Zealand (seismicresilience.org.nz). The Alpine Fault runs through the length of the South Island and the North Island Fault System — *always* a concern, attributed to the way it sits on the Pacific 'Ring of Fire' with hot spots well known for volcanic activity.

Many residents were still paying off their original mortgages for properties that were now in rubble, though, despite their 'rock bottom' financials, they gained additional mortgages to rebuild structurally safe new homes. Miraculously, within two years, Napier emerged from the grave as a new modernised Art Deco city, uniquely reconstructed within local tradition, with a hint of Spanish Mission influence. By the end of the decade, Napier was referred to as 'the newest city centre on the globe'. Today, Napier is considered to be the proud and colourful 'Art Deco Capital of the World', captured in Peter Wells' film, *Newest City On the Globe*.

Our roots can provide answers to the flavours and colours of our genetic brain architectural system, as well as our appetite for risk. Until I understood one 'part' of my cultural foundation, I wondered why I was so drawn to the simplicity of stucco buildings (cement, water, sand and lime) with their round, shapely curves and arches, as well as the 1920's era with its provocative colours and risk taking.

A blank canvass mindset begins by initiating your own decision to Reset — modernising our thinking and being prepared to adapt to a new set of circumstances. The Theme that comes to mind when I visualise my elders' darkest day is how the people became A Symbol of Optimism in the face of adversity. When a cultural mindset coagulates with a powerful visual optimiser, we *can* rebuild from disaster, even in the face of insurmountable obstacles. My relatives love celebrating our elders' challenging past, at the annual Art Deco Week in Napier, dressing up in 1920s-1930's clothing, joining with literally thousands of people who fly in from all around the world each year — in celebration of their Art Deco roots — relaying the story of 'Rubble to Ruby'.

Moore and Gillette (1990) remind us of Jung's collective unconscious theory that link us to the deep-seated beliefs and behavioural instincts from the collective experiences of humanity. Our genetic inheritance can maintain inherited patterns or, with our objective psyche, positively alter our future. Therefore, it's important to be responsible (or aware) of what we are not responsible for!

Gran was raised by loving parents. She *chose* to marry a brutal man. She told me that her engagement period was frightening, and she was aware of the cruel DNA splintered throughout my grandfather's family of origin ... which replicated throughout the lives of her own offspring. Gran, eventually divorced from cruelty, remained single, though sadly was often estranged from her children. Our genetic links and our connection to the intergenerational trauma of our ancestors (collective unconscious) can impact our own life, as it plays out within our instinctual patterns, particularly when we are forming our character in our earlier childhood years. Thank God, we can break the spiritual links to destructive genetic hardwiring, and rewire our personal foundational architecture: positively altering our characteristic human reactions!

Whilst Gran tried to live a champagne lifestyle on barely a chardonnay budget, my Nan (maternal grandmother) was afforded an upper-class lifestyle in Gisborne, New Zealand, due to my grandfather's career. My maternal grandparents abhorred class snobbery and discrimination, maintained values of honouring First Nations people, education and hard work, alongside their generous spirit, linked to strong family values. Nan's love of antiques, particularly Queen Victorian (1837-1901) antique furniture fascinated me and eventually slowly infiltrated the homes of most of our family, particularly after she passed.

Nan's antiques were symbolic of her parents' and grandparents' era in the 18th century and in many ways, she remained connected to the staunch values, ideals and routines of that era, easily seen in her decorating style from the Victorian, Georgian and Edwardian eras. Unlike the spontaneous, tangential nature of Gran who drew on the great outdoors for her serenity, my Nan was calm, ordered, planned and indoor-focused. It's important to understand that our roots can link us to sub-conscious patterns that are played out in parts of our life.

Laying aside notions of 'nature versus nurture' (genetics vs environment) — have we adopted a blame mentality for our childhood architectural system that now requires a facelift? Are we ready for a balcony extension or a partial renovation in order to welcome the warmth of the winter sun? Are we finely tuned to automatic responses that are tripping or overloading our internal brain circuitry? Are there any foundational flaws that give us the impression that we are on a journey without a roadmap?

Rational, Real, and Radical

The Open-Door Policy

Visualisation is powerful — open the light at the end of the tunnel and view your potential.

There are No Closed Doors. See, hear and then walk in the direction of your destiny.

3.2 — Strategy: A Decision with Visualisation — See, Hear and Walk to your Purpose

Decide to Move Forward. Visualise your Plan (Visualise to Actualise). Tell your brain where you are heading *without eliciting maladaptive emotions.*

See - What do you see in your new life? (goals/metaphors)

Hear - What are your ears saying? (theme)

Walk - What direction are your legs walking? (planning for action)

For example — my new life will be productive; I see financial independence and I can *hear* others encouraging me that 'it's time to move forward' (self-talk and tribal truth) ..... therefore, my *legs* are walking in the direction of *connection.* Adaptive emotion — Relief? Motivation?

Reset your future by refusing to be defined by your past!

Chapter 4
Parenting Styles, Developmental Stages & Adolescent History

Chapter 4 highlights a few of the *many* parenting styles that are discussed and publicised these days, alongside theories and models around developmental stages across the lifespan. Keeping in mind we are unlikely to fit neatly into a purely one-size fits-all parenting style, nor do we transition through our developmental stages in exactly the same way. Though, without an evolving and transparent plan for modern parenting, raising young people is, surely, like sailing blindfolded into the eye of a storm.

Once upon a time, parents looked at their wee babe through the vista of a bright, purposeful future. Now parents are crying out, 'Oh, God, where did we go wrong, and how do we prepare our kids for life down under within our strange new world order?' Can hindsight provide parents with answers, or is it now too late?

CAVE DAY SURVIVAL RULES

Back in the prehistoric 'cave days', emotions were generated as a calculated act of survival for the species. Historical records suggest that men between 15 and 50 years of age were expected to be on-guard and ready to fight to the death *at all times*. Men were considered no use to their tribe if they were not capable of rapidly inducing fear-based chemicals, such as rage-anger (within around 10 seconds) in order to prepare for battle, which *could* mean fighting to the death.

The notion of fear was once culturally linked to the notion of Loss — such as full tribal extinction, mutilation, attack, invasion or potential loss of autonomy. Today, it's obvious we've left our fear-based switch ON! — seen in the escalation of fear-based chemicals running rampant in our society (anxiety, panic and rage-anger) rather than our rationality winning the majority of the battles in our mind. Have we replaced our basic notion of 'survival' to one that over-focuses or prioritises fear-driven ego notions such as Separation (fear of abandonment, rejection, loneliness and spiritual disconnection) and False Ego (sense of worth, esteem, narcissism and codependency)?

Cave day men were powerful, lean, mean-protection-machines. They were deemed of no use to their tribe if they were weak and were subsequently killed by their fathers or elders. Cave day women were also expected to rapidly induce fear-based chemicals to protect those not involved in physical battle. The manic energy created by the body through eliciting fear-based chemicals ensured that there was sufficient 'retreating' energy to hide their kids, sick and elderly, while their men fought to (hopefully) protect their culture and land. If their men lost the battle, they knew their enemy would seek to destroy the remaining tribe.

Was it any wonder that brutal rites of passage and transition to adulthood practices were imperative for the overall survival of an entire culture in our prehistoric days? Moore and Gillette (1990: xix:4) point out that anthropologists universally agree that cave sanctuaries were created 'by men, for men' for the ritual initiation of boys into the mysterious world of male responsibility and masculine spirituality. Many ritual initiatory processes still survive in tribal cultures to this day. The crisis in mature masculinity feeds into the global crisis of our overall survival that we are currently facing as a species: the world needs mature adults if our race is to survive into the future.

Before 1920's — No Teens!

Prior to the 1920s, the notion of 'adolescence' didn't exist. You were either a child at school or an adult at work. Unless you were from upper-class families, it was common for children from around 10 years of age to transition straight from the classroom to full-time work. Children who worked from this age put food on the table for their families and they were *not* considered to be in need of care, nor was it considered child abuse or slave labour within their 'men don't cry' culture. The transition from school to work was once the rite of passage into adulthood. There was no focus on travelling abroad, sexuality, educational opportunities, gap years or extended time to contemplate career pathways. Children understood the concept of work-to-eat from a young age. A 10-year-old was once an adult.

Stanley's Adolescence

Although the first use of the word 'adolescence' appeared in the 15th century, described as 'growing up into maturity', it wasn't until 1904 that American psychologist Stanley Hall, was credited with the notion of 'adolescence'. This was influenced by social changes at the turn of the century, as well as legislative changes around child labour laws and universal education. Hall was reportedly not at all impressed, that under the new legislation, young people now had less responsibilities and more freedoms, believing that society needed to 'burn out the vestiges of evil in their nature', as adolescence was a time of overcoming beast-like impulses, engulfed in a period of 'storm and stress'. Identifying three key aspects of this phase as (1) mood disruptions, (2) conflict with parents, and (3) risky behaviour (Lerner 2005, p. 4).

Drawing upon the earlier work of Freud, Piaget (1936), Maslow, Erikson and Kohlberg in relation to lifespan developmental stages, child psychologist Peter Blos, otherwise known as Mr Adolescence, published his book, *On Adolescence* in 1962. Blos, a German-born American, focused on teen conflict and dilemma in terms of their desire for maturity and achieving independence by breaking free of parental constraint, at the same time as wanting to remain dependent. Blos suggested that maturity depends on independence with adolescence providing an important opportunity to explore 'a sense of self' and one's potential within a collective culture, valuing the overall notion of interdependence. *(Throughout the world today, there are still societies who don't recognise adolescence as a phase of life)*.

Although rights for education and the abolishment of the child working laws were a liberating move forward for young people, research from the 1970s suggests that society became overly focused on marking adolescence as a period of 'storm and stress', adopting a 'teen as broken' mentality, as opposed to adolescence as an opportunity to become self-sufficient.

By 1972 Parliament abolished military conscription in Australia. Literature on adolescence began to focus on risk and psychological diagnosis, addictions and suicidal ideation, alongside escalating sexism and cruelty/domestic violence. By the 1980s and the 1990s, adolescence was considered an important developmental stage and 'the process through which young people acquire the social, cognitive, and emotional skills and abilities required to navigate life' (University of Minnesota Cooperative Extensions, 2005).

History provides us with insight into the impact of legislative changes and evolving notions of adolescent psychology. Children's early transition into the labour force and the abolishment of forced non-identity, through military conscription, gave youth increased time to focus on 'self'. No longer *forced* Tarzans of the military jungle, nor were they expected to participate in 'discomfort to grow' regimes such as pseudo-rituals, left young people with increased opportunity to focus on mood, pathology, sexuality, gender identity, and targeted career/education choices.

Modern Life in Australia

Young people in Australia are no longer forced to take up arms, though parents often lay aside the fact that their sons are carrying a loaded gun in early puberty — boys can become fathers even before adolescence. Although the actual onset of puberty and fertility can vary widely for boys, it's possible for a young male to begin producing sperm as early as nine years of age, though commonly between 10 and 12 years. Males can impregnate by shooting their load from a strategic part of their apparatus when triggered, though today, overwhelmingly large numbers are stating that their navigational skills to strategically tumult their way out of the corner of a boxing ring, when in a state of agitation or distress (without becoming retreaters or aggressors), is sadly declining.

Hundreds of parents agree that had they known what the future would hold, they would *not* have let *their* minds nor the minds of *their young* become addicted and overly reliant on technology. Nor would they have let their young person shut their doors on their dilemmas and call their bedroom a 'social life' — while continuing to butter their big-kids' toast and bullet their fluffy milkshakes, disconnected from the unusual way their offspring meander out of their bedrooms for breakfast at 2pm.

Parents admit that less responsibility and increased addiction has caused the upper body strength of their offspring to be as fragile as their confidence, with their brittle-boned problem-solving feet often at a directional loss within strange ring-roads of confusion. Has the lack of open and honest 'uncomfortable' communication left our young people's defence and repair system wide open to invasion due to our lack of focus around building psychological immunity during the formative parenting years? At a deep level, parents of adult children are now well aware that the likelihood of their offspring being able to protect themselves, let alone our nation as a whole, is slipping away before our very eyes, diminishing more and more as the months and years roll by. Is it time to turn our hope towards our 10+ year olds?

Parents, with heads hanging low and a bucketload of 'it's too late' regrets tucked under their belts, *know* that Australia desperately needs 'our young men' to cut the apron strings that are incestuously attached to the boob tube and to broaden their moral conscience — to fight for our sovereignty ... before it's brain-chippin' too late.

Real Life Starts at 10 — The Age of Criminal Responsibility

In Australia, the age of criminal responsibility is 10 years. Google searches suggest that currently we have around 600 children in prisons in Australia. Boys behind bars, treated like men, deprived of their liberty, in chains without their carers for protection, forced to account for their choices. How would your young person cope without you, living in a prison cell, as a way of being held to account for his choices?

Since 1963, Australian Federal Laws state that the age of criminal responsibility, in terms of conviction and imprisonable sentencing, starts from 10 years of age. This is linked to research and developmental theories that suggest by 10 years we are capable of reasonable decision-making as well as understanding the consequences of our choices. In other words, if your child commits a heinous crime from 10 years of age, they can receive an imprisonable sentence.

The United Nations Committee on the Rights of the Child has urged Australia to consider raising the age of criminal responsibility to 14 years. If your child commits any serious or heinous crimes, they are charged with a criminal offence under the Youth Justice Act in their State or Territory. They often appear a number of times in court, supported by defence lawyers, the child's lawyer and justice officers who complete intensive family assessments, dissecting the history of the family system, and then presenting their labour-intensive findings in a pre-sentence report to court. Children can walk out of court in chains to their new bedroom life behind bars. After worshipping the pain or pleasure of their risky youth in the community, they are locked away from society — a tragedy with no winners.

In Australia, Legal Adulthood begins at 18 years. From 18 years of age you are no longer subject to the Youth Justice Act. You are seen as an adult in the eyes of the law and community. You can drink, vote, own a credit card, join the armed forces and so on. If you commit a criminal act, you can be sentenced to a term in adult prison, though you will not have any case workers advocating for your rights, nor is anyone paid to care. Landing in a cell on a wing and a prayer, to a new culture with the Big Boys of the prison world.

Neuroscience maturation age is 25 years (unless diagnosed as cognitively impaired). It is believed that by the age of 25 years, the maturation of the prefrontal cortex is fully accomplished, reaching full physical and intellectual maturity, as dictated by the region of the brain that assists with executive functioning, rationality, planning, empathy, reciprocation and reality fact-checking. However, these days ... is the topic of maturation fast becoming controversial, attributed to the increasingly large number of males who admit that although they are now indeed well beyond 25 years, they are *not* functioning as adults? Males are often quick to admit that their addictive culture and their reward-junkie and/or praise-dependent mindsets are clashing with their *need* to be raised in a consequent-dependent household.

Baby Brain

The brain is the command centre of the human body and our most valuable diamond. When a baby is born their brain is generally around a quarter of the size of an adult brain, doubling in size within their first 12 months. By around three years of age, it is estimated their brain will be approximately 80% of an adult's brain, and by five years of age it will be approximately 90%. The brain is the ultimate co-coordinator of our words, our relationships, our movements and our ability to pass on our genes.

Our brain architecture comprises of trillions of connections between individual neurons across different areas of the brain. Although new connections can form throughout life and unused connections can continue to be pruned, the early years are thought to be the most active period for establishing neural connections.

Attachment Theory

The brain begins to develop from the womb, though needs socialisation to mature. When a baby arrives having survived the potential graveyard of the womb (the battle between commitment, nature and contentious legislation), our parenting role begins with a complex mix of child protection and self-preservation. Our main role is to keep our child alive, as well as protected from influences that could constitute a breach in their human rights.

The way we form our early attachments can affect the way we seek, keep and end relationships throughout our lifetime. Psychological Attachment Theory suggests that children need to develop a relationship with at least one primary caregiver in order for normal social and emotional development to occur. Renowned childhood development theorists, psychologist John Bowlby (1960-1970) and Ainsworth and Bell (1960s) believe that from infanthood we have an innate need to form healthy attachments, and maintain psychological connection, which can have a lasting impact on how we relate to others as we grow older.

1. **Secure Attachment (autonomous)**
2. **In-secure - Anxious Attachment** (fears of rejection or abandonment)
3. **In-secure - Avoidant Attachment** - (ambivalent / resistant / detached)
4. **In-secure - Disorganised/unpredictable Attachment** (poor self-image, erratic behaviour, depression)

The psychologically invisible link between children and their primary carers is suggested to play out in the way they interact within their relationships. When adults respond sensitively, appropriately and consistently to their young child's needs, the child feels a sense of security within their attachment relationship and will duplicate this within other relationships as they grow. The Circle of Security is one (of many) popular attachment programs, focusing on the differences between secure and insecure parenting styles in terms of psychological growth as well as the impact of interrupters (such as family conflict).

Stages of Neural Brain Development

Our physical, social, emotional and cognitive development is strongly influenced by our environment and our early life experiences, with much of our neural growth believed to be reflected within a series of 'stages' — (1) Neurogenesis; (2) Cell Migration; (3) Cell Differentiation; (4) Synaptogenesis; (5) Neuronal Cell Death; and (6) Synapse Rearrangement.

Swiss psychologist Jean Piaget (1936) suggested that alongside our brain development, there are four stages of cognitive development, referred to as: (1) sensorimotor stage/object permanence (birth — 2 years); (2) preoperational stage/symbolic thought (2-7 years); (3) concrete operational stage/operational thought (7-11 years); and (4) formal operation stage/abstract concepts (11+).

This differs slightly from Erik Erikson's four growth stages (19021994): Infancy (birth — 2 years); Early Childhood (3-8 years); Middle Childhood (9-11 years); and Adolescence (12-18 years). Erikson modified Freud's controversial psychosexual theories, maintaining that there are eight stages of Psychosocial Development that secure our personality:

1. Trust vs Mistrust
2. Autonomy vs Shame and Doubt
3. Initiative vs Guild

4. Industry vs Inferiority
5. Identity vs Confusion
6. Intimacy vs Isolation
7. Generativity vs Stagnation
8. Integrity vs Despair

Parenting Styles

A retrospective sadness has fallen upon many post-war boomers and their offspring as they contemplate the consequences of their parenting styles within the context of our modern reality. The lost child-adults of the new millennium. Though they've fallen head first into the net, must they remain in the crib? When our crib-men continue to shut their bedroom doors and play in their polka dot pyjamas, it surely leaves our country, as well as our way of life, in a vulnerable and unprotected state.

A system is referred to as a group of interacting or interrelated elements that act according to a set of rules, forming a unified whole. Surrounded and influenced by its environment, a system is evidenced by boundaries, structure and purpose and is expressed in the way it functions.

Parents increasingly discover that their own upbringing (parenting styles and attachments — secure or insecure) can impact the *system* that they create for their own children. They often adopt a little piece of one style, and a snippet of another, chucking their children's hopes for the future into the simmering pot with the aim of surviving their messy world without being combat-rolled, as they tumble through the formative years of their children's lives.

There are as many different parenting systems and attachment styles as there are days of the year. Books, research, modern television shows and parents themselves constantly discuss styles of parenting ranging from Secure (autonomous) to Anxious (preoccupied) or Avoidant (dismissing) and Disorganised (unresolved) as listed below. Parenting, of course, would be a breeze if each child arrived with their own specifically tailored manual of 'How to Raise An Adult'.

Types of Parenting Styles:

1. **Disciplinarian/Authoritarian (Secure)** — tough love — patient and emotionally generous. Parenting experts suggest this is the most effective parenting style in terms of optimising academic, social, emotional and behavioural health. Parents have high expectations of their children, though expect even more from their own behaviour. Parents are not competing with their child's ego, nor are children competing with their parents' workplace or the local BottleO.

2. **Permissive or Indulgent (disorganised)** — child steers the family. Parents are non-directive, lenient, liberal with few behavioural expectations, though still very involved with their children. Parents place few demands or controls. Helicopter parenting — hovering and anxious. Parents fearful of rejection and continually 'worry'.
   Prone to *Empty nest syndrome* — depression, sense of loss of purpose, feelings of rejection, anxious about child's welfare, constantly questioning whether they've adequately prepared their child to live independently. Hovering around every phone call, ready to jump in and rescue. Parents describe difficulty balancing genuine risk with opportunities to grow, constantly fear the worst.

3. **Uninvolved (avoidant/dismissing)** — detached style of parenting, neglectful of emotional connectivity. Parents may focus on generating an income, career and assets, including

recreational pursuits, with children described as independent, latch-key kids.

4. **Dictatorship/Authoritative (high demands)** — harsh punishment and low responsiveness, little positive feedback or nurturing, often creates high-achieving children (elite sports, creative arts, child stars).

5. **Democratic Parenting (equality)** — draws on principles of equality and democracy. Decisions are made together and opinions of all members are respected.

   Parenting experts and parents suggest that, unless the young person is capable of reciprocation, this style is not appropriate for children under the age of 18 years given the disparity in financial responsibility and high expectation placed upon parents. Parents of 18+ suggest this style is optimal if all members of the system are willing to engage in family meetings and they participate in *equal* financial responsibility without being 'rescued'.

6. **Faith-based/Cultural-based Parenting Styles** — parenting guided by faith-based and/or culture-based ideals.

7. **Permissive/Addiction lead Parenting Style** — the addict/s are running the household.

   Technology (and other) addictions are leading the household. Common behaviours — intermittent explosive behavioural patterns, obsessive compulsive patterns, anti-social patterns linked to entitlement.

   Characterised by high addiction to devices with no plans for parents to reduce their own device usage, nor monitor the usage of their children. Family life is under the complete control of addictive technology. Parents believe in the technology potential of their children though ignore their children's right to progress their adulthood, often believing that their offspring will soon walk out of their bedroom as a multi-millionaire AP designer, resembling a 12-year-old musketeer.

When parents attempt to restrict use (interfere in the supply of), users become enraged, depressed or lost (at the same level as a full-blown alcoholic or drug addict). These parents are reluctant to consider a harm minimisation or cold turkey approach (even in school holidays) and report feeling like a hostage to their children with their addict (even as young as four years) running the household. How many rehabilitation centres are there for technology addicted young people in your local area? Probably nil!

8. **Career Parenting — ageing-parent dependency.** Adult offspring (grey hair millennials) are highly dependent on their ageing parents who continue to provide a home and lifestyle with no end in sight. A career parent does not expect adult children to pay full board ($350 p/w), nor participate with in-kind reciprocation. Adult children may not be living in the family home, though remain highly dependent upon others (including partners) for their survival.

   The numbers of career parents have risen in the past 20 years. Career parents are in an open-ended parental-adolescent system with their adult children who may be aged between 20 and 50+ years of age (including adult children with partners and children). There is an assumption that family wealth will be passed on to the next generation. There is little focus on preparing the next generation for the possibility of a lifestyle interrupter.

9. **Modern Realist Parenting (focused on legacy)** — parents walk 'alongside' as role models and view their offspring as adults.

Families believe in leaving a legacy for the succeeding generations and focus on building psychological immunity. Developmental milestones are met, whilst allowing room for interruptions and bounce-back.

The home environment provides the young person with a pseudo 'real life' in order to practice a wide range of communication and life skills to build their firewall within developmental norms and stages. Modern realist parents balance environmental fun, recreation, spiritual connection and global reality. They are not shy to debate notions of conspiracy, issues facing our First Nations people and other contentious issues.

Parents' *guide* learning rather than dictate or impose views and beliefs — encouraging young people to extend their rationale by bringing ideas or notions back to the 'talking' table. Parents help create an anti-scam centre by teaching children how to become scam-fit, leaving no room for cat-fishing or a decline in areas of normal developmental transition. Parents have a healthy or reasonable Swiss Cheese Layer style with plenty of 'others' connected to their family.

10. Single-Layer Swiss Cheese Parenting Style

The Swiss Cheese Model (J.T. Reason: 1990 — University of Manchester) draws on the image of multi-layers of Swiss cheese, stacked side by side, in which the risk of a threat becoming a reality is mitigated by the differing layers of defence, which are layered behind each other. Reason's risk and analysis principle suggests that when we 'layer' our defence and repair system we can prevent a single point of failure. **A single-layer Swiss cheese parenting style is a risk — this system will eventually insidiously turn in on itself.**

The first time a young adult faces a hurdle and is quickly rescued, it sends a very clear message — 'when a dilemma arises, I need rescuing'. The defunct single-layer Swiss Cheese Parenting Style attempts to prevent a hazard from penetrating their family system, by placing a parental barrier around their loved one — like an impenetrable wall, excluding outsiders from input. Like any layer, there may be holes and weaknesses, therefore, the risk of only one layer means that a hazard has the potential to break through the blood-brain defence-barrier to reach the core, reducing the social gold derived from others to mitigate disaster.

Healthy human systems are like multiple layers of Swiss cheese. Although there may be holes in one layer, when we work together in a 'village' mentality we strengthen our defences and mitigate a hazard from becoming a major risk. Single parents or co-parenting systems whereby children move between two households are often more likely to successfully transition to emotional adulthood due to learning *how* to be flexible and compromising. These young people are often highly adaptable and seek early independence.

Ears to See

Listening is an art: respectful two-way
conversation is our social GOLD!

Today's young people describe adults as poor listeners. Adults admit that listening without interrupting is extremely difficult, particularly stories that are one-sided or appear to distort reality.

Listening means listening to the deliverer, without interrupting, regardless of the content of conversation. Many parents report struggling to listen due to their inquisitive rational adult brain racing WAY ahead of the story, as they try to correct the content by responding or interrupting before the deliverer has even finished. These pressured (potentially anxiety-provoking) conversations do little to improve attachment patterns, often creating withdrawal from future interactions.

Consider the last time you engaged in a conversation about a controversial or difficult topic in a non-pressured setting? Were you interrupted? Were you taken seriously? Poor listening is a social divider. The brain of the young person is still developing — they need to be given every opportunity to analyse, problem-solve and to be heard. Whilst the developing brain can be difficult to reason with and concepts seemingly 'pie in the sky' or distorted, it is still the listeners' role to 'hear' the content and attempt to summarise the *context* before responding.

The reason anger explodes onto the public space is often attributed to the perceived lack of a 'fair hearing' or being misunderstood due to the listener's interpretation (or misinterpretation) of the speaker's reality. Once anger or fragile emotions are externalised, the system is then forced to focus on behaviour rather than the topic.

4.1 — Strategy: The Talking Stick.

1. The person initiating a topic owns the talking stick. The attention remains on the communicator.

2. When a full stop is placed on the conversation — the recipient then summarises what they believe is the content of the conversation before responding. For example:
'Correct me if I'm wrong, you believe ...'
'So, what I heard you suggesting is that ...'
'Can I check I heard you correctly, so you mean you would like to ...'

3   After Summarisation, the listener waits for:
Thumbs UP / Thumbs DOWN (result of summarisation revealed).
Listen to your young person's words within the walls of *their own story*, without interruption — with ears that are prepared to 'see'. (*The above is only possible, when there is an elimination of fear, aggression or any forms of abuse*).

Dealing with Aggressive Behaviour

'Anger' is one letter short of DANGER

If you are experiencing aggressive behaviour within your home, seek urgent consultation with police, mental health, child protection and/or domestic violence services.

When we are angry, we are a character in someone else's story: our child brain is interacting within an adult world.

Many parents are living in a war zone, crippled under the weight of ongoing aggressive behaviour within their households. Some parents remain fearful of triggering their children's erratic behaviour and reluctant to instil consequences. Reasonable requests, such as completing chores can result in reactivity likened to being teleported to the frontline of a battlefield. At the same time, young people report feeling 'loved' when their parents have the guts to instil boundaries and consistently maintain consequences for their behaviour.

Although young people enjoy their indulgent 'risk and reward' mentality, underneath all their many layers of bravado, they do not *actually want* to 'get away' with bad behaviour. Emotionally drained parents who decide to hand their kids' abhorrent behaviours over to the universe by only focusing on the 'good' behaviour, eventually discover that their child's character has turned into a learned (automatic) pattern of escalating entitlement and narcissism. This abusive system eventually transfers into love relationships and other systems, such as education and employment.

We are all eventually held accountable for our choices and our actions. Young people repeatedly report that they want parents to stop trying to be their friend by ignoring their bad behaviour. Out of the mouth of babes! Young people would like parents to know that their right for an education is *at the same level* as their right for discipline. Young adults are living in a real world where society has an accountability system that ultimately will not care about parents' socio-economic status, nor will parents be able to 'buy' their kids out of a legal system.

Past behaviour is often predictive of future risk. Intermittent explosive anger shows up when the primal child brain is running the story. At no time in history, nor in any society, is aggressive behaviour towards parents an acceptable norm. Families without a risk mitigation plan for aggression (or any other forms of domestic abuse) can assume that this behaviour will escalate, rather than improve on its own. Most aggressors are well aware that their behaviour is abhorrent, though don't actually believe the behaviour of their enablers will change. With their sense of entitlement fully ingrained, they know they've gotten away with *so much for so long*, so why will things be any different now?

Shame-blame systems lead to disruption of lives for all members living in this defunct system. Living in hope that aggressive behaviour will simply de-escalate without intervention is living in a system of DENIAL. Wake up! Unmanaged, non-consequential abusive behaviour within the family home is a serious regression system. Aggressors must learn that repeated hostility won't be tolerated, and may result in removal from the family home or other consequences such as police and emergency services.

Rejection-Aggression Plan — without a plan to reject aggression, the household is open to continued aggression-regression. If an individual minimises their risk to others, or there are repetitive patterns of Rupture and Repair, life will likely remain the same. Most young people deep down are disgusted that they 'get away with bad behaviour', particularly illegal behaviour. Although, often a force to be reckoned with, they are usually crying out for guidance, love and support.

When a jolt of reality is combined with an action plan, it sends a respectful message — there are consequences for your behaviours. For example, supporting the family member to temporarily leave the family home until others feel safe, joining family meetings, permanent removal from the home, written contracts, exposing family truth to outsiders, family removing themselves from the home for their own safety (and sanity!), behaviour charting or withdrawing privileges.

Graduated Return to Home Plans — can be highly effective, due to the strong focus on consequences and negotiation as a way forward. It's not uncommon for the duration of this graduated return to home (or transition to other suitable accommodation) process to be around 6-12 months, as the system moves around the U Curve of Adjustment. Unfortunately, Graduated Return to Home Plans are often interrupted or extended, attributed to enablers succumbing to the 'False Sorry's' without allowing enough time for evidence of change or healing for all members of the system. Ineffective early-return patterns are attributed to ongoing threats and manipulation, begging for forgiveness, jumping back into the Rupture/ Repair Cycle, rather than maintaining agreed timeframes, as well as rejecting the opportunity to include professional coaches or other social supports.

Protection Orders — aggressors are more likely to seek assistance, such as anger management courses or counselling, when 'the hands that feed them' have been cut off, evidently suffering under their reign of terror. Many families report success working with police under protection orders, justice conferencing and systems of external accountability.

We must ask ourselves important questions — is the home environment preparing all members of the system for life in the real world?

- Would the behaviour within the home behaviour be accepted or maintainable in the workplace, or within relationships?
- If this behaviour appeared in the workplace, would there be instant dismissal? Legal charges? Formal warnings?
- Is the home environment similar to a pseudo real-life community or workplace environment?
- Is my parenting style creating a basis for consequences and accountability?
- Adult trigger point bounce-back skills — can I switch from primal (emotional reactivity above 5/10) to a rational system (under 5/10) within four seconds?

When it's time, it's time — regardless of individual circumstances or history, we must ALL be held accountable for our choices and our behaviours. Calling the police for advice, or to report a crime within your family, and then adhering to court orders (including reporting violence within our education systems) sends a clear message — violence will not be tolerated.

Parenting from the Cells — Youth Justice

It was a humbling experience working with young recidivist offenders in the Queensland youth justice system between 2001 and 2008. My clients were all subject to involuntary legal orders under the Youth Justice Act, 1999. For some, they remained in the justice system for up to four years or until they 'graduated up' into the adult justice system. Although case workers are not parents, it didn't take long to learn that young men, regardless of their background, responded to secure boundaries in order to participate in society without offending.

The role of the youth justice case worker is to adhere to the law, as per their clients' court order, prepare pre-sentence reports and other legal documentation as well as journey with the young offender for the duration of their order. The overall goal is for the young person to divorce themselves from the justice system, and to get on with the life they are destined to live. The court prosecutes and sometimes incarcerates, though its main intent is to deter the young offender from escalating through the justice system.

The first meeting with our new clients was a time to talk about the conditions or 'special conditions' of their court order as well make it respectfully clear that *they* are in control of *their* journey, as well as when *they* will exit or end *their* relationship with the justice system. It was common for the initial meeting with our new client to be a somewhat smug affair, likely more focused on their busy street or addiction life, than the 'conditions' of their court order.

It didn't take long for my young clients to learn that I was prepared to go well over and above for them. Though EVERY single breach of *their* order would be followed through with a consequence. It was bullshit-free case work (even if it broke my heart at times). Meeting my young offender back in the police cells or prison as a result of *their* breach, and looking at them straight in the eyes, with the same tone — 'So, what's your game plan now? What would you like me to say to the Magistrate when we go back to court today?'

My arduous years spent working with offenders still remains part of my most rewarding career moments, particularly the hundreds of hours spent in intensive therapeutic sessions where these (mainly) young men let me into their private (and often horrendous) world. It was huge ride — the 40-hour court reports; the magistrates who didn't believe in my faith in my young offenders' ability to fight their addictions by attending rehab or detox rather than lockup; the long car rides with parents driving them to see their kids in prison; the youth justice conferences where the worker and police hoped and prayed that the outcome would reveal a restorative mindset rather than re-traumatise their victim; the parents who refused to let their kid back home — 'Let 'im rot in prison, it's time for tough love'; the horrific shock and debilitating rejection when realising there was no family bail-out; the first time a young person slept in a youth shelter or on the streets; the first time a young offender secured employment and the first time 'success' was marked by the completion of a court order.

Exit interviews were by far my most vivid memories. The court order had expired and the young person (and their family) were invited to attend a voluntary exit meeting to discuss their order — the good, the bad, and the ugly, including ascertaining their feedback about workers and other departmental processes. The most important discussion was the fact that they were getting rid of the legal system for (hopefully) good! The offending 'boy' had sometimes turned into a proud man.

It never ceased to amaze me during those exit interviews how many men stood up during the discussion to shake my hand, stating, 'Thanks for being the first person in my life to EVER give me consequences' or 'thanks for always following through', 'thanks for not giving up on me', 'I never knew what boundaries were', 'fuck you were tough, and I needed it'. When we neglect the role of boundaries and consequences, it is indeed a sad indictment that the justice system is forced into the role of growing the child to an adult, OR progressing the recidivist child offender into the 'big-boy' prison world.

The public often assume that lower socio-economic families and single parents are clogging up our justice system by raising dangerous recidivist offenders, as opposed to the hard-working parents of the middle-upper class. WRONG! My firsthand experience working with young offenders, writing countless presentence reports, interviewing families first-hand, sitting with whole family groups in court and completing hundreds of hours of therapeutic intervention was that white middle-class families were just as likely to raise recidivist offenders as any other group in society. In fact, single parents dropping their kids off to stay with their middle-class mates, *trusting* that these 'responsible' families would be protective, were often dumbfounded to learn that 'friendship parenting styles' had opened the door to their kids first opportunity for anti-social choices.

Regardless of class or circumstances, by the end of their son's or daughter's court order, parents were often brutally honest. Many urged me to share their regrets to mitigate against kids behind bars. On behalf of these parents, I'm passing on these typical cited 'parenting regrets' to the younger generation of parents.

The most common parenting regrets:-

- Overly 'forgiving' practices for the 'small stuff' and not enforcing boundaries around acceptable behaviour.
- Ignoring my child's first anti-social behaviour.
- Weak (or nil) consequences and playing quick-forgiving God in order to avoid social embarrassment.
- Naively believing that 'things' would just work out.
- Trusting other parents would do the right thing.
- Instilling 'tough love' principles far too late.
- Trusting that my co-parent would do the right thing.
- Not teaching empathy (reciprocity).
- No time-locks on devices (creating patterns of entitlement).
- Weak parental moral compass lines.
- My drinking patterns and substance abuse patterns used as an excuse not to instil consequences.
- Not taking responsibility for my own legal double-standards.
- Minimising nicotine and marijuana use as 'not serious' in comparison with 'hard' drugs.

We grow as a result of considering risk and testing (or not) that risk. If there is a weak line of reckoning, particularly in the presence of lenient parenting styles, our appetite for risk will increase, and so will our addiction to adrenaline-pumping activities that 'get off' on risk.

Once a young person develops a genuine baseline for their moral compass, they are in control of their risk appetite. Choice belongs to the individual: no one is holding a gun to our head forcing us to offend. I've lost count of how many offenders informed me that their primary addiction was the 'risk of getting caught', followed by the need for bigger hits of adrenaline, as their crime life became more and more sophisticated. Petty crime turned to home invasions. Home invasions turned to breaking and entering as well as assault occasioning bodily harm with weapons. The public assume that drugs and money are always involved with crime — WRONG! Offenders (and workaholics) can take many years to detox from their addiction to adrenaline (and other addictions) as well as develop the skill of empathy, such as considering the horrific trauma suffered by their victims as a result of their weak moral compass line.

The goal of parenting is surely to increase their young person's risk appetite by increasing their pro-social choices. For example, the risks associated with the pleasure and pain of love relationships, or taking up new or strange hobbies, geographical risks associated with relocation, the risks of standing up for ourselves (assertive communication skills) or disclosing bullies, dealing with workplace stresses and challenging workplace practices.

We are faced with numerous pro-social risks throughout our lifespan. The following are common statements from young offenders:

- The court system was too lenient, I got away with so much crime.
- I never had any consequences at home when I first acted like a little bastard.

- It was easy to talk my olds around when I started offending, they were so embarrassed.
- Piss-weak groundings didn't work for me.
- I got beaten bad when I did something small at home, so I figured it's normal to beat up people in the community, when they do wrong by me.

Payback and Vendetta

Poor impulse control is often excused as a 'condition'. Psychoanalyst, Albert Ellis (1962) disagreed with anger-related labels, urging society to understand and analyse the serious depth of a well-trained (automatically programmed) Payback or Vendetta belief system. The blame-game vendetta system suggests that 'if I believe you have done the wrong thing by me, you will (or have to) receive some sort of punishment'. Once this belief system is triggered, the body automatically produces a level of primal toxicity that responds to the *perception* of threat — mobilising the body for action.

Domestically violent relationships are often linked to one person who is operating within a vendetta or payback belief system, where the need for control and justification abounds — 'It's not my fault I go from zero to 10 in a second', 'I can't help it, it's just the way I am', 'it's because of my background', 'they *should* know by now not to push my buttons and what will happen when they do', 'they know exactly what my triggers are', 'everyone knows I have to respond', 'I'll have no cred if I don't'. Perpetrators often believe that although they are clearly the aggressor, they are, in fact, the actual victim, which justifies their violence, forcing the elicitation of sympathy from their victims.

It's an incorrect assumption to suggest that crime and other anti-social behaviour is always committed under the influence of alcohol or illicit substances. A vendetta belief system (payback mentality) is a calculated response to a learned behaviour — It will happen because it must'. Ellis suggested that a third of the population operate within this belief system, though most are not willing to cross a legal moral compass line. It's interesting to consider that enacting vendetta does not always rate on the anger scale, due to the incestuous notion that 'it must happen', whilst other vendetta acts are manifested under the dangerously toxic influence of unmanaged 10+ rage-anger — described as an outer body experience with no conscious awareness.

Together with robust parenting styles and determination, it is entirely possible to change our character and behaviour by focusing on our rules and beliefs. It's total bullshit to believe that it's impossible to change the reactivity of a repeat offender. I've worked with incredible people of all ages and witnessed the modification or deletion of malfunctioning rules and beliefs and NEVER return to their old ways, particularly when they *choose* to live within a boundary-enhancing home system. Unless cognitively or genetically impaired, the *person* is not a risk to society — their unchallenged belief system and their unchallenged moral compass line is a risk to society.

Prison sentences are another male social withdrawal system: a form of self-imposed mind control. Most adult prisoners aren't given any opportunity to re-program their brains whilst incarcerated, often finding themselves homeless post-release. Many prisoners are largely unaware that they are operating on a dangerous primal belief system that has been automatically pre-programmed (now a mega-superhighway neural brain system). They're living in prison as funded mind prisoners, *as well as* prisoners of the legal system. What parent would *ever* want this outcome for their child?

Secure Boundaries = Secure Children

Survey of kids and chores

Turning from incarceration and vendetta, back to general home life where the normality of basic chores, responsibility and accountability exist. I sent out a survey (2020) via a social media platform to parents in Australia and New Zealand to find out what chores are being completed by children without undue fuss. Disappointingly, I discovered that, on average, young kids are completing more chores than what older teenagers are! When I chatted with parents about this shameful, mathematically unsound system that suggests a rise in age is resulting in a decline in chores, I received answers that sadly reflected parental despondency and generational norming of attitudes.

The majority of parents agreed that indeed their role is a 'Bridge From Home To Adulthood' with the home base as a pseudo 'real world'. Though, somewhere along the line they admitted that their expectations decreased as their need to 'hold on' to their children increased — 'I'm not surprised about your research', 'there's no point getting into an argument with my son or daughter; they'll just ignore me anyway', 'I'd rather pay a housecleaner or just get the job done properly myself', 'my standard is so much higher than my kids', 'I can't bear the thought of living in a home with kids' standards', 'yea, right, get 'em to help, that's a bloody joke', 'I can't be bothered trying anymore', 'I think my kid is a narcissist', 'I get sick of nagging and being stonewalled', 'his reaction freaks me out and I'm not interested in dealing with it', 'I'm over it', 'I know my parents are elderly — but they do a better job helping me out than my adult kids', 'it's because I'm too busy with work; he'll hopefully leave one day, anyway', 'I can't deal with her screaming; she doesn't do her jobs properly anyway.'

Laying aside the wide range of parental excuses and defeatism, surely there is no justification for the delaying of growing our children to responsible adults?

Growing a boy to a man in less than fifteen minutes

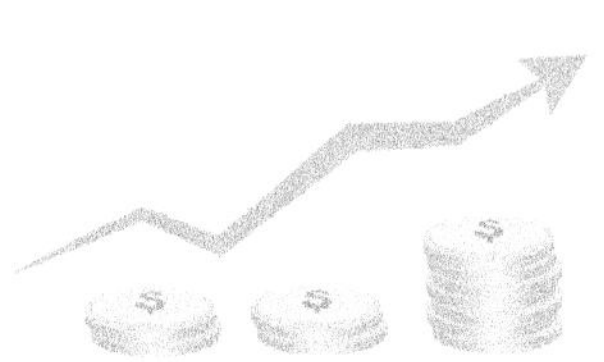

A typical conversation within a therapeutic session with young people referred to counselling due to parental-adolescent conflict.

Therapist: 'What's your credit point rating with your parents currently?'

Reply: 'Huh, what do you mean?'

Therapist: *(Draws a horizontal line in the middle of the white board that indicates the 0% line. Below the line represents negative 100% or negative 200%. Top of the line represents 0-100+%.)*

'So, hypothetically, if you wanted to be taken seriously right now by your parents, to negotiate as an adult, to borrow, let's say $50, how much "negotiation credit" do you assume you have? If I give you the whiteboard marker, where would you place yourself? Above the 0% negotiation line or would you be somewhere in the negative percentage area?'

Reply: 'I'd probably be around negative 200%.'

Therapist: 'I have three questions to check with you.'

(1) 'So, you're saying that your parents regard you as a child, and *you* also regard yourself as a child, which is why you currently have no negotiation respect and lots of conflict?'

(2) 'I'm wondering if your goal is to become a man or stay as a child?'

(3) 'If your goal is to remain as a child, would you mind if I refer you to you a child therapist, because I'm in the business of growing men, rather than regression. Regression means that you go backwards in your development, and you remain dependent upon your parents when you're older. Sort of like wearing adult-sized nappies and your mum breastfeeding or bottle feeding you all over again.'

Reply: 'Whoa'; 'What the!!!... 'My goal is to become a man — I'm not shittin' in no nappy!'

Therapist: 'Great, let's start with three things...'

(1) 'Name your top four chores — you know, the ones that are non-negotiable and likely you only complete when you've been nagged at (identify nagging-system of parents).'

(2) 'I'll write your jobs on the board.'

(3) 'Explain how long it takes you to complete them, and whether you ever instigate any jobs yourself.'

Example Reply: 'Unload dishwasher, take out the garbage every night, feed the dog, make my bed. I only do them after I've been nagged at around three times — I know how far I can push the old's until they lose their shit, and threaten to take my iPad (nagging style identified — moral line identification). Who actually instigates their jobs, anyway? It's not what we do, why would I actually *want* to do them?'

Therapist: 'When you instigate your jobs, you are acting like an adult. When you *choose* not to instigate a non-negotiable job, you are saying that you want to be a child, think like a child, treated like a child and to delay becoming a man. Another example of regression is when someone is forced to nag at you, or when someone else has to make excuses for you, such as your parent begging for an extension on behalf of you with your teacher or your parent talking to your boss. Any time an adult is using *their* adult (executive) brain to think for you, they are saying that you are too much of a child to be able to think for yourself. You are letting the adults in your life think that you don't want to be in control of your own mind. As you know, playing on the edge of your parents' nagging system is like a statement to remain in your child brain. Are you living in a child-adult bankrupt system?'

Reply: 'Hmmmmm — I'm probably negative 200%'

Therapist: 'Based on what you said a few minutes ago, I'm just checking that you're employing me to assist you to grow your executive brain from thinking like a boy to a man? Men don't need prompting, they know what needs doing, they're strong and focused and remain this way. They have plenty of room for negotiation because they're in credit. Even if it takes a week or so to maintain your above-line credit system, it's about moving away from your childish debit system.'

Therapist: 'I'm not sure if you realise, that when kids instigate their jobs, adults are shocked! In that moment they see you as an adult. That's because they're accustomed to thinking of you as a kid, and it messes with their brain architecture. They're so shocked, that without you (or them!) even realising it, you are given a bunch of credit points that move you closer to the negotiating line. If you keep this system going for a while, you'll surpass the 0% line, increasing your negotiable credit.'

Therapist: 'No Credit: No Negotiation. No credit means you are a child, living in a child system. After one week of maintaining your adult system, I would like you to have a conversation with your parents and make a fair request for something to trial your negotiation skills. When you've done this, you are welcome to book another session' (handshake commitment on departure).

Junior King of the Family — Through the Lens of Privilege

I recall an interesting conversation with a personable young man of 21 years (pre-2020) when I was out for dinner with his parents and a group of others. The young man appeared happy and healthy, citing his city goals and expectations, comfortable to chatter with everyone in the group. He was a lean-framed, pleasant-looking young bloke, liked playing drums in his church band, and hanging out with his muso mates, close to his family 'aside from Dad being a bit depressed at times'. His sisters had left home many years prior, working, married and now young mothers. He enjoyed spending time with his new girlfriend and was struggling with motivation to complete his TAFE course.

He knew I was aware of his family's socio-economic background, though he didn't refer to it when he began to answer my questions, 'So what's next for career and moving out of home? Are you paying rent now?' 'So ... what I've worked out', he replied, 'is that I'm not suited to being an employee, I'm more of a manager. I would rather work for myself, so that's what I'm thinking at this stage. I had a boss who I didn't really like, he put a lot of pressure on me. Well, I guess he was okay, *but* I've realised that I just want to work for myself at my own pace. I get a bit tired, so I'm staying home until I decide what business could be right for me.'

The young man's mother, who I'd known since before he was born, winked at me, and his father nodded with a half-smile. 'So',

I naively enquired from the young man, 'correct me if I'm wrong, what you are saying is that, you've had a try working for a boss once, and, although he wasn't a bad sort of boss you didn't really like some things about him, nor did you enjoy working full time. And, as a result of this experience, you've decided to go into business when you work out what type of business you want to go into, while you're still at home? What's more, you're pleased with your decision because you like the idea of being a "boss" as well as having a bit of a rest?'

'Exactly!', he smiled, appearing to feel validated. I smiled a little, as I wriggled a little in my chair, breathing through my dismay, as I thought about his generational norming and how often I'd had the same conversation with so many young people raised in middle-upper class families. 'So, what you are ALSO saying, if I heard you correctly, is that, although you don't actually have any area of specialisation yet, nor a long working history, nor robust finances, nor any particular industry or business you have decided to pursue, you would like to be a boss or an owner of a business. Though not wanting to work and study at the same time?' 'Yes, that's right', he replied with his endearing smile and sparkly blue eyes, maybe assuming I would be his cheer squad for his emerging entrepreneurial mindset.

Brazenly, I prodded further, 'Would you mind if I could just check out a few other things, because I'm sorta confused?' 'Sure', he eagerly replied as if I was the child, his back straightening up in a pre-managerial type of pose. 'So, what you're saying, is that although you *could* work full time or at least part-time for a boss, while you decide your business venture, you are choosing to be currently unemployed while living in your parents' home as an adult? That is, you're contemplating your future **through the lens of privilege**?'. 'What do you mean *through the lens of privilege*', he enquired, his smile replaced with a slight frown, as he cocked his head forward in my direction.

'Well', I began with a shift of pace and (hopefully) a calm tone, 'I just wondered if your goals and lengthy re-launch has been analysed through a slightly different lens than the rest of society?' 'Sure', he said with an air of class, his shoulders now square, waiting for my response. I continued, 'As you know, both your parents have worked full time all their working lives and have provided you and your siblings with an amazing lifestyle in your postcode envy suburb. Due to their sacrifices, you haven't had the opportunity to understand hardship, even feel hunger or pain, nor have you had to work full time from 18 years of age and your first car was purchased for you. So, because of this privilege, you're now able to stay at home, rest, play drums in the church band, hang out with mates and get to know the new young lady in your life without any pressures? Furthermore, I'm assuming you're only prepared to do maybe a few odd jobs when your folks ask you, and you're not pressured to pay board due to the fact you're home deciding on your future, right?'

The atmosphere at the table changed, the young man was centre stage, though he rose to his occasion, with a changed disposition. Looking at me clear in the eyes, his simple, albeit rather unenthused response, was no surprise, 'Yeah, errr, I guess you're right'. Taking further liberty in the moment, I asked him, 'What would happen, hypothetically, if your parents were forced to rent their house out permanently, or they moved to another country as missionaries and sold everything under you, or went bankrupt or divorced or died or were placed in supported accommodation, and you had no access to money or accommodation ... and if that wasn't tough enough, your girlfriend told you she was pregnant with triplets?'

'Far out, whoa! What the… well, hmmmmm', he said all in one breath, puckering his lips, 'hmmmmm, I know where you're going with this, okay, I know what you've done'. He lowered his head to the tip of his thumb, resting on his elbow, nodding with uninvited clarity. 'Well, I guess I would go back to my previous boss and ask him if I could get my job back. I'd have to work full time at that job to pay for my kids, and I'd probably have to study at night. I'd be stuffed. Though, I guess I'd *have to* do whatever I could do at the time, there probably wouldn't be any other options, probably be too busy to think about being tired, anyway'. In that brief moment, his collision with reality and his opportunity to adult stood staring at him square in the eyes. Would his transition to manhood be successful, or would his lifestyle and the choices of his parents still hold him back?

Mumma's Boy is not a Parenting Style - It's a Sickness

Pick me … Pick US

The transition to love relationships can be exciting, euphoric and turbulent, as we leave our carers and join together as one … or not? Whether we're living out of home, or still living at home whilst partnered, it's entirely possible to be unnaturally linked to parents in a type of unhealthy emotional web that causes our partner to be miserable. In her online article, 'How to Handle a Partner Who Is a Mama's Boy', Marni Feuerman suggests that rather than demonising the important role of mother, we need to appreciate the positive effect of males developing close attachments, such as increased empathy, confidence, ongoing emotional wellbeing and the ability to form meaningful relationships with women.

Though, sadly, the numbers of young women entering counselling due to her partner's 'Mumma issues' are increasing. These women are amongst the most emotionally battered and elevated, reporting robust mental health prior to their relationship, followed by extreme anxiety and depression after many years hoping and then wishing some more, that their boy-man would stand up for himself and protect 'their' relationship and family unit. This is made even more complicated in the presence of marriage, mortgages, children and health issues, alongside businesses entangled with his biological family.

Women spend the majority of their counselling sessions weeping, angry and often pacing. 'I just want him to pick me, *our* family. Why can't he break his sick relationship with his mother?', 'It's obvious that his Mumma owns him: she acts like a jealous school girl.' Victims of momma's boys can experience ongoing psychopathy, such as anxiety disorders, that can alter the geographical landscape of their brain and seriously decrease their general functionality. They can become a shell of their previous high functioning self.

Although not classified in the *DSM-5*, the notion of **Rejection Sensitive Dysphoria (RSD)** is one way of explaining this serious symptomology as a result of enduring ongoing rejection over a period of time, such as highly intense sadness, unusual outbursts of rage or panic, feelings of despair and hopelessness, chronic depression, and significantly lowered self-esteem. Rejection sensitive dysphoria can exacerbate pre-existing conditions, such as post-traumatic stress disorder, attention deficit hyperactivity disorders, and mirror behavioural patterns common for those diagnosed with personality disorders.

Leaving Father and Mother and becoming one ... or three? The overfocus on the biological family means there is an under-focus on his partner (and children). While his partner is screaming out, 'But, why the fuck *wouldn't* you want to choose me?' Unaware that Mother has no intention of letting him cut the apron strings, particularly in the presence of his unspoken dark secrets, his financial tie to the family, or his misunderstood anxious attachment issues he developed in his younger years (both fearing abandonment and/or rejection), on top of his genuine lack of understanding of the true meaning of love as a commitment to his new story.

Sometimes, he's unaware that he's been suffering a type of Stockholm Syndrome, or spooky entrapment since his early years, and lacks the ability to even *begin* to transition from his fear-driven relationship with Mumma, to the partner he believes he loves. Nor is Momma willing to give up her rein of power and control. With two women behaving like scorned lovers, he's enmeshed in a cycle of fear, confusion, broken love, mistrust and repeated lies, with no intention (or ability) to re-write his new story. Partners who were once robust and futuristic become shells of their previous self, seen as the overbearing villain in the wider family story, as they participate in unnatural, never-ending rupture/repair cycles, that they know deep down may not *ever* change.

For years, she chose to dream that he would de-toxify from the addictive, creepy allure of his mother, and simply know *how* to "stop sucking on his Mumma's breasts" — after all, why wouldn't he want to suckle on the firm, fit life that she's sacrificed for him? She remembers stonewalling her tribal wisdom. They had all urged her to 'just date for a while' before moving in together and 'you know the rules: you need to *really* get to know someone for at least two years' before marriage, mortgage and maternity'.

Eventually, after many years of over-giving, over-hoping, becoming parents, building assets together and simply hoping

Mumma would support versus control, she eventually wakes up and realises that her many years of fervent pleas have simply fallen on deaf ears. She blames herself for ignoring her gut instinct in the earlier days — 'Yes-but underneath, he's such a nice guy', 'his Mumma will surely do the right thing eventually', 'yes-but it'll work out'. She's now learned the hard way that a man who persistently, year after year, unnaturally prioritises his (otherwise healthy and able bodied) mother over his new family is actually *not* 'nice' — he's either very unwell or very cruel.

She remembers back to those strange initial months through the lens of her current stark reality. Her youthful hope and excitement that she'd found the 'nice' man of her dreams who would be a 'nice' father, as she visualised her happy kids and the cute puppies playing behind the white picket fence, enjoying life in her postcode envy suburb. In the beginning, she was kind, she was independent, she was innovative and bold — an alluring presence that fascinated her man though unnerved his mother. She recalls her first time, sitting at his biological family dinner table, sipping on her vino of hopeful acceptance, though was initially offered an entree of contempt.

In her confusion, she buffered her denial with optimism, whispering to herself during her mains, 'I'm sure it'll all work out, coz he's such a nice guy'. Though, little did she know that before she'd even sat down at the table, she'd already lost. As she sat next to her man and waited for him to boast their union and talk of their plans, he was strangely, yet 'nicely' dismissive. So, she focused on her dessert, trying not to own her secret despair, watching him interacting with his tribe, as they subtly closed ranks within their cultural banter. Deep down in her gut, the place where denial doesn't exist, she could hear the titillating giggle of his mumma's jealous voice and noticed how Mumma's eyes didn't leave his face

— she knows something is awry. Looking back now, it was obvious that the ol' girl and the bloodline had already won.

Sub-consciously, Mumma and the boy-man know that the *right type of partner* will need to be simple, undemanding and aware that she is secondary to The Queen. She will be a lover of the act of over-giving, and graciously learn from Mumma that the way to his heart is through the avoidance of discomfort and undue expectations. She'll likely own at least a snippet of a fear of abandonment, she'll detest the thought of being alone, she'll be eager to compromise, particularly if she believes her biological clock might stop ticking. The 'right' partner will be able to cope with Mumma, particularly if financial (or other) oversupply circumstances have the potential to decrease discomfort ... though, you don't *actually* marry your partner's family, do you? ... Bullshit!

Rather than a healthy transition to adulthood mindset and creating happy wider familial experiences, some matriarchal and patriarchal systems operate under a possessive 'Divide and Conquer' system. The controlling eldership often subtly 'works' on all parts of the family system to cause division, including older grandchildren when they finally come of age to manipulate. The tangled web of division and deceit gives the matriarch or patriarch meaning in their retirement, as they flitter between this one and that one, dropping subtle bombs on each family unit, as they try to become the hero (often the villain) of the whole family.

Whilst family systems are never perfect, with most moving in and out of regular (healthy and unhealthy) conflict, the systems I'm referring to are deep-seated — like a self-imposed dictatorship, refusing to compromise as they maintain power and control. These systems often avoid direct conflict or healthy styles of confrontation. Ross Rosenburg in his 2013 book, *The Human Magnet Syndrome: Why We Love People Who Hurt Us*, reminds us that codependency is a problematic relationship involving the relinquishing of power and control due to the connection to those who are either addicted (unfulfilled and undervalued) or who are pathologically narcissistic (intentional).

At the end of the day, your partner is either a man standing on his own two feet or he is a mumma's boy. There is no middle ground. If the truth is standing before you from the get-go, *you* are making a choice to 'buy into' this system. This system is a bankrupt partnership and without intervention, can lead to psychological and physical conditions that could, in time, become irreparable. It is no one else's fault that you chose to fast-track your relationship or become brain washed, particularly in the presence of tribal truth and genuine concern. Do you *then* expect your loved ones to be part of your painful reality, whilst *still* choosing to remain in denial?

The enduring anxious attachment that the son has towards his mother and the mother's need to dis-enable her son in order to meet her own needs, causes damage throughout an entire family. It also compromises the childhoods of otherwise happy children and grandchildren. There are no winners in this system. The adult son often finds himself eventually alone and seeking assistance for 'abandonment' issues. What parent would want to cause their adult son (or daughter) pain and heartache, as well as complicate the lives of their precious grandchildren and wider family?

Childhood Psychology Theories

Let's turn to psychology for the answers to the (sometimes) strange bonds between sons and mothers, as well as the bonds between girls and their fathers. Although there's very little clear evidence to suggest Freud's dream interpretation namely *The*

Oedipus Complex (1899) is real, in psychoanalytic theory, it is suggested that it's common for young boys to have a subconscious desire for sexual involvement with the parent of the opposite sex, and a sense of rivalry with the parent of the same sex. This is noted in some children who act possessively towards their mother and won't let Father touch her, or a child who insists on sleeping between parents when younger. For some children, this bonding becomes enmeshed long-term, subconsciously hovering around the transition bridge.

Sigmund Freud disputed Carl Jung's (1913) female father-fixated theory (as the counterpart to the Oedipal Complex), discussing *The Electra Complex*, which focuses on the period of psychosexual development, where a girl increases her possessive love for her father, by increasing conflict toward her mother. Although this stage is not referred to in the *DSM-5*, Jung suggests that it is part of the three to six-year-old phallic developmental stage where girls become aware of their bodies, develop a sense of penis-envy as they learn the differences between males and females. Increasing their time with their fathers, they may flirt or practice sexual behaviours without any actual sexual contact.

During puberty, there is a re-emergence of female-father-approval behaviours as she engages in cycles of conflict-competition with Mother. Attempting to be seen as endearing and worthy of admiration for her new intelligence and sexuality, often resenting her mother in cycles of competition-repression-identification-acceptance (the Id-Ego defence and repair system). Their female role model is often unaware that a game has even begun — a type of juvenile cat-and-mouse web that soon becomes a cycle of comparison-and-persecution as Mother is forced to participate in a system of debate and boundary pushing. I refer to this as attempting to 'dethrone Mum' by sublime means of coercion with Dad or other male role models.

To the outsider, this is nothing short of masterful, as her juvenile manipulation skills continue to become sophisticated. A wise mother gives her daughter the type of healthy competition that she too once imposed upon her own mother. A wise mother can separate the dysfunction and/or privilege from her own childhood, and see her daughter for what she is — a product of herself, and yet her own incredibly unique emerging adult with a lifetime of interesting complexities and opportunities ahead of her.

Commonly, mothers report an easier transition experience with their daughters, particularly by the beginning of their twenties. They are relieved that there is now less conflict and competition, as they begin to work towards more of a 'friendship' than foe relationship, at the same time, still admitting the double standard relationship with their sons. Mothers report a sense of overwhelming sadness within the early stages of their 'empty nesting' grief and loss months when they 'lose my boy', or believe they've been forced to 'hand him over' to his new love interest.

Parents are often heard asking — where are all the books teaching us how to avoid controlling our adult kids' lives? Why didn't someone warn us how *painful* it would be to let go of our children as they transition to adulthood? Why does it feel so unnatural to view our kids as adults? Why do I keep declaring that there are no meritorious applicants for the role of partner to my son? Why are there no rites of passage for this developmentally important stage of our journey? Is the name matriarch or patriarch one that is *bestowed upon* or is it right that we can *impose upon?*

It's suggested that young women transition to adulthood earlier than young men, due to their no-choice biologic rites of passage from their middle teens. Menstruation arrives — the girl is now *forced* to deal with monthly blood and discomfort for 35+ years, as well as her new adult responsibility that focuses on protection and reproduction. When that first blood-stained menstruation event occurs, her world has irreversibly changed. In the face of such complexity, she now considers what it would mean as a teen, to either place her own baby in the crib, or the possible lifetime of pain if she were to eliminate a life. She sets aside her toys and her boys and begins to bond with her new fraternity women, a sisterhood of blood and reproduction, where she's graduated into The Club — 'Hey, sis, you're a woman now'.

Prior to her new sisterhood, she was aware that there were emotional, behavioural and physical signals warning her that an unavoidable transition event was pending, though sad that her childhood years have now passed. There's no turning back, regression or opt-out. She's now forced to endure her monthly blood-stained years, as life becomes messier and personal, fumbling and mumbling with blood blockers and absorbers and dealing with her moods and broods, left in disbelief as to *why*, she was once so eager for this new club to arrive? The mighty young woman's voice is often heard crying out to their male counterparts, 'Oh, baby, why is your crib still warm and your Mother's apron strings so enticing, and when will you stop playing with your boys and your toys?'

As mentioned in the next chapter, traditional Aboriginal cultures have deeply imbedded transition practices, alongside clearly defined roles that are taught throughout childhood. For example, the avoidance relationship between a son-in-law and his mother-in-law. Is mainstream Australia becoming messier and confused within their relational systems? Is this due to a lack of clear transition markers, with parents increasingly developing helicopter parenting styles as they hover around like worry-fly-ing-machines? Has it become almost impossible for parents to proudly step back when their 18-year-old emerges onto the adult space? Are modern parents ready for their greatest challenge — to let go and believe in your young person's right to adult?

Chapter 5
Male Transition Practices

Similar to a rough uncut foxfire diamond placed in the fiery furnace for refinement, it's suggested that humans need to be given a dearth of opportunities to experience the full force of heat from life events, turned up to sometimes the absurd, in order to grow and then fertilise emotional resilience — whilst still respectfully remaining in the game of life. In other words — **No Heat, No Transition**.

Chapter 4 discusses a number of male transition practices, alongside a bunch of somewhat shocking tribal rituals and rites of passage customs within cultural norms around the world that provide initiates with graduated opportunities to build life skills and transition to manhood. Although many extreme male transition practices are now outlawed, the common thread within many cultures is the belief that **adulthood has arrived when the confidence or security of youth is appropriately lost as a result of a *forced* collision with reality.**

Today, with the systemic rupturing of male transition practices, the escalating rates of self-harm and the alarming level of diagnosed mental health issues (particularly since 2020), young Australian men appear to be genuinely struggling to claim their adulthood. They lack the awareness that they will, one day, be at the forefront of our society — while the rest of us are buried deep underground or aimlessly hanging around on our rocking chairs in our nursing homes. Though, one wonders, with the over-focus on alcohol-yard-glassing, technology, socials, pornography and gambling, how *can* 'Calibration Time' in Australia *actually* begin? The place where the merging of ego, hardship and privilege fuse into an individual who is ready to "adult" and participate in the real world — to a society that is waiting and so desperately in need of their participation.

Retrospective older people often proudly replay their adventures of survival against the odds with their traumatic, albeit heroic war stories and risk-taking exploits, turning the stomach of their listeners. They can quickly identify the bridge from childhood to manhood by enduring grizzly initiation practices as a way of calibrating ego with responsibility. A boy *sought* manhood. Men expected boys, at various developmental ages and stages, to *be ready*. Traditionally, mothers were proud of their role to grow their boys into men: *well aware* that their sons would one day be fathers, providers and protectors of their culture and way of life. The words 'nice and boy' were an anomaly.

Discomfort to Grow Through Transition Processes

Many cultural transition practices around the world are now obsolete, outlawed or pertain only to a particular culture or sub-culture. Though, research reveals that there is one main overarching transition-theme unique to the majority of cultures — **the building of psychological stamina is a vital life skill in order to maintain cultural integrity. By 'pushing through' significant physical pain barriers, the boy grows to a man.**

Transition to manhood practices historically excluded parents (or those who have nurtured the boy) from participating in ongoing graduated transition practices. This was attributed to the clash between the protective nature of the nurturing role and the (often) brutality of transitionary practices. Many cultures viewed the home environment as only *ever* an early-years nurturing station until the 'handing over' process began. For a boy to grow into his manhood, he was 'bridged' or handed over to elders through *graduated* group-based initiation practices. These graduated practices often took place over a long period of time, with some beginning from as young as five years of age.

In tribal societies, the child belongs to the *whole* tribe. During his raising, he's not sidelined, overly protected, kept away from others, nor is he indulged — he is raised for his role. Historical transition practices were once linked to whole of tribal survival and his 'training' was targeted on the preparation for warfare in order to protect their species. Therefore, the graduating male was well aware from a young age that his participation in cultural transitionary practices was mandatory. Growing the boy into a man was not optional, nor was it delayed — males were *expected* to fight for the survival of their species. Rites of passage rituals were characterised by mixing blood and fear through forced risk-taking, enduring horrific physical pain in order to cultivate emotional resilience.

A couple of articles to print out and dissect for our privileged young males, written by Brett and Kate McKay, outlines eight interesting (and insane) cultural rites of passage for young males around the world (some obsolete, some current). Although most cultures report a wide variety of transition diversity, the common thread is the overarching belief that both emotional and physical pain is required for a boy to pass the test of manhood — evidenced by the ability to display courage, endurance, and most importantly, the ability to control one's emotions.

Although the writers of the above article, are not suggesting these practices should be implemented in Australia, nor are they necessarily sane (in fact they would likely result in imprisonable child abuse charges in our current culture!), they share my concern that Australian males are unaware what it actually *means* to adult. Increasingly, males are questioning whether they have the skills to protect Australia from invasion or whether they have *actually* graduated into Manhood. This is believed to be attributed to: parenting dis-enablement styles, the lack of opportunity to be tested under fire and watered-down ceremonial or pseudo-initiations.

The question of 'reaching-adulthood' is answered when the young male meets his first major life-test — rather than stepping out of the fiery furnace through sheer psychological strength, he often retreats into his child self by waging a war upon the rulers of his own mind.

Today, not only is there a disturbing extension to adolescence well into the thirties and forties, there appears to be the disappearance of clear markers on their journey to manhood. Many believe that this is attributed to a distinct lack of Australian men and elders stepping forward in their community to publicly discuss this topic, let alone the provision of 'real' opportunities to build resilience.

The yearly harvest ritual in Vanuatu (land diving) includes circumcised males as young as five years of age, who are 'plunged into manhood' by jumping headfirst from towers of 100-plus feet at speeds of over 45 miles per hour, with a goal to shoulder-land-touch only. Miscalculations obviously result in horrific injury or, at worst, death. This barely compares to an Australian Aboriginal mob with circumcision and sub-incision practices that involve boys from 15 years of age, cutting off their foreskin and swallowing it as a way of eating their childhood away. Less dramatic practices exist within the Hamar tribe of Ethiopia, who require the young initiate to jump naked over castrated cows before fathers agree that he is an adult (*maza*) now worthy of marrying their daughter.

Two shirtless young rivals from the North African Fulani tribe enter into a battle of the fittest by enduring a horrific public whipping in front of the whole village. The boys take turns to brutally strike each other a number of times, with the winner chosen by the crowd as the one who has flinched the least and sports the bloodiest and deepest cuts. High mortality rates appear common for the Kenyan Maasi boys, who, with only a spear and rawhide shield, were expected to hunt riled-up deadly lions and cut off their tails. Today, this practice has been modified to pack hunting in groups of around 10 young males, due to the decrease in lion numbers, *not* due to the concern for their young males' lives!

The *okipa* ceremony for the Native American Mandan tribe expected their young lads to comply with a bunch of unnatural, brutal steps to reach their well-deserved grand finale into manhood. It's hard to imagine parents handing their sons over to such a sickening and barbaric practice, beginning with an extensive time enduring sleep deprivation and starvation, followed by a ritual to begin the horrific spearing by wooden poles, right through their body. They are then suspended from a ceiling and only released when unconscious. The 'moment' of manhood arrives if they wake, which THEN signals that it's time for the chopping off of their two small fingers, followed by running around with wooden rods still impaled — blood spews from their amputated fingers and other parts of their body which is all played out in front of their whole tribe!

Traditional Aboriginal Cultural Practices

For culture to thrive and survive, it is imperative that boys become men. Male initiation symbolises the fact that childish ways are ceasing and the mother's primary parenting years are over. When the boy becomes a man, the relationship between mother and son becomes vastly different — he is now an adult, with the privileges and responsibilities of a man.

From birth, within traditional Aboriginal cultural practices, there is a pivotal place with clearly defined roles for each individual within their collective. There are also expectations and graduated rites of passage rituals to calibrate youth into manhood. Beer, sugar, porn and pubs weren't part of traditional Aboriginal culture — our First Nations people were (are) proudly and collectively Tarzans of their own precious culture and land. Aboriginal people have cared for their land for tens of thousands of years, without the influence of white people. There was no opt-out clause for manhood, nor was there an opportunity to cave-hide emotional wounds, nor to ostrich-jive when wider societal issues emerged.

Calling a Man a 'boy' after initiation is a sign of enormous disrespect. A traditional Aboriginal man who adheres to his cultural norms, who rejects the contaminating influences from the white world, is truly an inspiring human being. He has endured a number of extremely arduous rites of passage markers that would sicken the stomach of most, if not all, white middle-class males. A fully initiated traditional Aboriginal man who rejects the traps of the white world, in my opinion, truly epitomises what it means to be a cultural man — lean, fearless, protective and culturally strong within his collective, seen walking with pride and purpose as he respects his unique relationship with his people, as well as his spiritual connection to his land and customs. If (when) Australia is under threat, it will be strong Aboriginal men who will be at the forefront of our protection — it is with this fact in mind, I say (in advance) thank you!

Discussing Men's Business within traditional Aboriginal culture, is simply that — Men's Business. Therefore, as a whitefella, I'm on somewhat shaky ground in my writing, so I proceed with caution, relaying a few of the very many insights provided to me during my time working and living with traditional Aboriginal people from 2011.

As previously mentioned, many years ago, as a naïve city worker, I relocated from Queensland's Sunshine Coast to live with a mob of special people, the Warlpiri people of the Central Desert region of Australia. Working in an off-road very remote Aboriginal community was a confronting privilege, particularly when I was accepted within the kinship system by being given a Skin name, which assists a white person to integrate into a cultural group for the duration of time in their community. Warlpiri provided me with the opportunity to turn weakness into strength and for strength to be re-aligned to the black way — it soon became glaringly obvious that the white way isn't necessarily the right way!

I slowly began to form an understanding of the way that Warlpiri culture divides people into different social groups called 'skin groups' with each group having a known set of relationships that determine responsibilities and obligations. The skin lines are linked to dreaming stories and obligations such as the relationship, duty and obligation to animals and the land.

Warlpiri taught me about the important relationship between **Land, Law, Language, Ceremony and Skin**. For society to maintain momentum, and function cohesively within traditional cultural norms, there needs to be a seamless transition between relationships. For instance, if Language becomes weak then they will not know the proper terms to address each other respectfully. If Skin becomes weak, social relationship are not being reinforced. Weak Skin means an inability to follow the Law which is important for the rules and responsibilities that are necessary between Warlpiri and country. Weak Law means it is not possible to run Ceremony and without Ceremony it is impossible to understand the rules and ecological knowledge to look after country. When country becomes sick then it cannot support Warlpiri and culture will fall apart — if one is neglected there is a breakdown of culture (refer to *Ngurra-kurlu: A way of working with Warlpiri people, Desert Knowledge, Wanta Jampiginpa pawu-Kurlpurlurnu* by Wanta Jampijinpa Pawu-Kurlpurlurnu (Steven Jampiginpa Patrick), Miles Holmes and Lance Alan Box, published by the University of Queensland in 2009).

While I was living with Warlpiri, I was well aware that cultural matters were not my business, even if, at times, practices appeared barbaric within my small worldview. It was evident that Warlpiri placed a great deal of emphasis on their young men's initiation processes, which varied in extremity, length and intensity — *all* vital for cultural survival. A few of their many practices included 'grabbing' practices from Alice Springs to out-bush male circumcision, payback (cultural justice — sometimes a spear in the leg of the person elected to receive payback) and the vitally important eldership rituals for initiates to be educated in the passing on of vital cultural knowledge, such as dreamtime stories.

As an outsider, it was mostly impossible to differentiate between male rites of passage practices, women's business, whole of family business, sorry business, land-based rituals, law as well as other important collective decision-making such as mining royalty matters and land-grab issues. I wasn't sure how Warlpiri managed to be so charitable to the white world who appeared to be constantly driving into their community uninvited, bombarding them with government expectations, often unknowingly (albeit disrespectfully), interrupting (or attempting to) important rites of passage (and other) matters.

Aboriginal Child-Rearing Practices

The overall way a culture views their babies and young children is surely a pre-determinant for graduation into adulthood? My work with the Warlpiri kids in Nyirripi and Yuendumu and the unique relationships with their parents and grandparents have been amongst the most valuable and life-changing experiences of my life, providing me with a privileged first-hand understanding of the huge differences between black and white parenting practices in Australia.

At the same time, I discovered an interesting report relating to Warlpiri cultural differences, *Aboriginal Child-Rearing Practice: For the Little Kids*, published in 2001, by Pipirri Wiimaku. This assisted me to form a cross-cultural comparison from my Kiwi roots that were linked to over 25 years as an Australian citizen, to avoid imposing my own white practices on a fiercely traditional Aboriginal culture.

Warlpiri, when looking at their newborn baby, do not see a helpless feeble little soul; they view babies as little adults who already have an important role and an important place within their community. A baby is viewed as a pending man or woman within a collective. Babies are born with a Skin name, with expectations around law and cultural responsibilities. For example, baby could be father to his elderly grandfather, which places this child in an ongoing Carer role for their grandfather. A fact largely misunderstood by white workers such as school teachers. This child learns from a very young age the importance of their role, as well as their future cultural expectations. Elders are not treated as 'old people' — they are held in high esteem for important historical cultural knowledge. Elders play a pivotal role with initiates as well as ongoing rites of passage ceremonies.

Could middle-class parents, blindsided in their white ivory towers in Australia benefit from an understanding of Opt-In non-negotiable Aboriginal child-rearing practices? Traditional Aboriginal people are dumbfounded when they hear young people say, 'I don't feel like an adult', 'I'm not in the *mood* today to adult', 'why aren't I adulting yet?' Traditional Aboriginal people remind me that when there are strong cultural norms of responsibility and reciprocation, there is no question of "adulthood".

When Warlpiri kids are small, general learning focuses on teaching through observation, role models and experiment as well as sign language, rather than excessive verbal instructions. As children grow older, listening becomes increasingly important as a way of learning about culture and history. Children are integrated into their environment early and understand the enormity of their responsibility to their land. They are not shielded from life and its extremes. They learn a sense of direction and guided risk-taking from a young age, often within bigger groups as well as important knowledge about their environment and the people in it. Play tends to be rougher and noise levels are not lowered to sleep. Fun is associated with lots of noise compared to other cultures where children are raised with lowered voices and delicately placed in quiet sleeping rooms.

Opposing capitalism and 'ownership', Warlpiri kids are taught from a young age that when they are given something, it's not exclusively theirs or they may be required to return it. They easily share toys, clothes and food and learn within their well-defined family and kinship system who can ask for things, who has equal rights to possessions and who they may be required to give things to. Learning is often observational and group-focused and does not 'shame' the individual by singling out acts of praise. Team sports are an example of collective achievement, significantly easier for those raised in cultures where young men are prepared to graduate through group eldership processes, as well as share the responsibility for their losses and wins as a collective.

Sporting the Mighty All Blacks

The All Blacks are referred to as the most successful rugby team in history, in any code. It's no accident that every team of big, burly blokes since 1903 has won worldwide recognition for their on-field prowess. Analysing the All Blacks' code of ethics reveals that rather than relying on good luck or mere physical ability, this patriotic New Zealand team proudly adheres to a particular language and code that they recognise as their collective, non-negotiable opt-in practice standards.

The fact that an entire small nation is unified in their support both on and off the field all year around, not only just for the duration of a series, is no coincidence. The All Blacks are a way of life in New Zealand and young boys dream of wearing the black jersey with the silver fern. When an overall cultural mindset shines their healthy (and somewhat fanatical!) mana (esteem) and expectation torch on 'their men', it's simply not possible to deter success.

The All Blacks know that being stewards of the future means collectively being a 'good ancestor'. Planting trees you'll never see — leaving the jersey in a better place. How is this achieved? The easy-to-read writing of James Kerr (2013) in his aptly named book, *Legacy: What the All Blacks Can Teach Us About the Business of Life*, discusses the unified language in their *Black Book*, providing 15 winning anchors, maps and mantras as a reminder that winning takes talent — though, to repeat it, takes character.

Character is considered the key trait to building physical talent. Choosing men who are (1) sacrificial and unselfish, with (2) strong working ethics and (3) strong body movers, who are prepared to die for the cause by leaving a legacy, is no easy feat, though considered *imperative* if the team is to maintain their century-long success. Building character traits and psychological strength begins with a brutal opt-in practice-under-pressure regime in order to grow the boy into an on-field winning machine.

Crudely speaking, being part of an All Blacks team means that no one is going to piss in your pockets. A professional rugby union career as an All Black means that you'll be told in no uncertain terms to 'front up or fuck off' and that 'no dickheads' are welcome. You are part of a unique, interconnected national team, where purpose meets strategy, attributed to strategic ground-zero leadership. All players are reminded that they must 'grow or go' and even when you are at the top of your game, 'change your game'.

The All Blacks' infamous ego-busting notion 'sweeping the sheds' has caught worldwide admiration and respect from sporting enthusiasts — whether or not they're shouting on the sidelines for an AB win! Stories of young people *initiating* their own 'sweeping the sheds' by not leaving any grandstand without clearing every piece of rubbish in sight in order to 'leave it in a better place' is evidence of a code of respect for self, others and the land. Reports of tenacious young people duplicating this code all around the world as they initiate their own Opt-In standards, by laying aside ego and choosing to sweep their own backyard sheds, has often left parents in awe.

Bravado, cheers-bro drink-and-sink dependency, laziness and grandiosity will eventually cut you off at the knees with no mercy in an All Blacks team. It will also result in a shameful legacy passed down your bloodline story-line for generations. Anchoring on an internalised framework (collective language) within a tight-knit, fiercely-loyal tribal mentality and prioritising character-skill-de-velopment ensures that 'Better people make better All Blacks', as each player is aware that they are not bigger than the team as a whole.

The transition from ordinary to extraordinary requires death to ego, putting one's balls on the line and ripening character to influence a generation. If the key ingredient to sporting success is character-building through psychologically high-heat intensive physical training, with little time for introspection, what uniform language do the All Blacks elicit for clarity of purpose? Kerr (2013:113) highlights the importance of harnessing the **duality of the Red and Blue emotional states, otherwise known as the Traffic Light system.** When the systematic duality between the Red (dark or fear-based primal zone) and the Blue (militarised, controlled executive system) is harnessed, there is a readiness to uniformly 'flow' on field.

The All Blacks attribute their century-long winning streak and international ranking to the way their 'inner life' is in sync with their 'outer life'. If there's a break in their defence, they head straight back to their core roots by focusing on their Anchors, Maps and Mantras to harness the mind, emotions and body by marrying pressure with pressure. This is evidenced by their readiness to adapt quickly and to know when it's time to reinvent by analysing their defence and repair system — Adjust, Readjust, Adapt or lose. Therefore, adaptation is not a reaction, it's a *continual* action plan.

The 'typical' Kiwi — the working class with their big, bold personalities who rarely shy from provocative debates, their outlandish spooning and forkish humour can quickly turn into a brutal psychologically edgy cliff-hanger movie. Learning is acquired through the school of hard knocks and sensitivity is often seen as a weakness. It's no easy feat for any New Zealander to shut their mouth and learn by 'hearing' their collective ancestral wisdom, that reminds us — to *actualise* we must *visualise* and then we will *ritualise*. A small, proud nation with an underdog mentality — 'on guard' and ready to take on the world.

The heart of New Zealand resonates with their sporting heroes, respecting their many years of excruciatingly painful physical and psychological training that requires the initiate to have sacrificed on the alter-ego of their boyhood years. They've been masterfully crafted into a graduated winning beast, who can hover in mid-air like a golden eagle in the eye of a cyclone. Every New Zealander knows that when their All Blacks run onto the field, like traditional owners of the rugby union fraternity, to begin their intimidating haka war dance of pending victory, each team member has *already* won, regardless of the final score.

Gangs, Guns & Gorillas Warfare

The same way that the All Blacks are synonymous to New Zealand's unique way of life, so too are the many grubby, patched gangs who, at times, hold the small country to ransom with their (often) deadly graduated-rites-of-passage customs often easily luring young males. Tourists experience decadent visual magnificence when visiting the land of the long white cloud — a far cry from the actuality of the sinister underground life in New Zealand, where character is defined at a young age: once one 'picks a side', it's often for life.

Kiwis often downplay the role of male gang initiation practices, evidenced by the large numbers of justified psychopaths who blame their tragic early-years abuse and trauma, on top of a child protection system that did little to protect them nor generate authentic masculinity, as a justification of their home-grown terrorism. The lost boys of the 1960s with their contaminated internal chaos, initiating what has become a seemingly never-ending patched revolt against society, in a bid to remain in total submission to their rage as well as their hunger for ultimate control. New Zealand's gang life is indeed a formidable force.

Most countries fear their evil gang elements and would rather deny than highlight gang prowess or their contribution towards highly ritualised male initiation as well as the overall lifetime membership. Leadership within gang life, similar to authoritarian, no-choice politics and the movements of sinister global elites, is united by money, sex and power. Initiates ignore the cries of warning from the graves of their ancestral roots. Devastatingly, when acceptance replaces feelings of loss or pain, and is jacket-patched within the closed walls of a brotherhood or elevated due to their natural bloodline rights, a sense of solidarity and purpose will always follow.

Gangs, similar to religious-based terrorism movements, share a unified language and purpose with graduated rituals for membership. They provide opportunities to 'bridge' the boy into his new un-adulted broken moral-compass world: as a new patched robot, cannibalised within his own unique digital currency. Gangs often form a cruel brotherhood of purpose that can hold a nation and its police force to ransom, and can *somehow* brainwash their government to donate millions of dollars to their cause. They prowl and scowl like daunting apes of the underground animal world, commanding fear-based gang respect — one only needs a snippet of 'a mob connection' to miraculously feel safe (or unsafe) in their bed at night, particularly within the average North Island Kiwi home.

As a kid growing up in Hastings, New Zealand in the seventies, we were invisible hostages to large-framed, heavily tattooed men in dirty old patched jackets, who were eventually buried in their grubby attire. Their un-adulted gang career had somehow secured their rights as our captors. We lived our lives within their ritualised murder-prison or money-drug-prison-release-torture lifestyles. I remember many nights desperately trying to sleep, forced to listen to the venomous sounds of screeching car tyres as deadly rival gangs were ramping up their ownership of the small dark hours, taking any opportunity to graduate their members into their new stunted adult life. Disgusting vile practices to prove gang-worthiness, particularly to women, even if it meant securing deadly stripes to slither up the ladder of gang-respect. Murder, rape, stabbings, dark alley mob violation, opt-in for life mandates, threats and violations to children, families and workers within the legal system, born 'n bred familial drug-running rackets — all synonymous with gang culture in the land of the shameful dark cloud.

My main ethos was 'if you can't grow then go' — and my main goal was to move out of the tiny inland North Island town as soon as possible. I wanted to find a safer place to live with a police force who weren't seemingly unarmed and 'in bed' with the gangs. I didn't regard myself a victim of my upbringing nor as a victim of gang violence, because where there's choice and an opportunity to visualise then actualise a new reality, the only *dilemma* is around making the *right choice*. When we have choice: we have freedom.

Pseudo-Rituals: Beer, Sport, Porn & Prawn

In the absence of traditional male transition practices or extreme rites of passages, it's more likely that 'manhood' in Australia is synonymous with pseudo-transition practices linked to porn, gambling, beer and pubs. One of the few times you see the words 'rites of passage' on television is when it's time for the annual schoolies' week. Beer and drug-stupor teens roam around the roads and beaches hoping that The Great Adulthood will arrive the day after they sober up from their culturally ritualistic transition-binge-rite.

Beer — the sign of manhood? Men often admit that in their earlier years they didn't even like the taste of beer, nor hanging around in pubs 'talking shit' though they needed to do this to remain connected to their peers and community. These Tarzans of the pub jungle forced themselves to 'acquire the taste' of beer due to societal pressures around maintaining their 'pack', eventually developing herd immunity. Transition to socialisation through beer and pubs — why is it any surprise that it doesn't take long until men agree that they've become expectantly dependent and adequately suppressed — unable to socialise without a form of mind control?

Women complain that men are hiding behind their toys and their dependencies and they are too superficial and robotic in their communication — citing an ever-declining emotionally responsive conversation, particularly when he withdraws to his man cave. At the same time, men complain that women over-focus on emotion — both theirs and hers. Men describe how drained they feel as women continue to exhaust them with their tangential personality disordered behavioural patterns and high expectations that far exceed their male counterparts' ability or motivation to change. Nor is it easy, men plead, to remain focused or connected to the large *range* of topics within these frantic conversations. Gray (1993:71) cautiously points out in his acclaimed book, *Men are from Mars, Women Are from Venus,* 'Men crave trust and respect and when this is in short supply, it's wise to never go into a man's cave or you will be burned by the dragon'.

No Sting, No Survival

Pollinate or Perish!

Albert Einstein once suggested that mankind would only last around four years without our bees. We're incredibly reliant on our little stingers for our ecological survival as well as our genetic diversity. Their vital life-cycle role for plant pollination within our society cannot be underestimated. In fact, globally nearly all seeds need to be pollinated. Poor pollination creates environmental stress such as climatic changes, persistently dreary weather patterns, invasive species, pathogen and even loneliness in the absence of flower clusters, particularly when too spread out.

When our dream songs are strangled within the confines of the isolated walls of the home-based interior and the external environment is shut out, pollination is simply not possible. If pollination practices continue to decline, the art of turning boys into men will be lost. Losing our youth to an incestuous form of self-imposed mind control will eventually kill the plants of opportunity that youthful bees were once industriously pollinating — creating sustainable food chains for population growth. If our youth are in early retirement villages located next door to their older folks' retirement villages, rather than pollinating their purpose and upholding our societal right for protection, does that not leave our society as unpollinated lambs to the slaughter?

Society is in loads of trouble when our young people lose their sting. When they stop dreaming. When they stop talking like fiery action-machines alongside their passion-on-steroids conviction. Today, many young people appear sad, lifeless and 'entitled', with their purpose hidden somewhere deep inside their wardrobes. I miss seeing youthful fiery-eyes darting around a topic during a social event, refusing to give up their future focused passion topic, like a bloody annoying bee-in-a-hardhat — leaving one gasping, albeit incredibly inspired, after hearing their conviction and truth.

For our future focused young people who have their sleeves rolled up — are we listening to their growing wisdom as they talk from their hearts? Are we hearing their generational warning for our planet? Young people see, they hear, they feel, they're given prophetic messages for our generation. Their feet are listening and they want to walk in their truth — like the apostles of the first century. Are we adopting and role modelling defeatist modern stagnation language or are we listening to their eagerness, their seemingly crazy ideas that oppose ours and their battle-cry concerns, even if we'd rather be chewing on our own arm than humbly listening? Captain, you must LISTEN!

Modern Anti-Social Language

The Undermining of our Social DNA?

Calling ourselves 'modern people' does NOT mean we need to adopt modern language and call it our own! Under the elusive power of suggestion and permission, the use of language can make or break us. Keeping up with the crowd by the use of modern language is surely a foolish way of travelling through life — like calling ourselves sheep *and* lambs to the slaughter?

Is the over-use of defeatist language that is not currently challenged, providing answers to the enormous rise of previously socially adept individuals who are now calling themselves socially withdrawn or 'permanent shut-ins'. Can we learn from countries such as Japan, who report an estimated one million sufferers who have shut themselves in their bedrooms and remain so for years, or even an entire lifetime? 'Hikikomori' (as per the Oxford Dictionary) provides a unified national noun to account for the alarming number of locked-in sufferers and their families who are struggling to cope with this devastating and debilitating reality.

A Japanese mother (name withheld) now an advocate and a public speaker on the topic of Hikikomori, the 'shut-ins' recalls standing with a knife beside her son's bed while he slept, as she contemplated murdering her son and killing herself. Her homicidal-suicidal intent was attributed to the chronic shame she felt, raising a son who she once labelled 'of no use to the world'. A culture where relentless expectations around education and career choices creates humans with chronic inferiority, who turn to the safety of their bedroom and devices by locking the world out. Many are unable to *ever* re-emerge into the public space.

Regardless of our past, current or future-projected 'social self', post-2020 finds us ALL living in a strange new world. We've lost much, changed much, grown in areas that we didn't think were possible and disappointingly grown down in other areas. We've become cynical and mistrusting at the same time as grateful for our blessings. We are passionate at the same time as dis-passionate — or we've simply dug our head in the sand.

Post 2020, a time when friends have turned to foes, opinions haven't always been welcomed, our styles of communication have altered and our humour has become rather awry. Many have simply taught themselves how to 'just get through' social events as a way of still respecting their host. Whether we are vaxed, vexed, un-vaxed, no-more-vaxed, no-care-vaxed, pollie dis-believers, believe in our Feds and our climate alarmists or we are not at all bemused with the musketeer-takover… there has *surely* never been a better time to join the madness, the sadness and the realities of our new world — rather than succumbing to the overall cultural undermining of our social DNA?

Social risk-taking is an opportunity to build emotional resilience skills. Are we now living in a world of complexity, confusion, deception and betrayal where socialisation is fast-becoming exercised by only the brave? A world where we can easily become broken by our brokenness. A world where we are learning to increase our avoidance of pain, as we reject the wiles of the poisonous pit viper that threatens our comfort and cannot be charmed. When we reject our community and let others or the home environment protect us, like a riled black mamba snake, whilst our conscience slithers around like a defeated king cobra, we turn backwards in our development to a life that resembles the very young.

Eradicate or Stagnate

NOW! Is the time to begin to re-build our social nutrients, while we all accept, we're a tad 'socially awkward' as we face the next stage of our Aussie future. In years to come, this time in history will be microscopically studied — we will represent the *forced-to-jab-under-trial vaccines* and the *forced-to-socially-isolate under imprisonable mandates*, generation. The period in history where one day, the topic of viral invasion and social isolation (and the effects of) will be discussed in classrooms and researched by our grandchildren and great grandchildren.

Socialisation is a learned behaviour

Have we become a new generation of adults (post-2020) who have 'unlearned' our previous flexible social skills? Have the last few years resulted in a somewhat forced synaptic weeding and pruning of our social self, resulting in a skeletal butchering of our social garden? Is it time to take back the years the locusts have eaten?

For our species to survive we must focus on our socialisation skills, not on our ability to deprogram our social brain — after all, who wants a species of robots or medicated fakes? When the media generationally norms our reality through the use of trendy acronyms (as elaborated below), this has the potential to undermine the social DNA of our whole culture. Media — you MUST stop, in fact ... fuck off! with all your publicising of new labels — you have no right to elaborate potential secondary conditions such as chronic social withdrawal, as if they are part of our new future. In a world where we are all just trying to survive — to keep ahead of debilitating illness or to simply put food on the table, why do you need to reinforce social withdrawal as if you have a licence to pathologize through sensationalism?

The Stupidity of Acronyms

The morning television show, *Weekend Sunrise* recently discussed or 'imposed' the atrocious new acronyms in town — introducing anti-social HOGO (Hatred of Going Out), presumptuous FOMO (Fear of Missing Out) and selfish JOMO (Joy of Missing Out). Collaborated by a dried-up old white, upper-middle-class celebrity, who is now all cashed-up hanging out in retirement after an admirable, high-profile career, now appearing to have nothing else better to do than reinforce new social-decline labels to our younger generation. *Supposedly*, this has been verified by empirical studies and interviews with thousands of citizens who tragically agree that they have no intention of changing their current (new) socialisation behaviour. Older people teaching the younger generation that it is okay to give up on our social-self, particularly when we can hide behind fancy new labels and remain uncommitted to social invites.

Has the proverbial YES now become a 'Maybe' or a cruel 'NO', assessed on the day of the event, based on 'so, how do I *feeeeeeeeeeeel* about going to the event?' The hatred of going out (HOGO) or the joy of missing out (JOMO) is often partnered to the fear of missing out (FOMO) evidenced by the way we choose to stay safely tucked away at home, regardless of the disappoint-ment that others suffer due to our choices. Selfishly, FOMO's report relief that they are still receiving social invitations, which reinforces their social standing and their perception of likability, particularly if this mindset maintains a future re-launch pad *if* they change their socialisation story in the future.

How tragic that thousands are resonating with their HOGO or JOMO as they transition through the next stage of their life by enjoying the relief associated with invitations to events, though happy to decline by not showing up in lieu of prioritising their feelings rather than the host. Surely! the three new anti-social cousins HOGO, FOMO and JOMO do not deserve a place in our language — chuck them out of the ring rather than letting them form an acceptable, selfish, brat pack alliance that has the poten-tial to dethrone the fabric of the Aussie culture.

Kindness and generosity are a choice. When we prioritise our negative feelings, over the prioritisation of the Joy of Others (JOO) or the Joy of our Social Self (JOSS) and decline an import-ant event, we are saying that the hosts are not important enough for us to risk discomfort. We are also saying that we do not value the potential for social gold to boost our emotional functionality — placing a higher value on the currency of 'avoidance'. When we elevate Discomfort, we Devalue our hosts. This is nothing short of a cruel, socially bankrupt economy, that will eventually increase the potential for FOMO and a bunch of secondary mental health and physical health conditions.

Let's turn the heat up on JOSS and JOO by respecting the potential for productive chemicals that oppose selfishness and promote happiness. Being the first one to leave an event is no sin, it's an indication that you have done the very best you could in respect of the person/s holding the event. It shows you cared enough about you *and* your host to turn up to the event, *despite* your discomfort. Even years later it's common to hear an appreciative 'thank you *so much* for coming' to a major event or milestone, reinforcing the 'loved up' chemicals of the people who instigated the event, particularly when the organiser was well aware of the sacrifices incurred by their guests.

Hospitality business owners are increasingly publicising their shock and disappointment as well as their 'financial crippling' due to incredibly large numbers of people not showing up to events, with hundreds of cancellations occurring at the last minute. Although unforeseen circumstances are inevitable, the rise of people who freely admit that they have no real excuse other than 'not feeling like it', is disappointing. Memorable occasions such as weddings, anniversaries, decade birthdays, graduations or just the simple Aussie barby are a way of celebrating the good times in life as well as the achievement of others. So why is 'turning up' on the serious decline?

When we are engaged in a self-reported rupture/repair cycle with HOGO, FOMO and JOMO, the after-event stage of the cycle often finds the event-disappointed person/s *forced* to deal with or appease their invited no-show counterparts' overarching feelings of guilt. How is this fair? So, why wouldn't our FOMO fears eventually come upon us as we morph into the new 'missed out' community during the next round of invitations?

In summary, our young people are an indication of the overall 'health' of a community at any given point in time. Though, when our role models, leaders and our older men 'give up' on the young, it too affects the spiritual umbrella under which a society thrives. Get involved in men's business, old guys, we still need you and *we* don't believe that *you're* a waste of time and that society should give up on *you*! Stop sipping on your café lattes in your local Blackrock Café with your robo mate Al Aladdin and Mr Elon-Gates and be the parents, leaders and loved ones that you are destined to be.

Impact of Christianity

Please Note: Reader beware! The next few pages relate to religion and Christianity. Nouns are used interchangeably such as pastor, spiritual leader and senior church leader. If this section is offensive or irrelevant, please jump ahead to Chapter 6 — The Financial Formula.

If Jesus teleported himself back to Earth today and had a chat with our generation of pastors about their role of growing boys to men, I wonder what he would say? It appears that the revolutionary, Jesus-style, feet-washing humility and strategic grassroots community development that opposed capitalism, notoriety and glamour is barely visible these days, let alone focused on male social withdrawal.

Before the state took over the role of welfare, the church *was* the social services. The church was once an instrumental part of a community. Churches knew the needs of their congregation and how to love their community through acts of service and charity. Faith-based families also once knew *how* to give and also when it was time to receive, as ultimate masters of the principle of reciprocation.

The gospel message, one of relationship *not* of rules, was once never watered down. Discomfort-to-grow was an expected and intentional part of preaching. No pressure, no growth. It was once impossible to walk out of church without the hairs on one's back standing to attention, after listening to preaching pumped full of Biblical conviction. You were never alone in your conviction or your intent, as you knew that your pastor was living and walking the preach, with Sunday simply the icing on the cake, not the main event. Reliance on the integrity and grit of young men was a given, with legacy and dying for your faith once considered the generalised norm of a Christian.

Today, church online platforms post-2020 has meant that the little local senior church leader in the little local church is now opened to the global stage, creating a whole new breed of neutralised, polished preachers who have moved from local platforms to worldwide acclaim — without the need to interact with actual humans. Have church leaders become their own socially withdrawn community, irreversibly linked to the not-for-profit conglomerates, easily cowering to government socialist or communist policies, hiding from their congregation and now living in their own deep state of despair?

Discussions between modern parents and pastors from Christian churches regarding the topic of growing boys to men suggests that there's a perceptual mismatch between the role of the church and the role of the family. Talking with active faith-based families reveals that the role of the church has a big part to play in growing their boys to men. This conflicts with discussions with senior leaders who deflect back to the family or junior (and volunteer) members of the church, suggesting that their role is far too 'generic', therefore 'they're not "able" to focus on one particular developmental stage'.

Could these perceptual mismatches be due to a decline in 'caring intelligence' causing senior leaders to lose their connection or people-skills, despite Luke 15 suggesting that the shepherd sometimes needs to leave the ninety-nine and reconnect to the hurting. Or does this scripture suggest that it's actually the *Shepherd* who has 'lost' relationship — or is it easier to elevate the shepherd and continue to blame the one who is seemingly lost?

Direct message to senior church leaders — Have you ever made an enquiry as to the levels of social retreaters (young people and adults) in your congregation or community? Do you see Sunday attendance as a reflection of true congregation numbers and motivation? Do you view your role as action-caring or as an inhouse coordinator with Sunday your main event?

Research suggests that the most effective way that social retreaters re-enter their community is through sharing their experiences with other sufferers, therefore the local church could surely provide a valuable role in creating a safe place, an overall awareness of the plight of the recluse (or addict) as well as ongoing group support? Many homebound individuals, caught in unfortunate cycles of social withdrawal and addiction admit that although they're struggling to leave their homes or cope within social interactions, they still regard their faith, their church and their church leaders as important. Many would like to interact with their mentors, though shame and awkwardness have broken through their firewall and are now clear barriers in terms of their perceived ability to initiate contact.

Many dearly wish their pastor was a mind reader and would take an interest in their life. As we are aware, brokenness can be temporarily incapacitating, though when we are back on our feet, we are often eager to 'give back' as a form of social reciprocation, creating a positive pay-it-forward ripple effect throughout an entire community. Is it fair to assume that the pastor from the pulpit has reneged his role within the Swiss Cheese Layer of male hurt and/or transition practices? Is this an acceptable practice? Or is it time for leaders to 'go' back *out* to the church to action their love. You know, like the old days, Jesus-style?

I remember sitting in a church service as a visitor, listening to the senior pastor of a large Sunshine Coast Church, shocked at the congregation's raucous laughter when he admitted he doesn't actually even *like people* and was glad that his role meant he could deflect pastoral care to his staff. I surmised that if people aren't his thing, then young people aspiring to church leadership roles as a stepping stone to the 'real world' of responsibility would be best under a pastor who values the notion of 'caring' rather than behaving like a heartless King and calling his church such.

Is it fair to assume that these days, it's hard to find a senior pastor who will humble themselves to home visit (or even tele link) with young people, particularly those they haven't seen within the church walls or youth group for quite some time? Nor, would they likely even know the names of those struggling with social withdrawal, assuming they've 'gone astray into the world'. Are excuses such as global health pandemics, mandates, 'too busy' and fancy titles now allowing leaders to hide behind their church desk?

Senior spiritual leaders, I urge you to exercise humility and consider the pain-behind-closed-doors community and clothe yourself with your multi-coloured Cloaks of Care and reach out, rather than leaving pastoral care to your administrators or other members of your team, particularly non-paid members. Keep in mind that sufferers of severe or long-term social withdrawal (generally) do not have the confidence to initiate support, nor will they likely suggest this to their parents, partners or loved ones. There are literally thousands of services held each week in Australia, attended by families who routinely flock together to enjoy their rituals, while their socially withdrawn young person (or partners) remain at home. The decline of males in your service may not be a reflection of lost faith, it may be a reflection of lost-in-bedroom-space with no caring pastor in anyone's face!

We must remain sensitive and reach out to the large numbers of individuals who have become a Priest of their bedroom, worshipping their emotional pain, becoming abstinent in their relationships and narrowing their vision of 'self' within their emotionally addictive walls of hell. Their emotional pain decreases their ability to display compassion for the suffering of others outside their world – a world where they would desperately like to return to one day.

In the early days, parents chat to their friends after the church service, boasting about their young person's 'V-Plates' as some sort of successful pro-virginal, anti-sex, faith-based parenting style winner. When talking with the same parent 10 years later, their child-man's V-Plates are now the topic of sadness, as well as his lack of transition and appetite for risks and love relationships – now talked about as a 'fail to launch'.

Has the media's justifiable exposure to the horrific ramifications of sickening deviance, alongside power imbalances and unlimited access to vulnerable people, frayed confidence in the proverbial church leader as a safe, caring role model? If there was ever an institution to highlight financial mismanagement, negligence, deviance and lack of consequences, the church is surely close to the top of the list. Though, in reality, there are thousands of genuine pastors and incredible churches all around Australia, as well as thousands of passionate young people who are active within healthy church life and eager to action their faith in their community. Remember that the 'health' of a church lays within the walls of acceptance as well as their out-reach to ALL their members not simply to the 'unchurched' or left to the social services industry.

Is it fair to suggest that the average pastor resembles a politician, located in their hard-to-reach ivory towers of protection, with their polished, scripted stage performances, backed by their cameras or trendy bands and singers? Often drawing on a watered-down *barely uncomfortable* Biblical notion of simply 'just ask and you will receive' that sports the new generational norm of 'Me-ism'? With an increased focus on capitalism and comfort, it seems easy for the church to increase their request for money, as long as the message *decreases the notion of discomfort and sacrifice*? Right? Wrong? It's not hard to wonder whether Christ is-OUT of the local church rather than Christ-IN?

Message to the Fat, Blobby Church Leaders

Emotional addicts?

For all the hundreds of pastors around the world who respect their calling and are doing a brilliant job, our community says 'thank you'...

It's nothing new that society craves the role of credible, strong leaders. An effective leader is one who regards themselves as a humble 'servant' with a defined calling, who knows their giftings, and, at the same time, seamlessly walks alongside others (not just their bloodline) to reach *their* potential. Although a leader is often centre stage, they thrive best as behind-the-scene givers. A leader is naturally drawn to the role of calibrating childhood with adulthood.

So, if callings and giftings are real, as well as the arduous years spent qualifying and walking in your relationship with God and your ministry, where does the pastor bloke with his big, fat belly, blobbing around the stage, in a large body mass of blubber fit with the story? You know, the pastors who *continually* joke about their 'belly fat' — to the sound of raucous laughter from their congregation, though are not prepared to action their truth, growing larger due to privilege and gluttony as the years roll on?

Let's compare my challenging or seemingly scathing remarks about our spiritual leaders, to the apostles of the Bible who were tough, lean warriors — who *all* eventually died for their faith. I wonder what they'd say to the blubbery pastor who is likely nothing short of a high-functioning food addict, as he proceeds to remind the church to maintain their faith, to get rid of shameful addictions, deal quickly with their unforgiveness and change their 'bad habits' as a reminder of the rewards in the heavens. The Sunday congregation pretend that their leaders' gut doesn't resemble a 'bloated beer belly', strangely blaming middle age as the culprit, rather than the possible truth that their senior bloke is struggling to button up his oversized shirt each week, possibly due to beer, packaged food, porn, sugar, addictions or Netflix?

In true double standards rhetoric, if a woman has curves and bumps and more to hug than what she'd like to — I say ... celebrate all that you are and all that you continue to become. You are a woman of your God, a kid of the King and a mighty warrior princess. In comparison with your male counterparts, your body from your teens has endured countless years of monthly bloating, nausea, swollen breasts, hormonal mood swings, stained under-garments, financed 34+ years of blockers, coped with contraception-medication, reproduction, baby feeding, sleep deprivation, dozens of costly bolder-holders and styles of clothing reflective of your size at the time.

Your grand finale begins with the internal flames of menopause, finishing somewhere 10 or so years down the track, when your true authentic self is expected to turn up — why would you *not* call yourself a curvy warrior princess? And, when *you* decide it's time to trim and slim, *you can* and you will because you have trained yourself from your teen years to face discomfort, to sacrifice and to achieve your goals.

In some cultures, big fat men were once considered to be the rich elites — food meant wealth, unlike millions of their starving peasants scarcely finding enough food for their bloated bellies. I'm not sure what the current cultural beliefs around obesity are, though our medicos would more than likely predict shorter life expectancy, and an array of health hazards. Middle age for men, therefore, is surely an excuse that suggests — I eat because I can?

Men of God, stop your hypocrisy and start acting like Jesus and his mates of the Bible. Turn off Netflix and stop playing with your secret socials and your online platforms, and turn back to your community and please re-assess your role of mentoring boys to grow into their intended adulthood. You are well aware that your medicos are sick of warning you about secondary conditions that will reduce your opportunity to fulfil your calling — your heart attack on stand-by, your early diabetes and spine problems are all but a few examples of your sugary attempts to eat away your stress and take your finger off the heartbeat of your congregation and community.

Pastors, is it time to face up to those red flags of privileged neglect that you have imposed upon your body — and to practice what you preach? Do you need professional assistance with addiction or will you refer to your book of wisdom for guidance? We agree when you remind us that 'it's how we finish the race' — so, what is *your* legacy and what is your commitment to authentic masculinity?

Leaders — can you answer these questions?
- What would Jesus say to you today about your focus on male transition?
- What is your commitment to the socially withdrawn members of your congregation?

- Are you concerned about your belly fat?
- Has any medical professional indicated concern for potential secondary conditions?
- Does your partner know all your passwords and can read all your socials?
- Are you prepared to action your double standards?

Stepped Aside for Nepotism

Many a promising young person, often an impressive wounded healer, has made enormous sacrifices, gained qualifications for church ministry and stepped up into adulthood with their calling. Humbled by their unique gifts, ripened for their go-give-feet-washing action-verb calling. At the same time, they nervously watch the pastor's kid (PK) grow up. Eventually PK 'comes of age' and is naturally elevated through the leadership gradient due to their bloodline rights, like the son of a King.

As we are well aware, when there is a lack of reality-based rites of passage markers and speedy career elevation through the bloodline of the senior pastor, it often weakens the authority gradient within church collegiate relationships, effecting the overall functioning of a church community. The ordinary battler (clearly called for the work) must step aside and exercise humility when in the presence of the chosen one.

Nepotism, a dubious and often destructive bloodline elevation currency, ripe for social capital bankruptcy, suggests that superiority is ordained from a birth*right* rather than through the blood of the lamb. It's often more than obvious that PK has been elevated into a role that was never ordained specifically for him, while the 'stepped aside' community suffers enormous emotional torture and lost dreams when they are informed that they are no longer wanted (though, clearly still needed). PK is unlikely to have experienced longevity within the non-faith world that requires repeated job applications, job interviews, job rejections, challenging bosses, annoying colleagues, initial low remuneration and slow escalation through the ranks, while the heat is turned up as a way of grinding his ego with his skills.

Initially, PK simply becomes an extension of the pastor's ego and an opportunity for the boy to work side by side (without interference from even a thin Swiss Cheese Layer) yet still remain as a kid of the father-boss-spiritual leader. Though, with all its grandiosity, PK eventually wakes up to the responsibility of nepotism, aware that they are now an easy opportunity for his father's quick get-away, particularly in the face of adversity and media attention such as in the stark reality of devastatingly poor earlier years decision making.

PK was too young and far too inexperienced to have adopted a Coastal Hazard Adaptation Strategy (CHAS) that analyses hazards such as coastal erosion, storm tides and sea level rises in order to reduce his own risk, as well as understand the depth of pain for the victims left behind in his father's wake. Afterall, why wouldn't nepotism increase the opportunity for secrecy, criminality, disastrous decision making and less financial transparency — particularly in the presence of gag orders and other family members who are employed in strategic positions such as law?

Gagging — a temporary gain, resulting in a lifetime of pain: truth is our legacy. The father-pastor who has elevated his bloodline to directly take over his dynasty is surely risking the sins of the father visiting his son? How does the son protect himself from the decisions of his father, if the Swiss cheese layers of accountability are thin, controlled or too weak? By the time the son cries out 'Houston, there's a problem', he knows he's simply been a lamb to the slaughter, his ministry forever tainted by the past choices of his elder, the ancestor of his children.

Bring Back Competition!

Has the white middle-class male been dethroned?

The only group in society *not* considered a 'minority' — the white middle class male with their once majority rule over the minority masses. Society was once in constant 'class' friction, attributed to the privilege of bloodline nepotism that provided certainty of wealth, assets and power. These days, with the rise of powerful global conglomerates, alongside the decline of family dynasties and fragmented nuclear families who continue to cultivate 'boy-ism' mindsets through tech addiction — has the game of life now become an odd type of evenness within the Australian culture?

I believe that life will always stop making sense when males abdicate their right for competition, purpose and full participation within their culture. Life will always stop making sense when young people form deep love-relationships with their addictions and devices that cause them to deviate their attention from the stark realities facing our era.

Device-hooked humans are beginning to resemble zombies in mind-locked bodies — has transhumanism arrived without the need to even brain chip our thinking? Undoubtedly, device-relationships have improved our technology intelligence, though our weak spines, obesity, myopia, shoulder and back complaints and ongoing migraines mean that most of us would barely pass Day One of a physical regime test.

Global elites are well aware that forms of mind control and home-grassing will reduce our ability to move forward as a society — when one group of society is at-risk, is this not a direct threat to our country's overall security? We desperately need our young people and their family systems to wake up, to participate in life through the principle of reciprocation and to rigorously oppose the incapacitation rule that has been imposed upon their life.

Chapter 6
The Financial Formula

Chapter 6 turns theory into action by reiterating the importance of equality and reciprocation within adult relationships — introducing the agent of growth: The Financial Formula. Reciprocation is a *learned* behaviour, reflecting our ability or genuine intent to *engage* in the act of two-way giving and receiving. Reciprocity does not require emotional analysis or assessing our energy levels or even motivation. **Reciprocity is a choice — followed by an action.** When role models neglect to teach this important principle, it sends very clear messages between givers and receivers.

When financial comfort forms the base for the lack of reciprocation, there is a clear dis-enablement message that sounds something like, 'If an individual has a lackadaisical or wealthy benefactor, then they are eliminated or isolated from normal contribution and other expectations that would otherwise be expected or imposed upon the rest of the population'. Therefore, the individual's behaviour is determined by an internal belief system that suggests — wealth creates special privilege.

The ways in which we 'give and receive' vary according to religion, culture, roles, capability and desire. In many families, love is considered an action verb rather than an emotion — there is a genuine commitment by all members to action their love through daily physical acts. The cyclical wheels of give and take enhance family cohesiveness and induce developmental growth, allowing the opportunity for *all* members of the system to balance work, rest and play.

The Principle of Reciprocation

One of the basic laws of social psychology is the principle of reciprocation — the response of a positive action with another positive action, a type of reward system for kind actions. When this system is flourishing, it is suggested that people naturally increase their kind acts and are more likely to be appropriately reactive to the needs of others. American sociologist Alvin Gouldner (1960) was the first to identify the existence of a universal, generalised *norm of reciprocity*, warning that the only members of society exempt are the very young, the sick or the very old.

The norm of reciprocity requires that we repay 'in kind' what another has done for us. This makes reciprocation a relatively powerful method for gaining one's compliance and building lasting relationships: at the same time as creating healthy hostility when there's an interruption to this system. Studies reveal that when individuals act within reciprocal frameworks, it has a positive ripple effect within all their systems, therefore they are less likely to behave selfishly when acting in other social contexts. Embedded principles of reciprocity such as 'pay it forward' also have an impact on our workplace productivity, played out in our commitment to collegiate relationships, organisational goals and the 'happy chemicals' associated with actioning our purpose.

International relations and treaties recognise the principle of reciprocity as benefits or favours generated by one country to another country, or the citizens of one state to another state, with the intention that they are *returned in kind*. Institutions such as democracy and capitalism can coexist when mixed with healthy cultural norms that enhance reciprocation and moral decency. When a country breaches the principles of a treaty, they can expect sanctions imposed upon them at the same level as their intent to disrupt the principle of reciprocation, particularly in the face of recognised leadership operating from a base of pure evil intent.

Our home environment provides us with our earliest opportunities to learn and participate in the principle of reciprocation, governed or witnessed by the behaviour of our parents and other role models. Our elders as teachers of our give-and-receive consequential behavioural system need to provide us with opportunities to action our relational intent both inside and outside the home environment. Are you thriving or are you merely surviving within your systems?

Reciprocity-deficiency in otherwise capable adults regresses our adult social skills as evidenced in an overall self-centred narcissistic system of take 'because I can'. You only need to look at the weeds in the gardens, the messy lawns and the overflowing washing basket alongside household members who have excessive time on their hands to know what type of system is currently in operation within your household. Why would *any* parent want to raise their children within a reciprocation-deficit parenting model that grows and festers unhealthy narcissism? A deficit model will always stagnate our opportunity to 'adult' (or to even *begin* adulting) and it will have a profound detrimental impact on the relationships around us throughout our lifetime.

Social Gold

Our social gold are the powerful chemicals we experience when we are actively engaged in quality relationships, which differs markedly from those disappointing experiences when friendship-kindness is not reciprocated. Although the roots of many friendships are often based in an imbalance of circumstances, most over-givers know that eventually one-way friendships sour or fall into a pile of rubble — a type of scorched earth compassion-fatigue.

Thankfully, for the socially astute, the reliable 2-way intimate bubble from our close connections means that we are buffeted from disappointments: a type of social kindness risk mitigation. When the principle of reciprocation is rocking and rolling, we are thought to be maintaining the seamless flow within our relationships, keeping our connections sexy and well-oiled, eliciting a range of mood-enhancing neurotransmitters, such as serotonin, dopamine, endorphins and oxytocin.

Regardless of our upbringing, role models or unique circumstances, there comes a time when the individual is living in an adult's body and must make their own choices. Constantly blaming others for not teaching us *how* to reciprocate reduces the focus on self as our own agent of give and change. One-way giving between adults usually continues until one party is *busted* for their lack of integrity, or one party *breaks down* such as emotionally, physically, psychologically or financially. What is *your* giving-receiving style?

Is your give-take system different within your other systems such as your workplace, education, peers or recreational groups? Do you engage in a democratically balanced system that entices equality within the home environment, which will, in turn, benefit the community or others? Are you an ideal one-way altruistic giver, with nil expected return for your kindness? Does your system only function in the presence of threats such as eviction or withholding privileges? Has there been an exhausting or coercive rupture-and-repair cycle that has been in place for many years?

Do you continually live in hope or faith that indeed one day the people in your life will somehow magically grow a conscience and return in-kind?

It's no secret that children are hard work, from their newborn beginnings until their emergence into societal adulthood at 18 years. Once adulthood arrives parents are suddenly forced to release their power and control and sit back and watch their offspring transition into the real world of unrestrained choice. Will they stay at home in their bedrooms or will they recklessly party on the Visa? Will they become addicts with their binge drug-drinking? Will they be responsible with their new cars or will they remain expectant of 'the good life'?

While our adult teens are enjoying their new sense of freedom, they are often still living in the family home and failing to comprehend the enormous commitment parents continue to provide towards their life. For tertiary students, the government expects parents to continue to fund their offspring (even with a combined income of 'fuck all') and remain financially committed to their adult children until somewhere between 22 and 25 years, depending on the policies of the day.

So ... we are now living in a society where young people can enjoy their adult freedoms from 18 years, take without giving, whilst parents automatically continue to give and give, hoping that the day of reciprocity will eventually arrive as they wait for their children to become independent.

The good news is that the day of reciprocation has arrived! The bad news is that if parents have not taught their children the VITAL principle of reciprocation or encouraged effective time management skills, financial management and work ethics before the age of 18 years, there will need to be an urgent systemic interruption. The key point is that young people who are studying or working or bouncing back from primary trigger events are never excluded from the principle of reciprocation within their home environment. They are waiting to be viewed as an adult, to be spoken to as an adult and to participate within their home environment as an adult. Is it their fault role models still view them as children?

A perfect storm is an opportunity to flip the script. If young people are not naturally participating in the overall principle of reciprocation by 18 years, it may be a reflection of *learned behaviour* rather than a character flaw. The word 'storm' does not mean anger, it reflects a major 'dilemma'. A dilemma means *choice. Therefore,* the focus of change must be off one person and placed on the family system as a WHOLE (please discuss risks with professionals or authorities before proceeding with change).

Is Altruism Reciprocation?

The *Oxford Dictionary* describes ideal altruism as selfless concern for the well-being of others for no reward or recognition. Pure altruism is a one-way street such as putting others before yourself, whether you have a tie to them or not. For example, voluntary work with the elderly or disabled for no reward or recognition. Reciprocal altruism is a sense of giving with limited or *minimal* expectations for future potential reward, compared to reciprocal actions that only that occur *after* the initial action or instigation of generosity by another party.

Parents often describe their sheer utter exhaustion at the end of their primary parenting years as they recall rewarding moments with their offspring, at the same time as the tiresome never-ending one-way street for many years. In the absence of cognitive impairment or other *major* factors, it is assumed that within healthy relationships at least basic concepts such as the Golden Rule of treating others as you would like to be treated and Mutual Goodwill, will be present and thriving. In other words, there will be a genuine desire or at least a growing ability to be working *towards* balancing the giving-receiving exchange by eventually *returning in-kind* those benefits to ourselves, others or our community.

When delving further into this topic with parents, many appear 'nervously hopeful' that their *now* adult children will in turn repay in-kind and become genuine employees, healthy partners and generous parents. Parents *hope* that their altruistic parenting acts will, one day, benefit others and society in general, even if *they* still feel emotionally and physically depleted. Though, is *hope* enough, particularly in the absence of role modelling and clear evidence of natural reciprocity during adolescence? Is it possible for an individual to seamlessly instigate the principle of reciprocation when they transition into their new adult systems such as love relationships or as colleagues? Or, unbeknownst to others have household members acquired a character fault from their earlier years that sends a clear message of future non-intent that sounds something like ..... 'I have an exclusionary clause on reciprocation'.

Cleaners (another example of our unsung heroes, those wonderfully professional gold bombers who leave our homes sparkly) are now increasingly citing how disturbed they feel when they are repeatedly asked to clean inside heavily-addicted adult Boy in a Bedroom's filth. When asking (otherwise capable) Johnny to kindly exit his room while the cleaner can attempt to decentise his room, he treats the cleaner with distain at being asked to pry himself from his devices while the cleaner is left gagging at the stench that is somehow their responsibility to neutralise.

Many cleaners are now refusing to clean the bedrooms of permanent bedroom dwellers and report interesting (and sometimes heated, other times highly embarrassed) discussions with parents (or partners) realising that this is possibly the first time the topic of the regressor's behaviour has reached the public space. Some cleaners state that they are not interested in being pseudo-parents in lieu of enablers who are too afraid (or not allowed!) inside a bedroom, nor are they enticed with 'I'll pay you more money' as they know their services are already in high demand with easier and more respectful jobs. Have our cleaners become our frontline voices of wisdom for enablers?

Perfectionism and Dictatorship

Young people constantly report that their parents' household standards are far too high. They believe they are living with either perfectionists or within a dictatorship system, which is the reason they don't participate in reciprocity within the home environment. They often view their parents as super humans with standards that seem impossible to reach, such as the Sergeant Major who cannot rest until standards are likened to an army barracks. Where perfection resides, procrastination will flourish.

Young people are often mistaken for being lazy and disconnected to the realities of routines and provision, though can actually be experiencing anxiety or low confidence in their ability to maintain an adult standard. When discussing this concept with parents, many *totally* agree that their high standards are an 'issue', at the same time as admitting that they can't bear the thought of living in a home with reduced standards. If adults are not prepared to moderate their standards to at least 'reasonable', they are unlikely to establish a foundation for reciprocation.

Perfectionism is the enemy of 'good'. Optimally, adults who focus on developing *life skills* (wisdom) through discomfort to grow opportunities by altering their standards to at least 'reasonable' (by sacking the dictator and the perfectionist) will eventually enjoy improved relationships within their home environment.

Young children who are constantly yelled at during dinner time, or yelled at for not managing morning routines or screamed at for not completing household chores or educational deadlines are at risk of developing anxious relationships with the morning, food, chores and study. When young people constantly 'hear' anger and nagging from adults, they will not only experience a sensory overload, they will develop protection responses to adult notions — behaving in a fight, flight, fright response system. This means that, from a young age, they train their primal protective brains to be switched to an ON-guard state, ready for the battle (fight), or on-guard for avoidance (flight, fright) in a war that they know they have already lost.

Young people respond best to healthy consequences, rather than focusing on a 'chore-care-system'. An assertive adult message that relays a non-negotiable 'no chores, no iPad' outcome sends a clear message. This is particularly powerful when younger children complete tasks 'alongside' adults until their routines or reciprocity becomes a natural part of their lives.

Parent-trapped couples of long-term social retreaters often plead to their counterparts to teach your kids how to delay gratification by role modelling *how* to participate in the principle of reciprocation from a young age. The era of hedonism within the home environment, where children are treated like Kings and Queens must stop! Whether a monarchist or a republican, the fact is, reciprocation and hard work was once a gen norm within the Aussie DNA.

The entire globe recognised the work of the Duke of Edinburgh in 2021 when he passed, still working and serving a few months shy of his 100th birthday. Our esteemed Queen Elizabeth II in 2022 passed away soon after she turned 96 years, seen on television welcoming her new Prime Minister only two days before her death after serving for 70 years as the longest working monarch in history. The only time our Queen took a break was when her health forced her, otherwise she worked and served. Our Queen superseded the legacy of her paternal great-great grandmother, Queen Victoria who served for 63 years. Royalty works and serves — so, why the *fuck!* are modern parents decreasing their contribution expectation and pretending their children are protected royal members of society?

Are you treating your adult children like a non-working or barely-contributory King or Queen? Plenty of parents have informed me that they truly believe their son or daughter was indeed royalty in another life. Regardless of our views or beliefs of who we believe we were in a previous (or next) life, we must not lose sight of the FACT that in *this* life we are all unique and vital and that we all need to fully participate in society for the cycles of life to thrive.

Boarder, Please Go

Imagine welcoming a boarder into your home. They pay one figure which covers rent, food and utilities. Initially the arrangement works really well. A 'nice' sort who works full time, pays in advance, even helps out around the home and doesn't mind doing the lawns occasionally in their spare time.

Unfortunately, a big shock stressor occurs — their relationship with the love of their life ends abruptly. They're understandably miserable and begins to withdraw from usual activities as well as changing normal routines. Though, rather than healing from their relationship wounds, your boarder begins turning to maladaptive coping strategies and regularly calls in sick for work. Initially the boss is understanding, though, it's not long before strange behavioural patterns emerge such as roaming around the house at night and then feeling too tired for work in the morning. Eventually your boarder is sacked — exacerbating their wounds.

Your boarder is now at home 24/7 and doesn't appear to be making any changes nor bouncing back from the shock of the break-up and sacking. They get behind in board with promises of 'catching up soon' for a grace period of a few weeks. They continue roaming around your home at night like a prowler. The power and food bills soar and there's no offer to assist with chores, which is surprising considering that they now have more time on their hands.

6.1 — Strategy: Adjust or Go

What would you, your partner or your friends suggest would be appropriate to do at this stage?

Write down your answers before proceeding

1. ____
2. ____
3. ____
4. ____
5. ____

Initially you may treat your boarder with respect, displaying empathy, compromise and generosity as you move towards 'bottom line' discussions. You might refer to the contractual agreement or maintain an 'I owe you' system. If nothing changes, as well as taking advice from your tribal truth, you would be forced to move to an eviction mindset — or even involve the authorities if your boarder remains in your home past the agreed date. As we are well aware — a boarder and a landlord enter into a mutually beneficial arrangement — until circumstances change.

Why would any parent neglect their role in teaching reciprocation and knowingly prepare their offspring for a life where they may be leper-ised and regarded as 'takers' as such as 6.1 above? Are you treating your adult children like free-boarders? Are you teaching them that when they experience a major hurdle it's okay to behave as self-entitled leaches? How will this transfer to the next place they live in after they've left home? Our young people often pay a huge price for long-term care bombing.

The Financial Formula

$350 Per Week every week

The breakdown of the Financial Formula is considered to be a moderate-only figure equalling $350 per week, attached to a debit/credit system.

If an adult is living in a household with providers who are largely covering the bulk of the living costs, the contributory figure of $350 per week is extremely low. Therefore, any figure under this amount is considered to be a catalyst for regression and an unrealistic adult system — unless of course the individual has severe (diagnosed) limitations or disabilities.

$100 per week board is a juvenile system

I've lost count of the large number of adult children who inform me that only paying $100 per week is the equivalent of 'living at home for free'. They TOTALLY agree with the $350 per week formula, though they admit to being 'highly unmotivated to change' a give-take system that provides them with a cash (or other) advantage! Furthermore, they admit $100 would likely only pay for a couple of days of their food or one night out with their mates. Many young people have looked at me right in the eyes with their sparkly smile and said '$100 is total bullshit and when I'm a parent there's no way I'd put up what I'm doing to my parents'.

This is in total contrast with parents' sense of pride that their loved one is being responsible by paying $100. Come on! Let's agree that $100 per week is not an adult system. Many enablers justify 'yes-but we're helping them to increase their savings', 'yes-but he's at Uni', totally oblivious to the juvenile system they've created, and the invited recklessness of increased cash for drugs, parties, brand new cars and other self-indulgences. You only need to raise this topic with indulged adults who have been living at home long-term, to hear their resounding agreement and stories of overdoses, criminal charges, addictions and bankruptcies to know how serious this topic really is.

The Financial Formula — Example	
200	Rent (leases, mortgage, bond)
20	Utilities and Insurance (power, water, land, car/house/contents/life insurances)
100	Food
30	Generosity (computers, devices, social media, transportation, asset depreciation, petrol, use of family assets/car)
350	**TOTAL**

If you have been blessed with financial wealth and you regard your young person's financial contribution to the family budget as unnecessary, I encourage you to consider the thousands of families in Australia who are currently living below the poverty line. Maybe you could do a 'drive by' tonight and see how many people are living in cars and parks in your local area and how many are losing their homes due to escalating interest rates and rental prices. Please give or donate, rather than dis-enable our younger generation, particularly if they are living like royalty as a seemingly warped bloodline right of privilege.

By completing the below questionnaire and reading the $350 weekly formula you have made the first step. Ask yourself – 'On what planet could I live on for only $350 per week and receive the type of lifestyle that is being provided to me or my loved one?'

Contribution Formula Questions

To be completed by the main providers within the family household.

Yes/No or N/A (not applicable)
1. Is your son or daughter under the age of 18 years?
2. Is your adult son or daughter living independently (without your financial assistance) in their own home/rental?
3. Are they working full-time? If yes, skip to 4.

    A. Are they regularly (weekly or fortnightly) working part-time for wages?

    B. Are they regularly (weekly or fortnightly) working for cash?

4. Do you know their earnings and what is in their bank account?
5. Have they been paying the same rent or board weekly without default over the past six months?
6. Have you seen documented evidence that they are completing University, TAFE, or other online studies such as recent course results and pay slips?

> 7. Are they connecting with peers or others weekly outside the family home?
> 8. Do they participate in their hobbies and interests outside the family home regularly (eg. every 1-2 weeks)
> 9. Are they completing all their household jobs daily, without prompting that equals the financial formula of approximately $350?

If you answer No to more than three questions, it is likely there is a process of regression and lack of reciprocity within your household.

Financial Formula Rationale

All capable adult members of the household are considered to be full contributory members of the household, regardless of their actual income. Adult students and workers are more than capable (or at least working towards) juggling study deadlines, cooking, washing, paying bills, chores, maintaining their own costs for running their own car, equally participating in relationships, raising children or caregiving for sick relatives.

Rent - $200 (less than general market)

The figure of $200 is a basic-only figure, unlikely to reflect the current cost of accommodation. The word Rent is important as it separates living costs, rather than a 'rounding up' of daily living into one overall figure.

Utilities and Insurance - $20

The figure of $20 for Utilities and Insurance is token only, barely reflective of the true costs of all utilities and insurances incurred on a weekly basis.

The topic of Utilities and Insurance is one that many young people would like parents to have discussed with them when they were younger, such as the ramifications of nil car insurance, exorbitant power costs such as the overuse of air conditioners and hot water. Why do we pay Council land rates? What would happen if rubbish wasn't collected? Do we take street lighting for granted and the way parks are magically maintained?

Food - $100 (groceries, beverages, costs of animals)

The figure of $100 for food is token only.

Young people who have not had opportunity to personally learn the value of the rising costs of food, or to regularly purchase groceries, or to fully complete the groceries-cook-clean-up process report feeling ill-equipped when they leave home. Very few young people raised in middle-class families have experienced a skeletal fridge or hunger pains! This is often one of the reasons they return back to the home of Mr and Mrs Bailout within six months of leaving the family home.

Budgeting means we are considered, planned and sacrificial. Single people suggest that they spend on average $150 per week on groceries, which does not include cafes, pubs, takeaway coffees, alcohol, restaurants, medications, vitamins and other hobby items. Some estimate their additional costs at around $200-300 per week.

Generosity - $20

The figure of $20 for generosity is a mere token amount.

The generosity category includes items that are taken for granted, including: family dinners out, wear and tear on the family home, vehicle costs, clothes, pets, therapy, holidays, updating technology, gardening, mowing, painting, upgrades to the home and so on.

There are thousands of adult children (and partners) living in privilege well into their twenties, thirties, forties and fifties who are unaware of the financial and emotional strain others are experiencing whilst providing their generous lifestyle.

There are also thousands of people living in comfortable lifestyles who are not initiating nor participating 'in kind' such as cooking, dishes, vacuuming, cleaning and washing — nor do they venture outside to assist with lawns, washing cars, renovations, painting or even weeding. Why would there ever be even one weed in the garden when there is an individual who is permanently at home?

Checklist - Implementing the Financial Formula

- Purchase Meeting Book.
- Prepare suggested Agenda items to discuss at first financial meeting.
- Refer to Chapter 7 — Moving Forward, and Chapter 8 — Family Meetings for ideas.
- In preparation for the financial meeting — write a list of all areas involved in the running of your household.
- Provide bank account details for all adult family members to begin immediate weekly/fortnightly rent payments.

Reality vs Secrecy

Many enablers are highly motivated for change, though they balk at the topic of financial privacy, suggesting that all household occupants have the right to their own privacy. If an adult is fully dependent on one system, surely the providers of this system have every right to know how that person spends their money as well as the dependent's plans for participation in the Financial Formula?

Privacy in our modern world is fast becoming an anomaly.

Does privacy now even exist in our modern world where our data is now the new gold? Where our every move is now tracked or traced? A pending new world order where even the last private frontier of our being (our brain) has technology that can (and intends to) computerise our thoughts? What do we say to the bank manager when our full financial history is required in order to secure a new loan or mortgage? Do we tell the bank to just hand over our new loan rather than breaching our privacy? Banks are increasingly becoming privacy no-care bombers, requesting every micro detail of our budget and spending history. They fully scrutinise our spending habits, assess our credit history and they are well versed as to how often we breathe or fart!

In terms of instigating new family systems of reciprocation, many parents report initial fears (with some becoming unduly distraught) at the thought of upsetting their children (or partner) as well as chronic fears of 'not being liked' (friendship parenting). They believe that due to long-term social withdrawal and/or addictions, change is now unlikely to *ever* be possible ('he's too damaged'). Others fear that they will experience hostility or disrupted relationships, including partners walking out of the relationship. In the absence of abuse, we must continually remind ourselves that the lack of belief in another (otherwise healthy) person's ability to participate in a system of reciprocation is not only a tragedy, it is a bankrupt economy.

Changing our notion of conflict means that we stop avoiding discomfort and increase our focus on resolution. The *Oxford Dictionary* describes healthy ways of viewing an argument: when two or more people express and validate their ideas through discussion: to dispute an argument based on the facts or evidence means to think about the action and decide on who it's most beneficial to.

Participating in the Financial Formula without an Income

Participating in the $350 per week Financial Formula requires creativity and an open mind. In the absence of employment, and the presence of other competing interests, there is still no exclusion clause from full participation in the Financial Formula.

All capable adults are responsible for fully reciprocating their existence. To do otherwise is participating in a self-centred system of 'take' that requires a cruel entitlement mindset and a lazy desire for comfort that is funded by others (low empathy individuals). *In-Kind* contributions can include a combination of financial and physical contributions that equals (at a minimum) $350+ per week.

Non-income-earning family members can participate in this adult system by *negotiating* their $350+ per week contribution, for example:

Taking over role of washing clothes	$150 = washing, hanging, folding, ironing
Groceries and cooking 3 meals	$150 = purchasing, preparation, dishes
Weeding	$ 50 = agreed area — ongoing project
$350	

6.2 — Strategy: The TO-DO List

List all TO-DO jobs such as renovations, upgrades, water blasting, painting, repairs, gardens, rubbish removal and other neglected jobs. Add to the Meeting Book or attach to fridge.

Role modelling or developing new systems takes time, as well as dealing with initial frustrations, such as waiting for clothes to be washed, dried and folded.

Word of Warning:

- **Abusive behaviour** — At NO time is ongoing abusive behaviour acceptable. It is your duty of care to protect all members of a household at all times. Child protection is everyone's business.
- **Involving others** is considered a major step forward. Change requires breaking patterns of shame and secrecy.
- **Professionals** — Canvass practitioners who are willing to work with (1) the individual, (2) the whole family or (3) couple-counsellors.
- **Keep the home base safe** — Avoid bringing practitioners or strangers to the family home without all parties in agreement. Home retreaters can regress further if they feel emotionally threatened. The home is their sanctuary and most are unwilling for a swift water rescue by strangers.
- **Respect bedroom** — Do not invite a practitioner or stranger into the bedroom of the long-term social withdrawer. This can have a catastrophic effect on progress as it can be perceived as an invasion of privacy. The bedroom may be the only place that the family member feels safe or has any sense of control.
- **Barriers for change** — Every member of the family has barriers for change — what are yours?

- **Threats of eviction** — Long-term social withdrawers do not respond to threats of eviction, particularly in the absence of employment, transportation or other accommodation options. *Threats to exclude* as a form of tough love, can cause further regression and overload a fear-based system. This can cloud the opportunity to negotiate: turning into a survival-only system.

Excuses and Reality

In the early days of change, it becomes glaringly obvious how ineffective and demoralising over-giving and constant care bombing is for ALL parties who are caught in a cycle of dependence. Physical decline due to extensive over-giving often manifests *at the same level* as someone who has underworked for years: physical deterioration and lowered immunity are the result of over-giving or underworking.

Most young people (under the age of 35 years) are adamant that when they are parents themselves, they will not let their kids get away with what they have gotten away with. At the same time, admitting that in the earlier days their manipulation, half-truths, alarm cards or minimisation of reality created an unfair advantage, placing parents in a no-win situation, such as citing severe financial hardship, suicidal ideation, addiction and prodromal states.

When the social retreater is aware that they are loved and that there is no direct threat of eviction, they often admit that they've been secretly *waiting* for enablers to increase contribution pressure. Many home dwellers are very resentful of their enablers despite the comfortable lifestyles provided to them for so many years. Rather than taking responsibility or verbalising their gratefulness for financial provision, they initially report a *deep loss of respect* for a system that has caused them to regress.

An adult is an adult, not a child. Temporarily take the baby photographs off the walls and replace with adult memories. Remember that the home environment provides the best opportunity to grow by increasing discomfort. Only then can we regain life skills, maintain routines, increase confidence and develop empathy.

Lazy Partners of Over-givers

Dependent partners often disrespectfully refer to their over-giver as someone who is letting them 'live off the pig's back', or who is 'choosing to be superhuman'. They are *well aware* that their moral compass is defunct, though secretly hope they will not be expected to return to the workforce. They often refer to their overworked partner as 'too demanding' such as when they walk in the door after a hard day at work. The at-home layabout feels insulted or even victimised particularly when discussing notions of reciprocation. As we are well aware in our strange society, it's very common for takers to believe that they are the eternal victim and to masterfully deflect blame in order to maintain their status quo.

Surely, we can agree that this is a form of domestic abuse, when otherwise capable people *still* expect to live off the pig's back - even when their working partner is diagnosed with chronic illnesses? The taker hopes insurances and income protection schemes will still cover the family costs as well as the lifestyle they are now accustomed to live. A chronic lack of reciprocation is rarely considered a form of domestic abuse, or part of a domestic violence cycle. Come on folks — abuse is abuse!

Sadly, when faced with pressure, many change-resistant takers often decide to talk with their legs and seek an alternative 'pig's back to live off'. This can be a hugely demoralising and emotionally fragile time for the person who has given until they're at collapsing point. The introduction of online sites has made it easy to become a predator, with the over-giver soon replaced with a younger, wealthier or older version — who, of course, soon becomes the next victim.

Opting-in to The Financial Formula means that the Bank of Mum and Dad (or a one-worker system) has now closed. You have opened an account called Reciprocation, which will operate within a debit-credit system, in preparation for the realities in our ever-changing world. Participants of the family system are all fully aware that life costs and all members of the system hold equal importance. **Life is Expensive — $350 every week from now on is the new family culture.**

In summary, Assertive Adulting is the middle state between a Child State (mood-driven hostages) and a Parent State (dictator or martyr). An Assertive Adult is fair and bold and does not focus on mood to dictate an outcome. An assertive adult is prepared to view *all* adults as adults. They are fully aware that the only time in our lives we are in our Parent State, is when we are parenting children under the age of 18 years. All adults (unless otherwise impaired) are capable of participation in an adult system of reciprocity.

Chapter 7
Moving Forward

Recovery Action Plan (RAP-it!)

Less Talk, More Action

Chapter 7 invites the whole family system to break their patterns of regression and move forward *together* by actioning the strategies (and highly repetitive themes!) offered throughout my writing. It's no secret that the transition from childhood to adolescence is one of the most significant adjustments for families, with many feeling ill-equipped at times for this arduous journey, particularly the final stage of adolescence — the adjustment to societal adulthood from 18 years. Young people inform me that they wait years for adulthood to arrive, a time where the adults in their life have less say in their decisions, though when they reach this milestone their 'adult self' is nowhere in sight.

Leading Japanese research suggests that the average age for social withdrawal onset is 15 years and the average age to begin therapy (if at all) is 19 years which represents a four-year time lapse, resulting in most losing their jobs, not attending educational institutions and not experiencing love relationships.

Many middle-class families can afford to hide their truth. For other families, particularly single-headed households, a social retreater or parasite single would constitute a financial disaster.

Has wealth become the great inhibitor for young people to transition to adulthood?

Mothers often report that their son's return to the family home (or his lack of transition from 18 years of age) provided her with something to do, avoiding the empty nest syndrome experienced by many of her friends. Sadly, while Mum was initially getting re-acquainted with her son and felt useful, she didn't realise she had morphed into her new permanent roles as Employment Officer, Worry Manager and Chief Martyr, whilst her son or daughter had signed a contract called 'No Power Over My Destiny'.

Stages of Withdrawal

- **Early Withdrawal:** 1-3 months — early intervention and prevention measures recommended.
- **Chronic Withdrawal:** 3+ months — Urgent need of intervention. Risk of developing secondary conditions.
- **6-12+ months:** highly urgent disordered state — an illness requiring intervention with the whole system urged to participate in a recovery plan. Keeping in mind, for long-term social withdrawal to exist there has been a long-term partnership of dependence — *the whole system is unwell.*

Major Transition Markers for Young People

- Transition between primary school to high school
- Transition between high school and tertiary education or employment
- Transition from education to formal employment (particularly full-time wages)
- Transition from home to independent living

Psychiatrist Dr Tamaki Saito (translated by Angles: 2013:117-130) reminds us that withdrawal is a desire for dependency therefore breaking these patterns is often very slow, helping a person through the maturation process all over again — starting with unconditional love. Respecting fears at all times is imperative in order to avoid further exacerbation of this serious condition.

Any change (even small) is likely to elicit a stress-response unless managed well. Volatile communication risks exacerbating the state of withdrawal such as mental health and physical health conditions, sometimes leading to hospitalisation or involvement with government first responder services. Therefore, it's important to remember that communication can be toxic unless it is a two-way connection based on *respect*. If we are talking 'to' rather than 'with', we are engaging in a dictatorship.

> **Moving Forward — be part of the solution ...**
> **not the problem**

The first stage of learning is silence
The second stage is listening (Kerr, 2020:110)

Respectful Communication — Avoid Blame

Slow, steady, empathetic and respectful communication cannot be underestimated. When individuals understand that they will not be the central focus of a targeted approach and that their direct needs remain safe, they are more likely to engage in a change process. Most of us have watched cringe-worthy television programs whereby a 'family intervention' model was forced upon one person who was told to sit in the 'hot seat' and then forced to listen to 'what went wrong' or 'what needs to change'. *This is NOT acceptable, particularly for those in long-term social withdrawal.*

For enablers who believe they have made genuine attempts to move the family forward, though your words have been falling onto deaf ears — please understand that this means your integrity has not been received as genuine. In other words — your words are not believable! You may be entrenched within a never-ending Rupture/Repair cycle — with your pleading simply heard as though 'swimming under water'. Thankfully the family meeting process (Chapter 8) provides a democratic system for all adults living in such a system who are prepared to move forward together.

It's important to avoid triggering a sensory overload. Verbal communication must not be loud, obsessive, repetitive or with undue pressure, particularly when an individual has not progressed their general living skills and they have been held up at home for an extended period of time. Start with a respectful tone and line of enquiry. Expression and tone are important, as well as avoiding attacks, blame-gaming, criticism and put downs. Take every opportunity for communication and maintain basic greetings, even if initially ignored.

Avoid Unfair Topics & Comparison To Others

It is vital that there is no comparison to other siblings, same-age peers or others. If your loved one is behind relationally (younger emotional age in comparison to their biological age) there is no point 'wishing' otherwise. Additionally, avoid discussing unfair topics that have no relevance in the present, such as getting married or buying a house. Gravitate to safe topics such as world affairs or topics relating to past areas of success.

Develop Interest Areas

Establish interest areas by *gradually* increasing the range of topics and opportunities for conversation.

Anticipate conversation starters even if they seem simple, ordinary or trivial. Maintain an interest, as well as a desire for communication. Empathy means developing an understanding of the overwhelmingly confined world of the sufferer. Humour is important, though may be in short supply during the initial months. It's important not to be offended if this is the case.

Communication outside the bedroom is important, even if the family member is inside the bedroom. Respect the young person's bedroom. At all times, avoid powerful, controlling, demanding, condescending or superior language.

Secret Grudge

It's important to understand that, although there's been a long period of dependence on each other, it does not mean that *inner fragility* has been communicated within the family system before this time. Working towards increased communication for participation in the family meeting process often means the occasional bomb explodes on to the public space. Saito (2013) suggests that one sign that you are Moving Forward is when the Secret Grudge hits the public space or the Dumping Ground becomes messy.

Although truth-bombs, as a result of pent-up frustration over a long period of time, are not always easy for the recipient to hear, they can be an indication of a major step forward as well as increased confidence *(this does not include forms of abuse)*. Although there's a limit to parents or others taking all the blame or being unfairly 'dumped upon' for extended periods of time, particularly when personal responsibility is in short supply (and truth is skewered), this process can provide the base or foundation to move forward.

Assumptions & Anchoring

There may be a pattern of avoiding or denying previous positive stories and achievements. Keeping in mind that these happy chemical stories are often filed or hidden away subconsciously, though down the track can become highly retrievable (refer to strategy 1.3 — Anchoring).

In time, communication moves to a 'reflective/accepting' style and meetings become a natural part of life, with every member speaking freely from their *own* perspective without unfair assumptions. After all, we know that to *assume* can make an ASS out of U and ME! For example, 'he doesn't *want* to work' rather than the actual *truth*, which may be that the long-term social retreater doesn't actually *believe* they have the *ability* to work (laziness vs self-worth).

Discussing topics such as the principle of reciprocation (The Financial Formula) is best left for the family meeting or a copy of the Financial Formula has been provided to all members to read in their personal time. Keeping in mind that the longer the withdrawal period, the more likely there is a significant change of value in systems such as the relationship between money, relationships and assets. In other words, there may be a genuine dis-association with values such as work-to-eat — 'You let me regress so you must want to provide for me?'

The Social Media Tribe

The topic of Social Support Networking (refer to strategy 2.2 — SSN) may have altered from previous social practices. The Social Media Tribe may be the new 'community' given the way that social media has formed hidden new social communities. If so (outside of reportable criminality) this means that the social withdrawer *has* actually maintained a sense of connection with the outside world, even if it's a highly secretive form of tribal community (often with no face-to-face or verbal contact linked to the notion of 'friendship'). These underground or virtual connections may need validation, rather than disrespecting the sufferer who may perceive their community is being judged. This 'community' may have been their main (or only) form of social support for many years.

Refer to the below list of strategies as a preparation for the Family Meeting process.

A-Z – Prevention & Intervention Strategies

**If you're not growing anywhere
You're not going anywhere (Kerr, 2020:101)**

A. Adult language

Household members who are 18+ years of age are adults. Treating a child as a child is solely dedicated to 'child-hood'. Unless significantly impaired, each member of the household is responsible for progressing *their* adulthood. Invite adults to be part of the family meeting process. All members agree to talk to each other as adults, replacing words such as 'my baby and 'our boy' with suitable pronouns and nouns such as Man, Woman or my adult children (refer to strategies 1.5; 1.8).

B. Bedroom is for sleeping ONLY

Theme: Decreasing bedroom dependency

Creating a bedroom 'for sleep only' can take time. It is important to ensure boundaries are crystal clear and well negotiated without bullying or threats of eviction.

Colour, music, sound, light and smell impact our mood. Our interpretation of sensory information sends signals to our nervous system. For example, light makes contact with the retina of the eye and our hearing produces pressure waves. If we spend considerable time in a toxic space that lacks light or disconnects us from our environment, our life will eventually reflect this. Soul-destroying gaming, music or dark, dreary colours and wall decorations with toxic images will do little to enhance a positive view of the future. Improving our life often starts with focusing on our senses.

An adult changes their childhood toys and lives in a room that induces sleep and serenity in order to fulfill their purpose. Is your adult son or daughter living in their childhood bedroom? Do you walk into your bedroom and feel a sense of calm and peace that induces sleep? Is there a seamless connection to light? Do the pictures on the walls reflect positivity?

Long-term social retreaters often live in bedrooms that become disorganised and full of clutter, whilst other bedrooms are minimalistic and highly ordered with obsessive rituals associated with exit and entry. Although the long-term bedroom dweller has likely found a great deal of comfort and protection from their bedroom, pending change can be frightening. Therefore, it's important to discuss changes well ahead of time such as moving into temporary rooms or other accommodation. It's important to discuss the property market and future possible downsizing options related to ageing realities *well ahead of time.*

7.1 — Strategy: Spring Cleaning

Spring cleaning was once a *thorough* yearly event and all rooms of a home were deep-cleaned, sometimes repainted, carpets cleaned and all clothes and items re-sorted with unwanted items donated to charity or binned. Discuss plans for a complete bedroom spring clean (or wait until the family meeting). If the bedroom dweller is in paid work, discuss them paying for cleaning and other costs. It may be time to upgrade furniture or swap bedrooms as they begin developing the skill of adjustment.

7.2 — Strategy: Storage & De-clutter Boxes

Leave boxes outside the bedroom as it will give the bedroom dweller autonomy to take responsibility for their own bedroom overhaul. It's important to keep nostalgia such as photograph albums or maybe re-frame important milestones and memorabilia. Reminders of past success or awards can assist the individual to view positive aspects of their past.

C. Change Book (Meeting Book)

The Change Book (Meeting Book) provides a paper trail of family decisions and future planning. The Change Book is not intended to be managed by one person — it is a democratic system and belongs to all members of the household system

7.3 — Strategy: Change Book (Meeting Book)

Purchase a blank exercise book (preferably hard cover) to reflect pending new agreements for systemic change.

D. 'Dilemma' is an opportunity to speak into the future

When we sack the react-ionary word 'problem' and adopt a Dilemma mindset, we begin to speak into the future (refer to strategy 2.3). The *Oxford Dictionary* describes the word 'problem' as a thing that is difficult to deal with or to understand. This contrasts with the executive word 'dilemma', which means we have a choice between things of equal importance. A Dilemma provides our rational brain with the opportunity to visualise *movement towards* a solution-focused action.

Constantly thinking and problem-solving for others is saying that we believe the other person is incapable of handling a situation without your assistance and lacks a belief in a person's ability to adult. 'Walking alongside' is a caring partnership between adults that suggests .... we are doing life together, not '*for*'.

Examples of dilemma-focused sentence-starter language:
- 'Correct me if I'm wrong' ... 'I'm assuming that' ...
- 'What's your game plan?'
- 'I think I heard you say ...'
- 'Let me know if you need any ideas ...'
- 'Your room is being renovated — let me know your plan' (eg. couch, other room, temporarily moving out).
- 'Do you need another listening ear/advice or have you got this?'
- 'I imagine you would have probably felt... disappointed/frustrated/confused/ when ....'

E. Employment — working to eat, rest and play

Superannuation and Secret Retirement — Reality Checking

Secret or early retirement is exactly that! If we are not participating in regular income-generating activities nor building our superannuation nor providing evidence of our earnings to those who are providing the main source of income for our survival, we are likely secretly retired, or we are choosing to remain unemployed (*This doesn't include those raising children, caring for the sick and elderly or those with clearly defined roles where both parties are in full agreement as to the division of labour*).

Household members who are choosing to remain unemployed, such as parasite singles (or partners) who have no other reason for non-action other than laziness or the belief that they are 'owed' the luxury of non-participation, not only break relationship trust, they decrease their skills for the future and reduce their overall participation in society. At this time in our history, there are literally hundreds of businesses around Australia facing bankruptcy due to nil availability of workers. The number of suicidal farmers in this country is utterly devastating. This point is nothing short of a disastrous indictment on our society.

Dedication to our Business Owners

Outback communities are the backbone of our country, often situated in extremely harsh climatic and geographical regions trying to cope with constant natural and manmade disasters (floods, famines, fires, changeable government policies, cloud seeding, land grabs and mining interruptions). Our big, burly farmers who generally have a no-frills approach to life, are labouring to their early deaths (including alarming levels of suicide) and yet, there are thousands of otherwise able-bodied people at home, who are not willing to relocate to low resource areas, nor are they willing to participate in a society where the *desire* to work was once a normalised part of life.

Our Employment Minister is currently launching a campaign in an attempt to move young people from the youth allowance to their local working world by contacting each of the 'suspect' 122,000 recipients individually, admitting that 'people can't just sit under the doona'. Is it fair to suggest that any parent who neglects to teach their 'at home' offspring of their country's harsh working realities, must take responsibility for the part they are playing in the overall decline of our society?

Has the luxury of home-based over-nurturing become a new un-adulted Harbour Town? While we leave our salt of the earth employers floating around on their own desolate islands, are we harbouring our capable young person and agreeing that $50 board per week or only working part-time is 'good enough' for their adult offspring? Do enabling adults need to hang their heads in shame — or is it easier to continue to pathologise and focus on individual responsibility?

2021 Newspaper and television headlines:

'Restaurants close because Aussies refuse work: Battle of the Bludge.'

'Aussies avoid the hard work.'

'They have managed to barely scrape through the pandemic lockdown but the state's restaurateurs and farmers are now faced with a new threat to their livelihoods — lazy Aussies.'

'Eateries are being forced to close several nights a week due to a lack of willing workers.'

'Restaurants going bust with bludging: Welcome to Lazy Town.'

'Popular Sydney eateries are being forced to turn away hundreds of customers and close several nights a week due to a lack of staff, while orchard growers are watching their businesses wither on the vine — literally — because there are no temporary migrants here to do the work that unemployed Australians are refusing to do.'

'Without the staff I'm turning away about 200 people who want to eat here a week.'

'I'm getting to the point of begging people to work.'

'You put an ad out in the paper for bar staff or kitchen staff, and you try to organise trials and some don't even turn up.'

'About 220,000 overseas workers left the labour market between December 2019 and March this year.'

'A lot of visa workers went home and 10,000 jobs a week are advertised in our industry. We want to employ Aussies but we can't because they're not applying.'

F. Forgiveness: victims of abuse

It's common for victims of abuse to hide their secret pain by behaving in anti-social behavioural patterns for years, despite the supportive relationships around them at the time. The biological age at our trauma point can sometimes stop in its tracks as the primal brain has been forced to jump into a protective 'survival' mentality. The alluring call of the bedroom offers safety and security, buffering historical abuse from disclosure.

Analysing our past within the context of our boundaries and our pending future can provide us with an opportunity to purge our internal pain, as we 'hand over' the cruel behaviour imposed upon us by others. Forgiveness is considered one of the greatest acts of self-care (Refer to the U Curve of Adjustment and Grief & Loss Mapping in Chapter 2).

It's important to validate the enormous impact of abuse and the bravery associated with disclosure. Disclosing past abuse sometimes occurs during family meetings, particularly when the sufferer feels emotionally 'safe'. Loved ones are often shocked when disclosures of abuse are externalised (prompting counselling outside the meeting process). We must salute our broken as they bravely climb out of the pit of their pain and begin to slowly move forward. We must also be aware of the shock and broken hearts of loved ones when they realise how long their loved one has been suffering in silence.

Bullying is one (of many) examples of abuse and costs our country multi-millions of taxpayer dollars every year. The numbers of victims are not declining. This includes bullying within the school system from primary school to high school; within the workplace, peer groups or anywhere else 'entitled' people roam. Many workplaces throughout Australia provide free counselling for their employees under their employee assistance program (EAP) including free counselling for family members (face to face; telephone or video).

G. Ground Rules

Ground Rules are brief action verb statements that guide the way we participate in meetings. It is important that each member of the system participates in the formulation of Ground Rules and adds such to the Change Book before the first meeting or during Meeting 1. Please keep in mind that social retreaters can be HIGHLY sensitive to the changes around them and they may not have participated in a meeting process for quite some time (or ever). The fear of change or exposure is very real considering many have been suffering in silence since the onset of their primary trigger event. Your biological age at the time of the initial trigger may now reflect your current emotional age. For example, a 30-year-old may feel closer to their trigger age of 15 years. Therefore, communicate to the 15-year old whilst still *visualising* the 30-year-old.

7.4 — Strategy: Establish Democratic Ground Rules

In preparation for the first Family Meeting, consider the below list of potential Ground Rules (or transfer to the back of your Meeting Book).

- No blaming.
- One talking at a time.
- Opt In: There is no Out Clause.

- All members have an equal right to share their opinions without interruption.
- All members are now in a process of change.
- There may be an increase or decrease in household responsibilities.
- There may be changes to the bedroom environment.
- Me Statement: Each member agrees to write ... 'It's important that you know this about me' into the Change Book/Meeting Book. For example: 'It's important that you realise that I'm very embarrassed', 'it's important that you know I'm at breaking point', 'it's important that you don't tell me I'm an addict, I'm aware that I have a problem in...'
- *Boys in Bedroom: The Prison of the Mind* — I agree to highlight relevant sections of the book that I have been unable to communicate to/with you. Keeping in mind that this book is NOT an opportunity for enablers to highlight the faults of others. It's about owning your *own* thoughts, feelings and behaviours.

H. Health Checks

Living in a body embedded with long-term toxic stress hormones disrupts our life rhythms. It is highly recommended that Physical Health Checks and Mental Health Assessments are completed. Seek medical clearances prior to beginning a family change process.

7.5 — Strategy: Health Checks

After booking and completing health checks, complete your own mental state examination (MSE) by analysing your relationship between your appetite, sleeping patterns and energy — your answers will give you an indication of your overall current mental health.

1) Appetite/Diet — erratic? reasonable? three meals a day? use of suppressants or stimulants?

2) Energy levels — fluctuating? flat? hyperactive? Wake tired?

3) Sleeping patterns — erratic? poor onset? wakeful?

Messy Life Rhythms — mood turned to a deep brood?

It's no secret that disordered rhythms of life such as changes in our sleeping and wake patterns can have a catastrophic impact on our mental health and our physical health. Once our rhythms of life are disordered, our energy levels are messy and we can begin to feel anxious, depressed, irritated, exhausted or hyperactive. It's easy to begin to alter our perception of life as we grab for emotional blockers to manage our slippery emotional life (refer to Chapter 1).

In order to boost the functionality of our brain circuitry system we need enough melatonin in our system to sleep and enough serotonin in our system for our daily energy. By focusing on the sun, our diet and our sleep patterns we can avoid our mood turning to the brood. For our 24-hour sleep/wake circadian clock routine to be highly effective, a simple daily morning walk for 15-20 minutes or even standing outside in our nutrient rich environment every morning will significantly improve our melatonin-serotonin relationship.

There's a plethora of informative professional writing discussing balanced lifestyles, such as internationally acclaimed Dr Michael

Mosley in his books, *Fast Asleep* (2020:149) and Just One Thing (2022) as well as Cooper (2009), *Overcoming Bulimia Nervosa and Binge Eating* (2009) who encourages the reader to use language such as 'meal planning' rather than 'diet' and to avoid fixating on weight and addictive exercise or distraction patterns.

Mosley's use of metaphorically rich descriptors to explain the link between our brain circuitry and our gut health (psychobiotics — the mind-gut connection) is fascinating. Creatures live in our gut which affect our microbiome and the way we function in our daily life — in terms of our brain, body weight, appetite, cravings, energy and our immune system. So! If we are seeking balance, we had best get to know our gut garden bed cultivation system!

Eyes, Spine and Sugar

The rates of increased spinal problems, undiagnosed diabetes and eyesight deformities are reaching epidemic levels (refer to Chapter 3 — The 20/20 Rule). Optometrists are increasingly concerned at the way society is 'turning a blind eye' to myopia — now endemic worldwide within the younger population attributed to less time spent in the nutrient-rich environment and abnormally long hours spent on close-focus devices, compared to 'back in the day'.

I. Involvement with PROFESSIONALS — get involved!

Adjusting to involvement with Professionals

For those serious about change, it's highly likely, at some stage, professional input will be canvassed — so why delay? It's common for families to regularly access doctors, therapists, couple-counsellors and psychiatrists. It can be helpful to let your loved one know that the 'family' therapist has invited them to be part of the process and would like them to join a session at some stage.

It's important to calmly extend the invitation to all members, on a regular basis, close to the appointment time, rather than creating stressful anticipation over a longer period. Most will eventually attend an appointment. The relationship between client and professional is important — trust, patience and empathy are integral in developing an effective long-term (or short-term) relationship, so there is no rush for a quick fix. Continue to write the appointments on the family calendar or the family diary and continue to invite without pressure or negativity.

Positive signs are when you are asked how the appointment went today. Let your member know that attending counselling is not about forcing medication or ganging up on them. Any psychotropic medication discussions are entirely between doctor and adult and not the business of others. Most medication isn't necessarily helpful nor is there necessarily specific medication for 'withdrawal' although some anxiety/depression medication can have benefits for reducing symptomology (after a trial period assessing side effects).

J. Jane of the Jungle — You're sacked!

Jane of the Jungle — the days of swinging from many different branches in a strange circus style of chaos in order to please everyone all the time needs to cease! Balancing a working life and managing a home environment (including financial responsibility) whilst maintaining a compulsive over-giving rupture-repair cycle/s is called a "bankrupt social system". This has been built on a one-way street called Fail Avenue. Is it time to stop sipping on your wine of denial or your beer of bullshit?

Chronic fear of failure, fear of disapproval of others, perfectionism, procrastination and constant people-pleasing are determinants for failure. Though, easily treated within psychology, particularly when we focus on trendy words such as Equality, Democracy and Reciprocation. Jane, smother yourself in self-love as you climb into the spa bath full of bubbles and chocolate and contemplate your new life that does not involve thinking on behalf of others.

K. Karen the Great — Cut the bobbing and become the new YOU!

Hey Karen, grow back those locks, stop calling the manager, stop walking into the male changing rooms to talk to the sports coach and stop barging into the classrooms to make demands on the teachers. Lower your nose and look at yourself right square in the eyes. The world can survive without your boisterous exhaustion. You've given of yourself right down to the bone and now you're chewing on your own arm in the name of survival and family giving. Adrenaline and anger are likely your addictive mates. You stepped in when others abdicated their role. You always meant well in your actions and you'll always be society's unsung hero, though now it's time to prioritise your own needs — it's time for you to do 'YOU' and let your people "adult".

L. Listening creates Empathy

Empathy is a learned skill. Developing empathy is imperative for our species to survive and develops as we ripen our emotional intelligence through interaction with others. Healthy adults can prioritise their own vital needs, at the same time as exercising empathy: evidenced in our social interactions.

Studies and research suggest that empathy is relatively innate from in utero. Nurses working in antenatal care remind us that newborn babies are highly sensitive to the distress of others. The visible signs of empathy for their counterparts is heart-warming as they move their tiny heads to ineffectively intervene, often becoming visibly upset in their powerlessness. Other studies suggest that in utero babies empathise with highly stressed mothers throughout their pregnancies, often becoming empathetic children who are more aware of others needs and can form functionally close attachments. *(This book does not focus on the opposing attachment-disordered research that suggests highly stressed mothers produce children that can become anxious and problematic as adults).*

Are you capable of taking off your own shoes and stepping into the shoes of another person .... by seamlessly:

1) **hearing** what *the other person* is saying (not what we assume they are saying)
2) **summarising** our interpretation of their story (regardless of whether we agree or not) and then
3) waiting to hear whether we have correctly **interpreted** the above (validated the other person) – thumbs up/thumbs down. (Refer to The Talking Stick Strategy – 4.1)

M. Major Disclosures

It is common for each member of the family system to have a major disclosure/s that has been hidden away for quite some time. Although hidden matters of the heart are entirely personal to the individual and often remain so until the day they die, calling a moratorium on reactions within the safety of a meeting process can elicit truth in order to eventually move forward. The dumping ground within the safety (and privacy) of the family system can be an opportunity to share burdens and create a 'real' sense of primary-trigger-truth, for example; financial mismanagement, addictions, nonattendance at university (whilst still pretending to be a student), secret retirement, criminality or other sobering 'truths', as an explanation for long-standing inaction.

N. No means NO — Stop lying!

Young people constantly report their disdain for 'wishy washy' (fence sitting) parenting styles that can easily be manipulated, as opposed to a sense of security when a YES means YES and a NO means NO. Rupture-Repair cycles are not bottom lines or consequences — they are idle, lazy, meaningless, manipulative false sentiment within a never-ending cycle of 'swimming under water' threats and pleadings, that simply continues to repeat itself for year after exhausting year.

Please note:
- **Compromise** means that you are open to negotiation and debate with a view to an alternative solution.
- **Bottom Lines** means that you have made a fixed and final decision. Your No means No and your commitment to the topic is sincere.

O. Opt IN — There is no OUT clause

Japanese research indicates that without the full involvement of both parents (or all enablers) change is unlikely. It's sadly common for parents, particularly fathers, to quit way too early during the early stages of the change process. Making a decision to move forward is saying YES. It is a lie if you have no intention of participating in the change process. If a member of the enabling system does not participate in the change process, it is a clear message that they have no desire to assist in the process of maturation. In other words, regression is acceptable.

YES, means that we have all made a decision to move out of our comfort zone (or for some out of their chronic denial state) and to not give up, even when the going gets tough. This means that we have begun a 'Visualise to Actualise' system (Kerr, 2020) and there is now no 'OUT' clause. Technology has provided us with FaceTime, video links, mobiles, iPads, computers and laptops so that all members can continue to participate in family meetings — *regardless* of their location or time-poor lifestyles. It is common for one member of the system to link in to a family meeting (via telelink) from another room, another state, another country or while at work.

P. Postponing big changes

While the family system is embarking on a change-process, it's important to consider postponing significant changes, such as moving residence, building a new house, adding further household members to the mix, or making significant changes to the home environment. This is extremely important for members who are long-term social retreaters.

Many families plan to sell the spacious family home, eager to downsize or move into units, townhouses or retirement living. During their 'planning' they often believe (without any evidence of such) that, despite their long-term home dweller's extended years of dependence upon them, they will *somehow* ... suddenly be able to cope without them or find alternative accommodation, as well as walk into full-time employment or have the motivation or confidence to upskill *just in time* for their ageing parents to move onto the next stage of *their* life. It can indeed be quite a shock for aged parents after they've moved into smaller, more manageable accommodation to find their dependent in a desperate state, on the front doorstep, pleading to 'come back home'.

Many aged parents find themselves miserable as they try to cope in crammed living spaces, compromising their Golden Years. Sometimes escaping into even smaller retirement-type accommodation where the rules are strictly no extras.

Chronic Dependency

For the seriously disenabled social withdrawers who are forced to leave the family, though make a genuine attempt to transition to independent living, they often find themselves left in the cold, or couch surfing, permanently homeless (or severely compromised) triggering serious physical and/or mental health risks, including suicidality. For some, they join the 'living on the streets' community and become permanently dependent on the welfare system for the rest of their lives. They continue to beg extended family members for assistance and continually move between adult households, often struggling with addictions and relying on welfare assistance and increasing their psychotropic medication.

Elder Abuse — the dangers of doing nothing

Many parents relocate or downsize under the proviso that their adult son or daughter will only be living with them *temporarily* in the new home, though soon report the shocking truth as to the severity of the level of dependency of their loved one. Although they knew there was an overall 'lack of general life skills', they believed that if pressure was placed upon their family member, they would somehow rise to the occasion by becoming independent on cue — somehow it would eventually 'all just work out'. The risk of rejecting a Family System Change model or not listening to their Tribal Truth in the earlier years, was very steep indeed. The term 'unto death' often becomes a reality due to the lack of intervention within the earlier years of dependency.

For ageing parents who succumb to the reality of Career Parenting and do not plan to change this reality, they will likely be forced to include their son or daughter as part of their retirement plan. They will need to budget for the extra expenses associated with mature aged caregiving, which will be drawn from their pensions or savings. A budget in place, of course does not negate the importance of a legally binding health directive, as (often) the first signs of cognitive or physical decline results in the quick emergence of older children becoming officially paid carers or Enduring Power of Attorney or Executor of the Will, until death. For the kind and capable carers, this can provide a source of income and an official carer role for adult children as well as maintain a home (versus government funded assistance) for all parties.

This home-based system can also result in less dependency on the government funded welfare system as well as less dependency on the aged care system, considering that most systems involving the elderly are currently under the pump due to the overwhelmingly large numbers of baby boomers reaching old age. Sadly, many independent siblings report long-term dependency is often an opportunity for one adult child to inherit the family home after years of carefully planned 'takeover' goals. This causes enormous concern for the welfare of parents, as well as resentment, pain and litigation for other biological adult children who have often been independent for years. When accusing the dependent of 'parent abuse' or attempting to legally intervene by reports to the authorities, intervention is often nowhere in sight or changes are very slow.

Many stories are bleak. Love is often tested as parents age, or are *forced* to be fully cared for by dependent adult children, who are not versed with elderly caring realities, though of course well versed with the benefits of a free existence. It would be hard for any parent to imagine, even in their *wildest* dreams, to *ever* believe that their treasured child, now all grown up and in the role as Senior Carer, would leave them to rot in their nappies, while continuing to live under their enabled roof — then deflect their truth, during conversations with concerned family or government workers, that 'it really *is*, all okay'.

The rates of escalating elder abuse are staggering. The government is concerned. Organisations are concerned. There are Royal Commissions and continued publicised shock for what is happening to our dearly beloved aged people. The rates of passionate aged care workers who refer themselves to counselling (particularly through their employee assist programs) is also escalating. The shock of witnessing their client's care severely compromised by adult children is far too painful for many workers to maintain their employment. This is the reason I have laboured this point — as a tribute and an opportunity to thank our brave (and often underpaid) aged care workers, at the same time as reiterating the importance of continuing to report the miserable plight of aged-children's abusive practices towards their vulnerable elders.

Aged care workers who were once passionate and optimistic, believed in a system that protects our vulnerable elderly, soon become disillusioned and powerless. They report horrific accounts of our frail elderly left for days in nappies, left unshowered and medically neglected. Official reports not followed through by their organisation management, workers being accused of being 'whistle-blowers' when they contact their CEO's or police (or Ombudsmen or the media), often causes chronic worker breakdowns and diagnosis of PTSD, eventually managed under Workcover as a psychological injury.

There are hundreds of aged care workers who have now left the industry and will never return due to the ongoing abuse of adult children towards their now, dependent parents. Reports of our frail elderly abused, such as the lack of medical treatment for days (particularly over public holiday periods) is causing highly skilled workers to never return to an industry they were once so passionate about. It's hard to believe that in the 'lucky country' of Australia some of our elderly are treated like animals, and our workers are suffering avoidable mental health conditions similar to walking in from a war-torn country.

Is it fair to assume that (otherwise capable) adults who abuse their parents in this way have, at some stage in their life, been overindulged, chronically enabled and treated like royalty, at the very time when they were meant to be taught the principle of reciprocation within their intended adulthood? Many of these behind-closed-doors abusers of their parents simply wait for them to die. When eventually questioned by the authorities, these smiling assassins deny reality and blame their aged parent, quickly forgetting the comfortable lifestyle that has been provided to them for so many years. The cycle of life — with parents eventually becoming a full-time hostage to their children.

(If the above doesn't scare the living shit out of enablers, then I'm not sure what will!)

Q. Quitting is not an option — be part of the solution

Fathers, do not be a 'typical' statistic for quitting.

Change requires all members of the system to be equally as committed.

R. Recovery Goal

A recovery goal is a short, sharp, concise statement of future intention – an Action Verb. It is important to establish a Recovery Theme based on your overall goal as a family system.

7.6 Strategy: Create Recovery Goal

Please remember that individuals who have been in long-term social withdrawal patterns may not be capable of establishing a recovery theme.

Examples – 'Moving Forward'; 'Breaking Old Patterns'; 'One Step at a Time'.

Ask each member to name their recovery goal.

Name your Recovery Goal/Theme

7.7 - Strategy: Recovery Actions

In preparation for the first Family Meeting, list possible pending changes. For example:

Parent 1 – (full-time working adult – source of all family income) – no further housework

Parent 2 – increase household chores/ideas to generate an income

Adult children – take responsibility for one major role eg. washing/cooking

Adult children — recovery — taking over all tasks associated with outside of property, such as weeding, mowing lawns, gardening, painting

S. Sacking toxic language

Remorse vs Guilt

Guilt is a dangerous and extremely unhelpful emotion to maintain. Most of the time, guilt does little to provoke change, other than help us run around like a headless chook maintaining our defunct mindset and bruising our brain.

Remorse is an executive action-verb that induces change by strategically action-planning a new reality. Remorse is associated with insight, empathy and realism.

Sacking 'Yes-But' and 'Nice'

Create a family dollar jar for each time anyone uses the defunct justification blame-game word 'but'. Eradicating 'Yes-But' will close the door on inaction and compulsive or addictive over-giving. Let's stop butting heads with the 'Yes-Buts'. By changing unhelpful language, we cease deflecting responsibility.

'Nice' is simply a learned behaviour and deflects attention. If someone is providing for us and not placing any pressure on us to change, most of us would behave in a 'nice' fashion. Come on! Though, of course, there is nothing *at all* nice about someone constantly taking, while others are left over-working and over-giving whilst waiting for responsibility and empathy to arrive.

When asking people what they mean when they refer to someone as 'nice', they often respond by suggesting that there's an elimination of 'not-nice' behaviours such as violence, verbal abuse, criminality or sexual deviance. So ... does 'nice' describe an individual who is gentle or not a criminal? Parents talk about their 'nice boy' who wasn't sexually active in his teens nor loud or obnoxious or overly demanding and kept to himself. When asking how 'nice' now fits with the current picture when one party is at break-down level due to long-term over-giving, a blank face stares back at the questioner. Let's face it 'nice' is simply a stumbling block!

T. Tribal Truth — Rounding up your People

Accountability Coaches (refer to Strategies 1.10 & 1.11)

Our Tribal Truth are loving individuals in our life who (although brutal at times) aren't afraid to speak their truth — our cheer squad. The professional community can also serve as tribal truth until we gravitate back to the people in our life we trust. Regular contact with Accountability Coaches, such as friends, family, counsellors, pastors, school personnel is important.

U. Umbrella

Draw an umbrella and consider the people and professionals in your life you trust or who are positive examples of where you are heading. Who supports you to achieve your goals and challenges you in a way that motivates you to focus on your future?

V. Visualisation

Talk to the Future, not the Present. Visualise to Actualise your Future. Working towards a new future means not focusing on the dysfunction of the present.

Talk to a new situation — for example, 'when you're ready to quit smoking, it will be easy because you're a strong person and that's how I raised you'. As opposed to 'you're addicted to smoking, you should quit, it's disgusting'.

Why state the obvious when we are opening the door to the future of possibility? It is an absolute waste of time nag-festing, when we can talk to the future — we must action-verb our talking, rather than word-vomiting the past or the present.

W. Workstation as a Pseudo-work Environment

Many parents have stated that their biggest parenting regret has been co-locating technology in children's bedrooms from primary school. This downward slide entirely changes the role of the bedroom as a sleep-only space. It also creates disrespect for parental discipline, addictions and long-term bedroom-dependencies. Try negotiating with a hostile, hairy, six-foot teenager who has enjoyed free-range technology since pre-school or primary school and has no intention of changing. Then visualise in 10 years, then 20 years until aged parents become reliant on their baby-adult for their basic survival.

7.8 — Strategy: Create a new Workstation

Create an open-plan workstation outside of the bedroom. Make every effort to move all technology and social media to a communal space of the house.

If possible, set up a workstation in a bright, well-ventilated area of the home. Remember that the younger generation are constantly reminding the older generation that they are apt at multi-tasking their devices, at the same time as meeting educational deadlines, so they are more than capable of adapting to a change of environment within the home. Set up your home-based workstation that best reflects an open-plan working environment (pseudo office) that would be typical within many workplaces.

Remember that we are raising the next generation of employees and managers, not the next generation of babies.

X. X-Rays

Exacerbation of prior injuries is common when we maintain a sedentary lifestyle for longer than three months. Is the big morph impacting you — Stress-Injury-Condition?

7.9 — Strategy: Complete X-Rays before first meeting

It's vital that all pre-existing conditions are assessed for further exacerbation. Depression, back pain and chronic migraines may be a reflection of a medical condition that has changed from a strain to a serious preventable injury or has morphed into a new phys-ical condition. Consider co-morbid conditions, new underlying health conditions, prodromal states and cease from Dr Googling (Refer to Chapter 3 — (Avoidable) Secondary conditions).

Y. YO-YO Ping Pong — Stop!

Let your word be your word and stop your wishy-washy dou-ble-standards. Are your words focused on the future or are they simply gurgling or spluttering like they are swimming under water in a never-ending Rupture/Repair cycle?

Z. ZERO Tolerance for Violence Policy

(Refer to Dealing with Aggressive Behaviour — Chapter 4)

It is imperative that the family establishes a Zero Tolerance for Violence Policy. Violence or other forms of abuse within the home environment is a crime. All crime must be reported.

One person (at least) is murdered every day in Australia as a result of family domestic violence. It is rare for murder to occur as a first-time or single event. Abuse has a starting point and likely will not change without consequences, therefore no matter what age or stage we are at, it is vital we do not excuse bad behaviour at *any* time. It may not be appropriate to begin a family change process if there are concerns for safety to self, others or the community. If proposed changes pose a risk to anyone in your household, it is advised that police, child protection (or other) assistance is sought before proceeding. There are no excuses for minimising risk.

Zero Gaps – Checkpoint Assessment

A   Adult Language
B   Bedroom is for sleeping ONLY
C   Change Book (Meeting Book)
D   Dilemma is an opportunity to speak into the future
E   Employment – Working to eat rest and play
F   Forgiveness
G   Ground Rules – Establish Democratic Ground Rules
H   Health Checks
I   Involvement with Professionals – get involved!
J   Jane of the Jungle
K   Karen the Great – Cut the bobbing and become the new YOU!
L   Listening creates Empathy
M   Major Disclosures
N   No means NO – Stop lying!
O   Opt-In
P   Postponing big changes
Q   Quitting is not an option – Be part of the solution
R   Recovery Goal
S   Sacking Toxic Language (guilt, nice, yes-but)
T   Tribal Truth – Rounding up your people
U   Umbrella
V   Visualisation – Talk to the Future not the Present
W   Workstation as a Pseudo-working Environment
X   X X-Rays – Complete all major assessments
Y   Y YO-YO Ping Pong – Stop!
Z   ZERO Tolerance for Violence Policy

**Ideas from A-Z to begin to implement or discuss
at Family Meeting/s.**

Chapter 8
Family Meetings

Meetings are a helpful way to *move forward* as a whole family system (including non-familial households, where adults are cohabitating together). Family meetings are an opportunity to engage in a democratic, transparent process, to generate ideas and track progress.

Family meetings are practical in nature. They are not an avenue to spotlight an individual nor are they therapeutic interventions. They are a place of emotional safety. To adult is to treat one another as an adult and to view each member as an adult. Meetings are not an avenue to think on behalf of another adult. Adults do not need to be dictated to, controlled or manipulated. Love is an action.

Family meetings are a commitment to the change process — an Opt-In. Your Yes is Yes, not *maybe*. For members of the system who are reluctant or unmotivated to be part of this progressive system, or who indicate a 'maybe', it is important to view this as a clear statement of current non-intent. **Research indicates that fathers are more likely to Opt-Out.**

Unwilling participants may still wish to read, highlight and share relevant sections of this book as a first step. You are welcome to instigate any number of the wide range of strategies scattered throughout this book.

The following meeting formats are a *suggestion only*. Many families report that a consistent style, particularly one that is written in the meeting book, creates a seamless way of achieving outcomes, tracking progress and importantly to ensure ongoing emotional safety for all participants.

Assessing Levels of Dependency

Social withdrawal can be a temporary form of 'time-out' within the home environment, providing comfort and support as a result of healing our life-war wounds. However, as reiterated throughout this writing, inaction or not resuming previous functionality after three months can interrupt future progress within our relationships, work to eat values, the environment as well as our overall life goals.

Social Withdrawal Timeframes

- **Early Withdrawal** — 1-3 months — the individual still has secure memory of social interactions (muscle memory) as well as their ability to participate in their community.
- **Chronic Withdrawal** — 3-6 months of inaction or nil return to previous functioning in all areas of general life. Urgent need of intervention and connection to external supports. It is recommended that you begin with assessing risk, sleep and diet hygiene and to complete medical assessments.
- *A state of withdrawal is a sign or desire to enter into a relationship of total dependence, therefore treatment sometimes involves helping a person through the maturation process all over again, starting with unconditional love.*

- **Highly Disordered State** — 12 months – 3+ years. Considered to be a complex and highly disordered state — an illness requiring intervention, with the whole family system needing to participate in recovery.
- **Milestone Birthdays** — Non-action at a decade birthday (such as 30 years) often results in a further 10 years of regression.
- **Important Transition Times** — Primary to high school; high school to university, flatting and working; changing jobs; relocation — locally, nationally, internationally; relationship breakups or changing dynamics within relationships.

Preparation for the Family Meetings

- Purchase blank exercise book and place on kitchen table.
- Name Book — such as 'Family Meetings'; Change Book (or discuss in first meeting).
- Start an Agenda — all members to add/delete to the topics.
- Provide copy of *Boys in Bedrooms: The Prison of the Mind* to each member of the system — highlight all relevant sections of the book (avoid placing pressure if members do not wish to read book).
- Professional contacts — write names and contact numbers of local professionals such as doctors, therapists, couple counsellors in back of book.
- Set the date, time and place for the first meeting. The date must be agreed by all adult members of the household. Use of electronic calendars or placing dates/times on fridge, txt reminders, video invites etc. are also helpful.

Meeting 1 – Set-Up

The purpose of Meeting 1 is to discuss the Notion of Change and the practicalities of Moving Forward as a whole system.

Key words: Democracy, Reciprocation, Empathy, Honesty, Risk and Action.

Suggested Theme: Moving Forward

- Establish length of meeting: Begin meeting on time as per agreed date and place.
- Meeting Book: All members of the system to discuss how they would like to run the meetings and whether each person agrees/disagrees with the current Agenda items (or whether to transfer to Meeting 2).
- Establish Roles and Rules: Chair, Secretary and Recorder (change roles each meeting).
- Risk Assessment: Respectfully ask each member if there are any risks, disclosures or hesitancy. Discuss referral pathways (to be canvassed every meeting).
- Canvass date for Meeting 2.
- The honesty rating 'Suggested Meeting Checkpoints' list 1-6 (outlined on the following page) is an example of a strengths-based system.

Suggested Meeting Checkpoints

P — Participant   Rating Scale: 1 = Low; 5 = Reasonable; 10 = High

Beginning of Meeting

Qu 1.   <u>Motivation Assessment</u> — On a scale of 1-10 how comfortable am I to begin the Family Meeting Process?

P1....../10   P2 ....../10   P3 ...../10

Qu 2.   <u>Positive Report (current strengths)</u> — What is working well?
(eg. meeting together as a family, willingness to consider changes, motivation, Opt-In)

P1 ____
P2 ____
P3 ____

Qu 3.   <u>Reality Checkpoint A</u> — What are my concerns?
This is what I would like you to know about me at the moment
(eg. I'm anxious; I'm reluctant; I'm finding this process challenging)

P1 ____
P2 ____
P3 ____

Qu 4.   <u>Reality Checkpoint B</u> — What needs to change?
(eg., you need to let me adult; I realise I need to step back; you need to believe in my potential; I need to be more involved)

P1 ____
P2 ____
P3 ____

End of Meeting

Qu 5.   <u>Motivation Assessment</u> — How comfortable am I to continue family meetings?

P1....../10   P2 ....../10   P3 ...../10

Qu 6.   <u>Actions/Follow-Up</u> — Who is doing what? Timeframes?

P1 ____
P2 ____
P3 ____

Suggested Meeting Topics:

- **No Out Clause** — Adopt an Opt-In clause. Agree that all members are fully committed.
- **Principle of Reciprocation and the Financial Formula** — Initial discussions only as well as references to written material — provide copy of Financial Formula.
- **Through the Lens of Privilege** — Explain the notion of 'privilege'. If parents agree that their blessings and financial tenacity as a family unit have placed them in the 'middle or upper middle class' echelons of society, they may need to explain this fact to their family member.

  Please Note: many young people disclose during counselling sessions their genuine lack of awareness of privilege, believing that most people live like them. Others state that due to their bloodline privileges, they believe that they've been raised to take over the family assets, therefore delaying their adulthood until the 'handing over of their bloodline rights' (calculated dependency). Some also believe that they actually own the family home: 'It's mine anyway, or at least it will be formally one day'.
- **Apology for Lack of Education** — Parents may need to apologise for the lack of education around notions of reciprocation. This can also apply to parents with elite sports children and those raised with hired help throughout their childhood (particularly when spending time living in other countries) or those who were not respectfully taught that Life Is A Two-Way Street.
- **Involvement of Others** (Swiss Cheese Layering) — respectfully remind all participants of the possible professional involvement with others, such as counsellors, couple-counsellors and doctors (re. medical assessments).

Practical:

- Swapping Books — if members are comfortable, suggest reading and highlight relevant personal sections of Boys In Bedrooms: The Prison of the Mind, particularly words that you have been unable to verbalise. This is not an opportunity to victimise members of the system or 'tell' others what you want or expect.
- Meeting Book — Agenda items and Actions established for next meeting.
- Next Meeting — Date for Meeting 2 agreed by all participants

NOTES: ____

____

____

____

____

____

____

____

____

____

____

____

____

____

____

____

Meeting 2 – Moving Forward

Purpose: The Financial Formula

- Minutes & Actions from Meeting 1 – Agree? Changes?
- Agenda Items – Agree what topics will be discussed today?
- Roles Agreed (Chair, Secretary, Recorder). Decide date for Meeting 3.

Suggested Meeting Checkpoints

P – Participant   Rating Scale: 1 = Low; 5 = Reasonable; 10 = High

Beginning of Meeting

Qu 1. Motivation Assessment – On a scale of 1-10 how comfortable am I to begin the Family Meeting Process?

P1……/10   P2 ……/10   P3 …../10

Qu 2. Positive Report (current strengths) – What is working well?
(eg. meeting together as a family, willingness to consider changes, motivation, Opt-In)
P1 ____
P2 ____
P3 ____

Qu 3. Reality Checkpoint A – What are my concerns? This is what I would like you to know about me at the moment (eg. I'm anxious; I'm reluctant; I'm finding this process challenging)
P1 ____
P2 ____
P3 ____

Qu 4. Reality Checkpoint B – What needs to change? (eg., you need to let me adult; I realise I need to step back; you need to believe in my potential; I need to be more involved)
P1 ____
P2 ____
P3 ____

End of Meeting

Qu 5. <u>Motivation Assessment</u> — How comfortable am I to continue family meetings?

P1......./10   P2 ..../10   P3 ....../10

Qu 6. <u>Actions/Follow-Up</u> — Who is doing what? Timeframes?

P1 ____

P2 ____

P3 ____

Suggested Meeting Format:

- Risk Assessment — Ask each member if there are any risks present?
- Feedback — Ask each member for Meeting 1 feedback and Agenda items. Any changes or new ideas? Has anyone started counselling or completing medical tests? Validate feelings of all members.
- Adjusting Family Environment — Discuss the gradual softening of the protective walls that have separated the withdrawer from the rest of the family. Discuss practical ideas such as: spring cleaning, decluttering, painting, storage and temporarily moving room. Record who will do what?
- Discuss the Principle of Reciprocation and the Financial Formula. Discuss initial steps (ideas) to increase or decrease contribution.

Practical:

- Swapping Books — Has each member read and highlighted relevant sections (do not place pressure if not read).
- Meeting Book — Agenda items for next meeting established as a group. Leave on kitchen table.
- Next Meeting — date for Meeting 3 agreed by all participants.

NOTES: ____

____

____

____

____

____

____

____

____

____

____

Meeting 3 – Contribution is a Verb

Purpose: Implementing the Financial Formula - $350
(please refer to Chapter 6)

Suggested Meeting Format:

- Read Minutes from last meeting – Agree? Disagree?
- Agenda Items – Agreement that each topic will be discussed today?
- Roles (Chair, Secretary, Recorder)
- Risk Assessment – Ask each member if there are any risks present?
- Feedback – From each member of the group – how was Meeting 2? Any agenda changes or ideas to put forward? Has anyone completed medical tests, started counselling, shared their story?
- Adjusting Family Environment – Progress on changes within the family home (refer to Chapter 7 – A-Z).

Suggested Meeting Checkpoints

P – Participant   Rating Scale: 1 = Low; 5 = Reasonable; 10 = High

Beginning of Meeting

Qu 1.   <u>Motivation Assessment</u> – On a scale of 1-10 how comfortable am I to begin the Family Meeting Process?

P1......./10   P2 ..../10   P3 ...../10

Qu 2.   <u>Positive Report (current strengths)</u> – What is working well?
P1 ____
P2 ____
P3 ____

Qu 3.   <u>Reality Checkpoint A</u> – What are my concerns?
This is what I would like you to know about me at the moment
P1 ____
P2 ____
P3 ____

Qu 4.   <u>Reality Checkpoint B</u> – What needs to change?
P1 ____
P2 ____
P3 ____

End of Meeting

Qu 5.   <u>Motivation Assessment</u> – How comfortable am I to continue family meetings?

P1......./10   P2 ..../10   P3 ...../10

Qu 6.   <u>Actions/Follow-Up</u> – Who is doing what? Timeframes?
P1 ____
P2 ____
P3 ____

Suggested Meeting Topics:

- Contribution is an action-based system of accountability - structured intention to reciprocate 'in kind'.
- The Financial Formula - $350 per week, *every* week, 52 weeks a year. If an individual does not meet their $350 per week target, they are in arrears. Discuss other tasks that can be completed in lieu of finances, and ways of maintaining a credit system, rather than living in a deficit model. Explain banking models, transparency and workplace expectations.
- Support People — Who is your tribe? Name your account-ability coaches? Would they be willing to extend this role to others in your system? Are their contact details written at the back of the Family Meeting Book?

Practical:

- Meeting Book — Agenda items for next meeting established as a group. Leave on kitchen table.
- Next Meeting Date for Meeting 4 agreed by all participants.

NOTES: ____

____

____

____

____

____

____

____

____

____

# Meeting 4 – Equal Contribution

Purpose: Feedback of Implementing Financial Formula

All members of the family are participating in the $350+ Financial Formula — discuss debit or credit?

Suggested Meeting Checkpoints

P — Participant   Rating Scale: 1 = Low; 5 = Reasonable; 10 = High

Beginning of Meeting

Qu 1.   <u>Motivation Assessment</u> — On a scale of 1-10 how comfortable am I to begin the Family Meeting Process?

P1......./10   P2 ..../10   P3 ...../10

Qu 2.   <u>Positive Report (current strengths)</u> — What is working well?
P1 ____
P2 ____
P3 ____

Qu 3.   <u>Reality Checkpoint A</u> — What are my concerns?
This is what I would like you to know about me at the moment
P1 ____
P2 ____
P3 ____

Qu 4.   <u>Reality Checkpoint B</u> — What needs to change?
P1 ____
P2 ____
P3 ____

End of Meeting

Qu 5.   <u>Motivation Assessment</u> — How comfortable am I to continue family meetings?

P1......./10   P2 ..../10   P3 ...../10

Qu 6. <u>Actions/Follow-Up</u> – Who is doing what? Timeframes?

P1 ____

P2 ____

P3 ____

Suggested Meeting Format

- Minutes from last meeting – Agree? Disagree?
- Agenda Items – Agreement that each topic will be discussed today?
- Roles (Chair, Secretary, Recorder)
- Risk Assessment – Ask each member if there are any risks present?
- Feedback – From each member of the group – how was Meeting 3? Any changes or ideas to put forward? Has anyone changed their contribution measures, started counselling or completed medical tests?
- Adjusting Family Environment – Progress on changes within the family home.

TOPICS:

- Financial Formula – Progress? Debit? Credit?
- Financial Formula – Weaknesses – changes needed?
- Delay next meeting until all members are comfortable (and operational) with the Financial Formula. Ensure medical (or other) assessments are completed, as well as identification of supports/accountability coaches. Consider the range of secondary conditions and risks that may need addressing at this point. Remember that progress may be slow. This process is not a race.

Practical:

- Meeting Book — Agenda items for next meeting established as a group. Leave on kitchen table.
- Next Meeting — Date for Meeting 5 agreed by all participants or delayed due to areas for follow-up or inaction.

NOTES: _______________________________________

Meeting 5 – Preparation for Community Reintegration

Purpose: Plans to Relaunch

Discuss ideas and plans for community reintegration. This is considered a huge step forward for long-term sufferers. For some this is a potentially frightening process, therefore Meeting 5 is a 'discussion only'.

Suggested Meeting Checkpoints

P – Participant   Rating Scale: 1 = Low; 5 = Reasonable; 10 = High

Beginning of Meeting

Qu 1. <u>Motivation Assessment</u> – On a scale of 1-10 how comfortable am I to begin the Family Meeting Process?

P1......./10   P2 ..../10   P3 ....../10

Qu 2. <u>Positive Report (current strengths)</u> – What is working well?
P1 ____
P2 ____
P3 ____

Qu 3. <u>Reality Checkpoint A</u> – What are my concerns?
This is what I would like you to know about me at the moment
P1 ____
P2 ____
P3 ____

Qu 4. <u>Reality Checkpoint B</u> – What needs to change?
P1 ____
P2 ____
P3 ____

End of Meeting

Qu 5.   <u>Motivation Assessment</u> — How comfortable am I to continue family
meetings?

P1......./10   P2 ..../10   P3 ...../10

Qu 6.   <u>Actions/Follow-Up</u> — Who is doing what? Timeframes?

P1 ____

P2 ____

P3 ____

Do not proceed without full participation from all members of the system. If necessary, seek professional advice and discuss with your accountability coaches

Suggested Format

- Minutes from last meeting — Agree? Disagree?
- Agenda Items — Agreement that each topic will be discussed today?
- Roles (Chair, Secretary, Recorder).
- Risk Assessment — Ask each member if there are any risks present?
- Feedback — From each member of the group — how was Meeting 4? Any changes or ideas to put forward? Has anyone changed their contribution measures, started counselling or completed medical tests?
- Adjusting Family Environment — Progress on changes within the family home in preparation for community integration. Has there been connection with employers, trainers, at least one peer, canvassing (online) employment or recreational pursuits?
- *It is imperative that the dependent is fully engaged and in control of the formulation of ideas throughout the process of community reintegration and they do not feel threatened such as exposure or eviction from the family home.*

Practical:

- Meeting Book — Agenda items for next meeting established as a group. Leave on kitchen table.
- Next Meeting — Date for Meeting 6 agreed by all participants or delayed due to areas of inaction and lack of follow up.

NOTES: ____

Meeting 6 – Moving Forward
Community Integration Planning Meeting

Purpose: Time to Launch

- Minutes from last meeting – Agree? Disagree?
- Agenda Items – Agreement that each topic will be discussed today?
- Roles (Chair, Secretary, Recorder)
- Risk Assessment – Ask each member if there are any risks present?
- Feedback – From each member of the group – how was Meeting 5? Any changes or ideas to put forward?

Suggested Meeting Checkpoints

P – Participant   Rating Scale: 1 = Low; 5 = Reasonable; 10 = High

Beginning of Meeting

Qu 1. <u>Motivation Assessment</u> – On a scale of 1-10 how comfortable am I to begin the Family Meeting Process?

P1......./10   P2 ..../10   P3 ....../10

Qu 2. <u>Positive Report (current strengths)</u> – What is working well?
P1 ____
P2 ____
P3 ____

Qu 3. <u>Reality Checkpoint A</u> – What are my concerns?
This is what I would like you to know about me at the moment
P1 ____
P2 ____
P3 ____

Qu 4.   <u>Reality Checkpoint B</u> — What needs to change?
        P1 ____
        P2 ____
        P3 ____

End of Meeting

Qu 5.   <u>Motivation Assessment</u> — How comfortable am I to continue family meetings?

        P1......./10   P2 ..../10   P3 ...../10

Qu 6.   <u>Actions/Follow-Up</u> — Who is doing what? Timeframes?
        P1 ____
        P2 ____
        P3 ____

Topic Suggestions:

- Establish Safe Community Systems — Sporting group, church, previous peers or colleagues?
- Support Groups — Parents support group (start your own!)
- Peer Group Support — Research indicates that the most helpful source of support is when the social withdrawer interacts with other sufferers. Peer-to-peer support is important. Although this is lacking in Australia, there is nothing stopping you from reaching out and starting your own peer group. You only need two people to call yourself a group!
- Acknowledge Previous Re-integration Skills (muscle memory?). Refer to past successful or 'reasonable' adjustments, such as from primary school to high school or new job or relationship, hobby (refer to strategy 1.3 — Anchoring).
- Enlisting Assistance from Support People — Connect with people or services who will accompany you in the community. Check with others, agencies or medical practitioners as to who they may recommend. Ask for assistance — you are important!!

NOTES: ____

____

____

____

____

____

____

____

____

Statements from Young People – Barriers for Community Integration

'Parents need to teach us about the principle of "no work, no eat" BEFORE we reach 18, for example – if you live at home after 18 years you *will be* expected to contribute as an adult.'

'I feel useful when I'm an active part of our household and useless when others make excuses for me.'

'Ask me *why* I'm in the bedroom or *why* I don't want to leave home, and stop pretending that things are going to change just because you *want* them to change.'

'Stop telling your friends that I'm going to be a rich, famous programmer one day, it's embarrassing, it's probably not going to happen, it's just an excuse.'

'Why is it taking so long for you to ask me to begin changing: I'm lazy.'

'It's only "blah blah" when I'm constantly threatened, I'm not even listening' (Rupture/Repair Cycle).'

'Parents are totally ONE SIDED when they listen to our stories. We just need you to listen to our grievances, not to *do* anything about them. When you interfere, we stop talking or trusting.'

'Most of our panic stories are a bit *distorted* at the time. The trouble is that parents listen with their "literal" ears and end up panicking like us. We don't always give adults the whole story or the *other side* of the story. We need parents to be adults and stop letting us manipulate them.'

'We need to be able to make mistakes, not to be supported to drop out of school or quit our jobs with no other plan in front of us.'

'We need parents to convince us not to quit and not to give in to our fears or other emotions.'

'How do you think we'll have the guts to find another job if we know you'll keep rescuing?'

'We need to learn to be true to ourselves rather than being fearful of what others think about us. This takes time to learn. Stop telling us stuff that sounds like we're wounded.'

'I have so many regrets for all the shit I've caused my parents. I dug a hole and it got too big.'

'You need to listen to our regrets, as well as our shitty stories about your parenting mistakes and not take it to heart.'

'COVID — although the world seems messed up at the moment, it's going to be our world one day. Our parents won't be around holding our hands and they won't get to mess thing up any more'; 'Why don't adults care about legacy?'; 'Most of us believe in climate change and reducing omissions, listen to us'; 'The decisions you lot are making now will bite the next gen on the arse, so grow up!'

**Feedback from industry professionals
To: parents of young people under the age of 30 years:**

(The below statements are from industry managers, CEOs, mining bosses, engineering managers and tradie bosses.)

Overall Theme: We just want the bloody job done.

'Thanks to all the parents who let us get on with the job and who raise kids who like working and can speak up when they need to.'

'The manager is *not* your son or daughter's father or mother or therapist. A boss is a boss.'

'A mummy-boy is a workplace liability: fathers never call us.'

'Mothers need to stop calling managers and bosses when their kids are *just* getting used to their new work environment. Calling us is NOT OKAY.'

'We don't care about your personal life, or your sexuality or even getting those pronoun things right — we just want the f'kn job done.'

'Parents should teach their children assertive adult communication when they are young so they can manage difficult workplace situations.'

'Young adults are more likely to get sacked from the workplace if their parents constantly contact managers, particularly if they go above the line manager.'

'Stop telling us how to do our jobs, you have no right. You are not on our payroll and we are not accountable to any parent with a son or daughter over 18 years of age. In fact, it's a breach of their privacy.'

'We'll find all sorts of excuses to issue first, second and third letters of warning to young people who can't cope without their parents constantly interfering, until we eventually get rid of them, *even* if they've got decent skills.'

'We don't care about losing unfair dismissal cases because we only need to pay out around six months of income, and that's much easier than putting up with parents. We don't want dickheads and we don't want parents on our backs.'

'We're sick to death of parents contacting the workplace to complain. It's an embarrassment. For fuck's sake let us get on with our jobs and stop babying your son. We don't have time for soft cocks in the workplace, if he's working in a blokey industry, that's what he needs to be, a bloke.'

'We don't have time to stroke egos. It's not our fault you told him he was "a good boy" every five minutes he did something minor. We're not going to tell him that here, we expect him to work without constant praise, so don't ring us and tell us "we don't speak to him like that in our family". The workplace is not your family, it is a working place that meets deadlines for pay-packets.'

'It's really easy to tell if your young bloke has been given any consistent responsibilities and projects around your home environment when he was growing up. It shows up in their confidence when learning new skills or being put on the spot or when giving "feedback" versus perceived criticism.'

'What happened to "paying it forward" — are parents teaching their kids to "pay it backwards?".

'If the young person is honest about their heavy stuff, like recovery from addictions, we'll give them a fair go if they want to work. Most of us here don't have our shit together. Being a bit messed up doesn't mean you're not going to be a decent employee.'

'If we're doing something wrong, he can talk to the manager himself. We have complaints processes and human resource departments ya know.'

'If your son or daughter isn't coping with being "the new kid on the block", they can talk to us, we're not here to stroke ego but we'll listen so the job still gets done.'

'If he doesn't want his pay packet, tell him to work somewhere else.'

'We'd rather employ the oldies these days. They just get on with the job and we don't have mummies to deal with.'

Summary

**Without pushing oneself out of one's comfort zone spiritually, emotionally, relationally, physically, geographically or financially
… one does not grow or become informed.**

I sincerely hope that long-term sufferers of social withdrawal will begin to bravely step forward and re-integrate back into their community ……. in order to walk their new talk and enjoy the life they are destined to live.

Introduction – Ad Lib
Controversial Notions (optional reading only)

During the final months of writing this book, I began to reflect on our last two years of global disarray and the astronomical changes to our way of life. As if the story of male social withdrawal wasn't disastrous enough, mainstream society began joining our environmentally starved Boys in Bedrooms, when Stage One of our new 2020 social isolation lockdown life arrived. A leaky virus at ground zero had found its way to our nation, thanks to Bat Woman and her accidental gain of function cronies, or was it the start of WW3? Our borders were shut and so too were our shocked minds... We could scarcely believe that the world had come to a grinding halt.

The world plunged itself into the sudden, new, global stay-at-home-community, and the government began borrowing just to keep us at home. Fear propaganda, confusing new health laws and strange draconian orders began messing with our proud career-driven minds. As our generations' new home prisoners, ISO life for some, began to turn in on itself within the four walls of our new hide 'n gloom, as our new race-to-trace life, called 'protection and survival', steamrolled ahead.

In the beginning weeks of our novel adjustment to LockyD we had no time for Orwellian theories nor notions of evil global elites hellbent on economic control, and most of us refused to entertain *notions of sinister panda-engineered bioweapons. Our hearts broke for our virus victims, our brave mega-super heroes on the medical (and other) frontlines, and our bankrupt businesses, as we began transitioning into new workers or learners from home. We sat in our collegiate video sessions in our above belly-button professional self, bemused by our bottom half, sporting our pj's 'n slippers or tracky dacks 'n uggs.*

We learned to stay at home with our pots and pans, as we attempted to keep up with our deadlines and growing waistlines, while the government worked on their own plots and plans that included messing with our microbes and weakening our brain architectural system — knowing only too well the insidious impact on our mental health and physical health when we alter our relationship with our precious nutrient rich environment. There were repetitive fear-campaigns that opened with 'don't panic' and closed with increased offers of borrowed money to hide. We became entrenched in our new roles as the new paid-to-hide community. We began mowing our bedroom carpets and we were rewarded with easy doe (job keeping/job seeking), with many earning more in their 'hidden life' than in their previous working and/or non-working life.

Negative thought strands and foreign ideas ran rampant, and it soon became clear that the name State meant 'Superior Premier Control' as the armed Feds and the local police brigade thought it best to play local antagonist. Our Victorians, hidden away in the most locked down, curfew-bound city in the world, felt powerless. They became stressed and confused, their new looped thinking, spinning around, inside out, becoming well versed in their new roles as Chief Analyst, though often dubbed as the mighty antagonist. They knew they'd been left for dead — the media, pollies and meds, scripted and gagged and now all festering together in bed.

The VICS, with their gut instinct intact, together with the sound of the trump, knew there was 'something' happening deep inside their city within the small hours of the night? Disturbing allegations of trillion-dollar global-drugsters and human exploitation rings, left to run rampant in a State conveniently now curfew-bound — streets that were left bare every night, for week after week after sinister week. Well aware in the presence of filthy greed and evil desires ... addicts of money, sex and power will reside.

With no checks or limits imposed upon swamp creatures and secret global elites, who are best buddies with obsessive trillion-dollar global economic population-culling elites, who all own shares in the global pharmaceutical trade and are competing with the brain chipping crowd ... we knew that the bodies and the minds of the ordinary folks were in trouble, big trouble.

Why weren't we paying attention to the bloke from Melbourne (Synchron) who had jumped in bed with the Australian Government and America's military with his brain-chipping implant scheme, who was FDA approved in 2020 to begin human trials in 2021? Was this really occurring, right in the middle of a global health pandemic, in the most locked down city of the world, under the guise of benevolence - helping humanity ranging from Parkinson's to paralysis' despite the warnings that losing the last part of our privacy, our brain, to computer-controlled devices and placed in the wrong hands, will create a 'new' irreversibly altered human species who will be robotically controlled through computers?

Though, for those less focused on bioweapon labs, brain chipping, transhumanism, population culling or notions of doctors-in-bed with big pharma, most agreed that by the end of 2020, Australia, as a whole, had dug themselves into a dark financial hole. Rather than our PM controlling our geographical landscape, we learned that we were all living in our own bubbled up, border-controlled dictator State. For those clever enough to live on the Isle of Denial, they simply dug a hole in the sand, rocking the ostrich-jive, finding peace in their establishment ... even for a while, simply to stop all that mess, in the weary ol' head.

By 2021, we were all forced to 'pick a side' – the bats had turned us into large adult-sized laboratory rats. We were introduced to stringent new vaccine mandates, with 'choice' meaning the difference between livelihood and recreation; or our gut instinct and principles – our new legislated Conquer and Divide life had now begun. We were introduced to QR check-point shopping, alongside our controversial new dirty words of the year - 'adverse reactions', 'no immunity', 'minimal protection' and 'natural immunity' – as we turned into one big nation of 25 million lab rats. Most rolled up their sleeves for the jab as they, indeed, 'gave a rat's', whilst pro-choicers didn't seem to give even the smallest of rats.

The new vax season was simple: (1) get jabbed and join the pro-establishment party, in the new vax passport laboratory program to receive your reward of keeping your jobs, as well as the privileges you had been enjoying the day before, or (2) no vax one-way ticket to Mr and Mrs Doubt-Pfizer's anti-bio weapon leper colony, where Delta wasn't singing centre stage anymore, Alpha was nowhere in sight and mild new act Omni (and the breakout crew) were now on the floor. Joining the leper colony meant that some lost their work contract and some of the privileges you'd been enjoying the day before, monitored through the new dictator in town – QR Checkpoint Charlie.

Regardless of choice or whether your device sported the brand new big green tick of two-jab societal approval, it soon became sadly clear that the virus and the gene therapy drugs were no *respecter of persons. The notion of 'protection' turned to 'waning', with the Booster crew moving into town. Many avoided being local antagonist, following the guidelines for viral protection, by double-jabbing, then tripling up, before their flu jab winter time. We were expected to behave by being masked, mandated, border obeyed, told how to think, what to say, who to avoid and who not to trust.*

Eventually, our feisty, satirical, tangential minds, after large doses of extra time on our hands, began to reflect and mourn our old life — our last few decades of comfort and convenience in our once-privileged peace-time slumber. Deep down-under, we knew we'd become heavily addicted and device-dependent, now owned by big tech elites who'd sold our minds to the data-rich cloud — so why wouldn't our data now be considered the new gold? We started listening, questioning, researching and debating ... at least, more than we'd been bothered to in the past.

Some stayed pro whilst others began joining their conspiracy mates. Hey, so what are de-centralised cryptocurrencies? Is cash set to become globally digitised after the cash-crash? Will cars really drive themselves at the same time as study our data? Will our bodies and brains be chipped so we can be told what to think and what to buy? Is it too late to reduce our omissions and save our precious planet? What exactly is the Internet of Things and ... why the fuck is intelligence artificial?

We knew our collective identity was seriously at stake. Our heavy hearts continued to mourn our forced changes, our jobs and the deep loss of our dearly departed. As the new parted-border-controlled community, we attended weddings and funerals and our group discussions online. We discussed the breaches to the Nuremberg Code and the Declaration of Helsinki and wondered if they were now merely a myth?

It was no laughing matter when publicly opposed changes to public health orders began altering job titles — had the title 'Premier' been superseded to 'Unelected Narcissistic President of the State' or were we just hoping that totalitarians would somehow magically cannibalise together with their dungeon mates? Had our human rights, under the Hippocratic Oath, been superseded to the new Hypercritical Order, assisted by the ever-increasingly gagged doctors and media, all owned by Mr or was it now, medically non-credentialled, Dr Gates?

The Great Resignation, a time when groups of tens of thousands of pro-choice protesters barely fared on our frontline news and the words of joe-average were cut off at the knees. Now living in a divided society, one that had turned bosses against workers and fathers against sons with friends turning to foes. Thousands upon thousands of pro-choice or adverse-alarmed doctors, nurses, midwives, pilots like Hoodie, tradies, allied health workers, truckies and teachers began walking from their posts in a deep state of despair ... as the pretty-dressed, sports-worshipping truth-gagged media, as our scripted puppets on a string, light-heartedly, wished us a happy new year!

The king of the tennis world, Mr Double-flip, No-Vax Djokovic faulted his visa, and was denied his on court swings, as Australian opened in 2022. Our Aussie baby rooster's talent rich/primal-poor swings sent him walking, as usual, through our tennis hall of shame. Though, thankfully our nation's pride was restored at the awe-inspiring Barty party, crowned as our (now retired) impressive new Tennis Queen of the world.

PCR testing began floating to some hard-to-reach planet, and lab rats were given their own hard-to-locate RAT tests, as we stood in long lines under threats of non-disclosure fining, where the word 'negative' had now become our new 'positive', with ambulance ramping and code browning starting to muddy our minds. At the same time the media were in a frenzy, assisting the government to delay the start of the new school year, with reports of baby-lab rat testing stations — introducing the medication-before-education policies and the opportunity to blindside parental rights. The media neglected to report 8,000+ Queensland teachers and other government workers who began walking from their posts, questioning whether education now not even a human right?

Hundreds of parents in their pro-establishment frenzy ignored international medical warnings and jabbed-before-learning their kids, whilst other parents were heard screaming, 'keep away, I'll teach my kids at home'. Kids were either eager for the jab, fearful of the jab, angry with their parents for forcing their jab, with some kids taking up their posts to publicly protest the jab, and others being told that jabbing doctors may co-locate with teachers? Why was a kid, though well under 18, now deemed their own capable vaccine-trial decision-maker, despite our national policies linked to evidence that suggests executively otherwise? Was Gillick running the score?

Had our country gone mad? Was it any wonder that in 2021, the word 'anxiety' was voted children's word of the year? A world where doctors were blindsiding parents, and pollies truly believed they were chief doctors, and it seemed that everyone other than the individual, had full guardianship over their bodies, due to a sinister John Travolta-style multiplying virus.

It was the end of January 2022, and we wondered if our next Fed election would occur before Russia plunged us all into war?

Were biolabs and bioweapons the greatest risk to our civilisation? Or was cloud seeding, flood bombs, seed control, dislocation and land grabbing? Would China, North Korea or the terrorist movement begin to stir the global pot? Or was the brain-chipping dreams of billionaire king-of-the-financial-global-world, Elon Musk and his brain mission (Neuralink) set to space-cadet our future?

Not satisfied with his space colonisation plans and his world-leading automaking, Elon was reported to be desperate for FDA approval in order to keep up with the other global telepathic brain-chipping crowd, though warning us of the dangers of misuse in the wrong hands. Where were the provocative citizen discussions regarding this dangerous neurotechnology? Were there any concerns for our mental liberty, cognitive liberty, mental privacy and psychological continuity? Though, the warnings seemed clear that unless one wants to be a monkey in a zoo, and have 'snake stents up your jugular vein and into the vasculature that supplies your brain with oxygen, permanently implanting a distributed series of sensors (stentrode) to constantly record your entire brain's activity', then we must be aware of the multi-trillion dollar elites' plans.

If history repeats itself, initially we'll be sucked into the benevolence of new brain-chipping technology (particularly if we're already body-chipped) as there will be promises of protection and improved health. For example, for those with spinal cord damage, promises to help patients to walk again through neuro-stimulation therapy (thought of as a hearing aid for the spinal cord by manipulating neural pathways). Seriously! Technology that can ultimately create brand new neural pathways, read our thoughts, direct our legs, cut and paste our memories into the body of others, most definitely has the potential to turn humans into robots — likely to arrive subtly under our noses, while we're sitting in our homes watching Americanised Netflix transhumanism movies that seek to seamlessly drip-feed us into our next reality (*Implanted; Lucy; Knight Rider; Limitless; Gattaca; The Island; RoboCop*).

Is the era of transhumanism just around the corner? While countries such as Australia, prefer to teach citizens how to maintain denial and distraction, thankfully international neuro-techs are already a step ahead of the brain-chipping crowd, creating technology to create privacy firewalls within our brains that may (or may not) protect access to particular parts of our brain. Really? In the future, will the words 'protection' and 'permission' shift to the levels of access we allow to the various departments of our brain, as well as the impact of others reading, sharing or selling our personal neuro-data?

While neuro-techs have been building highly specialised firewalls between a person and the digital world to protect our brain against intrusion or alteration, internationally savvy neuro-ethicists have become highly alarmed about this pending new technology. Will Australia follow in the steps of world-first Chile by enacting our own Neuro Rights Act to protect the Aussie brain from privacy invasion? Or is our connection with America and other messed-up nations too entrenched to stop what is already occurring under our noses? Is Australia merely a baby lab rat country for this dangerous neuro-technology? (Stephen Rainey: Oxford Uehiro Centre for Practical Ethics; Marcello Ienca: European bioethicist; Tom Oxley; Grant).

It's surely not difficult to imagine our new neuro-tech brain-chipped world, where our thoughts are read and our brain is owned. Initially, we'll be a little hesitant, until we hear the word 'mandate'. We've already become accustomed to being puppets on a mandate string, therefore new slogans such as 'no-brainchip-no-job', or 'no-brainchip-no-education', or 'no-armed-force-no-life' would hardly be a surprise. Imagine brain-chipped soldiers as weapons of mass destruction? For the cynical, what would you, then, call a direct brain link to a weapon?

The good news! For now, we simply need to Move Forward. We also need to be prepared to learn how to fight the war in our mind and remain psychologically strong. Afterall, at this time in history, NO ONE has access, nor the right, to control the last part of our privacy that we still own — OUR BRAIN!

Bibliography

American Psychiatric Association. *Diagnostic and Statistical Manual of Mental Disorders: Fifth Edition: DSM-5*. Arlington, VA. American Psychiatric Association, 2013.

Beattie, J. *Codependent No More*. USA. Hazelden Foundation, 1992.

Bloss, P. 'On Adolescence: A Psychanalytic Interpretation'. APC PsychNet. Free Press of Glencoe. 1962. URL: https://psycnet. apa.org/record/1962-06265-000

Cooper, P. *Overcoming Bulimia Nervosa and Binge Eating: 3rd Edition: A Self-help Guide Using Cognitive Behavioural Techniques*. London. Robinson, 2009.

Drabek, T. *Social Dimensions of Disasters*. Maryland. Federal Emergency Management Agency, 1996.

Chilton, Dr S, Rusktalis, Dr M, Gregory, A.J. *The Rewired Brain: Free Yourself of Negative Behaviors and Release Your Best Self*. Baker Publishing Group, U.S.A., 2016.

Dispenza, Dr J. *Breaking the Habit of Being Yourself: How to Lose Your Mind and Create a New One*. 9th Edition. Hay House, Australia. February 2016.

Feurman, M. 'How to Handle a Partner Who is a Mama's Boy'. 12 April 2021. URL - https://www.verywellmind.com/ways-to-handle-mamas-boy-husband-4050817

Gouldner, Alvin W. 'The Norm of Reciprocity: A Preliminary Statement.' *American Sociological Review*, vol. 25, no. 2 (1960).

Goleman, D. *Emotional Intelligence: Why It Can Matter More Than IQ.* London. Bloomsbury Publishing, 1996.

Gray, J. *Men Are From Mars Women Are From Venus: A Practical Guide for Improving Communication and Getting What You Want in Your Relationships.* New York. Thorsons/Harper Collins, 1993.

Kerr, James. *Legacy: What the All Blacks Can Teach Us About the Business of Life.* London. Constable, 2020.

Leaf, C. Dr. *Who Switched Off My Brain?: Controlling Toxic Thoughts and Emotions:* Revised Edition Inprov Ltd. USA, 2009.

Leaf, C. Dr. *Switch On Your Brain: 21-Day Brain Detox Plan: The Key to Peak Happiness, Thinking, and Health.* Baker Books. USA, 2013.

Lerner, R.M. (2005) Promoting Positive Youth Development: Theoretical and Empirical Bases. Workshop on the Science of Adolescent Health and Development, National Research Council/Institute of Medicine, Washington DC, 9 September 2005, p. 92.

McKay, B & K (1020). 'A Man's Life. On Manhood. Rites of Passages: 8 Interesting (And Insane) Male Rites of Passages From Around the World; and Why Father's Shouldn't Initiate Their Sons In To Manhood'. URL: https://www.cracked.com/article_20075_the-5most-terrifying-rites-passage-from-around-world.html

Moore. R. & Gillette. D. *King Warrior Magician Lover: Rediscovering The Archetypes Of the Mature Masculine.* New York, USA. Harper Collins, 1991.

Mosley, M. *Fast Asleep: How to Get a Really Good Night's Rest.* Cammeray, NSW. Simon & Schuster, 2020.

Mivision (December 2021: Issue 174: pg. 84) — 'Myopia Management: Why Eye Length Matters'. URL: https://youreyesite.com' what-is- myopia-can-it-be-cured

Northern Territory Government, 'Little Children are Sacred Report'. Akelyernernane Meke Mekarle (Aranda) (In our law children are sacred because they carry the two spring wells of water from our country within them), 2007.

Oberg, K. (1960). 'Cultural Shock: Adjustment to New Cultural Environments.' Practical Anthropology 7, pp. 177-182.

Pape, S. 'The Barefoot Investor.' Melbourne, Australia. John Wiley & Sons Australia, 2018.

Patrick, S.J, Holmes, M., Box, L. (1988). 'Ngurra-kurlu: A way of working with Warlpiri people: Desert Knowledge:, Wanta Jampijinpa Pawu-Kurlpurlurnu by Wanta Jampijinpa Pawu-Kurlpurlurnu'. Published by The University of Queensland, 2008.

Rosenburg, R. The Human Magnet Syndrome: Why We Love People Who Hurt us. Premier Publishing & Media. Bellingham. Washington. 2013.

Saito, T. & Angles J. (Translator). Hikikomori: Adolescence Without End. London. University of Minnesota Press, 2013.

Sarason, B.R., Pierce, G.R., Shearin, E.N., Sarason, I.G., Waltz, J.A., & Poppe, L. (1991). 'Perceived Social Support and Working Models of Self and Actual Others.' Journal of Personality and Social Psychology, 60(2), 273-287. https://doi.org/10.1037/0022-3514.60.2.273

Stringer, S. 'On Eagles Wings: He Can Because He Believes He Can'. Eagle Publications. U.S.A. 1983.

Wiimaju, Pipirri. 'For the Little Kids — Aboriginal Child Rearing Practices'. Waltja Tjutangku Palyapayi Aboriginal Corporation. NT. Australia

2001. URL: https://www.snaicc.org.au/about/